THAT OTHERS
MAY LIVE

Also by Sara Driscoll

Lone Wolf

Before It's Too Late

Storm Rising

No Man's Land

Leave No Trace

Under Pressure

Still Waters

That Others May Live

AN FBI K-9 NOVEL

THAT OTHERS MAY LIVE

SARA DRISCOLL

KENSINGTON
PUBLISHING CORP.

www.kensingtonbooks.com

KENSINGTON BOOKS are published by

Kensington Publishing Corp.
119 West 40th Street
New York, NY 10018

Library of Congress Card Catalogue Number: 2023942115

The K with book logo Reg. U.S. Pat. & TM. Off.

ISBN: 978-1-4967-4398-5

First Kensington Hardcover Edition: December 2023

ISBN-13: 978-1-4967-4399-2 (ebook)

10 9 8 7 6 5 4 3 2 1

Printed in the United States of America

In Memory Of:

*Ann Vanderlaan (1949–2022), co-creator of
the FBI K-9s.*

*The ninety-eight lives tragically lost on June 24, 2021,
when Champlain Towers South fell in Surfside, Florida.*

You are loved. You are missed. Rest in peace.

Author's Note

Most readers of this book will make the clear connection between this fictional building collapse and the real and tragic collapse of Champlain Towers South in Surfside, Florida. After the building fell on June 24, 2021, Ann Vanderlaan and I watched the news coverage closely. Not just because we, as so many others, held our collective breaths, waiting and hoping for any bit of good news to come from the disaster—be it a live rescue or a recovered cat—but because search and rescue is our professional niche. As we watched the incredible bravery of the search-and-rescue workers, paying special attention to the use of dogs to find victims buried in the debris field, and as our hearts broke for the families and friends of the lost, we knew we were witnessing something remarkable—the incredible efforts of hundreds of people, putting their own lives on the line on the small chance just one more person might be alive in the rubble.

Almost a year before Ann passed away in July 2022, she suggested a title for the book that would become known as *Still Waters—That Others May Live*. I loved that title but felt it needed a larger story, a story where more lives were on the line, and where the dogs' and handlers' lives were also at risk. In June 2022, as we were preparing to start working on this book in a few months, we agreed we would use that title for a scenario similar to that of Champlain Towers South. Following Ann's unexpected passing a month later, I continued with our original idea, not because I wanted to write a thrilling tale at the expense of irreplaceable lives lost and their families' pain, but because of the bravery and dedication I saw from rescue crews at that site. This is a story told from the point of view of first responders, of their courage and determination to bring everyone possible out alive, while agonizing over the loss of those they couldn't reach. We mourn those lost, but we thank those in Florida that day and in the weeks that followed, and all other first responders around the world, for all they do for us, often at their own expense.

CHAPTER 1

Schematic Design: The first phase of the structural design process, involving conceptual drawings of both the interior and exterior of the proposed building.

Monday, December 17, 8:12 AM
Jennings/Webb residence
Washington, DC

Meg Jennings finished the last of her coffee and set her mug down next to her empty plate. A glance at her fitness tracker told her she had only a few more minutes to linger, and then the team needed to get moving.

The other half of the team rolled over in his bed near the fireplace, stretched, and then relaxed back into the fuzzy cushion with a gusty sigh, his favorite red dragon tucked close, one yellow wing poking out from under his foreleg.

"Hawk, nearly time for work."

The black Lab opened one eye in response to her words and then closed it again.

Meg chuckled. She had no concerns that the moment she picked up her go bag—the search-and-rescue backpack she carried everywhere in case she and Hawk were deployed to an incident—and gave a real command, he wouldn't be raring to get to work. This was part of their job in the FBI's Forensic Canine Unit—to be ready to deploy at a moment's notice to wherever they were most needed. Minutes could mean lives, and Hawk had learned three years ago, when they'd joined the Human Scent Evidence Team, to take his rest when he could, because once they walked out the door, it might be a long time before he would find himself at his ease again.

They'd been up for nearly two hours by this time, and Hawk had eaten a hearty breakfast before heading out to their large shared backyard.

Meg had lived in the Cookes Park brownstone with her partner, DC Fire and Emergency Medical Services firefighter/paramedic Todd Webb, for almost six months now, with her sister Cara and her partner, *Washington Post* investigative reporter Clay McCord, moving in next door the month after Meg and Todd. One of the first things they'd done was remove the fence dividing their respective backyards, giving their dogs—Hawk, along with Cara's two dogs, Saki, a mini blue pit bull, and Blink, a brindle greyhound, and McCord's energetic golden retriever, Cody—space to run.

This morning, the dogs had enjoyed a romp over grass stiff and sparkling with the season's first heavy frost. Cara had leaned out her back door far enough to wave at her sister before shivering and disappearing inside. Meg had retreated inside, as well, and had enjoyed the warmth with a second cup of coffee while the dogs frolicked together, easily visible through the sliding glass door.

As far as Hawk was concerned, nothing was better after a good breakfast and a run with friends than a nap with his dragon, and he'd been happily dozing since he'd come back in.

Meg's gaze was drawn to the other side of the fireplace in their open-concept kitchen and family room, where a tall, fully decorated tree stood, its multicolored lights throwing a warm glow over the space and sparkling off reflective balls and through glass ornaments. Adding to the festive flavor, lights twined and twinkled through an evergreen garland draping the mantel; stockings labeled MEG, TODD, and HAWK hung below, flanking the fireplace; a stuffed elf lay in the dog bed behind Hawk; and an evergreen-scented candle burned on the stove.

The entire setting made her think of peace and family. This was both couples' first Christmas living together, and Meg and Cara were looking forward to jointly hosting the family for the seasonal celebration. Meg had booked some vacation days over Christmas and was eagerly anticipating a little time off to relax and revel in the season. To rest and recharge, to enjoy family, as well as the holiday treats.

A break would also allow time to fit in a little wedding planning. Their summer ceremony was coming up fast, and there was still so much to do.

After pulling the elastic off her wrist, she gathered up her long dark hair—a gift from her paternal black Irish grandmother, along with her fair skin and ice-blue eyes—and tied it back into a ponytail. Pushing back from the table, she stood, then snagged the zip-up hoodie she'd tossed over the back of her chair and shrugged into it. Casual wear—her usual outfit of an athletic long-sleeved tee, yoga pants, and a hoodie—was a perk of life in search and rescue. You had to be ready to deploy at any moment, so you dressed in the morning for the ten-mile wilderness trail you might have to run with your dog later in the day.

She worked out of a building full of male and female FBI agents of various ranks, and every one of them wore some variety of business suit. She was happy to be in the active minority that got a pass on formal office wear.

Meg was just latching the dishwasher after loading in her breakfast dishes when she heard the sound of a key in the front door lock. With trepidation, she stepped toward the kitchen doorway leading out to the hallway and the front foyer. Todd had left for his eight o'clock shift almost an hour before, and there was no good reason for him to be home from the firehouse so soon.

The front door opened, and McCord stepped into her foyer on a chill gust of wind that ruffled his blond hair and wrapped around Meg's ankles fifteen feet away. He was clearly in a rush, having not taken the time to put on his winter jacket but simply looping it over his arm. His intent, strained expression, and the way his gaze sharply locked on her, then shot to Hawk behind her, had the bottom dropping out of her stomach.

Normally, McCord would knock on the locked door and wait for Meg to open it instead of letting himself in with the spare key he and Cara kept for emergencies.

Something was wrong. Something so wrong he deemed the time it would take for Meg to answer the door was simply too much to lose.

"Hawk, come." Meg's voice was quiet, but the command in her tone had him scrambling upright. In a moment, her dog was sitting obediently at her knee as McCord strode toward them, his cell phone pressed to his ear.

"That's all you know so far?" McCord's words were rushed and insistent. "Yeah, I get it. It's early. I'm with Meg now. Can you run over it again for her? That will give me a chance to make notes." McCord jabbed an icon on-screen before setting the phone down on the table. "You're on speaker." He dug in his back pocket, and pulled out the battered notepad he always carried, a pen jammed down its spiral ring. He met Meg's eyes and cut right to the chase. "We have a major incident. Sykes just called me with it."

Meg's gaze shot to McCord's phone, where the words

"Martin Sykes" glowed in white block letters against the black screen. Sykes was McCord's editor at the *Post*, and a call from him, especially outside regular work hours, meant a story. She sank down into a kitchen chair beside the phone. "Martin, good morning. What's going on?"

"Have you been deployed yet?" Sykes's words carried the same stress and rushed cadence as McCord's.

Meg looked up to meet McCord's wary blue eyes behind his wire-framed glasses. "No. Should we be?"

"Maybe Beaumont doesn't know yet," Sykes said, referring to Meg's boss, Special-Agent-in-Charge Craig Beaumont, who ran the FBI's Human Scent Evidence Team. "A building collapsed downtown."

"*What?* Where?"

"Talbot Terraces on I Street NW."

Meg closed her eyes, conjuring a map in her mind. Instead of running in a neat line, I Street NW ran in a series of jagged disconnects from just short of Union Station in the east to nearly all the way to the Potomac River in the west. The building's location could be anywhere from the city's main transportation hub to the heart of the nation's political capital to one of the country's most prestigious universities.

Correctly reading her silence, Sykes said, "The corner of I and 9th Streets NW."

Meg's eyes flew open to find McCord beside her, head bent, pen flying over the notepad. "That's not even three-quarters of a mile from the White House."

"I know."

"Is there—"

"We have no idea," Sykes interrupted, clearly reading her question about national security and the safety of the president simply from her tone.

"Sykes, give her the rundown of what you know."

McCord was still head down, writing, not willing to waste a second. "We need to be out the door in two minutes."

"If not right now." Sykes blew out a breath. "What I know so far: A twelve-story building collapsed minutes ago in the heart of downtown DC. It's too early to know why, whether it was a structural failure or a malicious attack. Early reports say it just folded in on itself with no warning."

"Twelve stories," Meg breathed, already calculating the difficulty of a search at such a complex and massive site. "It's a residential building?"

"Partly. Ten stories of high-priced condos, with a fancy pool and terraces on the roof. Shops and restaurants took up the extended first floor, so there was no true second floor."

"And the whole thing collapsed?"

"I don't think so. Early reports are chaotic, and the scene is mostly hidden in a massive cloud of concrete dust, but it sounds like part of the building is still standing. If it is, they're going to mount a rescue for anyone trapped inside."

Mount a rescue. And the first responders will come from DC Fire and EMS.

Meg's hand locked around McCord's wrist, and he stopped making notes long enough to look up, the tightness of his expression and the set of his jaw telegraphing he was already two steps in front of her.

"I know Webb's on shift today," he said. "Which means they'll send him in."

"If it's as bad as it sounds, DCFEMS will send in everyone on shift and call for anyone off shift as well. And will already be calling in mutual aid," Meg said, referring to the agreement fire departments had with their neighboring departments to help each other out in times of crisis, no questions asked. If so, Todd's two brothers, Luke and Josh, both of whom had followed their father into the Baltimore Fire Department, might be on their way to DC shortly.

Meg stuffed her concern for Todd down in the face of her own challenges. If this scenario was as bad as she feared, she needed to be on point. Fretting about her partner could cost lives. He was smart, strong, and capable. Additionally, he would have his company with him. As always, they looked out for each other. She would have to depend on that to ease her fears so she could concentrate on what she and Hawk could do. "At this time in the morning, some of the residents would have left for work or school, but surely some would still be in their apartments. And if the entire height of the building has collapsed, even for just a portion of the building, they're going to need the dogs to search for survivors in the rubble."

"That's why I wanted you to know right away," McCord said. "Craig needs to mobilize the teams."

"He's my next call, but it's going to be from the SUV. Can you give me the exact address?" Meg stood to retrieve her go bag and the extra equipment she knew this kind of site would require.

"Once we're in the SUV, sure."

She noted his use of the plural. "McCord, this is a rescue operation. You're not rescue personnel."

"It's the only story in town today, and likely for the next few weeks. I'm coming no matter what. If I come with you, it saves clogging the streets with one more vehicle when every emergency person in the city is headed there. Do a guy a solid. I brought you the story after all."

She knew she didn't have time to argue with him. "Fine." She turned back to the phone. "Thanks for the heads-up, Martin." Meg pushed McCord's phone toward him and jogged to the mudroom to get her bag and the gear she'd need for this kind of search.

Within a few minutes, they were speeding toward downtown in Meg's SUV, with Hawk lying in his canine compartment behind them, visible through the mesh separating the front passenger seats from the large area that took up the space where a back seat would normally be. He'd been trained to rest in that compartment, as once they arrived at any search site, he'd have to hit the ground running.

They'd just made the turn onto P Street NW when Meg's phone rang. One quick glance at her handset, securely mounted on the dash, told her Craig had saved her making the call herself. Answering the call from her steering wheel, she skipped unnecessary salutations. "Craig, I know about the collapse. McCord and I are already on the way. You've deployed the teams?"

"You were my first call. McCord alerted you?"

"Yes. Calls came into the *Post*, and Sykes looped in McCord, who came to find me. We're about fifteen minutes out under normal circumstances."

"Going to be hard to get there, as they're already locking the area down. Flash your badge to get through. I'm coming too. Can you call Brian? I'll take care of Lauren and Scott."

"Can do. I'll call you when I'm on-site, and we can figure out where incident command is."

Meg hung up and immediately called Brian Foster, her partner on the Human Scent Evidence Team. Her fingers tapped the steering wheel impatiently as his phone rang three times before Brian picked up.

"Morning," Brian said, a cheerful note in his voice. "Are you—"

Meg cut him off. "Grab your gear and get downtown.

You'll need coveralls, your hard hat, and steel toes. And winter gear for underneath. We could be outside for hours."

"What happened?" Brian's congenial tone was wiped clean away, replaced by pure business.

"Twelve-story building collapse at I Street NW and 9th Street NW. Mixed business and residential."

Brian sucked in a sharp breath. "Any idea about casualties?"

"None. It literally just happened. Craig's scrambling the teams and is meeting us downtown. Hawk and I are en route."

"Lacey, come."

Meg could picture Brian's German shepherd, Lacey, morphing from relaxation to work mode at that single command.

"We'll be out the door in sixty seconds," Brian said, "and will get there as soon as we can fight our way through traffic. Call you when we're there." He hung up.

Meg white-knuckled the steering wheel a little tighter, cursing the single lane of traffic open to her as a row of parked cars filled the curb lane.

"Don't strangle the steering wheel," McCord said. "It's not going to get us there any faster."

Meg forced herself to loosen her hold slightly and gave McCord a sideways glance where he sat in the passenger seat, his own tension revealed in his stiffly upright posture rather than his normal casual slouch. "You know, you talk a good story about trying to keep the downtown core clear of traffic, but don't think I missed your real angle here."

"And what's that?"

"Every Metro PD cop in the area is converging on the site, and they're locking down the area for blocks. But I'll get in because I can badge my way through the barricades. You'll get carried along for the ride."

"All it's going to do is gain me some time. You know I'd get through one way or another on foot. This early on, there's no way they'll be able to block every access point." McCord's usual irreverence was entirely missing from his tone, replaced by a dogged insistence. "You're saving me annoying a bunch of cops who will already have their hands full." He stared out the windshield, his fingers rhythmically clasping and unclasping his knees. "This is going to be bad."

"Yeah." When silence stretched, Meg felt she owed it to McCord to give him more detail. She might give him a hard time for using her to angle for a story, but she didn't blame him. Especially when she knew full well any story in his hands would be told fairly and truthfully. "Hawk and I, we've been deployed to earthquake sites several times, which is the closest experience I can draw from for this. It's . . . hard."

"Because you can't reach people in time?"

"That, yes. But also because you find a lot of people died instantly. You'll spend hours searching and often won't find anyone alive. And time is a real factor. Often, you don't find anyone after the first day of searching. But in a collapse site like this, sometimes you're days away from tunneling down to anyone who might have survived the original collapse." The car in front of them turned right; Meg hammered the gas, and they jumped forward into open road. "I just want to get there. I can't imagine the terror of being trapped in the dark, waiting for some-one—anyone—to find you. Hawk can do it. He can find them."

McCord leaned forward, peering through the wind-screen, as Meg approached Dupont Circle. "And here's your way to speed things up. Right . . . there!"

As McCord pointed over the steering wheel, past the driver's side mirror, the long wail of a siren sounded as a white SUV, with blue-and-red accents and lights flashing, sped toward them.

"There's only one place he's going," McCord stated. "Get in behind him. He's not going to take the time to stop to ticket you—"

"I've talked myself out of tickets and into a police escort before," Meg interrupted. "But I agree, he's not going to take the time to pull me over."

The cruiser shot past, and Meg swung into the circle behind it, pushing the pedal to the floor so they slipped in before any other vehicle, and sped after it. As cars pulled off to the side to make way, she stayed behind the cruiser.

Traffic was no longer a problem. As McCord lapsed into silence, Meg took the time to get into the right headspace. Today was going to be a hard day, but miracles could happen.

Craig's words from the Jamie L. Whitten Building bombing twenty months earlier rose in her mind. *Bring home the ones you can.*

She knew what it meant: Save every life possible, but leave the lost behind when you leave the site. Don't carry them with you. Concentrate on life.

She had a bad feeling she was going to need that miracle to come out of today with any kind of win.

CHAPTER 2

Foundation: The lowest structural element of a building, designed to support the entire structure and transfer the total gravity load to the ground beneath.

Monday, December 17, 8:47 AM
CityCenterDC
Washington, DC

Tailing the police cruiser got them all the way to the historic Carnegie Library. After that, they stopped only long enough for Meg to show her ID and roll down the back window for the officer blocking traffic to see Hawk and wave them through.

She turned onto 9th Street NW. Then shock eased her foot off the accelerator, letting the SUV coast, as Talbot Terraces came into view.

Or what was left of it.

"Oh my God . . ."

McCord's stunned murmur echoed her own thoughts as she struggled to piece together the downtown core she knew with the current reality. She'd driven these streets for three years, ever since she'd joined the FBI. Especially since moving to Cookes Park, she'd often use 9th Street NW as her conduit south to the J. Edgar Hoover Building.

She regularly passed the luxury condo building, which took up over half the block, a towering structure of pale spears of concrete; wide, glass-fronted balconies, supported by lengths of decorative I-beams that ran the breadth of the building; and what had to be panoramic views of the nation's capital from long stretches of unobstructed windows. And then there were the terraces for which the building was named—tiers of gardens stepping down to the rooftop pool. In summer, the terrace greenery tumbled over the railings, as if reaching for the streets below. As someone who loved classic architecture and who would lecture Brian during their crack-of-dawn jogs through old residential DC about her favorite aspects of the Federal or Beaux Arts houses around them, even Meg could see the appeal of Talbot Terraces for those who liked a clean, modern look.

Now an unnatural hole in the cityscape revealed the sky beyond as the backdrop to the crumbling wreck of the tower.

It took her breath away.

The building was partially masked in a haze of suspended concrete dust, but the scope of the disaster was undeniably clear, and Meg knew in that moment any kind of miracle might be out of reach. She had an impression of hazy height on the west end of the building, but she couldn't tell how much of the structure was still standing. What she could see more clearly was the devastation at the east end of the building, which abutted 9th Street NW.

She'd never counted the floors, but Sykes had said there were twelve. Those twelve stories had crumbled, falling as if in a coordinated fashion on a slight angle, one floor at a time, each layer above pancaking down on the one below it. The stepped levels of the different floors were clear, but instead of occupying twelve stories, all that concrete, glass, and steel was only about three stories tall.

She couldn't see the historic Gerrard Apartments behind Talbot Terraces. It was four stories itself, so it should have been visible. Was it also down, or was it still standing and hidden in the cloud of dust and behind stories of packed debris?

How many could still be alive in all that?

Meg's foot hit the accelerator again, and the SUV jerked forward from her sudden need to get there, to get onto the pile. But they made it only about twenty feet farther before being stopped by a mass of emergency vehicles. Knowing this was as close as they were likely to get, and any time spent looking for parking could be counted in the last breaths of victims, Meg pulled off to the side of the road, ignoring the NO PARKING signs along 9th Street NW, and cut the engine. "We'll go on foot from here."

"Yeah." McCord remained frozen, his gaze riveted on the devastated structure still visible through the windshield, over the open-air parking lot to their right. "How could . . ." He trailed off, as if trying to find a way to put his question delicately. "What are the chances . . . anyone survived that?"

Meg was already climbing out of the SUV to circle to the back and pop the hatch. "We're going to be searching for voids or anyone close to the surface or the edges." She paused, her hands fisted around the straps of her go bag, as her gaze drifted past McCord, still in the passenger seat, and through the windshield. "Otherwise, no one survived that."

She slid her pack on and then closed the hatch as dread at the probable futility of what they were about to attempt roiled through her. She opened the compartment door to the sidewalk. "Hawk, down." He jumped down in a single fluid leap, and she snapped the leash on his collar. Looking up, she found McCord beside her. "Stay with me. We'll likely still have to badge our way into the site proper."

She pulled out her phone as they started speed-walking down the sidewalk, and waited as the call connected to Craig. "We're here."

"Me too. Meet me at incident command. They've set up in the Park at CityCenter. You know it?"

"Yes. Todd and I were there a few weeks ago, when they held the annual tree lighting." Her memory of that night was lit by a happy glow—surrounded by a large crowd, already well into the holiday spirit, she and Todd had stood holding hands, each with a hot chocolate, their faces illuminated by the white twinkle lights outlining the bare branches of every tree as the seventy-five-foot fir at the far end of the park transformed from darkness into brilliant, joyful light. Someone nearby had mentioned the tree held 150,000 lights and nearly 5,000 ornaments, and she believed it. It was magnificent and had made the night truly magical.

The thought of that location, a place of such joy only a few weeks ago, now the operations center for a scene of death and destruction was an extra kick to the gut.

"That's the place," Craig continued. "I don't know where you're parked, but you need to avoid I Street until we get started. When the building fell, part of it collapsed into the street."

Cold horror rose in a wave. Meg knew what downtown DC was like in the morning—everyone trying to get somewhere as fast as possible. She herself had to build in extra time to get to the Hoover Building, because traffic in the city's core could be stop and go at best. I Street NW would have been packed with traffic at that time of the morning. Not to mention the added pressure of holiday shoppers trying to get an early start to their day. "But . . . rush hour."

"I know. We don't know how many cars and pedestrians are under there. Hurry. We need to get started.

DCFEMS is already on-site and is starting to mount rescues."

Which means Todd is here somewhere. And since Engine Company 2 is physically closest, unless they were already out on a call, then he and his men were first on scene. That makes his chief the incident commander.

"Is Chief Koenig IC?"

"I think that's what he said his name was. I quickly introduced myself so he knew our teams were incoming, but then I got out of his way. There needs to be three of him right now."

"They're lucky the closest house is staffed with one of the few battalion chiefs in town who also happened to be on duty. We're in good hands. See you in a few." She hung up.

"This way. Hawk, come." Meg broke into a jog, and Hawk instantly matched her pace. She cut into the half-full parking lot, heading east, and jogged through lanes of parked cars to come out on the far side, onto the wide, tree-lined sidewalk of New York Avenue NW. A glance over her shoulder showed McCord behind her; then he closed the distance to run beside her. Beside them, the tall, mirrored facade of the Conrad hotel reflected both the bright blue morning sky and the postmodern granite and glass building opposite, an image that struck Meg as painfully normal on a day turned upside down. They barely paused at a red light at 10th Street NW, the mostly deserted streets giving them clear passage.

Across from them lay the Park at CityCenter. Part of the five-acre CityCenterDC area, which included both Talbot Terraces and the Conrad, the park was a small, triangular oasis bounded by New York Avenue NW, 10th and 11th Streets NW, and an eleven-story steel and glass office building to the south. Slate and granite pavers stretched throughout the park, broken only by a scatter of treed gardens, empty now with early winter's chill, and a fountain, its water still gurgling and running down ridged, topographical spillways. At the far end of the park, the Christmas tree towered, magnificent even with its lights dulled in the brightness of morning.

Meg's gaze was drawn to the emergency vehicles at the edge of the park, lights flashing in bursts of red, white, and blue. Fire engines and ladder trucks filled the street, interspersed with police patrol cars and SUVs. Uniformed officers and firemen in helmets and black turnout gear were everywhere, and the buzz of radio chatter filled the air. But it was the red-and-white SUV at the end of the park, where I Street NW took a jog to the right a block north, that caught her attention. The back hatch of the SUV was open, and even from there, Meg could see the incident command board: a long open case holding two white boards—one upright, one flat—and several smaller foldout boards. Todd had explained to her that this was how the incident commander at any fire scene kept track of who was where in the operation. It was a system designed to ensure every person was accounted for at all times, and it also laid out the incident action plan.

Meg's gaze cut back down the street to the vehicles from what had to be at least five companies and every man available.

That board isn't going to cut it for this.

She scanned the crowd for Craig's familiar stocky frame and salt-and-pepper hair. Then she heard her name being called and glanced back to see Craig standing about fifteen feet from the chief's SUV, waving one arm over his head. With a quick look to McCord, and his answering nod, they redirected.

As they approached, Meg could hear Koenig barking into a handheld radio. "Set up the staging area on New York Avenue NW. It's three one-way lanes in each direction, separated by a boulevard. We can keep the trucks in line, still have room to move vehicles through, and use the boulevard for equipment, supplies, and personnel."

Meg watched Craig, whose gaze was fixed on McCord as they jogged over. "Have they started size-up?"

But Craig stayed focused on McCord, speaking to him directly. "I need you to stay with me. The site can be accessed only by professionals."

"That's fine," McCord agreed. "They have work to do. I just . . . I can't be out there wondering. I need to be here." McCord had worked with the team often enough that he understood their job, and they understood his. In fact, he'd worked with them long enough that when he disappeared last August, the entire team had shown up in the middle of the night to stage a rescue. He was one of them now.

"I get that. But the last thing they're going to want is a journalist tracking their every move."

"I'm not going to—"

"I know that." Craig cut him off. "But they don't. Unless anyone asks directly, we're not saying who you are or what you do. Keep the note-taking and the pictures on the down-low. And anything you use goes through me first, if not Public Affairs."

"Got it." McCord scanned the scene around them. "This looks like chaos to me, but I'm sure it's organized chaos. Where are we?"

"Just getting started." Craig turned to Meg. "FEMA's incoming. This is DCFEMS's show, but they're going to be part of unified command."

Meg's gaze flicked to Koenig, now bent over his board and moving small magnetic rectangles around, each one representing an officer or a truck—who commanded operations, who was the safety officer, which company was taking which role in the incident. "That's early for them to be involved."

"Very. With the exception of the Whitten Building bombing last year, the 2011 Virginia earthquake, and the Pentagon in 2001, most of their incidents aren't local. But they're only fifteen minutes away; it makes sense they'd lend their expertise. DCFEMS is a damned good department, but . . ." Craig's gaze cut to the activity going on down the street. "Did you see it?"

"Partly." Meg followed his gaze. "Hard to see the details from that far out under a cloud of dust, but it looked . . ." She stopped, struggling for a way to describe the destruction she'd witnessed.

"Catastrophic," McCord said, the single word clipped.

Craig turned away from the site. "FEMA is deploying the two closest Type 1 USAR teams to start. Virginia TF1 and Maryland TF1. But they know they're going to need more."

"You're losing me," McCord said. "USAR? TF1? Type 1? These aren't the usual terms you toss around."

"Urban search and rescue," Meg said. "DHS and FEMA's National USAR Response System has twenty-eight task forces, or TFs, across the country. They specialize in exactly this kind of event—hurricanes, earthquakes, bombings. Structural collapse is their specialty, no matter how it happened. They'll come with search personnel, structural specialists, medical support, and a *lot* of rescue equipment. DCFEMS has plenty of equipment, but not enough to support an incident of this size. Without getting into the nitty-gritty, a Type 1 task force is big enough to split into two full twelve-hour shifts. It will also come with all the equipment a Type 2 task force would have, but will have additional capabilities to handle a hazmat situation."

"You think you're going to need that here?"

"Collapse sites can be incredibly toxic. The dust raised can put people into respiratory distress. Older buildings can have airborne asbestos or lead dust. Carbon monoxide, Freon from older refrigerators and air-conditioning units, pool chemicals, cleaning supplies . . . all those containers pulverized, and then the force of the collapse sends it all up into a massive toxic cloud."

"And you're going into that?"

"Not for long," Craig interjected. "As soon as PPE arrives, you'll be wearing it." He held up a hand as Meg drew in a breath. "No, we're not waiting for it."

"Good. As soon as size-up is complete and the other teams arrive, we need to get out there." Meg searched 10th Street NW for any sign of the other dog teams. "There's not enough of us yet. We're going to be shorthanded to start."

"That's where the incoming task forces will help."

"You said there's enough for two shifts. There will be strength in numbers at that point?" McCord asked.

"Each task force will be sending seventy to eighty people, which seems like a lot, but it's not when you think about twenty-four-hour coverage and rotating shifts. Reflex time is going to be an issue." Meg side-eyed McCord. "Meaning how long it takes to pull personnel in, load the equipment, and get here."

"Both teams are in motion," Craig said. "They're only an hour out each, but it will take three times that just to get ready for an active deployment of this size. But three task forces per major incident is standard, so Pennsylvania TF1 is also incoming. They'll probably take more like twelve hours to get here."

McCord shaded his eyes with one hand as he squinted down the street. "So nothing is going on so far?"

"Not at all. DCFEMS is already doing peripheral rescues of anyone who is at the edge of the incident or who is lightly trapped. If they're easily accessible, that's where they're starting." Craig looked down at Hawk. "But that's not where we need you two. We need you on the pile. Koenig has one of the deputy chiefs doing the initial size-up of the area and locations where we can safely get started with the searches." His gaze rose to the part of the building still standing, visible down at the far end of the adjacent block, partially obstructed by the historic three-story bank building that faced 10th Street NW.

The dust cloud was starting to settle, and the standing section of the building—the entire western wing, which was about fifty feet deep before a jagged cutoff into the void—looked like it had gone through an aerial strike. Even from this distance, significant cracks in the concrete gaped black against dusty gray, and the glass-fronted balconies were shattered. Near the dividing line that could have meant life and death as part of the building collapsed, the exposed structural steel supporting the balconies was torqued, a testimony to the unbelievable forces applied to it. But, worst of all, the structure looked as if it were listing to the southwest.

How long would they have before that part of the building fell?

Two people burst from the building, out the front doors at the northwest corner and onto to the deserted sidewalk, left as a buffer zone between the rescuers and the unstable structure. Three firefighters ran toward them, then shepherded them away from the building, leading them toward 11th Street NW.

"At least some people are getting out on foot," Meg said.

Craig nodded. "About a dozen so far, from what I understand."

"Have they got triage set up already?"

"They're going to clear out the parking lot on 9th Street

NW, set up tents, and use that for triage and operations, but until then, they're using a closed section of I Street NW and diverting emergency vehicles down 8th Street NW."

Motion caught Meg's eye, high up on the front face of the structure, two floors from the top. A figure stood in the open doorway that led out to the balcony, waving something bright red—maybe a towel?—over their head. Meg was too far away to hear anything over the din of the voices, radios, and running emergency vehicles, but she could only imagine that individual screaming for help at the top of their lungs.

She pointed toward the balcony. "We have at least one victim near the top."

Craig and McCord followed her indication.

McCord whistled. "You have to assume they're trapped, or they'd try to get out on their own."

"When a building comes down like that, only partially, the forces on the rest of the building are severe," Craig said. "Inside the standing structure, walls could be coming down, doorways collapsing, stairs crumbling. There literally may be no interior way down. And depending on the layout of any space cleaved in two because of the collapse, there may not be a way out of the living space." His phone rang, and he pulled it out of his pocket before glancing up at Meg. "It's Brian." He accepted the call. "Where are you? Good." He quickly sketched out where to meet them and hung up. "He's close, coming down 10th."

Meg scanned 10th Street NW but couldn't see her partner or his German shepherd, Lacey. "What about Lauren and Scott?"

"Should be here soon. Wait here for Brian. Koenig put down his radio, and I need to see if we have the all clear to enter the site, even if just at the outskirts." He headed for Koenig.

Meg turned to look toward the building and scanned

the black-clad firefighters. Already she could see groups of firefighters at the edges of the collapse, could hear the roar of a K-12 saw cutting through metal or concrete. But it was a sea of black helmets.

McCord didn't need to ask what she was doing. "Do you see him? I mean, could you pick him out under all that gear?"

"All I need is the helmet. Firefighters are black. Chiefs and captains are white. Lieutenants are yellow."

"Don't see any yellow."

"Me either. But he's there somewhere." Meg didn't say it, but her gaze rose unwillingly to the structure itself. A shout from her left broke her gaze, and she swung around to find Brian and Lacey jogging up to them. Like her, Brian wore steel-toe boots and navy coveralls, with FBI in yellow block letters above the left breast pocket and on the back, and he carried his go bag over both shoulders and a red hard hat in his left hand, leaving his dark hair uncovered. Like Hawk, Lacey was wearing a collar instead of her FBI work vest as she easily loped beside Brian on lead.

"Hey." Brian slowed to a stop and then pointed past Meg and McCord. "And the gang's all here."

Meg turned to see Lauren Wycliffe, tall and statuesque, her blond hair pulled back like Meg's in a no-nonsense ponytail, striding toward them with Rocco, her black-and-white border collie, on lead beside her. Behind them came long, lanky, blond Scott Park, keeping pace but somehow still managing to look like he was just slouching along, with Theo, his droopy bloodhound, looking more perky than usual. Many bloodhounds were energetic. Theo was not in their number, but he had an unbeatable nose, and Scott always knew how to motivate him. As the best nose on the Human Scent Evidence Team, Theo would be a godsend. Both dogs were wearing only collars, and Lauren and Scott were similarly attired to Meg and Brian.

They were ready to go. All they needed were their orders.

Craig jogged back to the group. "Good. You're all here. Thanks for the quick response."

Lauren's gaze was locked on the scene down the street. "This incident is huge; we're not going to be even remotely enough manpower. Who else is incoming? And do they have dogs?"

"Virginia, Maryland, and Pennsylvania USAR are on their way. Virginia and Maryland could be here as early as early afternoon, and Pennsylvania by tonight. All three are deploying dog teams, but you guys will start us off. They're lucky we're based downtown and no one was deployed. Let me give you the rundown of what we know so far, keeping in mind there's a lot we don't know. But understanding the little we do know could help you deduce where victims might be until we get the building layout." Craig sucked in a breath, his shoulders rising.

Meg had seen Craig give an untold number of briefings in the field, but this one had clearly hit him hard.

Had hit them all hard.

She met Craig's eyes and gave him a short nod, trying to convey her support with nothing more than sympathetic eyes and a gentle quirk of her lips. *We're all in this together. Help us help them.*

He gave her a short nod in return and let go of the breath, sending some of the tension in his shoulders with it. "The building fell just after eight this morning. Metro PD was first on the scene, and they immediately jumped in, trying to help anyone they could see. Bystanders pitched in, and a not insignificant number of victims were pulled clear or identified for rescue in the first fifteen minutes. DCFEMS was on scene by then, and they took over the rescue efforts, freeing officers to talk to witnesses and lock down the area.

"Talbot Terraces is L-shaped, with the short wing running north–south and the longer wing running east–west along I Street NW. The building went up around the historic Gerrard Apartments, which is why it has that shape— to best use the space available to them on that block when every square inch of downtown land is precious and you can't touch a historic building. Early word is that the middle section of the building, the section running along I Street NW that wasn't part of the rectangular wing that ran north–south along 10th Street NW, fell first."

"So . . . about the middle third of the building as it ran along I Street NW?" Brian asked. "But not the whole length?"

"Not at first. The middle section fell first, and it was constrained by parts of the structure to the east and the west, so the debris spilled out over the street, trapping any cars and pedestrians on I Street NW underneath."

"The rest of that wing couldn't have stayed standing long," Lauren stated. "Without any bracing and after that kind of applied force and with the resulting structural damage?"

"It didn't. It swayed for about six or seven seconds, which was a godsend, because it actually gave some people on the street level time to run or abandon their cars. Then it too came down, twisting slightly and falling partially over the collapsed middle section."

Meg thought back to the pile as she'd seen it from 11th Street NW—the stacked, staggered layers. "That explains the stepwise stories. The east end didn't come straight down."

"Right. We're doing everything we can to figure out who might have been inside and where, so occupancy lists and building plans have been requested, but they're going to take time to pull together. Not to mention it was morning, but not first thing. If we're lucky, a lot of occupants will have already left to go about their daily activities. But a number of them were still on-site at the time of the collapse. They might have still been in bed, or in their bedrooms, getting dressed for the day. Or the bathroom or the kitchen. Maybe less likely they'd be sitting in front of the TV, relaxing. Once we have the layouts, that will help us figure out where it might be more likely to find victims, so we can focus our searches."

"What about the retail space underneath?" Brian asked.

"That hasn't been reviewed yet, because we're so early into the incident. But a list will be made, and companies will be tracked down and asked to assist. If we're lucky, it might have been too early for the stores to be occupied."

"If we're unlucky," Lauren stated flatly, "people might have come in early to deal with stock before they opened their doors at nine. We're in the thick of holiday shopping." She shot a glance back to the building and said what they were all thinking. "The holidays will be a nightmare for too many families now."

"Let's try to minimize that number." Craig pulled his radio off his belt. "We're taking channel twelve. If you need any assistance, go through me, and I'll liaise with Koenig or the new IC once command transfers to whoever will be head of the incident management team. Or, once things really get set up, whoever takes lead on operations. This site is going to be dangerous, so I want everyone to be extremely careful. I'm going to set up search areas in close sequence so if any dog alerts, we have a second dog nearby to confirm. There's going to be a high degree of effort to pull anyone out of the collapsed areas and we can't afford to waste a moment of the rescue personnel's time. For now, until an exclusion zone is officially set up around the standing structure, once they determine how stable it is, we're going to concentrate on the outskirts of the pile, up the stepped layers."

"That's going to have the best chance of survival," Meg agreed. "The layers are close. Unless there are significant voids, no one in the middle or the bottom of the pile survived. But at the edges, where there's less mass . . ."

Brian nodded. "We have a chance."

Three minutes later, they had their search areas and stood at the curb, waiting as another ladder truck drove through and toward the standing structure to join two other rescue vehicles already extending their ladders to prepare for balcony rescues.

As the truck passed, Meg took a deep breath and looked down at her dog. "Hawk, come. Let's find them."

CHAPTER 3

Overburden: Nonstructural materials, often decorative, built over structural elements, such as tiles, pavers, or a colored or stamped topping slab.

Monday, December 17, 9:12 AM
Talbot Terraces
Washington, DC

I Street NW looked like a war zone.

Meg led the teams down the street at a jog, Hawk keeping pace at her knee on lead. She could hear Brian's footsteps behind her and knew Scott and Theo, and Lauren and Rocco, brought up the rear.

They had their designated search areas and were ready to hit the pile on the far side of the building. First, though, they had to get through the chaos of the rescues in progress.

As they approached what was left of Talbot Terraces, Meg got her first good look at the disaster. She thought she was prepared, but the simultaneous assault on all her senses struck her like a physical blow.

A cacophony of sound cut through the clouds of dust: car alarms blared from under the rubble, adding to the rumble of running engines from emergency vehicles; K-12 saws roared as they sliced through concrete and rebar; metal screamed as the Jaws of Life were used to extricate a driver at the edge of the debris field; and cries for help and the yells of first responders working together rode over it all. The air smelled of burnt electrics, plastics, and rubber, and smoke hung thick with concrete dust, which Meg could feel as grit between her teeth with each indrawn breath. The sight of millions of pounds of debris piled over the sidewalk and spilled into the street chilled her blood.

She darted around the back of a DCFEMS engine and to the far side of the sidewalk, where a woman sat on the curb, a shrieking toddler cradled in her arms, as a fire-fighter crouched down in front of her, a comforting hand on her knee. Blood tracked down from the woman's hair-line, trickling over her dust-coated temple and cheek to splatter on the collar of her coat. The child's coat and romper were torn, but thankfully, he appeared otherwise unharmed. The young mother accepted a blanket from an-other firefighter, wrapped it around her child, and rocked him, trying to comfort in the midst of chaos, all while re-sponding to the firefighter's questions. Behind them, at the edge of the debris field, bystanders helped anyone mobile, the dust-covered staggering away from the disaster with an arm around a non-dusty counterpart. A woman in dress pants and a cashmere coat ignored her expensive at-tire and climbed onto a jagged slab of concrete and, brac-ing her hands on rubble, leaned in as if to talk to someone. Turning, she waved an arm over her head and shouted for assistance.

Another victim found.

As they ran past paramedics loading an unconscious man on a gurney into the back of an ambulance, Hawk suddenly whipped his head toward the pile and broke his stride, bumping into Meg's legs. Not able to hear anything over the din, Meg nonetheless knew her dog might be able to pick up something no human ear could detect. Slowing slightly, Meg spotted a navy sedan, half buried by concrete and steel, and the terrified eyes of a child in the back. Small fists beat on the glass as the girl looked directly at Meg and Hawk, her mouth open in a silent scream, at least to Meg's ears. Meg stumbled momentarily, drawn by the need to help, especially to help a child, but then a fire-fighter ran toward the car, the hydraulic spreader of the Jaws of Life in his arms, followed by two others carrying the generator needed to power the equipment.

Meg picked up her pace again and forced herself to turn toward the pile. That was where she was needed. Not where the victims could be easily identified and it was sim-ply a matter of brute force and equipment to extract them, but where the victims were hidden, where no one came to their rescue. Where they waited in the dark, terrified and alone.

The dogs would be their rescue.

They jogged to the corner of the debris pile, and Meg dropped to a walk. Brian caught up with her nearly imme-diately; Lauren and Scott, only seconds after. As a group, they turned to look at the pile.

"God almighty . . . ," Brian whispered.

This close to the three-story pile, close enough that the dust no longer blocked the view, they had their first real examination of the debris. As bad as Meg had imagined it might be, the reality was even more jarring, even more of a shock to the system.

Pieces of ten-inch-thick concrete lay scattered in every size imaginable, from pulverized stones to shattered sec-tions of wall, still held together by the web of rebar orig-inally reinforcing it. Wispy scraps of yellow insulation poked from between tangled snarls of steel. Shattered glass glinted, and textiles—curtains or bedding—snaked through concrete cinder blocks and around crushed PVC piping. At the top of the pile, a series of HVAC units staggered in a drunken line atop a dark smear of roofing materials.

But it was the jolting disconnect of the personal items mixed in with the building materials, visible even from this distance, that pulled at Meg's heart—a broken kitchen chair, a torn section of rug, a crushed refrigerator, a mattress. A couch picked up and tossed upside down near the top of the pile. A sink ripped from its moorings to teeter on a sharp angle at the edge of a slab. Signs of an everyday life—now almost certainly those of tragic death—shockingly interrupted and on public display.

Scott whistled. "This is going to be hard going. For us and the dogs."

"Yeah," Brian agreed. "And as much as I'd like to get Lacey into her boots, at a site like this, she's going to need her pads to feel every surface. We're going to have to check them on the regular for cuts and abrasions. That steel will be razor sharp." He paused for a moment, as if his brain was trying to reconcile what his eyes were seeing. "It's not just going to be looking for voids. It's going to be finding someone in a void who hasn't been impaled on rebar or had their skull crushed by concrete."

Meg sent Brian a sidelong look but didn't reprimand him. His words were brutal, but she knew it was his way of trying to force them all into realistic expectations about the challenges of this mission. To force himself into a realistic expectation. Brian was, after all, the most optimistic of the group. She could hear in his tone that he was trying to temper his own instincts.

There was only one problem with that though.

"Maybe." Meg pitched her voice higher. "But we have to keep the dogs' spirits up."

Brian straightened his spine and put a chipper note in his tone to match Meg's. "Yeah, we do."

Meg's gaze dropped to Hawk, who stood silently at her knee, his eyes on the debris field, his tail low. *He already senses it.* Meg knew well that while a lack of live finds was hard on the handlers, it was even harder on the dogs. A dog who didn't find live victims could become depressed, which would affect their ability to continue to work a disaster. In those cases, handlers often asked first responders unknown to the dogs to "hide" in the rubble, so the dogs could find them.

It had been a strategy used immediately after 9/11 for the same reason. The last live person was pulled from the World Trade Center debris twenty-seven hours after the buildings fell, but the searching went on with live find dogs for thirteen days before the disaster switched from rescue to recovery. Fooling the dogs into thinking they were making live finds was what got them through those last twelve days, exhausted but convinced they were successful in their efforts. It was harder on the handlers, who knew the truth of the situation yet had to act like their spirits stayed high so the dogs didn't pick up on it.

Dogs were incredibly sensitive, and when a dog and handler had a bond like the Human Scent Evidence Team pairs did, it was incredibly hard for handlers to hide that kind of sorrow and depression from their animals. But every single one of them would do it if that was what their partner required.

None of the Human Scent Evidence Team members had been old enough in 2001 to be in the field, but they'd all learned from those who had. And looking at Talbot Terraces, Meg knew every one of them was drawing comparisons to the World Trade Center. A much smaller scale, but she had a bad feeling it would have similar results.

Meg put on the hard hat she'd been carrying while she jogged, and pulled a KN95 mask from the pocket of her coveralls, slipped it on, and fit it around her nose. Craig had said he'd get proper respirators for them all once equipment started flowing into the site, but for now this was the best they could do. Unfortunately, the dogs would be exposed to any toxins on-site, but there was nothing they could do about that. The key to their use here was to be able to inhale every scent particle possible. Hopefully, the handlers would be able to pass the search off to other dogs as more teams were incoming, so no one dog got a truly toxic dose of any chemical in the air. Granted, for now, her current mask protected her only from dust, and in some ways, she felt better being on a more even footing with Hawk. She didn't want to ask him to do anything she wouldn't do herself.

She turned to the other handlers to find them also masked and wearing their hard hats. "Ready? Let's do this." She ran a hand down first Rocco's back and then Theo's. "Good hunting." She looked up at Lauren and Scott. "Be safe."

"You too." Lauren tightened Rocco's lead. "Rocco, come." She crossed the street, heading for 11th Street NW, to skirt the edge of the debris field.

"Theo, come." Scott followed Lauren.

"Ready?" Brian asked Meg.

"Yes."

"You're going to be okay up there?"

Meg's gaze rose to the top of the debris field, three stories up. Her fear of heights wasn't a well-known fact in the group. Brian knew, and while she suspected Lauren had an inkling, Craig wasn't aware at all. Nor would he be, because she wouldn't allow any shortcoming of hers to slow Hawk down when he had work to do. "Going to have to be. More important things on the line here than my little fear of heights. I can do it." She looked down at Hawk. "We can do it."

"Good girl. Call me if you find anything. I'll do the same."

They crossed the street and split up at the bottom of the pile, Meg taking the corner of the building, Brian starting about thirty feet farther down and climbing in parallel.

Meg unleashed Hawk and then unsnapped his collar. It was a breakaway collar and should give way if it got snagged on something but at a site like this, with an un-told number of potentially lethal hazards, she didn't want to take that risk. It was safer that all the dogs worked un-encumbered. She jammed the leash and collar in the side pocket of her go bag, zipped it shut, and resettled the bag securely on her shoulders. "Hawk, find them."

In response to her command, Hawk jumped onto a bro-ken slab of concrete with giant cracks running through its ten-inch depth, creating large gaps in the material. He im-mediately put his nose down and started scenting.

Meg scanned the area around them. Craig had laid out their search areas as a grid, with each of them taking a strip on the grid and working their way through it. Meg's grid was largely over the edge of the building where paral-lel lines of the balconies marked each level. Because the building had twisted slightly as it fell, toppling toward the center of the structure, each level lay slightly offset from the one above it. The glass-fronted balcony walls had all shattered, but the supporting structural steel was mostly intact, marking each level.

She could count only eight of what would have been originally ten floors with balconies, with what was origi-nally the fifth floor now essentially at street level. Which put the first four floors of the building underground, cratered into the parking structure beneath. Finding anyone who might have been in the stores, let alone rescuing them, if they survived the collapse and found themselves in a survivable void, would be incredibly challenging. The USAR teams would be bringing in cameras and listening devices, which would be needed as soon as the teams arrived to direct the rescues.

But in the meantime, they had the dogs.

Meg clambered after Hawk, keeping her eyes firmly on the debris in front of her and not the street lying behind her as she climbed higher.

The first thing that struck Meg was the oppressive silence of the pile. They weren't far from the chaos on I Street NW, but as she climbed higher and higher, and the sounds of the rescues eased away, there were no added sounds save for the chill whistle of the light wind. Balancing on a chunk of concrete that would have been the seventh floor, she spread her arms wide to help keep her balance and ordered her dog to stop. "Hawk, hold." She pulled in a lungful of air and yelled as loud as she could, "Hello! Can anyone hear me? Call out if you can hear me! We're search and rescue! Can you hear me?"

Seconds ticked by as she and her dog listened for any sound—a voice, a tap, a scratch. But there was nothing.

"Okay, Hawk, free. Slow, but find them."

She let him work without her micromanagement; her main guidance in this situation was to keep him in their area of the grid, to make sure that no sections were missed. In normal outdoor searches, a person or an object in the distance released scent particles that spread out with air currents forming a cone the dogs could identify and then work as the cone's diameter decreased until they zeroed in on their prize. However, this search was a matter of trying to find live scent that filtered up from below. In some ways, it wasn't so different from some of the water searches they'd done only a few months before in the

Boundary Waters Canoe Area, where scent had needed to trickle up through the water from the bottom of the lake until the wind scattered it at the surface. Their greatest luck today was that while there were air currents, they were relatively minor, so hopefully, fresh scent would remain close to the victims.

They could use every piece of luck they could get.

Her gaze was drawn up to the standing structure still towering precariously eight stories overhead. The open side of the building was a horrific gaping wound. The left side of the severed section was a solid concrete wall, possibly the back of an elevator shaft or a reinforced stairwell, but the right side was a nightmare—floor after floor of what had once been living spaces, brutally ripped in half. Rebar and vinyl flooring drooped from concrete slabs, while signs of daily life—framed pictures, a couch, a toppled coffee table, a flat-screen TV still attached to a wall—hung in midair. Shards of shattered drywall filled every space, and a lacework of reinforced concrete dripped from each level. Near the upper floors, several HVAC units dangled, held in place by God only knew what, ready to crash onto the pile below.

Widow-makers, as search-and-rescue crews called them.

They had yet to set the exclusion zone around the building, but that word would come down as soon as the structural engineers, now hurrying to the site, could make an assessment. In the meantime, the Human Scent Evidence Team pairs knew to give the standing structure a wide berth because they wouldn't risk their dogs to the hazards of those interrupted living spaces. Later, when the heavy equipment and the cranes were in place, and some of those risks were picked off, secured, or otherwise neutralized, more of the site would open up. For now, they'd stick to the open edges of the pile.

It was tough and slow going over the pile. The debris

was overwhelmingly heavy—jumbled pieces of concrete studded with chunks of cinder block. Tangles of rebar confounded any straight path, and ragged spears of the supporting metal jutted from every surface. Fragments of pool tile popped jarring bits of bright color; small pieces of broken glass were sprinkled throughout; and long lengths of steel of all shapes and sizes—from balcony supports to window frames and doorframes, to sprinkler system pipes—twisted in and out of the rubble. The conformation of the steel, so much of it bent beyond recognition of its original purpose or twisted into knots, told the tale of the incredible forces applied to it.

The kind of forces soft tissue wouldn't be able to withstand.

Meg gave her head a shake. *Stop it. Miracles happen. You've seen it after hurricanes and earthquakes.*

She turned her attention to the rubble around her, to her dog. Together, they continued the search.

It wasn't simply the physical difficulty of the search for Meg; it was the constant battle against her own nerves. She knew she slowed them down slightly, constantly looking for a handhold and not trusting solely her balance when a fatal fall could result. She'd worked with higher sites than this before and had learned to live with her heart pounding in her ears and her palms sweating inside her gloves. She just kept her eyes on the pile, exactly where they should be.

On top of that stress was the emotional battering of the search. In many ways, she was glad Hawk wasn't aware of what he searched through—mangled family photos, a shredded backpack, a torn pair of blue jeans, one end of a computer keyboard, a lone sneaker. All signs of what had been normal lives up to a few hours before. She kept her emotions tamped down hard. They had a job to do, and she needed to stay on task.

That determination slipped badly when Hawk stopped to scent a stuffed rabbit. Originally a fluffy white, it was now a dingy gray, grimy with concrete dust. One ear had been ripped off, a jagged tear ran over its midsection and padding spurted through the gash. The rabbit was jammed into a nook, between a chunk of concrete and what might have been the side of a kitchen sink, and she couldn't help but feel a wrench of pain for the child who owned and loved it. Was he or she here, under her feet, never to cuddle a stuffed toy again? She swallowed hard, blinking back the tears that wanted to rise, and, bearing down, followed her dog up to the next level.

They'd been at it for just under an hour when her radio buzzed and Brian's voice came over channel 12. "Meg, Lacey may have found something. Can you get here? Bravo side, about halfway up the pile." He referred to the directions used by search and rescue at fire departments across the country for building descriptions—A, or alpha, for the front side of the building, and then B, C, and D, moving in a clockwise direction, for the other sides of a typical four-sided building. This building, due to its L shape—even though part of that shape had collapsed— would have E and F sides as well.

Meg pulled her radio from her belt and hit the TALK button. "Yes." She shaded her eyes with her hand, scanned down the pile and to the south, and finally spotted Brian's bright red hard hat. She waved at him. "I see you. Give us a few minutes to work our way toward you."

Meg noted their current position for when they returned, called Hawk, and together, they slowly made their way to Brian and Lacey.

"I don't want to point Hawk at it, but where's the approximate area?"

"Lacey alerted by that mangled patio chair at the edge of that balcony. I can't tell if there's really someone there or if it just smells like people because someone stood out on their balcony, having a smoke, before going to work."

"Let's see what Hawk thinks." Meg brought Hawk to within fifteen feet of the location. "Hawk, find."

Hawk carefully and methodically began climbing over rubble, his nose down, his tail waving proudly.

"He's in the zone." Meg kept her eyes on him, watching for any sign of hesitation that might lead to an alert. "If the scent is there, he'll find it." However, within a few minutes, as Hawk passed by the area and kept going, Meg glanced uncertainly at Brian, who shook his head. "Give him a few more minutes."

Meg had him make a second pass, but he never gave any indication of scent. "Sorry, Brian. He's not picking up on anything."

Brian shrugged, but lines of discouragement cut in around his mouth. "Worth double-checking."

"For sure. Mark this spot. We don't have enough hands on-site to start digging when we don't have a solid hit, but we should come back to it. And it wouldn't hurt to have Theo take a pass. Just to be sure."

"Agreed. Thanks."

Meg gave his shoulder a rub, and then she and Hawk picked their way back to their search area.

After two hours, she led Hawk down to street level, to the rest and rehab area, watered and fed him, downed an energy bar herself, and followed it up with a bottle of water. Then they took ten minutes to sit and rest. Constantly balancing on shifting materials for several hours at a time gave a thorough leg and core workout. And while they were both in excellent shape, fortified by regular five-mile jogs with Brian at the crack of dawn, it was necessary to take a break, even if just for a few minutes. When reinforcements arrived, she would allow herself and Hawk to rest a little longer, but until then, the bare minimum would have to suffice. Hawk had an easier time of managing the debris field than she did, due to four feet and a lower center of gravity, but she didn't dare overtire him, or he could make a mistake. Or she could. And a single mistake on top of a three-story pile of razor-sharp steel, jagged glass, and chunks of concrete could end their careers in search and rescue. If not take their lives. In a job where it was both of them together or neither of them at all, they both needed to be safe for the sake of each other, their current mission, and their long-term careers.

Still, every moment Meg sat idle grated on her. She knew it was necessary, but nonetheless, she felt guilty resting while someone could be slowly dying under tons of concrete. She watched the clock as her dog lay at her feet, his head on his paws. He knew the drill—rest when you could, because otherwise, it was work, work, work until their shift was over.

The second the ten minutes were up, they were on their feet and headed back to the pile, picking up exactly where they'd left off.

Now there were more people on the pile. No other dog teams yet, as those were still coming, but firefighters wearing the turnout gear of other cities were searching as well, and more were grouped at the edges, making plans and considering options. I Street NW was even more jammed, and the parking lot across the street was being emptied of cars and was filling with ambulances as triage took form. Tent city—the incident management area of a disaster site like this—would pop up in the parking lot and in the Park at CityCenter as the site went to twelve-hour rotating shifts twenty-four hours a day, in all weather. At this time of year, they'd bring in propane heaters for the management staff, as well as for searchers who needed warming. Luckily, so far today, it was chilly but not cold.

It was as Hawk was working his way up the pile from what was once a seventh-floor balcony to the eighth that his posture changed. He was slinking under a twisted steel support beam when he froze, even his tail going still, as his nose went into overdrive with a series of short inhalations. Then he was back in motion, clearing the beam and starting to squeeze under the mostly intact concrete slab that was originally the floor for the ninth level.

"Hawk, careful buddy. What do you have?" Meg tested her weight on a mangled piece of rebar jutting from a block of concrete, found it solid, and used it to hoist herself up to Hawk's level. She studied her dog carefully, hope growing. His alertness, the tense play of his muscles, his tail high and proud—all signs of him on the scent.

Hawk backed out of the crevice and sat.

His alert signal. He'd found someone.

Meg gave herself three seconds of elation before letting reality kick in as she reached for her radio. "Brian, I need Lacey. Hawk's alerting. Alpha side, near the alpha/bravo corner, eighth-floor balcony."

"On our way," came Brian's response.

"Craig, this is a strong alert. Can you have a rescue team ready to go if Lacey confirms?"

There was a crackle of static, then Craig's voice. "Affirmative."

The four minutes it took Brian and Lacey to make their way carefully across the pile felt like the longest in Meg's life. Hawk's, too, because he was acting like there was someone just out of reach and kept wanting to squeeze into the gap. Luckily, in that section of the collapse, the floors had fallen in a staggered fashion, so each level had only the weight of a single slab lying across it.

It was the kind of area where there was the possibility of survival.

But that survival would still take an immense amount of

luck. The twelve feet of original space per story was now down to possibly only twelve or fifteen inches. At most. Likely less, the farther into the pile you delved.

Meg grabbed any small chunks of debris she could find—concrete, drywall, splintered wood—clearing an area for the dogs and for herself and Brian. She couldn't shift the steel support beam, but some of the shorter sections of metal she could move, grateful for the heavy gloves she wore to protect her hands at a site like this.

The sound of concrete shifting above drew her gaze upward to find Brian and Lacey about twenty feet away and working their way around the corner of the building. Finally, Lacey hopped onto the cleared slab, and Brian slid in behind her. Meg pulled Hawk back as far as she could while still staying on the slab.

"Okay, Lacey-girl. Find." Brian gave the command but then stayed as far out of Lacey's way as possible, not wanting to influence her in any way.

No influence was required as Lacey put her nose down and immediately zeroed in on the same area as Hawk, then tried to push her way under the slab before pulling back and sitting, alerting to a live find.

"Good girl, Lacey!"

Brian, Meg, and Hawk joined Lacey. Brian clapped a hand down on Meg's shoulder and squeezed, and she returned his hopeful smile as his eyes crinkled above his mask.

They'd found someone.

Now only questions remained—were they alive, and could rescuers get to them without bringing the pile down on their head, ending the rescue before it even began?

CHAPTER 4

Excavation: Preparing a building site for the below-grade foundation by removing soil and rock.

Monday, December 17, 11:56 AM
Talbot Terraces
Washington, DC

It seemed to take another lifetime for rescuers to reach them.

Brian and Lacey returned to their searching, wishing to stay for the hopefully good news of a live rescue but not wanting to tie up both dogs when one of them could still be actively searching. With a promise to keep him in the loop, Meg sent Brian on his way.

While she waited, Meg explored the space, trying to see if there was any easy way to reach whoever might be under the rubble. There was a mound of concrete jamming the space between the floors, as if part of the floor above had fractured unevenly as it fell, filling the space with its bulk, leaving the possibility of a survivable void behind it. Either that or a bulky piece of furniture, perhaps something like a refrigerator, wasn't crushed flat during the collapse and contributed to a void space. She didn't dare try to actually shift any materials under the slab for fear she might make the area unstable. For now, all she knew was Hawk scented a person.

Was that person alive and exhaling and therefore detectable, or were they dead, having left behind waste products and fresh blood, which Hawk smelled?

Meg put her money on life, so every few minutes, she'd call out to them, explaining search and rescue had found them, that she and Hawk wouldn't leave them alone, pleading with them to hang on, and assuring them that help was coming. She watched Hawk for signs of any response from inside the pile, knowing his ears were more sensitive than hers, but, while alert, he never indicated any response.

Activity down below attracted her attention as a large crane drove slowly onto I Street NW, and emergency crews cleared a way for it to park near the ruptured end of the building, likely to deal with the killing weights dangling from the structure. At the far end, a bulldozer and a front loader were working at the edge of the pile, moving debris off and away from any trapped cars.

Now we can really dig into the pile. Good.

She turned back to her section of the pile and called out again. Still nothing. Trying a different tack, she picked up a small chunk of concrete, stretched her arm inside the crevice as far as she considered safe under what might be an unbalanced slab, and sharply rapped a rhythm against the concrete.

Four fast taps, four slow, four fast, four slow.

Wait. Listen.

Nothing.

Again. Four fast taps, four slow, four fast, four slow.

Wait.

Beside her, Hawk gave a low whine, his ears perked high and tipped forward, his head tilted to the side.

Did he hear something?

She tapped the sequence again, but this time she pressed her ear to the concrete, hoping she might be able to hear a faint sound more efficiently directly through the material. And waited.

Then she heard it. Faint, but unmistakable. Four fast taps, four slow, four fast, four slow.

Their victim was alive!

She beat a rapid tattoo to let them know she'd heard their message.

She reached for her radio. "Craig, what's the status on the rescue team? I can hear tapping. This victim is alive."

She heard Brian's whoop of joy, not over the radio but over the curve of the pile, and it brought a smile to her lips. It was what they all needed. It didn't matter who had found the live victim; just knowing someone had survived gave them all a kick and would push them that much harder.

"They're coming up to you now," Craig responded. "DCFEMS Special Operations, and they're bringing all the equipment they'll need. Just hang tight."

A few minutes later, a group of six DCFEMS firefighters gathered at the corner of I and 11th Streets NW, carrying K-12 saws, pressurized water tanks, and bracing equipment. They looked up toward her, and she waved. They waved back and then started up the pile with their equipment.

A tall, umber-skinned man with broad shoulders under his turnout coat and a white helmet gave her a nod as they reached her level. "Captain Harris, Special Operations. Where's the dog alerting?"

Meg quickly brought the team up to speed with everything she knew about where the victim was and their status.

"That sounds promising," said Harris. "Let us get in there. We'll brace the area and try cutting through with the K-12 saws. Go back to searching. We'll let you know how we do."

In that moment, Meg understood even more how Brian felt—not wanting to leave, but knowing that she too had a job to do. "Thanks. Good luck."

Harris ran a hand over Hawk's back. "Let us know if this smart boy finds anyone else."

Meg nodded her thanks, called her dog, and moved well clear of the Special Operations team. They were the extrication experts and knew what they were doing, and all she'd do was get in their way. But as she and Hawk searched, Meg found herself glancing back often, watching their progress as they used circular saws to cut carefully through the heavy concrete, their synthetic diamond-studded blades kept cool by the water pumped over them. As they burrowed into the rubble, they braced the slab above and slowly, slowly tunneled forward.

They'd stop every so often and call into the pile; Meg had no idea if they had any response, but hope kept her heart light. She would believe in this particular miracle until convinced otherwise.

When the saws went quiet and the men packed around that one spot, Meg finally couldn't take it anymore. "Hawk, stop." She marked their location. "Come." And led him toward the rescue operation.

She arrived just as the Special Operations team pulled a young boy into the light. He immediately raised his hands to cover his eyes, blocking them from the bright light of the midday sun. Meg pegged him at maybe eight or nine. He was dressed in grime-covered jeans and a hoodie—just a regular kid getting ready for a normal day at school. On what would become the least normal day of his entire existence, the day his life turned upside down.

Harris spotted Meg and Hawk and waved them closer; then he bent down to the boy. "Mark, do you want to meet the dog who found you?"

Mark dropped his hands, revealing a face covered in dust and smudged with blood, with tear tracks cutting paths down his filthy cheeks. He nodded.

Meg gave Hawk the hand signal to move forward. He carefully picked his way over the slab as firefighters moved down a level, and prepared a backboard for Mark while Hawk kept him distracted. Mark reached out to run a hand over Hawk's neck, then curled around it, pulling the dog closer to bury his face in his fur as Hawk balanced carefully beside him.

She couldn't imagine the terror of being alone in the dark, thinking no one would find you and you'd die there, scared and isolated. She wasn't sure how she'd handle it as an adult, let alone as a child.

Harris gave Mark only about thirty seconds with Hawk; then he looked back at Meg, and gave her a hand signal to pull her dog away. "We need to move him. The paramedics are waiting to start field treatment for crush syndrome, and then they're taking him to George Washington University Hospital for full treatment." He bent down, had a few more words with Mark, who reluctantly released Hawk, and the dog stepped back to stand with Meg. Then the rescuers carefully shifted him onto the backboard, strapped down his head, torso, and legs, and two firefighters carefully carried him down the pile to the waiting paramedics.

Harris turned to Meg. "Can you check this area again? Mark said he was in the apartment with his mother. She was in the kitchen; he was in his bedroom. We need to check to see if your dog alerts on anyone else."

"Absolutely. Pull your men back. Maybe don't go too far, but Hawk needs a clear space without conflicting scent."

"Affirmative. There are enough teams on hand now that I can put us on temporary hold. If we have to move, we'll let you know." Harris and his men retreated to the sidewalk and watched as Meg and Hawk started the search again.

They tried for a full thirty minutes, concentrating on that level and where the footprint of the apartment might have landed. But Hawk didn't alert again.

Meg trudged down the pile with Hawk to Harris and his men. "I'm sorry. There's nothing." She scanned the faces of the men, seeing no surprise or disappointment, simply resignation. *They never thought we'd be successful.* "Which is what you expected."

Harris nodded grimly. "We had to be sure. But she was farther inside the apartment, according to Mark. He was near the outside wall when the building collapsed, near the balcony." He met Meg's eyes, and she saw the flat acceptance, the weight and sorrow of it. "He was lucky enough to fall into a void space, one large enough for him and under a lighter debris load than in most areas of the building. They're treating him for compartment syndrome now; he's young and should make a full recovery. But his mother . . ." His gaze slid up the pile. "We didn't think you'd find any trace of her, but I promised Mark I'd try." He turned to his men. "Okay, boys, back to it." Harris activated his radio handset on his shoulder. "Harris to IC. No trace of the boy's mother. Returning to command."

Meg watched the men trudge away and then dropped to a crouch in front of her dog. She ran her hand over

Hawk's back and wished she could remove her mask so he could see her smile of pride. "Good boy, Hawk. You found Mark, and he's going to be okay."

Hawk wagged his tail enthusiastically, as if he understood her perfectly.

Meg pushed to her feet. "Now let's do it again." She turned to face the pile, her dog ready at her knee. "Back to it, Hawk. Come."

They climbed up onto the pile. Meg was hoisting herself onto what was once the seventh floor when a low groaning sound rumbled through the air and the debris under her feet vibrated slightly. Her gaze shot to the standing structure in alarm, her heart rate jumping as she studied the building, waiting for something to happen. She couldn't help but think of all the first responders lost in the Twin Towers, those who entered the buildings with only the intent to find and rescue those inside but who lost their lives when the buildings crumbled.

Todd.

She was sure he was somewhere inside the standing structure. She knew him—he wouldn't hesitate to run into a burning building or one on the verge of collapse if there were people inside whose lives were on the line. If that structure fell . . .

Her gaze dropped to the millions of pounds of concrete, steel, and glass at her feet, fear streaking through her. They didn't know how stable the remaining part of the building was. Was that the sound of it simply settling into its new balance without two-thirds of its mass, or was that the sound of columns nearing a breaking point?

The warm weight of her dog leaning against her left leg pulled her attention down to him, and she found him gazing up at her, his brown eyes full of love and support. And drive. She could practically here him thinking, *Come on, we have work to do.* She stroked a gloved hand over his head. "You're right, buddy. We have work to do." Here was where the victims needed them, so here was where they would be. She took a deep breath and centered herself. "Ready, Hawk? Find them."

They continued their way up the pile.

And yet she couldn't help glancing one more time at the shattered structure towering overhead.

CHAPTER 5

Live Load: Transient loads applied to structural elements in a building, such as by moving cars or people.

Monday, December 17, 12:34 PM
Talbot Terraces
Washington, DC

For Lieutenant Todd Webb, the world contracted into the beam of light coming from the side of his helmet. Everything else was utter blackness.

"Smaill! Kowalski! With me!"

"Right here, Lieutenant." Firefighter Chuck Smaill swung into the inky blackness of the stairwell, the gloom now slightly lessened by two beams of light. "Kowalski is staying on seven. O'Dwyer found some tenants, so they're staying paired."

Webb turned around, automatically keeping his light beaming above Smaill's helmet, while Smaill dropped his chin to keep his light clear of Webb's eyes. "They're going to radio in?"

"Affirmative."

Apprehension crawled up Webb's spine. He'd led the first team into the shattered building hours ago. They hadn't even taken the time to wait for structural engineers to arrive, which could have taken up to an hour...or more, if luck wasn't on their side. They'd simply gathered their forcible entry tools, and he'd been the first in the building, with seven men and women behind him. They'd known from the moment they'd set foot into the structure they were up against both time—how long could this building stay standing?—and rapidly degenerating conditions following the partial collapse.

The interior was dim, and the light level dropped further as they moved into the building and away from any windows or external doors. The building had been dark when they arrived; still, the only thing that had kept them outside was ensuring all power to the building was shut off. There would be enough hazards today without worrying about anyone accidentally brushing a live wire. There would be plenty of loose and shredded wires inside; they had to ensure the safety of not only the firefighters but also the surviving residents.

Every firefighter had the slim LED lamp attached to the brim of their helmet switched on for hands-free lighting. They had only to step into the lobby for the destruction to be clear. Just past the security office, part of the main hallway had collapsed, the ceiling and a wall crumbling to fill almost half the hallway. Light fixtures and wires dangled from the ceiling, and a two-inch-wide crack ran down the opposite wall, beside the dark bank of elevators, like a jagged lightning bolt. Webb had radioed in that he was leaving two firefighters on the first floor to ensure all the community rooms were clear before joining the rest of the team he would lead up the emergency stairwell. They'd start on the third floor, where they would clear apartments one at a time, ensuring everyone was out, moving as quickly as possible, ever conscious that the building might not hold.

That had been nearly four hours ago, and while the

structure was still standing, the groans and vibrations coming from it were truly disconcerting.

It was a slow process working their way up the building, floor by floor. They knocked on every door. If no response came, they attempted entry to ensure no one unconscious was left inside. If the door was locked, it was forced open using a Halligan bar—a thirty-inch steel tool with a curved fork at one end and an adze and pick at the other—with a little extra force applied with a flatheaded forcible entry axe.

At this point, the damage they did to any door was immaterial when the rest of the building was crumbling. Firefighters were an "ends justifies the means" kind of people to begin with—whatever it took to make the rescue a success was A-OK with them. But even more so now, when time was of the essence just for all of them surviving the day.

It did cross Webb's mind a time or two that every door they opened weakened that wall as a whole by removing another fraction of its stability. And they knew early on the entire building had shifted, as knocks were met with cries of help from the other side when residents couldn't open their door because the frame had changed shape. Some doors they could force open; others wouldn't budge, requiring an external rescue by ladder truck.

Most buildings weren't truly square at the best of times, but he had a bad feeling this one was approaching a parallelogram.

Webb had been a firefighter for over thirteen years and had never seen a situation like this before. Fires, car accidents, medical emergencies, those were the norm. He'd even been caught in a building collapse in the spring, during a hoarder fire, and had survived because he worked with the best damn firefighters in the business, who had rescued his ass for once, and not the other way around.

But none of them had been in an incident like this. They knew their stuff, but to a certain extent, they were making things up as they went. Like when they made it to the fourth floor but found the emergency stairwell buckled between the fourth and fifth floors, causing them to backtrack to the ground floor and then outside, where a ladder truck got them up to the fifth floor to continue the search.

Ladder trucks lined the street in front and to the side of the standing structure and were doing a lot of the heavy lifting. Residents who were injured were strapped to backboards and carried out to their balconies and then to a rescue platform on one of the trucks. Anyone above the fifth floor had to come down to another rescue platform, which picked up those who couldn't access the stairwell. Residents came out with their pets in cages, and firefighters rescued more animals that had been alone in empty apartments when their owners went to work. The local animal shelter was collecting and holding any unclaimed animals, noting where they'd come from, even the cat found wandering the sixth-floor hallway alone.

They'd cleared over twenty residents so far, but there were more above. Many had called in to 911, who stayed on the phone with them as they waited for rescue. And Webb was afraid there were more than just those. It was the injured and the elderly who concerned him the most. Those who couldn't call for help, who waited, alone and in the dark, for someone to find them before the wing fragmented.

He was sure it was only a matter of time.

Webb gripped his irons—the married set of Halligan and axe—in his left hand and motioned to Smaill to follow him as they hit the stairs. He needed more firefighters again. Finding tenants was great, but he needed more men, as each discovery required two firefighters staying together in case either of them ran into trouble or in case of multiple victims. But doing so repeatedly had shrunk his search team, and so time and again, he'd requested additional support. Fortunately, as more first responders had arrived, that support had been provided.

"We need more guys. Again," Webb said.

"I guess it's a good thing that we keep needing additional support, because that means we're finding more residents."

"Yeah. But I know they're worried about how much live load is active in this building. Too much movement could be a problem in a building balanced on a knife edge, so they don't want to send guys in unless they're needed. No help for it, though, at this point. Time isn't on our side." Webb activated the radio handset in the top pocket of his heavy coat. "Engine 2 to Command. Lieutenant Webb and Firefighter Smaill are proceeding to the eighth floor. We need additional manpower."

"Command to Engine 2. Message received. Three additional mutual aid teams from Arlington are now deployed. Are floors one to seven cleared?"

"Affirmative. Cleared or in progress. Send the new teams to the eighth floor once they enter at the fifth. Staircase is manageable."

"Message received."

Webb released his radio. "Let's go."

They climbed the stairs in the dark, their ears attuned to every creak and groan coming from the structure around them as they worked their way upward, moving farther into instability, farther away from an easy escape if the building shifted and started to fall. Even the emergency staircase wasn't a way out anymore. If they needed to evacuate quickly . . . Webb didn't want to consider that option, because it no longer existed.

For a day that started like any other, it had certainly gone sideways in a big way. He'd climbed out of bed, grabbed a shower, sat down to breakfast with Meg, had time for an extra cup of coffee, kissed her goodbye, and told her he'd see her the next morning, hopefully home in time to catch her before she left for work. Into his truck and downtown in plenty of time for his 8:00 AM shift. At the firehouse, they'd been preparing the list of the day's tasks—reports needing completion for Webb, firehouse and truck cleaning for everyone else—if the shift was un-eventful, when the tones had echoed through the fire-house.

He wouldn't soon forget the shocked look on Ox's face at the announcement over the PA system. "Attention Engine 2, Rescue Squad 1, Medic 2. Collapsed high-rise apartment building at 920 I Street NW." Then everyone sprinted for their turnout gear and vehicles and pulled out in under a minute, Firefighter Barrett at the wheel of Engine 2.

The updates coming in via radio as Webb sat in the passenger seat beside Barrett told him they had a major incident. At least half of a twelve-story condo building gone. They were going to need every unit in town, which they couldn't do without leaving DC's population at large vulnerable to the normal emergency and fire situations that occurred daily in a large metropolitan area. Which meant mutual aid.

He picked up his cell phone and dashed off a quick text to his brother Josh. **You on shift today?**

The reply came almost immediately. **Yes.**

Not out on a call. Webb knew Josh and their youngest brother were on the same shift at the Baltimore Fire Department, their retired father's department, though out of different houses, so that meant Luke was on duty as well. **Watch for a mutual aid request. Major incident. Condo collapse downtown. We need help.**

You dispatched?

En route now.

Webb directed Barrett to avoid I Street NW for as long as possible and instead take H Street NW, which ran parallel to their final destination. As soon as they made the turn onto H, the dust cloud from the collapse was evident; and as they streaked past 11th Street NW, sirens wailing, on their way to 10th Street NW to circle around, Webb had a glimpse of empty sky, piled debris, and frenzied activity as ordinary people sprinted in to help in any way they could.

As an officer, he'd taken FEMA's Incident Command System training. He knew that in a major disaster involving a collapsed structure, up to 50 percent of the victims, even if injured, might not be trapped at all or might be only lightly trapped, and nearby untrained civilians could spontaneously leap into action to assist. In fact, those civilians were crucial to the effort in a large incident, as they left the professionals free to tackle the more dangerous scenarios.

In the few minutes since the collapse, civilian rescue was already underway. Webb only hoped the structure was stable enough that no one got caught in a secondary collapse.

They went north on 10th Street NW and then circled the north end of the block. And drove straight into chaos.

Mere minutes after their arrival on scene, Chief Koenig, Battalion 6 chief, had stepped in as incident commander. Units had flooded in from across the city, and as Webb knew, the call for mutual aid had gone out immediately. Neighboring cities had responded in droves. He'd heard about it and seen the evidence only in his brief stints outside the building, but it had been a boost to everyone's morale.

Together, they were going to get every living person out of this hellhole.

He and Smaill now pushed on to the eighth floor,

though forcing their way through the stairwell door required that both of them put a shoulder into it. They stepped into what was now a familiar sight—a dark hallway, its cracked and crumbled walls lit by their helmet torches, parts of the ceiling collapsed. To their right stood the elevator bank. One of the two doors hung at a slightly drunken angle; the other door was either missing completely or stuck open, so only a black hole beckoned beyond.

The forces in this part of the building must have been incredible. As an experienced firefighter, Webb had a comprehensive understanding of building techniques—knowing materials and how structures were built could save your life and those of your colleagues in an inferno as you would be able to predict how flames moved. In this case, he suspected the bank of elevators was what had kept this part of the building upright when the rest tore free, thanks to the structural stability of the concrete walls encasing it. But the damage was done. What was left of the building simply couldn't stay standing. The only question now was, Would it come down on its own—possibly while residents and rescuers remained inside—or would experts have time to bring it down safely?

He and Smaill passed the elevators and made their way down the hallway. As they had on previous levels, they started at the far end of the hallway, the end partially involved in the collapse. Bypassing debris and skirting areas where the ceiling looked tenuous, they reached the apartment door at the northernmost end of the standing structure. Webb pounded his fist on the door twice. "Fire Department! Is anyone there?"

The only response was a subtle moan from the wall to their left as the building shifted minutely again, the live load within creating stress points.

Webb exchanged an uneasy glance with Smaill. "We

need to move now." He pounded again. "Fire Department! We're coming in."

Webb tried the doorknob. Locked. After separating his Halligan from his axe, which he handed to Smaill, Webb jammed the curved fork of the Halligan into the gap between the door and the jamb a few inches above the lock, with the curved bevel facing the door. "Ready."

"Hold steady." Smaill set his irons on the floor behind him. Then fisting both hands around Webb's axe handle, he slammed the flat back of the ax-head into the blunt end of Webb's Halligan bar, driving the teeth between the door and the jamb.

A half dozen solid hits and Webb judged the teeth were in the right place. "Hold." Grasping the bar in both hands, he gave it a rough shove. The door resisted for a moment before wrenching open. After taking his axe back, Webb pushed through the doorway. "Fire department, coming in!"

He'd entered three of these border apartments, and it still gave him a kick of adrenaline to go through a door to a room that opened out to the cityscape beyond instead of possessing walls, framed pictures, and cupboards. Instead, through the settling cloud of dust, he could see straight through where the structure had once stood, all the way to the facade of the glass and concrete health center on the far side of 9th Street NW. A chill breeze blew into what was left of the apartment, rippling through the horizontal blinds that hung drunkenly over the empty gap that was once a picture window.

"You know the layout. Take the remaining bedroom. I'll take—" Webb stopped, another gust washing a new scent over him.

Urine. Which usually meant death.

"I can smell urine. Someone's here. Check the bedroom."

"Yes, Lieutenant." Smaill peeled off to the left, toward

the single bedroom. "Don't get too close to the edge without a line."

"Affirmative." Webb's gaze cut to the other side of what had originally been a neatly appointed living room. He knew this layout now. What had once been a one-bedroom apartment with en suite bathroom, luxury kitchen, living and dining space, and a long balcony with an impressive view of downtown was now reduced to the bedroom, the en suite, and a fraction of the living room, with the kitchen and dining room lost to the rubble below. A three-seater couch, its back to Webb, dangled partly over open air; framed pictures lay mangled and shattered on the floor; a lamp was upended over an armchair; and a flat-screen TV had toppled facedown on the debris-strewn carpet. But beyond the blinds shivering in the breeze, nothing moved.

He opened the front hall closet to his right, then scanned for any person or animal hiding in fear. It was unlikely but not impossible, and every apartment would be cleared only once, but thoroughly.

No stone left unturned.

He was turning away from the closet when a slight sound reached his ears over the constant rumble of engines and searching below. He froze, straining to hear when it came again. A thump, as if someone was hitting something.

He hurried to the couch, circled it, giving it space, because it hung partly over the edge of the chasm.

When he saw the woman, he paused only for a moment, taking in every detail, before he moved. "Smaill! In here *now!*"

She was easily seventy, if not eighty, and lay beside the couch, her feet mere inches from the ragged edge of what was left of the concrete slab floor. She was in a dangerous position as it was, but as she shuddered with convulsions, her body jerked across the carpet toward the edge, making her situation all the more precarious.

His paramedic's eye instantly identified a bilateral tonic-clonic seizure, but medical treatment was secondary. If she went over the edge, there'd be nothing he could do for her.

He moved in close, keeping his eye on the open edge as the breeze swept over him, carrying the scent of urine, which now made perfect sense to him. Not death—a seizure, likely brought on by the stress of the situation.

Avoiding her flailing arms, Webb hooked his gloved hands under her armpits and dragged her away from the edge, then glanced behind and pulled her an extra six feet for good measure. As Smaill jogged in, Webb dropped to his knees, ripped off his heavy gloves, glanced at his battered black wristwatch to time what remained of the seizure, rolled her onto her side so she was partly resting against his thighs, then lightly clasped her hips—not to restrain her, because that would only hurt her, but to keep her on her side to help maintain an open airway.

"What can I do?" Smaill looked like he was about to drop down to help, but Webb waved him back. "She's having a grand mal seizure." He stuck to the more well-known terminology, suspecting Smaill wouldn't know what a tonic-clonic seizure was. "Radio in. I need a med pack with benzodiazepines, preferably IM midazolam. And make sure they bring oxygen and a non-rebreather mask. There's no way they'll be able to get close to us here, because of the debris field, so they'll need to ladder it all up to five and then run it up."

Smaill nodded and activated his radio. "Engine 2 to Command. Lieutenant Webb and Firefighter Smaill have found an elderly female in medical distress in 704. Patient is experiencing a grand mal seizure. Lieutenant Webb can treat on-site and requests a med pack with benzodiazepines, preferably IM midazolam, immediately. Also, portable oxygen and a non-rebreather mask. Then we'll need a backboard for transport to the fifth-floor platform."

"Command to Engine 2. Message received. Sending in a med pack and additional support. Command out."

Smaill crouched down and started clearing space around the woman's body, sweeping fragments of concrete and glass away so she wasn't cut on anything sharp. "What do you need to do?"

"I need to wait this seizure out. There's nothing to do while she's seizing. But I didn't hear her when we came in, not until after you'd gone to check the bedroom." He leaned in, bending over her, and checked to make sure any fluids in her mouth could drain out the side and not choke her. Then he grabbed a pillow from the floor, gave it a shake to make sure there wasn't anything stuck to it, gently lifted her head as she thrashed, and lowered it onto the cushion. "I don't think this is her first seizure. That's why I could already smell urine. That can happen during a seizure. But then I heard another seizure begin." He reached down and undid the top button on her collar, giving her a little extra breathing room. He glanced at his watch again. "I don't like how long this is going on. What did you find in the bedroom?"

"Evidence of two people living here, but no one and no pets. I checked the closet, under the bed, and the bathroom. Evidence of a walker, though, if not two, from the tracks on the carpet."

Webb glanced over his shoulder toward the gaping void only ten feet away and then back to the dull gold wedding band on the woman's left hand. "You're thinking her husband went over."

"Possibly. If they both had limited mobility, when things went to hell, they wouldn't have had time to get up and walk ten feet to the other side of the dividing line, even if they knew what was happening and how to save themselves. He might have disappeared literally before her eyes."

"That kind of stress could definitely cause a seizure if she's epileptic. She's wearing a MedicAlert bracelet, so I can check that." Webb watched her movements start to slow. "She's coming out of it." They watched as the woman's convulsions gradually stilled, leaving her limp on the carpet. Webb glanced at his watch. "Just under two and a half minutes from when I started timing." He flipped over the medallion on the bracelet. "Confirmed. She's epileptic." He looked up at Smaill. "Run back into the bedroom and bathroom. Look for medications."

"One sec." Smaill quickly strode toward the bedroom.

The woman now lay limp and unconscious under Webb's supporting hands, so much so he thought if he released his light hold on her hips, she'd likely roll off the pillow to lie facedown on the gritty carpet. He leaned over her to check for breath sounds—present, thank God—lifted one eyelid, and purposely angled his head so his LED lamp shone down on her face. He felt a spurt of relief when the pupil dilated normally. Unconscious, but the brain was still in control.

"Ma'am, my name is Todd, and I'm with DC Fire and Emergency Medical Services. We're going to take care of you." He studied her face as he slid two fingers over her slender wrist, her skin cool under his touch. He kept his eyes on the digital seconds on his watch as he counted off heartbeats before doing the math. He removed his fingers, found the pulse again, and took it a second time for confirmation. As he'd expected, she was tachycardic, her heart rate at 130 beats per minute.

High enough that he needed to watch for signs of cardiac arrest in this postictal stage. He flicked a glance toward the open doorway. He needed that oxygen now.

Chances of cardiac arrest were higher when oxygen was low, as it would be currently, even with an open airway.

Smaill hurried back, carrying a brown leather handbag, open at the top, with prescription bottles sticking out. "There were a bunch on the bedside table and bathroom counter. I pushed them all into her purse because I figured we'd need that too."

"Good thinking. Trade places with me to hold her still. I'll go through them, and when the med pack comes, I can get to work."

Smaill slipped in beside Webb, who slid sideways to make room and took the handbag.

"Do you need to do anything for her before we package her for transport?"

"She needs oxygen and to be put on a heart monitor and pulse ox. I think she's had two seizures in a row and could be in the middle of a seizure cluster. I'll administer midazolam to stop any more seizures that might be coming." Another look at the doorway. "I need that pack now, before we're in the middle of one again."

"You know they're coming as fast as they can. Just moving through the hallways is hard."

"Yeah." Webb started to sort through prescriptions. "Two names here. Margaret and Neil Pfeiffer." He bent down toward the woman again. "Margaret, it's Todd. I'm still here with you. And so is Chuck. We're going to keep you safe and get you to a hospital." He studied her face, but there was no evidence she'd heard him. Still, he knew unconscious patients were aware of more around them than they showed. He picked up another bottle for Neil, turned it around to show Smaill, who glanced toward the chasm ten feet away and then shook his head.

Webb nodded grimly and then returned to sorting, trying to get a medical picture of his patient, separating out medications for Neil, who he suspected was not going to be found alive. Atenolol for high blood pressure, Pradaxa as a blood thinner, Synthroid for a hypothyroid condition, a statin for cholesterol. All typical pharmaceuticals for senior citizens. Then he pulled out a bottle of lamotrigine. "Bingo. Epilepsy meds."

Voices echoed through the hallway.

"In here!" Webb shouted.

A male and female firefighter in Baltimore Fire Department turnout gear appeared in the doorway. The male in front carried the leading edge of a backboard under his arm and a med pack over his shoulders. The woman carried a cylindrical black pack over both of hers and the other end of the board.

Webb sprang to his feet and met them in the doorway. "Thanks for the assist. Did you have trouble getting up here?"

"Not at all. They brough the rescue platform up to a balcony on seven where a sliding door was off its runners so we could enter through that apartment and come through to the hallway. Faster than the emergency staircase, from what I hear." He turned to the woman behind him. "Parker, let's set it down here." They leaned the backboard against the doorway, and they both removed their packs, then handed them to Webb. "Firefighters Clement and Parker from the BFD. What can we do to help?" Clement eyed the floor of the apartment. "Is it safer for you if we stay back here?"

"For now, yes. I'm not sure how much live load this floor can take, and I don't want to move her again until we're ready to package her."

He returned to Margaret and Smaill to kneel again, then opened the oxygen pack just enough to reveal the top of the tank with its on/off valve and regulator. After opening the med pack, he dug until he found the non-rebreather mask, quickly connected the tubing to the tank, turned on the tank, tested the gas flow, and then gently lay the mask over Margaret's mouth, sliding the elastic around the back of her head. Another quick check of her pulse reassured him that at least her heart rate had stopped climbing. He found the vial of midazolam, a syringe, and pulled back a 10mg dose. But as he turned to Margaret, she stirred for the first time, her eyelids blinking rapidly and the fingers of her right hand opening and closing.

Webb laid a hand on her shoulder, gave it a gentle squeeze. "Margaret? Margaret, I'm Todd. I'm going to take care of you." Normally, he'd ask if she knew where she was, but he didn't have the heart to as they huddled in the midst of the ruins of her home.

Her eyes opened, a watery blue, and she struggled to focus on his face.

"That's it. That's good. Margaret, you've had a seizure. I'm going to administer a needle with meds to keep it from happening again. Do you understand?"

A single nod.

He opened a few more buttons on her blouse, pulled down the collar far enough to expose her shoulder, and administered the midazolam into the muscle of her upper arm. Then he pulled out the multivariable vital signs monitor, attached the cardiac leads to her chest, and pulled the blouse closed so she'd feel more comfortable surrounded by strangers who were mostly men. He connected the lead for the optical finger sensor and clipped it over her index finger.

As Webb sat back on his heels, a grinding sound came from the wall to their left. He looked up sharply to find Smaill's worried gaze locked on his face. He did one quick overview of the monitor—heart rate was 122 and coming down, and oxygen was 90 percent and coming up—and considered her safe enough to move.

She could be on death's door, and he'd consider her safe

enough to move if the floor was about to give way under them. Blood sugar monitoring could wait for the ambulance.

"Slide over the backboard, but stay where you are," Webb said. "I don't want any more weight on this section of the floor."

Webb and Smaill worked fast, getting the backboard into place, carefully shifting Margaret onto the board, strapping her in place securely, and loading the monitor on beside her slender thighs. Webb passed the med pack to Smaill and then secured the oxygen tank in the pack, slipped his arms through the straps, and gave it a bump to settle it into place on his back.

Webb bent over Margaret again to find her eyes, clearer now, looking up at him. Her lips formed a single word— *Neil*—but no sound came out. "We're looking for him, ma'am. Search teams are out there. In fact, I bet my own fiancée is there right now with her search dog, Hawk. They'll find everyone they can." He could see his words weren't reassuring her; she knew if her husband had been caught in the collapse, chances of his survival were minimal, at best. But he couldn't dwell on that. His job was to get her out; there wasn't anything he could do for her husband.

He suspected there wasn't anything Meg and Hawk could do either.

He rose to his feet, went to the head of the backboard so the tubing from the oxygen tank he shouldered still had slack. "Smaill, on three. One, two, *three*." They lifted her smoothly and in only a few steps were at the front door to the apartment. Webb knew there was no true zone of safety—hell, the whole building could go at any second— but some of the cold stress of being so close to the line of life and death lifted from his shoulders. "Can we get down the same way you got up?"

"Yes. They left the platform in place, knowing it was a medical rescue," Parker said. "Let us lead you back."

As they went out the door, Webb glanced one last time over his shoulder at the chaos and destruction behind him. At the apartment where just that morning a woman had sat down with her husband of possibly forty or fifty years for coffee and an utterly normal day, one that instead became her worst nightmare. Now she left the shattered remains of that happiness, homeless and most likely widowed, with her health and possibly her life hanging in the balance.

Sometimes life could change in the blink of an eye, with everything you knew wiped clean, leaving you with absolutely nothing and, worse, nothing left to live for.

CHAPTER 6

Reinforced Concrete: Concrete strengthened by embedded steel rods to increase the material's resistance to tensile stress/stretching.

Monday, December 17, 8:38 PM
Jennings/Webb residence
Washington, DC

Meg could have wept when she came around the corner to find an open parking space directly in front of her house, allowing her to park nearby instead of having to trudge a full block or more home, as happened some nights. The frequent lack of parking was the only negative of their house, which she otherwise loved. But tonight, after a day where she mostly felt luck wasn't on their side, this small sign of some for herself eased a little of her misery.

As opposed to those who lived at Talbot Terraces, if they'd survived at all, she had a place to come home to. Todd wouldn't be home until the next morning, so she'd be alone tonight, but at least she'd be in her own bed. Hawk was almost never allowed up on the bed, but tonight she might make an exception. She hadn't seen Todd all day, as she'd been on the pile and he'd been inside the structure. She was sorry she'd miss him tomorrow morning, as she needed to start at 8:00 AM on the pile, just as his shift ended at Firehouse 2.

She wanted to see him not only safe but alive and vital. After so much anguish and death, she needed to reconnect with him like she needed to breathe.

That would have to wait. In the meantime, she and her dog needed to get cleaned up and to eat, in that order.

She got out of her SUV, but before she could circle the hood to let Hawk out of his compartment and onto the sidewalk, the door to the far side of the duplex opened and Cara stepped out. She took one look at Meg, pulled her front door closed behind her, and started down the stairs.

Despite their eighteen-month age difference, most people thought the sisters looked like twins, with their shared black Irish coloring and considerable height, but there was no mistaking one for the other now as Meg stood by her SUV, filthy and exhausted, her long black hair gray with concrete dust.

Meg could read the intent in her sister's eyes as she approached, and held up a dissuading hand. Part of the required decon coming off the pile was to strip off her coveralls and spray down her boots, but she could still feel the dust and grime in practically every pore. "No, no. I'm filthy. You don't want to get this on you."

"I don't care." Cara stepped around Meg's extended hand and wrapped her in a tight hug. "You need this more."

Meg resisted for all of two seconds before giving in and relaxing into the embrace. "How did you know?"

Cara pulled far enough away to stare Meg in the eye. "I'm your sister, dummy. I only have to look at you." Her half smile died away, and her eyes went serious. "I also followed the news coverage today, knowing you were there, as were Clay and Todd. It must have been awful."

"You have no idea."

"Would you feel better talking about it?"

"Maybe. But I need a break from it first."

"And a meal. Did you get a break for food at all during the day?"

"Not really. I took the time to feed and water Hawk, but I mostly survived on energy bars." Under her sister's withering gaze, Meg simply shrugged. "I didn't have any appetite anyway. People were buried alive." A shiver ran down her spine as the phrase called her mind back to an open coffin in a partially exhumed Arlington grave, the lid of the coffin deeply gouged, as the occupant had tried desperately to save herself. She shook off the image. There'd been too much horror already today to add on more from the past. "People *are* buried alive."

"You know there are more survivors than who you pulled out today?"

"We have to hope, or else the job is simply unbearable."

Cara squatted down in front of Hawk. "And we have to keep this boy's spirits up." She kept her voice light and positive. "Right, buddy?" She ran a hand down his back and came away with a palm coated in concrete dust. "Let me help. I'll clean up Hawk, you worry about you. Go take a shower. I'll take Hawk to my place and shower him in our walk-in shower stall."

"You're sure?"

"I wouldn't offer otherwise. Then I'll be back with all the dogs, and I'll get you a meal."

"I'm not hungry."

"You doing this again tomorrow?"

"Eight AM."

"Then you're going to eat."

Meg couldn't help the half smile that tugged at the corner of her lips. "Yes, Mom."

"You know Mom would do the same thing. Now go."

Twenty minutes later, Meg came down the stairs to voices in her kitchen and the mingled smells of coffee and frying bacon. As she stepped off the bottom stair, Hawk trotted out of the kitchen to meet her. His fur was still slightly damp and spiky, and his collar was off, but his head was high and his tail waved happily. She bent down to kiss the top of his head and caught the scent of the honey and oatmeal shampoo both she and Cara used on their dogs. "Hi, buddy. How's my boy?"

He tipped his head up, and caught the underside of her chin with an enthusiastic lick, making her laugh.

Straightening, she patted his back. "That's my boy. That's what I need right now. Come on. Let's see what Cara is up to." She walked into the kitchen, into light and warmth, and nearly straight into McCord. "McCord! When did you get here?"

"About ten minutes ago. Grabbed an Uber."

"I'm sorry. I should have checked in with you, but I just wanted to get the hell out of there and couldn't think of spending another half hour searching for you through the hordes of first responders. I'd had enough."

The coffee maker beeped the end of the cycle, and McCord walked over and started to pour steaming brew into mugs set out on the counter. "No worries. I didn't know if you'd already left or if you still needed to stay, and I didn't want to bother you, so I walked out of the locked-down area and arranged for a pickup." He raised a mug. "You want?"

"Oh yeah." Meg wandered to where Cara stood at the stove, and hooked her chin over her sister's shoulder. "Breakfast for dinner?"

"Fast, hot, and lots of protein. You're going to need that for tomorrow."

"I will. Thanks."

"It'll be ready in about ten minutes. Go sit and have your coffee and—" Cara cut off as the front door lock shot back and the door opened.

All three of them stepped toward the hallway in confusion and surprise, but it was Meg's gasp that spoke for all of them. "Todd!"

Todd radiated exhaustion from where he stood in the doorway, two men behind him, backlit by the outdoor light. He wore his winter jacket over his navy DCFEMS station wear—something she'd never seen him wear home—and his short-cut dark hair was in disarray, as if he'd sweated under his helmet for hours and hadn't cleaned up afterward. There were shadows of fatigue under his dark eyes, but he gave her a smile as he raised a hand in greeting.

Meg flew down the hallway, and he met her with open arms, pulled her in, and then simply held on, his head bent to hers, one hand fisted in the back of her shirt, as she wrapped her arms around his neck.

Home.

"I spent all day watching for you," she whispered. "On the street, from the pile, I never saw you. I spent the whole day worrying. You were inside, weren't you?"

"Yeah." He loosened his hold on her, pulled back a bit to be able to meet her eyes. "I didn't see you either. You were there all day?"

"Yeah. It was . . . Oh God, Todd. Those people."

"I know." A shuffle behind them caused him to glance behind. "Um . . . I hope it's okay. I brought company."

"Tonight?" Meg couldn't help the thread of stress winding through that single word.

"I don't know." The words came from behind Todd. "Are we really 'company'?"

Meg straightened, recognizing that voice. She leaned around Todd to take in the two men, one a near carbon copy of Todd, and the other of his mother. The stress melted away. "Never."

She pulled away from Todd to hug first Josh and then Luke Webb.

"I told them to bunk here, rather than drive all the way home, only to come back for tomorrow morning."

Meg drew the brothers into the foyer and closed the door behind them. "Of course they're welcome." A thought occurred to her, and she turned back to Todd. "Why are *you* here? I didn't expect you home until end of shift tomorrow morning."

"And here I thought you'd be happy to see me." Exhaustion edged his slight chuckle as Meg drew in a breath to respond. "Kidding." He grasped her hand, threading his fingers through hers. "Koenig sent us all home. We'd been working for over ten straight hours—really stressful, physical work—and were exhausted. And so many departments responded when we put out the call for mutual aid, all our stations were covered. The place was lousy with firefighters." He thumped a hand on Josh's back. "Like these two lunkheads."

"Baltimore pitched in?" Meg asked.

"And then some," Luke said. "The story is all over the news, and we had off-shift guys showing up at their stations, asking how they could help. Which gave Baltimore FD a lot of mutual aid to send, and still be able to cover our own region."

"They needed hands here more than anything else," Josh added. "There are only so many trucks you can get near the building, though we brought a lot of rescue and extrication equipment with us. But it let us leave a number of fully staffed and equipped houses ready to respond at home."

"And now their guys are in our house, and Koenig sent us home with orders to rest up and report to incident command tomorrow for our assignments. We switched shifts with the guys doing the B shift from 8:00 PM to 8:00 AM, and we'll be back at 8:00 AM to spell them. For now, all regular shifts are off. This is where we're needed, so this is where we'll be." Todd stopped, sniffed. "Is that . . . bacon?"

"It sure is." Cara's head popped into the kitchen doorway. "And there's more where that came from if you haven't eaten yet."

"None of us have. And I'd love to sit and eat." Todd looked down at Meg. "But first, I'd kill for a shower. I bet these guys would too."

"Let me take them next door while you clean up here." McCord came down the hallway, a wide grin for the men he'd worked with only a few months ago to free Meg of a charge of murder, as well as a false accusation of animal abuse made by an actual abuser. He held out his hand and shook with first Josh, then Luke. "Good to see you guys. You need a change of clothes?"

"We came in our turnout gear, with our station wear underneath. So yeah, we're hot, sweaty, and could use a shower and some fresh clothes."

"I have stuff they can borrow," Todd said. "Let me grab you some clothes, and then we'll clean up."

"And then you'll eat." Cara waved a spatula at them. "Go. I'll stall it a bit, but dinner will be waiting when you get back."

"You'll have enough?" Meg asked.

"I'll run next door and pilfer from my own fridge. That will round us out."

"You're a miracle."

Cara grinned. "I'm not Eda Jennings's daughter for nothing."

Thirty minutes later, they gathered around the kitchen table. Heaping platters of scrambled eggs, bacon, and toast, along with an impromptu fresh fruit salad, were passed around; coffee cups were filled and refilled; and then it was all consumed at what seemed like light speed for that amount of food. By this point, everyone had experienced enough of a mental break that each could talk a little about their day.

Todd described the initial alarm, the firehouse response, and the chaos they found at the site. Luke and Josh told of arriving in the late morning and joining the current shift, working mainly to move the debris that had overflowed I Street NW, concentrating on rescuing anyone trapped under the pile. Those lucky enough to be in vehicles had a much higher chance of survival; the few pedestrians they'd managed to unearth had all perished under the crushing weight of so much concrete with nothing to shelter them.

Watching them, it was clear to Meg that there was much the brothers weren't saying, instead skirting around the trauma to many of the victims. Because she'd experienced some of the same, she knew some of what they skipped over was the trauma they themselves had experienced at the sight of such violent and bloody loss of life.

She and Hawk had searched long enough that she'd learned that often what he scented was only bloody traces. It had quickly become clear that while they were looking for survivors or perished victims, often they found only human remains once workers came to assist and bucket lines formed to move debris in the afternoon. In the end, their morning win had needed to hold them for the rest of the day.

She'd heard from Brian that Theo had managed to find a woman on the southern side of the pile. She'd been pulled out after hours of careful excavation but had died of her injuries in the ambulance on the way to the hospital. Brian and Lauren hadn't been able to find any survivors.

By the end of the day, even the dogs had been discouraged.

When it came around to her turn, Meg concentrated on the positive, describing how Hawk had identified Mark and skirting over his missing mother with only minimal details.

They'd all gone through hell today; there was no need to dwell on it.

There would be time tomorrow for that.

CHAPTER 7

Structural Integrity: The ability of a structure to withstand normal loads, including that of its own weight, without deformation or failure.

Monday, December 17, 9:44 pm
Jennings/Webb residence
Washington, DC

After dinner was finished, they shifted to the family room. Instead of sitting down, Todd moved to the fireplace, stepping over Cody where he was sprawled partly under the Christmas tree. He knelt and started to pull quartered logs and kindling from the firewood rack on the hearth to lay the fire. After the fire caught, he stayed for a moment, holding his hands out to the heat from the growing flames.

McCord claimed Meg's ugly yet comfortable old recliner. It had been with her through multiple moves—and looked like it—but she could never bear to part with it. Ever since McCord had come into their lives, he couldn't either. He tugged Cara down into his lap as she walked past on the way toward the couch.

"Hey!" She struggled briefly, but without any real vigor. "What if I don't want to sit in your lap?"

"Look around." McCord waited while she eyed the seating around them. Meg took the armchair, while Josh and Luke sat on the couch, leaving just enough space for Todd. "We need to conserve space." He waggled his eyebrows at her.

Studying him, Meg wasn't fooled by his chipper facade. McCord had been uncharacteristically quiet over dinner, and she knew he was feeling the devastation of the day, just like the rest of them were. And from the placating look Cara was giving him, she knew it too.

Cara patted McCord's cheek. "You keep telling yourself that." But she hooked one arm around his neck, settled her legs over the arm of the recliner, and relaxed against him.

"You don't have to submit an article tonight?" Meg asked. "Don't you usually have a midnight deadline for tomorrow's edition?"

"Article is mostly written." He lifted his hips, causing Cara to hold on a little tighter as he levered her upward, and reached into his back pocket, before dropping them into the chair again as he pulled out his cell phone. "Wrote a lot of it standing there with Craig. Because I was boots on the ground right there, and further embedded than any of his other reporters, Sykes wanted me to cover the rescues and incident command. He has a slate of other writers running around looking at potential structural issues, engineering reports, permits, blueprints, construction history, that kind of thing. He wants to be able to cover when it was built, who designed it, who built it, and who paid for it."

"If there's any chance this was an engineering failure, others will want to know all that too," stated Josh.

"So they know who to sue," Luke added.

"Exactly."

"Not the direction Sykes is going with it," said McCord, "but yeah, you know with this amount of loss of life, property damage, and mental anguish, there will be lawsuits. Anyway, my article is going to need a polish, but 'I can take an hour to recharge. That still gives me time to clear my head so I can come back to it fresh, and Sykes isn't expecting anything yet."

Todd dropped onto the couch beside Josh and gave him a good-natured push to get a little more room. "He's staying up for it?"

"On a day like this? Yeah. Everyone is working overtime."

"You didn't comment on what you did today." Meg kept the statement light, giving him an out if he didn't want to talk about it.

"I spent the day with Craig. Well, most of it. Once I'd proved I'd be a good boy and wouldn't get in the way, he turned his back a few times when I wandered. Luckily, I'm a newspaperman, and not a TV news broadcaster. No one identified me as media based on my tiny byline photo. I made it all the way down to the pile. I was sure someone would stop me, but I kept my distance and didn't get in anyone's way, so I got through." He opened an app on his phone, scrolled for a moment, selected something, and then blew it up on his screen. He turned his phone around to face Meg. "And there you were."

In the photo, Meg stood with Hawk, balanced on a slanted section of concrete slab. Hawk had his head down, scenting. At their backs, the ragged floors of the standing structure rose above them.

Meg took the phone from his hands, studied the photo, and then returned the phone. "Hawk did a great job today."

"You're once again leaving out half of the team. I

watched you work with him for a while. He kept going because of your encouragement, and with your direction, to steer him toward more likely locations of life. It was a team effort."

"He's the nose."

"You're the brains." McCord looked over to the dog bed on the far side of the Christmas tree, where Hawk lay in a warm pile with Saki and Blink. "Not that he's not supersmart himself, because he is, but you understand the challenges and the logic of the search and where he's needed. You're definitely a 'sum being greater than the parts' kind of deal." His gaze slid to the fire, and he watched the flames dance silently for a few seconds, before he looked directly at Meg. "Did I ever tell you what happened on the second day I was an intern at the *Washington Post*? I'd just started a co-op placement as part of my journalism degree."

"I don't think so, no. Not your second day specifically."

"I was shadowing Vic Costa, one of the senior investigative reporters. He was showing me the ropes when I was totally wet behind the ears. My first day was September 10." He paused. "Two thousand and one."

With a chill, Meg understood. "That made your second day 9/11."

"Yeah. "

McCord's eyes went unfocused, and Meg could see he'd gone back to whatever he'd experienced that day.

"They sent us out to the Pentagon after American Airlines Flight 77 hit. Standing there today, looking at that pile, it was like standing across from the smoking wreck of the Pentagon again. Maybe not with the same level of shock, and with the knowledge of everything else that had happened that day and knowing that America would never be the same again, but it carried the same horror.

There could be easily as many people lost." McCord looked up and met Meg's eyes. "You know. You saw the pile. You saw *into* the pile."

Meg had to hold back the shudder as a slide show of images shot through her head. "And what we saw today? On day one? This is nothing compared to what we're going to see as we move farther into the pile." She jerked in surprise when her cell phone dinged. She reached into the side pocket of her yoga pants and pulled it out. "It's a group text from Craig." She scanned the message. "He says the mayor is about to give an update if we want to tune in." She grabbed the remote from the coffee table, turned on the flat-screen over the mantel, and flipped to the local station.

Meg instantly recognized the backdrop as incident command, which was still packed with the command team as firefighters and urban search-and-rescue personnel, now on-scene, ran in and out. In front of the organized chaos stood a Metro PD tent, which, based on the geography of the park visible behind it, was pitched on the slate pavers at the corner of New York Avenue NW and 10th Street NW. A microphone stand, loaded with about a dozen cabled microphones, each ringed with the call sign of a TV or radio station, stood at the front of the tent.

A tall, slender woman with skin the tone of burnished copper and shoulder-length, curly black hair pulled into a ponytail stepped into the frame. Meg instantly recognized Kelly Reardon, the mayor of Washington, DC, even though she wasn't dressed in her usual neat business suit and heels. Today she wore jeans, sneakers, and a parka to fend off the chill night breezes. She looked exhausted, and Meg suspected she'd arrived not long after Meg that morning, after grabbing the first clothes she could lay her hands on and securing her hair with as little fuss as possible. Meg recognized the look because she'd worn it herself often enough.

It's a good look. A look that says she cared less about her own standing than just getting to where she was needed.

Reardon stepped to the microphones, and a number of other people filled in the space behind her. Meg recognized senior Metro PD and DCFEMS personnel, as well as the head of FEMA and the at-large nonvoting delegate of the District of Columbia to the US House of Representatives. It was the picture of a united front from local to federal levels.

"Good evening." Reardon paused as murmuring voices quieted. "I've been able to periodically update you throughout the day, but I wanted to give you a last update this evening to summarize the day's activities and to outline what to expect tomorrow and in the coming days. We've suffered an unthinkable tragedy here in DC, and our thoughts and prayers are with the victims, their families, and friends. To the families of those missing, I understand your desperation. But please know we are just getting started on the rescue operation. I know you need answers, and we'll do our best to provide them to you as soon as we can. In the meantime, please hold on to your hope. We are hopeful, and it's fueling our determination to find survivors.

"Following the collapse of the building, DCFEMS responded immediately and commenced rescue operations. That included rescues from the edge of the debris field and from inside the standing section of the building. Those operations began within fifteen minutes of the collapse. Shortly thereafter, DCFEMS was joined by the search-and-rescue dog teams from the FBI's Human Scent Evidence Team, all of whom are currently stationed in town and were able to deploy immediately. Through their combined actions, they were able to rescue thirty-one persons from the building, six from the edge of the debris field, and three from the debris pile proper, although, sadly, one of those rescued passed away en route to the hospital. An additional nine persons were able to exit the standing structure on their own. Fourteen of those rescued from the building were treated on-site, with five of them being transported to the hospital for further treatment."

"I heard all the nearby hospitals were on high-alert standby, waiting for a massive influx of patients." His voice flat, Todd's eyes stayed locked on the TV. "It never happened."

They were hoping for a flood of survivors, which never came.

"So that's a total of forty-two persons from the building, forty-one residents and the security guard on duty at the time of the collapse," continued Reardon. "We were able to adjust our earlier estimates and now have one hundred seventeen unaccounted for and sixty-five safe. As of right now, we have seven confirmed dead, three from the main debris pile and four from the overflow onto I Street NW." Voices sounded off camera, and Reardon held up a hand as she angled to the side. "We'll collectively take questions after our statements, so please hold them until then."

She turned back to the mass of microphones. "While we started with local resources this morning, we now have urban search-and-rescue task forces from Virginia and Maryland on-site as well. They arrived with specialized equipment and dogs and are out on the pile now. These are top-notch teams, among the best in the world, joining with our already excellent local resources, and everyone is working as hard as humanly possible. We're running in two operational periods, from 8:00 AM to 8:00 PM and then 8:00 PM to 8:00 AM. The urban search-and-rescue task forces have split their teams, so they'll cover both shifts.

"Task Force 1 from Pennsylvania's urban search and rescue will arrive first thing tomorrow to join the 8:00 AM shift, so combined with mutual aid from surrounding fire departments, we have more than enough resources for the rescue and recovery. Additionally, structural engineers from the US Army Corps of Engineers are examining the building, and by tomorrow morning we hope to be able to decrease the exclusion zone around the standing structure, if they feel it's safe to do so." She turned and motioned to a man standing behind her. "I'd like to ask Congressman Sharpe to say a few words."

Sharpe, wearing a full-length winter coat to ward off the breeze that ruffled his salt-and-pepper hair, stepped forward. "Good evening. I asked Mayor Reardon if I could speak to the federal response. As the mayor has declared a state of emergency for the District, that opens up a full federal response. We're fortunate to have FEMA"— he turned and nodded to a man behind him wearing a navy winter coat with the FEMA crest stamped high on his left breast—"so close by, and we welcome them into the unified command team along with DCFEMS and the mayor's office.

"I've been keeping the White House and the president personally up to date, and let me assure you, this is an all-hands-on-deck response. The White House is granting all our requests, both for the heavy equipment, such as the cranes and excavators needed to move the pile, and for the resources for rescue efforts, housing, funeral services, and eventual cleanup. They're also fast-tracking travel visas for international family members, allowing them to come to DC in the wake of this tragedy. I'll have more updates tomorrow, as the response continues. Thank you." Sharpe melted back into the phalanx of personnel behind him.

Reardon stepped forward to the microphones again. "I can take a few questions if you have them. Then I'll be back at 8:00 AM, following tomorrow morning's briefing, and will be able to update you on the night's operations." She pointed to someone off-screen. "Yes, you."

"It doesn't look like there's much activity going on now. Is that just because more people are coming in?"

"Partly, yes, but there's much more activity than you think. Depending on where you're getting your bird's-eye view from, you're not seeing all the work going on. It's on all sides of the pile, and it's also underneath. Urban search-and-rescue teams, along with DCFEMS firefighters, have access to the underground garage through the second entrance off H Street NW. As a result, they have access to the pile from the upper garage level."

"That sounds dangerous," said the off-screen voice.

"These are highly skilled individuals, and they're doing everything required for safe work and shoring as they go. As the building collapsed into the underground parking, they have hopes of being able to access some victims that way." Reardon pointed to someone on the other side. "Go ahead."

"How will they work through the night? Will there be adequate light and power to support a full shift?"

"There is already. These urban search-and-rescue teams are quite skilled and know exactly what they're doing. And have all the equipment they need for round-the-clock work. Next?"

"What are the chances of finding anyone alive?"

Reardon opened her mouth, then closed it, but before she could try for an answer, a DCFEMS officer stepped forward.

"Good," said Todd. "That's the head of Special Operations. He's the right person for that question. The mayor doesn't have that answer." He met Meg's eyes. "Assuming he'll be straight with the media, it's not good."

"I spent the day on that pile." Meg's tone was grim. "I agree, it's not."

The man moved in front of the microphones as Reardon stepped to the side, her expression grateful.

"I'm Assistant Fire Chief Keenleyside, and I'm in charge of Special Operations for DCFEMS. I'm going to be honest with you. From what I've seen today, chances aren't great. As the building fell, it pancaked, one layer on top of the next. What we need to find the living is void spaces large enough for survival. Could those spaces exist? Yes, so that's what we're concentrating on." He glanced at Reardon, who indicated the microphones with a "Keep going" gesture. "I can take some of the more technical questions, if there are any." He scanned the group on the other side of the camera, then pointed. "You."

"Any theories as to what caused the collapse? Was it a catastrophic failure? Faulty construction? Are we under a terrorist attack?"

Keenleyside jumped in before the reporter could launch into a greater list. "Those are excellent questions, but unfortunately, not ones anyone can answer currently. Though I can say no one is taking credit for the collapse, which perhaps makes a targeted terrorist attack somewhat less likely, because those groups like to get credit for their activities. Though it's not impossible. Those are questions for the coming days. Our priority now has to be rescuing any survivors and recovering all victims. But, rest assured, there will be answers for your questions, though it may take considerable time. Next question?"

"Do we know how many were in the building at the time of the collapse?"

Reardon smiled her thanks to Keenleyside as she took the lead once again. "We're working with the building owners to compile a list of residents and their location inside the building. But someone owning an apartment inside the building doesn't mean they were inside at the time of the collapse. At that hour of the morning, some were on their way to work and school. God willing, many were." She looked directly into the camera. "If anyone lived at Talbot Terraces or knows anything about someone who did, please contact my office, DCFEMS, or the American Red Cross to assist us in compiling that list, so we know who we *aren't* looking for. We also have a Facebook page set up—just search for 'Talbot Terraces' and you'll find us—where people are checking in to let friends and family know they're safe."

She glanced at her watch. "I think we'll wrap up now for tonight. I want to close with some of the good I've seen today. This is a great city, with great citizens, and when disaster struck, people stepped forward. From the local grocery store owner who showed up first thing with cases of water for the rescue workers, to the restaurants that sent food to support our rescue teams, to the hotels who opened their doors for out-of-town search-and-rescue personnel as well as the survivors of the collapse, and to the citizens who offered clothing and shelter to those who escaped with nothing more than the clothes on their backs, I'm so proud of all of you. You warm my heart in the midst of so much sorrow. Many thanks to every one of you. Now, I'm going to let these fine folks get back to work, and I'll be here tomorrow morning at eight o'clock." She turned away from the mics, and the screen switched to two newscasters sitting behind a desk.

Meg flipped the TV off. "I guess that's about as reassuring as we can expect."

"It sounds like they're being very clear about what their chances are," said Cara. "Like they're managing expectations."

"That's exactly what they're doing," Todd confirmed. "For the families, for the community. They're trying to help people prepare for the worst. Because I think that's what we're looking at."

"You don't think they'll pull anyone else out alive?" Cara asked.

"Chances are low. We know the expectations if it's an earthquake collapse. They call the first twenty-four to thirty-six hours the 'golden hours,' because that's your greatest chance of success. Survivability in the first hour is about ninety-five percent. In the first day, it's eighty percent. By the end of day two, after forty-eight hours, it's about forty percent. By day five, it's about seven percent."

"We're still in that 'golden hour' time period right now," Cara pointed out. "Haven't even hit the one-day mark yet."

"All true. But that's for a generalized earthquake with a mix of buildings going down. Two-story houses, five-story apartment blocks. But this collapse . . . From what we hear, it was a bottom-up failure, each floor dropping down to crush the one below it."

"Right, so you're looking for empty spaces."

"Sure. Except that kind of collapse in that kind of concrete slab structure doesn't tend to have those void spaces. There's simply too much weight from each slab, and then the lower ones are crushed further by the weight of the upper slabs crashing down. We're going to look. We're going to spend days or weeks looking, but at some point, this is going to move from rescue to recovery, because the straight truth is it's an unsurvivable event." Todd turned to Meg. "I'm sorry. Maybe I shouldn't be so blunt when you have to go out there and try to find life in the midst of all that death."

"You're managing my expectations, just like they were for the families and the community. I get it. But that makes it hard on the dogs. It will be days before the FBI sends in the Victim Recovery Team and the decomp dogs. But that is coming."

"I'm afraid so."

Realizing she still held on to the remote, Meg tossed it onto the coffee table, where it slid across a thick magazine.

Josh followed the track of the remote, then leaned forward, plucked the magazine off the table, and flipped through it, a parade of flowing white dresses flashing past. He glanced sideways at Todd. "How's the wedding planning going?"

"Fine. But if you want the real story, talk to Meg. She's doing all the heavy lifting there."

Josh tipped the magazine toward Meg. "Planning?"

Meg's gaze dropped to a slender woman wearing a mermaid-style dress, a clingy style that hugged her figure to the knees, then exploded outward in a spray of satin and tulle. "It's coming. Cara's been a huge help with the research. We have some time. The big stuff is all booked—the venue, the officiant, the florist, and photographer . . ." She trailed off, her eyes on the magazine, a crease forming between her brows.

"What?" Todd asked.

When she didn't answer, he tried again. "Meg? What's wrong?"

That jerked her out of her reverie and her eyes up to his. "Wrong? Nothing."

Luke snorted a laugh. "Ah, the all-purpose female answer."

Meg threw him a sour squint, and when she looked

back to Todd, he'd extended his hand out to her between the couch and her chair. She automatically laid her hand in his, and he closed his fingers around hers.

He gave them a little squeeze. "Want to try again?" He turned her hand so her platinum and diamond ring, custom made for her with a surprisingly robust bezel setting inside a swirling filigree, allowing her to wear it on the job, sparkled in the light. "Unless you want to dump me, and then maybe you could do that in private?" He gave her a wink, so she knew he wasn't serious.

"No, it's not that." She let out a quiet sigh. "It's just . . ." She paused again, struggling to line up her conflicting emotions. "I look at that, at the expensive dresses and flowers and fancy meals, and after today, it all feels like overkill. The people who survived, sure, they lost their homes, but I know they're grateful to have been twenty or thirty feet from the dividing line that meant life or death this morning. For those who died . . . Their families would give everything to have them back. Not the stuff, not even the family heirlooms. Just them. So all this"—she threw her free hand toward the glossy pages, still dangling from Josh's hands—"seems like all glitz and glamour and no heart." She met Todd's eyes. "Does that sound crazy?"

"Not at all. I'm a guy. A lot of us don't tend to be as invested in the details of a wedding. It's not that we don't want something nice. It's that we didn't grow up with the white dress fantasy. As I said from the beginning, I may have an opinion, and I'll certainly let you know if it's something I don't like, but by and large, I'm pretty easygoing about it. Whatever you want is probably going to be fine with me." He gripped her hand a little tighter. "Now isn't the time to make a decision. The day's been too difficult and too full of emotion. But if that feeling sticks, then we make some changes, okay?"

"Yeah. Thanks. I'm probably being overemotional because it's been a horrific day. With some bright spots, mind you, but overall, a nightmare. I'm sure things will look brighter, if not tomorrow, then in a week or two."

The conversation started to flow again, everyone making a conscious choice to discuss anything but the day's tragedy. But Meg's gaze kept coming back to the bridal magazine Josh had dropped on the table.

She wasn't so sure a week or two would change her mind after all.

CHAPTER 8

Catastrophic Failure: The sudden and complete failure of a major structural element from which recovery is not possible and which causes the immediate or eventual loss of the entire structure.

Tuesday, December 18, 6:58 AM
Jennings/Webb residence
Washington, DC

The next morning saw Meg and the three Webb brothers up long before the sun and down in the kitchen by six thirty. By tacit agreement, there was no chatter, but they all started making breakfast, Josh handling the coffee, Luke pouring juice and setting the table, and Meg feeding Hawk and then chopping the apples Todd had peeled when he started a large batch of his family's traditional recipe for apple-cinnamon oatmeal. They sat down to hearty, steaming bowls of oatmeal at the table, and Todd flipped on the TV to see if there were any updates before they started their day.

A young brunette woman in a formfitting navy blue dress stood in front of a weather map. "There's still a fair amount of uncertainty as to the storm track. If the system moves out over the Atlantic as expected, Washington will escape the worst of the storm's potential. If the storm instead tracks west, this may be the earliest winter storm Washington, DC, has seen in years. Stay with us this week for the latest in weather updates, and we'll make sure you're ready to meet your day. Back to you, Natasha."

Two unusually grim-looking broadcasters sat side by side behind the news desk, looking as perfectly put together and stylish as usual, but without their usual sunny smiles and morning exuberance. Behind them, block letters declared *MEET THE DAY*.

"Thanks, Dominique," said Natasha, a willowy blonde in a bright blue jacket over a V-neck blouse. "It's the top of the hour, and we're returning to our continuing coverage of the Talbot Terraces collapse. The mayor will be giving an update at eight this morning, but there are two new pieces of information we can share right now. First of all, witness reports coming from individuals on the street at a distance at the time of the incident describe the sound of an explosion coming from the building immediately preceding the collapse. One witness characterized it as a boom coming from the parking garage below street level. We'll be talking to that witness in about a half hour to get her personal experience."

"Damn," Josh said. "Now everyone is going to be thinking terrorism or sabotage. I mean, it also could be a gas leak, but that's not going to be anyone's first assumption."

"Or it could have been the beginning of the collapse itself," Todd suggested. "Which must have been deafening. Maybe it was the sound of columns explosively failing."

The man in a dark suit and a maroon tie who sat on the right side of the desk fiddled with the pen he held between his fingers, unconsciously revealing his unease. "We're also hearing the incident commander is describing the collapse as an MCI 4. A mass casualty incident, level 4, meaning they expect there will be between one hundred and one thousand victims."

Icy fingers trailed down Meg's spine. "My God. A thousand? Surely it can't be that high."

"No," Todd agreed. "Especially when you consider those killed versus injured. But it could be over one hundred dead, especially when you consider the added fatalities from those on I Street NW on their way to work and school. You remember how I told you last night how the hospitals were standing ready for patients that never came? It's because they were anticipating injuries, serious ones, but injuries. But there just weren't many who were simply injured." He took a sip of his coffee, his gaze returning to the TV.

"For those just joining us this morning," the male newscaster continued, "newly released security footage from one of the adjacent buildings caught the collapse of Talbot Terraces." The screen switched to a grainy color image of the condo building. Having been on-site the day before, Meg recognized the angle—the camera had to be part of the Conrad's security system, meant to capture the street and sidewalk around the rear of the hotel and the retailers on the first floor of Talbot Terraces. It captured street level perfectly, the color image featuring a road packed with rush hour traffic flowing in both directions, and pedestrians hustling down the sidewalk on their way to work, to shop, or to breakfast.

But in this case the camera had caught so much more.

As Meg watched in horror, a spoonful of oatmeal frozen inches over her bowl, the whole middle section of the building simply dropped, floor upon floor collapsing so quickly, she couldn't mark the passing of each. Trapped between the two ends of the building, concrete, glass, and steel collapsed into the parking garage below and then rolled out over the street, crushing any cars and pedestrians in their path. As the top floor crashed to the ground, the far end of the building seemed to twist slightly, swaying. Meg knew how this footage would end, had felt the remains beneath her boots as she climbed over the pile the day before. And yet, despite that knowledge, she found herself chanting, *Stay up, stay up!* in her head, even as gravity and instability won and the east end followed the center section straight down to the ground.

The whole collapse had taken only about twelve to fifteen seconds. A catastrophic fraction of time.

Most chilling was the silence of the security footage. The downward rush of all those building materials must have sounded like a 747 roaring forty feet overhead, but the utter silence of the carnage left Meg breathless.

She dropped her spoon into her bowl, all appetite gone.

Todd flicked off the TV. "Maybe we can wait for more of an update after all."

"You know," Josh said, "as horrific as that footage is, it's going to be really important. The structural engineers will be all over it. It doesn't say what caused the collapse, but being able to see that it gave way first at ground level and was a progressive collapse from the bottom up in that middle section and then out, that has to tell them something."

Meg stared sightlessly at her oatmeal, and jerked when Todd's hand came down on hers.

"What are you thinking?" he asked.

She glanced back at the TV, dark now, but she could still see the image of the building as it crumbled to the ground. "They never had a chance. The people in the section that went first, they might not have known anything, but those in the end section, they might have had seconds of terror, of knowing something was very, very wrong. But past that, no one had a chance. No time to escape, nowhere to run. With very few exceptions, it was instantly game over."

"Maybe that's a blessing," Luke said quietly. "For the children, for all of them. They didn't suffer. Most probably had no idea what was going on, it happened so quickly. And for those who knew they were in trouble, it didn't last long. I'm glad it didn't last long."

"Yeah." Meg picked up her spoon and pushed the thick cereal and chunks of apple back and forth a few times.

Todd tapped the back of her hand, drawing her gaze. "You need to eat."

"I know." She scooped up a spoonful, but before she could raise it to her mouth, Hawk appeared at her side, rested his chin on her thigh, and gazed up at her with liquid brown eyes. "Hey, buddy." She dropped a hand to the top of his head, then ran it down his silky fur to his back. He wagged his tail, his entire rear end undulating with his enthusiasm.

"I think your dog is trying to tell you something," Josh said. "Right, Hawk?"

Hawk raised his head, ears perked, as he stared at Josh.

"He's an extremely smart boy, and yes, he's reminding me that we have a job to do. But we'll do it together, right, Hawk?"

More tail wagging and a lick to her hand was her confirmation.

"And to do that job right, I need to fuel up, since we may not have a chance to eat if today is anything like yesterday. Food and coffee, and then we can meet the day."

"That goes for all of us," said Todd. "It's going to be another hard physical day." He met Meg's eyes. "And remember, just because the deck is stacked against us doesn't mean we have no chance of success. It's December, so it's cold, but it's still survivable. There may still be live victims in the pile. If there are, we'll have additional equipment and hands today. Keep the faith. Don't count us out yet."

Meg dug into her breakfast, one hand still resting on her dog.

Having a partner like Hawk made keeping the faith easier. Without a second thought, he would hold it fast.

So, then, would she.

CHAPTER 9

Structure: A collaborative system of interrelated components arranged to support external loads and resist forces.

Tuesday, December 18, 7:46 AM
Incident command, the Park at CityCenter
Washington, DC

"Thank you for coming a bit early. It gives me a chance to bring you up to speed so you're ready to pass off with the teams on the pile shortly." Craig stood, surrounded by his teams, all dressed once again in coveralls and hard hats, their dogs sitting at their sides, partway along one of the paths in the Park at CityCenter. He'd chosen the spot not only to keep the dogs away from any emergency vehicle and heavy equipment traffic but also to put some space between themselves and the main incident command tent, a noisy communication hub, with the constant buzz of discussion, the squawk of radio chatter, and the strident peals of cell phones. Craig had also purposely placed them away from the media, which was gathering again at the corner of New York Avenue NW and 10th Street NW, at the media tent.

Not that it was currently easy to see for any distance with the smoky haze that had settled over the site.

Brian waved a hand, as if to clear the air, and Meg raised her eyebrows at him. "That's not going to work."

"This is all from a fire under the building?" Brian asked.

"Yes." Craig glanced sideways at the incident command tent, where a group of men and women were huddled around the main table. "Started last night, and they're having trouble getting it under control. Had to actually stop some of the top work for about forty-five minutes last night. Then they thought they had it out, only to find it had started up again."

"What's burning down there?" Scott asked.

"Electric vehicles started the problem. The batteries can burst into flame when they're damaged, and they're damaged, all right. And from the briefing I just had, this causes a thermal runaway reaction that keeps burning, so it takes a *very* long time to burn itself out. Add together all the EVs down there, and then the gasoline spilled as cars and their gas tanks were crushed in the collapse, and it's a big issue. They've decided to dig a firebreak—a trench that will run from north to south in the middle of the collapsed wing, about twenty feet wide and forty feet deep. It won't keep the batteries from burning, but it will remove some of the fuel for the spreading flames. And it will open up a search area at the same time. We'll need to work around that excavation. On top of that, the ongoing fire in the section of the garage that's accessible is causing trouble, because DCFEMS and one of the USAR teams want to tunnel into the pile from below."

"They can do that?" Lauren's tone carried a mix of surprise and disbelief.

"It's risky, there's no doubt about it, but they're stationed under the plaza, where it hasn't collapsed. The parking garage continues past the building and occupies the space under the plaza, almost all the way to the Gerrard, with the second entrance leading out to H Street

NW. They've gained access through that entrance and have shored up the space below. Now, if the standing structure falls, that may not keep them safe, but they're hoping it will counteract any collapse from the sheer weight of the pile. That's essentially an additional edge of the pile, and they're hoping the shear wall may have helped create some void spaces."

"Tough working conditions if they're managing a fire at the same time," Meg stated. "They'll all have to be in respirator masks, if not their air tanks and regular fire-fighting masks."

"It's why they've had to stop a few times and pull out. Conditions and the lack of visuals down there as smoke filled the space, then filtered out to blanket the pile meant they had to put a stop to the pile searches. Fortunately, it's been back on for a while now."

"Are there more dog teams searching today?" Lauren asked.

"Yes. Both Virginia and Maryland USAR Task Forces brought in K-9 support. They've been at it all night at this point and are definitely ready for a break."

"Any luck?" Brian asked, his tone guarded, as if already guessing the answer.

"Two deceased pulled from the pile. Overnight they worked the bucket lines, clearing the debris from the top of the pile by hand, passing it down the line, circling back with empty buckets. But there's still a large exclusion zone."

Meg turned and looked eastward, down I Street NW, studying the site through the haze. "Were structural engineers here all night?"

"So I hear. At this point they've passed off with a second group. There are concerns about collapse of the standing structure. I caught some of the discussions around it because while DCFEMS cleared the building of humans yesterday and all the animals they could find—from dogs to cats, to caged rabbits and a guinea pig—they apparently missed two cats."

"With that amount of chaos, most animals' first instinct would be to hide," Scott stated. "And not come out at the sound of strange voices."

"That's what they think happened. The families, who both have children, are extremely upset that they might lose their perfectly healthy animals because they were not in the building at the time of the collapse."

"We all understand," Meg said, looking down at Hawk. "Dog, cat, rabbit, whatever . . . you get attached to a pet. They're true members of the family. To stand back and wait while one starves to death or dies of crush injuries . . ." She forced herself to stop. "Anyway, if that was me, and I knew my family pet was in there, I'd be losing my mind. They've already been on their own for a full twenty-four hours." She studied the building. "Just knowing they're there is going to stress me out."

Brian rubbed her arm. "That's no surprise. You're the person who doesn't blink at people getting killed in a movie, but if anyone harms an animal, you're done."

"And you aren't?"

"Well . . . when you put it that way, yeah, I am." He shrugged in a "What can you do?" gesture.

"Anyway . . ." Craig hauled the discussion back to the task at hand. "There was a lot of talk about shear walls, catastrophic failures, and a progressive collapse. The bottom line is that firefighters are going in again. They know exactly which apartments and will go in through the balcony to minimize time in the building. The hope is that the animals will at least stay in familiar spaces and not wander the floor because the doors were all forced open and no one tried to close them. It's going to be a volunteer endeavor only, and they'll be in and out. After that, no one is going in again. Families have asked for personal items, but the command team is firm. If it's not breathing, no one is going in for it. The risk is simply too high. There were some who didn't want firefighters going in for the pets, but they settled on no one being ordered to and it being a volunteer mission."

Meg didn't know where Todd was that morning and had to wonder if he'd be in a position to volunteer. It was exactly the kind of task he'd take on.

"Past that, the engineers will stay on-site and are constantly monitoring the building," Craig continued, drawing her attention back to her own task. "The moment they think the standing structure is at risk of collapse, the site will be evacuated. There are some real fears about the building falling, partly based on location—in the heart of downtown DC, so close to the White House. But the real issue is how close packed the buildings are here. The building at biggest risk is the Gerrard, which has already taken some minimal damage. It's at greatest risk of substantial damage or collapse if the rest of Talbot Terraces goes down."

"Surely it's been evacuated by now," said Scott.

"Yes. But while it's been renovated to luxury apartment status and is the home to some of DC's richest and most influential people, it's on the National Register of Historic Places because it was built in the late nineteenth century. It's why Talbot Terraces was shaped the way it was. The developer wanted to use as much land as he could in the precious downtown core, but the Gerrard couldn't be touched. So they designed the building in an L shape to go around it. What I picked up eavesdropping this morning is that L-shaped structures have inherently less stability than a solid rectangular or square building, which may have contributed to it being unable to withstand whatever forces were applied to it. Anyway, that's for the experts to work out. They're worried if the standing structure falls, it will damage or take out any buildings in its vicinity. However, if it stays standing until all victims are found, then it will be safely brought down by demolition at that time."

"Is this instability going to affect the exclusion zone?" Lauren asked.

"The biggest issue today around the exclusion zone is the stuff dangling from the standing structure. And I don't mean the personal belongings from the severed apartments, though some of the furniture at the edge will have to be dealt with." Craig pointed down the street, where all the fire trucks, minus three ladder trucks, had dispersed to the staging area.

Now, a huge mobile crane—the one Meg had seen move into place yesterday—was parked at the edge of the debris pile, its outriggers stretched out to fill the remaining width of the street, stabilizing the massive piece of equipment. The crane's telescoping boom was extended, and it stretched out until it disappeared behind the standing structure. In front of the crane, an excavator with a large claw was pulling into place beside another excavator with a massive set of pincers, from which dangled part of the air-conditioning system.

"Some heavy equipment arrived yesterday, but more came overnight. They're using cranes to remove the largest slabs of concrete, which can't be moved by human hands. Excavators and a 'picker' are pulling off any hanging columns or dangling HVAC equipment. Once all that is gone, then the searchers will be able to expand their grids without fear of being crushed by a ton of falling concrete, which would also obliterate any voids under it in the pile. There will still be an exclusion area close to the building, but it will be smaller. The other thing to know is engineers are limiting the number of people allowed on the pile to one hundred fifty for now. There are real fears about it shifting from too much weight on top. Any shift could collapse what had been, up to that point, a survivable void, killing anyone inside. You're all expected to be on the pile, and you'll be joined by USAR teams, but nothing above that cutoff."

"Is there a strategy for the search they'd prefer?" Brian asked. "Certain sectors covered, with a maximum amount of added weight per sector?"

"Yes. And I'll give you your search grid location, like we did yesterday. But we have a lot of hands today, so we need to be even more methodical. It's going to be a very different search site than yesterday, but the dogs are just as important." Craig glanced at his watch. "Eight o'clock is shift change, but instead of hitting the pile, there's going to be a pause. Virginia, Maryland, and Pennsylvania USAR Task Forces are now all here at full strength, and they brought electronics."

"Cameras and acoustic listening devices?" Meg asked.

"Yes. And they need specific conditions to use them. We can't have excavators dragging slabs around or moving materials, causing vibrations, or have searchers yelling at each other. So, at eight o'clock, minus the mayor's media circus over there"—he jerked a thumb toward the media tent, which was already swarming with reporters—"which will still be going on, when shift change happens, all work stops for at least fifteen minutes. All equipment engines off, everything held in place. They're already setting up, and they'll turn on the acoustic devices in various parts of the pile and will try to pick up any sound or vibration. If they detect anything, they'll try to confirm with dogs, though a victim might be too far inside the pile for scent to carry. Even without confirmation, they'll move to exca-vate at that location."

Lauren was shaking her head, her skepticism clear. "I've seen them use those devices following earthquakes with decent success. And I know they pick up certain specific frequencies that will cover voices or someone tapping or knocking, but what kind of depth will that cover? This isn't a two-story house collapse. It's millions of pounds of concrete."

"They know it's going to be difficult. How well sound travels depends on the material it's traveling through. In this case, we have multiple kinds of materials all interrupting each other. And apparently, some kinds of materials—carpet, drywall, and vinyl—aren't great conductors and can interrupt the signal. But they're going to try and will use an array of sensors to approximate survivor location." His gaze drifting to the activity down the street, Craig frowned. "It sounds like they're realistic. They don't think there's anyone at the bottom of the pile who survived, simply due to the sheer tonnage of materials overhead crushing what might have been a survivable space. Anyway, they have the pile until at least eight fifteen, and then we'll get started. They'll be using the cameras while people are on the pile, as that activity won't affect their ability to visualize anyone."

An amplified voice coming from the media tent attracted his attention momentarily. "Oh, one other thing. They now have proper safety gear, so everyone going onto the site will be wearing respirators to protect your lungs from toxic fumes. And smoke."

"I hate those things," Brian griped under his breath.

"Yeah, but we have to wear them," Meg murmured back. "I wish we could offer the dogs the same protection, but it would wipe out their sense of smell, and then why are we here?"

Wearing their masks and hard hats, the teams made their way down to the pile, wanting to be in place in order to get to work as soon as the all clear was called.

Coming through the haze, Hawk on her left, at her knee, Meg studied a group of five handlers and dogs standing on the sidewalk, watching the USAR members on the pile. Meg's gaze fixed on a tall woman with auburn hair pulled into a ponytail under her aqua hard hat. She was wearing navy blue coveralls but had her profile to Meg, so she couldn't see which group she was with. Then Meg spotted the golden retriever at her side, and recognition dawned.

Pam Dennihoff and her retriever, Goldie. Pam worked with the Search Dog Foundation, but the moment disaster struck, FEMA called her in to organize additional dog teams from all over the country to assist in rescue operations.

"Pam." Meg raised a hand in greeting as the FBI teams approached.

As Pam turned, the FEMA patch on her left breast pocket became visible. "If it isn't my favorite group of FBI live find dogs. Were you here yesterday?"

"First thing in the morning," Brian confirmed. "All of us were in town, so Craig was able to deploy the whole team. Hawk and Theo both identified live victims in the pile."

"Well done." Pat bent and ran a hand down Hawk's back. "Good job, Hawk." She turned and repeated the praise with Theo. "What's it like up there?"

Meg met Pam's eyes. "Not good."

"Pretty much what I expected. Not that I've done a site like this before. Hurricane collapses, but not something of this size, weight, and density."

"We're having trouble finding void spaces and live victims," Scott said. "There are some, but they're few and far between."

Pam's gaze flicked back to the pile. "The victim count is still so low. I can't imagine it won't climb significantly higher."

"That's because they're not counting human remains," Lauren said, her tone flat and detached. "The dogs are alerting on blood and body fluids, thinking it's an injured victim. Most often, it's not anyone who's survived. In fact, it's not even an intact victim much of the time. So . . . be prepared. It's going to be hard."

Pam sighed and nodded in resignation. "Thanks for the heads-up."

Meg took in the debris field and tried to take Lauren's words to heart. It had been hard yesterday and might yet be harder today. She needed to be prepared.

Not that you could really prepare for where they were about to go.

CHAPTER 10

Shear Wall: A vertical panel or panels of reinforced concrete designed to resist lateral forces, such as wind and seismic activity. Internal shear walls are often positioned around stairwells and elevator shafts.

Tuesday, December 18, 7:52 AM
Talbot Terraces
Washington, DC

Webb stood in the underground garage with a group of rescuers, some dressed in DCFEMS turnout gear, some wearing the heavy work pants, shirts, and jackets worn by USAR. Part of the group was DCFEMS Special Operations, specifically the tactical rescue crew, distinguished by their use of hard hats instead of the standard firefighting helmets other DCFEMS firefighters wore. Everyone wore respirators in the doubly toxic environment of smoke and chemical fumes.

Behind the group, a row of large industrial fans had been set up. They were powered by generators outside on the sidewalk, power cords running down the K Street NW driveway to where the fans sat near the entrance, pulling smoke out of the garage to disperse it into the outside air.

The fire had been out now for over forty-five minutes, and the air was finally starting to clear.

Webb hung back with three other firefighters, watching the USAR and tactical teams discussing next steps.

It was more than twenty-four hours since the collapse, and no living victim had been pulled from the rubble in over eighteen hours. Word had filtered through as to how the surface searches were going, and it wasn't good. Once building plans were received from the owners, and as the missing were reported and names were compiled, one of the USAR groups had run a simulation of where people might have been based on their apartment layouts, the time of day, and who might have been home at the time of the collapse. It was only an initial estimate, but it gave crews on the surface somewhere to start tunneling into the pile based on where they thought victims might be. The initial reports were not encouraging. Where rescue teams had been hoping for at least twelve-to-eighteen-inch void spaces, they were finding a maximum of eight inches.

It simply wasn't survivable. This was why they were consistently finding only human remains and not intact victims, let alone survivors.

But hope still lived, and the searching continued, even here in the upper level of the parking garage. There was no access to the lower level, as the driveway down to it, as well as both emergency staircases, were beneath the rubble pile, leaving access to potential survivors only on the upper level.

Webb had his doubts when he first arrived at this section of the debris pile. With the roof half caved in and the debris stacked in close-packed layers, he had a hard time believing anyone could have survived the initial collapse, let alone a full twenty-four hours. As a dual-trained firefighter/paramedic, he knew too much about the human body to be so naïve as to think it likely anyone could be at the bottom of this pile, curled up in a void space, waiting for rescue. At the very least, anyone who had fallen stories and then had the crushing weight of millions of pounds of concrete and steel rain down around them would be suffering from multiple fractures and possibly internal hemorrhaging. If they'd survived past the first few minutes, the chances of them holding on for a full day and not bleeding out before being found were infinitesimally small.

At least they still had ambient temperature on their side. The human body was much more susceptible to high temperatures than to low ones, and last night had fortunately been warmer than the average, with a reported low of 44 degrees Fahrenheit. And while temperatures like that would definitely induce hypothermia, over a twenty-four-hour period, it might not kill. Individuals could stay alive as long as their body temperature didn't stay below 70 degrees Fahrenheit for too long. If those temps persisted for much longer, no one buried here would survive, but for now they had a chance, especially down here, where the fires had created extra heat. The downside to the fires was the smoke. If air was moving through the debris, it would carry smoke with it, and a live victim could die of smoke inhalation. If air wasn't moving through the pile, a victim could use up all the oxygen and suffocate.

Damned if you did, damned if you didn't.

All they could do was move as fast as possible without bringing the entire debris pile down on their heads, with the standing structure following it. The USAR crews had been the first allowed in the space and had braced the ceiling as they moved in farther and farther, installing the industrial steel posts they'd brought and using the multi-directional swivel feet to shore up the ceiling at any angle of collapse. The garage was a forest of shore poles, as the only way to tunnel into the pile was by using saws and chipping hammers, and they had to ensure the vibrations they produced wouldn't trigger a new collapse.

On top of that risk, they also had to hope they didn't get stalled again by the fire, which kept reigniting deep inside the pile as well as in the more accessible areas of the garage. Fortunately, that fire was down at the east end of the garage, while they stood at the west end, but all the water they'd used to put out the fire rose halfway up their shins, making it a constant slog to move around.

Firefighters understood the need to move away from fossil fuels, and electric vehicles were a logical choice to accomplish that goal. But every firefighter in the country hated the batteries—impenetrable, watertight boxes that contained a runaway chemical reaction during a fire. You couldn't use foam or dry chemical extinguishers on them, because where smothering would put out most fires, it did nothing to a fire that was strictly the result of a chemical reaction and didn't need oxygen to continue to burn. It was why the deep-seated fire under the pile was so problematic—it could keep producing smoke and the most toxic of fumes—and why they'd been forced to use trenching in the pile as a firebreak. For an electric vehicle fire in an exposed garage or out in the open air, the strategy they often used—let it eventually burn itself out and just protect everything around the car—wasn't possible here, for the sake of rescuers and possible survivors alike. Which left *copious* amounts of water as the only option to put out the EV fire and any spilled and incredibly flammable gasoline.

The fire had stalled rescue efforts for much too long, but now they were finally making progress.

Webb listened to the USAR and tactical guys planning their strategy, which made sense to him logically. They thought the best chance to find someone, anyone, alive at the edge of the pile down here was in association with the concrete shear wall just to their left. This was the line that marked the divide between the living and the dead he'd seen from above the day before. Constructed of concrete containing two embedded layers of bidirectional rebar, with two short connected perpendicular walls to brace the elevator shaft, the shear wall had withstood the forces of the east wing of the building falling. As each floor had ripped away, the shear wall had stood firm, protecting the structure behind it. It was this unyielding support they were hoping to use. If they were lucky, as materials had fallen, some of them might have become jammed against the shear wall at an angle, creating a survivable void space. Their best chance was at the edge of the debris field at this level, in locations that might not have the full weight of the rubble resting right over top, the kind of weight that would crush void spaces out of existence.

Like the rescuers aboveground, the rescue crews in the garage were going to use the work stoppage at 8:00 AM to listen for any possible sounds. They were going to try to tunnel into the debris field no matter what, but if they heard any sounds, it would give them a direction.

A radio squawk echoed through the enclosed space, and one of the USAR crew members near the edge of the pile radioed back. After a short conversation, he put his radio on his belt and turned to the rest of the group. "The pile is quiet. We're going to start listening now. Everyone needs to stop what you're doing, and someone needs to kill the fans temporarily. Then be as still as possible." At that instruction, one of the firefighters sloshed his way through the water to the fans, which sat a foot above the waterline.

Another man—Webb had heard someone call him Holt—stood at the edge of the pile, holding a compact black monitoring unit. Two cables ran from the back of the unit, one over the rubble in front of Holt and the second to his right. A series of six three-inch-tall hexagonal orange sensors were spread out over the rubble, all sitting on horizontal concrete surfaces and daisy-chained together with additional long cables. The sensors were spread out to listen to as much of the pile as possible.

Holt adjusted one side of the headphones he wore; then he held up an index finger, reinforcing the need for quiet, made an adjustment on the unit, and then bowed his head, eyes locked on the six indicator lights on his display. Each had a vertical bar, and as sound was detected, the bar would light up. The louder the sound, the higher the bar would go.

After twenty-four hours of constant noise, the silence was unsettling. Webb scanned the men around him and saw the same uneasiness as several of them stood with their gazes turned upward. With nothing to do but take in their surroundings, it struck home hard about what they were doing and where they were standing.

As Webb's gaze, too, swung up to the ceiling, he couldn't hold back the memory of the accident the previous spring, when he and his crew were fighting a residential fire in a hoarder's house. Webb had been leading the hose line when the ceiling above him gave way, burying him under a pile of flaming debris. It had taken precious seconds for his men to reach him, and even longer for them to free him. So long they'd had to be replaced by a fresh team with full air tanks. They'd found him unconscious, had given him air just as his own tank was running out, and had pulled him to safety. But for as long as he lived, Webb would never forget the knife stab of fear as the ceiling had opened up over his head. He hadn't had long to prepare— just long enough to get his left arm over his head, resulting in a dislocated shoulder—but it had been long enough for the fear to stick with him. And standing under that sloped ceiling angling down toward the debris pile, he felt the sharp stab of it again.

On the bright side, if the ceiling collapsed, he wouldn't have long to feel the terror of his oncoming death.

He and fear were old friends. Smart firefighters felt the emotion but did the job despite it, even using it to keep themselves sharp. Only an idiot would run into a raging inferno, even with the correct gear, and not feel any misgivings about where they were heading. Every year, firefighters died while doing their jobs as safely as possible. The fear was real. The trick was to work through it. Because what was on the line was too important to let it stop you.

Webb looked down in time to see several bars on the monitor light up. He moved closer, vying for a better view. The indicator lights for sensors one, two, and three were pulsing, leaving a single spot illuminated on the bar marking the highest sound level. Sensor one was highest, with two and three progressively lower.

Webb had seen this technology before. Normally, rescuers would call out into the pile, trying to get victims to call back. But with multiple rescue teams spread out across the pile, all listening at the same time, they couldn't risk one USAR team mistaking another for a victim. After a full day of constant noise from the active rescue, they were counting on the silence of the pile to alert anyone conscious inside that this was their chance to be heard. However, depending on the depth and the interfering materials, using their voice might not be the best way for victims to indicate their presence. Tapping the debris around them might be more effective, as sound vibrations would transmit farther in solid conductors as opposed to air.

If there was any air in there in the first place.

Staring at the monitor, Webb suddenly realized the

lights pulsing up and down the bar indicator were in a pattern. Three fast. Three slow. Three fast. Pause. Repeat.

SOS.

Holt turned around, and there was genuine surprise in his eyes. "We have a survivor." He kept his voice low so as not to interfere with other groups trying to detect survivors. He scanned the pile. "Normally, I'd move the sensors and try to narrow down the location, but with this minimal amount of offside access, we'll have to go with these readings. Based on the sensor locations and the strongest vibrations, our initial thoughts are correct, and the victim is up against the shear wall."

"Any idea how far in?" someone asked.

"Impossible to say with the sensors in their current position against the side of the pile. And if we went up top to be directly above the victim, he or she might be too far down to actually hear. From here, the tapping sounds are clear, but I don't hear a voice. We can listen in again or request another short tactical pause, if needed, but we're going to have to start tunneling."

As soon as the quiet period was over, the USAR and tactical crews started organizing and bringing in the equipment required for breaking and breaching concrete—jackhammers for lower-set pieces, chipping hammers for vertical or overhead pieces, K-12 saws for concrete and rebar, more support materials to shore up as they tunneled. Devices to monitor movement in the pile. They also stationed structural engineers on the surface on alert to monitor the standing structure in case of any shifting.

They got to work. Webb and his fellow DCFEMS firefighters let the tactical and USAR guys lead the way but helped out in any way they could—bringing equipment, carrying away broken pieces of concrete and tangles of rebar as they were freed, running for more shoring materials as they moved into the pile, breaking away when the fire started to smolder and needed to be controlled yet again.

Hours of backbreaking work passed, but they kept at it, one or two of them breaking occasionally for food or water but coming back as soon as they could. Other teams offered to help, but none of the men wanted to stop—a life was finally within their grasp, and after all the pain, anguish, and trauma, they wanted a part in saving it. They traded places often, allowing each other a time of rest while someone else took over hammering, chipping, or sawing.

Every few hours, without calling for a work stoppage above, because those above the surface needed rescuing as well, Holt would listen in to the pile, tap out a sequence on concrete with a Halligan bar, and wait for a response. The first time, he receive an echoed response; the second time, he didn't.

Had their victim lost consciousness? Died?

Webb felt the impulse to work harder, faster, but knew it wasn't possible. Anything they did here could trigger a chain reaction in the pile around them. Slow and steady, bracing the pile as they went, was the only way to work it. But the contained intensity of the men around him told him he wasn't the only one feeling the pressure.

They'd been at it for nearly eight hours when Holt requested a short work stoppage above to listen in again. Holt situated several of the sensors inside the tunnel and had one of the USAR crew members call out from their deepest location. This time Holt heard a male voice respond. Better than that, even without the sound equipment, so did the USAR rescuer inside the tunnel.

The work continued, above and below.

Webb was just returning from carrying away a bucket of debris when he caught a snatch of conversation between Burt Melnyk, one of the DCFEMS tactical team, and a USAR responder with VIRGINIA TF and KOVAK stamped on the front and side of his electric-blue helmet.

"Are we nearly through?" Melnyk asked.

"Close," Kovak responded. "We're hoping to be through inside of an hour."

"Are you prepared to assess the victim before pulling him out of the rubble?"

"We'll do a quick assessment, but time is of the essence."

Webb was glad Meg wasn't standing beside him, because he knew she wouldn't like the offer he was about to make as he paused beside Melnyk. "Send me in."

Kovak eyed his uniform, from his turnout gear to his firefighter helmet. "Why you?"

"I'm dual trained as a paramedic. I get that time is of the essence, but if there are back or neck injuries, we could paralyze the victim during the extraction. You need someone who can assess and stabilize in place, if needed. Would you guys be able to judge lucidity, respiration, or a cardiac event?"

"We have first aid training, but I'm the first to admit this situation is beyond what most of us have ever dealt with before."

"Then send me in. You'll have already done the hard work of tunneling through. That's not where my training lies, but field triage is. It's going to be difficult in a confined space, with the risk of the pile falling on our heads, but we need to take a few extra minutes to get this right. You don't want to pinch or sever the spinal cord or tear the aorta if the existing injuries are severe. If we kill the victim getting him out, what was the point of all this time spent and of the weakness this tunnel is going to leave in the pile?"

"Sounds sensible to me," Melnyk said. "If Webb can't

maneuver the guy out on his own, he can at least get him ready to move."

Kovak took long seconds to consider, then relented. "All right. But I'm pulling the plug on it if there's any risk to our men. If it's between pulling the victim out quickly and damning the injuries or having the tunnel collapse, he's coming out quickly."

"Affirmative," Webb said.

"What will you need?"

"I'll get it. There's a full med pack on the truck for when we're out on a call. We'll need a backboard. And I'm thinking a McGuire sled."

"A sled? In there?"

Webb was ready for the pushback, as he'd already had the argument in his own head. The McGuire sled—a three-and-a-half-foot-by-six-foot rectangle of tough military-grade fabric surrounded by six sturdy handles and equipped with several carabiner clips—was used in an active fire to carry out the injured. One had been used to carry out Webb himself after the ceiling collapse.

"We know the vic is awake, at least intermittently, but he's going to be hurt, and we don't know how badly," Webb said. "We don't know how mobile he'll be, if at all. The tunnel you're carving is only big enough for one man, or else you increase the risk of bringing the pile down on whoever's in there. Unless it's a bigger void than we think it is, I'm not going to be able to climb in there with him. I'm not going to be able to help him out except by dragging him, because I'm not going to be able to be beside or behind him. If I can get the sled in there and can help him get onto it, then I can use it to pull him out in a one-person drag. Assuming that's even possible to do. It may be too rocky to attempt without actual injury to him, but I think we need the option."

"I think we need all the options we can get," agreed Melnyk.

"I'll go grab everything and be back long before you get through."

It was a relief to step out of the water and smoke they'd been working in for the entire day and to walk into sunlight. Even though the emergency lighting in the garage was brilliant, it was pointed at the pile, leaving much of the rest of the garage shrouded in gloom. He stepped into the last of the afternoon sun, and being able to remove the respirator and breathe the crisp, chill air was a revelation. His eyes were gritty from hours inside with the remnants of smoke, and the fresh air felt deliciously soothing.

Not wanting to take too long, he jogged down H Street NW, past the standing structure, and headed up 10th Street NW to the staging area on New York Avenue NW, where he found a number of DCFEMS engines. He grabbed the med pack from his own engine and checked the contents, ensuring there was a cervical collar, a saline bag and IV lines, a defibrillator, and aluminum splinting materials. He put on the pack and grabbed the long, narrow backboard and the folded McGuire sled. He jogged back, the round trip taking him less than ten minutes.

When he got back to H Street NW, he stopped at the mouth of the driveway, where it dipped down into the parking garage. The pile spread out before him across the plaza, a hive of activity of what had to be over a hundred rescue workers. He automatically scanned the pile for Meg and, more specifically, for Hawk, as one coveralled and hard hat–clad rescue worker looked much the same as the next.

His hand was automatically reaching for the cell phone in the pocket of his turnout coat when he thought he saw her on the C side of the pile. His fingers closed around the phone, and he froze, indecision streaking through him.

You shouldn't bother her.

This isn't bothering her. You may not come out of the tunnel.

She'll just worry.

She'll never forgive you if you don't give her the chance to say goodbye, even if she doesn't come right out and say it. And don't you want that same chance?

There was no arguing with that.

He pulled out his phone and speed-dialed her number.

On the pile, Meg paused, pulled out her phone, no doubt expecting Craig or another teammate, and halted briefly again when she saw his name on the screen. She answered the call. "Todd?" Wariness was already in her tone.

"Hey." He hesitated. *How do you tell the woman you love that you're about to do something so dangerous, you might never see her again?*

"Is everything okay?" she asked. "Word filtered through that you found a survivor."

"We did." *Just do it. Dragging this out will only scare her.* "That's why I'm calling. I wanted to let you know . . . I'm going into the pile to get him."

"*What*? Hawk, stop." On the pile, Hawk returned to Meg to stand at her knee.

"They've tunneled through to him, and they need someone to go in."

"And you volunteered." It wasn't a question.

That brought a slight smile to his lips—she knew him so well. "Yeah. They need someone with medical skills. I'm the only one."

"They could call in someone else."

Her words had been blurted out, and he knew if she'd taken a moment to think, she never would have said this. But right now, she was riding on pure nerves. Meg was one of the bravest people he knew, but she was less brave when it came to the chances *he* took.

She'd nearly lost him eight months before in the cave-in, and he knew she was seeing the similarities, just as he had.

"There's no time," he said gently. "We need to get him out while the tunnel is stable. We don't know how long that will be."

Silence met that statement, and he knew she was biting back a response.

"I wanted to call you before I went in. To let you know." He paused. "To hear your voice."

"Don't you dare—"

"I just wanted you to know. I'll call you the moment I'm out. I love you."

"I love you too. Please . . ."

He could hear all the things she couldn't bring herself to say as she stood on top of the pile, surrounded by rescue workers, the dead under her feet. But she didn't need to say them out loud. He knew.

Be careful. Take care of yourself. Move quickly.
Live.

"I will, I promise. I have to go now." He wouldn't say goodbye. "Talk to you soon." He ended the call.

He took one last look at her standing motionless in the last light of day, in the midst of frenzied activity, her dog at her side. She couldn't hear his promise from across the plaza, but he said it out loud anyway. "Wait for me. I'm coming back." Then he turned away and jogged down the driveway toward the parking garage.

Webb dropped his supplies on the dry pavement above the waterline, put on his respirator, stepped from sunlight into darkness, and paused for a moment as his eyes adjusted. They were still tunneling, but from the chatter, he knew they were getting close to reaching the victim. After joining the group, he studied the tunnel, which started a half foot above the waterline in the garage.

They'd done a good job of tunneling parallel to the

shear wall without touching it, in case their work directly affected the standing structure. Though they knew any major shift of anything in the pile could do the same thing, there was a difference between taking tools to the shear wall as opposed to something that leaned against it.

If anything compromised that wall, the remaining structure could fall and every rescuer on-site could die.

The tunnel was rough cut and showed the different layers they'd gone through, from concrete to steel to wood. Every few feet inside the tunnel, two steel shores straddled the gap and a squat I beam lay over them, balancing the load across the top of the tunnel. The opening between the shores was only wide enough for a single rescuer to slide through. Currently, all that could be seen of that rescuer was the light coming from his helmet about thirty feet away as he lay on his belly, his chipping hammer, connected to a generator by a power cord, seated on several stacked chunks of concrete to keep it free of the water. The rest of his body was lost in shadows.

The chipping hammer fell silent, and then they could hear him speaking. The hammer ran for a few more minutes, then fell quiet, and there was only the sound of shuffling. It took the rescuer a full three minutes to inch his way backward out of the tunnel, slowly, carefully, bringing his equipment and dragging some debris clear of the tunnel. Finally, he inch wormed back into the garage.

He looked up, his face filthy but his eyes lit with excitement. "We're through. And he's conscious."

Webb took a step forward. "What's his condition?"

"I couldn't really tell. His face is covered with streaks of blood. Looks like he has a head wound that bled like hell. His eyes are open, and he's talking in full sentences, though not comfortably."

"What kind of space is he in?"

"He's in a triangular void, under an angled section of

slab that's jammed against the shear wall. The void is roughly at the same level as the tunnel and lies perpendicular to it, so we tunneled right in. He's lying on his side, and he'll need to turn around enough to come out. I don't know how mobile he is. I told him we had a medic here who needed to evaluate him." The man looked back to the tunnel. "Evaluate quickly."

"That's the plan." Webb turned to grab his gear, only to find a DCFEMS colleague already holding it. "How risky is it to have two people moving through the tunnel?"

"We've hit that pile with jackhammers and chipping hammers to get through it. Any movement isn't great, but if you go slow and don't touch the shoring system, you should be okay."

"I'm going to go in without the med pack until I know what's going on." Webb stared down the tunnel, which disappeared into inky blackness. "I don't want it behind me, blocking my way, if we have to suddenly move fast. I'll take some basic supplies with me, but I want an ambulance on the street outside and paramedics with a gurney waiting as close as they can to the driveway so they can come down and get him."

He turned to the firefighter holding the med pack and turned it in his arms so he could open and sort through it. He pulled items out of the pack—an IV bag and tubing, needles, morphine, a rolled splint, an assortment of first-aid supplies—grateful for the deep pockets in his turnout coat and bunker pants, which took long items like the flattened cervical collar. "Thanks." He unclipped the LED light on his helmet and took it off. "I need to swap this out for someone's hard hat. I need something with a smaller brim." Then he took off his respirator, knowing the space was going to be tight and he was going to need every tiny bit of freedom of movement possible. The rest of the protective gear had to stay.

He took his first breath of garage air and nearly choked on the acrid mixture of smoke combined with the toxic remnants of burned rubber, fuel, plastics, and electricals. Layered over it all was the reek of sulfur dioxide, given off by standard car batteries as they burned, mixed with the slightly fruity scent of burning lithium-ion batteries. The combination made his stomach roll greasily, and he swallowed hard to keep what was left of his lunch in place.

"Take mine." One of the DCFEMS tactical guys took off his hard hat and exchanged it for Webb's firefighter helmet.

Webb clipped his light onto the side of the hard hat, put it on, checked to make sure his radio was securely tucked into his left breast pocket, and grabbed the McGuire sled, which he quickly rolled into a long cylinder. "I'm ready. I'll radio if I need anything."

Melnyk nodded. "Affirmative."

Walking forward, his heart rate kicking upward as what he was about to attempt truly hit home, Webb studied the gaping maw of the tunnel.

Past the first few feet, illuminated by the garage emergency lighting, all that looked back at him was utter blackness.

The kind of blackness that would come if the tunnel collapsed and the weight of the pile crushed the life out of him.

CHAPTER 11

Survey: The use of drones to gather data about a building site, in the form of photos and topographical maps, to infer equipment usage and to navigate hazardous conditions, thereby increasing the safety of human workers.

Tuesday, December 18, 8:20 AM
Talbot Terraces
Washington, DC

Meg and Hawk were on the pile as soon as the USAR teams on the surface reported picking up no sounds. After that, people strategically poured onto the debris field, covering both the pile proper and the edge that overflowed I Street NW. A bulldozer and several backhoe loaders worked on I Street NW, trying to clear as much of the overflow as possible to allow the heavy equipment to get closer to the pile itself.

There was an entirely different mood on the pile today. The shock at the devastating silence of yesterday, with no voices calling out for help, had been replaced by a concerted mood shift—one of determination, camaraderie, and support, as they held each other up through the horrific experience of searching hopefully for life, yet knowing most of what they'd find was death. Meg had seen this on searches before, including the ones following Hurricane Michael and Hurricane Cole as well as earthquakes and mudslides. First responders deployed, and whoever stood shoulder to shoulder with them was a comrade in arms, so to speak. There was no time to learn to trust or to question skills; you simply leaped in with both feet and found out that the person beside you knew exactly what they were doing, just as you did. You might have different skill sets, but those differences most often made the team stronger.

More than just with skill sets, the USAR teams came with all the portable equipment needed for work on the pile, all powered by rechargeable batteries or gas: jackhammers, chipping hammers, diamond-blade concrete saws, cutting tools and chisels, and an unending stream of plastic buckets to move the pile by hand. The task forces had brought everything they'd need to take apart the debris field by hand when the heavy equipment was otherwise occupied or the work demanded the delicate touch of human hands.

The heavier equipment was already making a dent in the side of the pile as the firebreak trench started to form between the A1 and A2 search grid locations, and the rescuers were all aware of it as an extra hazard, both during and after its creation.

The K-9 teams had spread out to their assigned search grids. Several bucket brigades had already formed in different locations, including a group of five or six USAR members near the top of the pile who worked in tandem with a long line of fifteen or twenty people trailing down to the street and then to a large open disposal bin. The workers at the top dug through the rubble, filled their buckets, then passed them down the line before starting on the next empty buckets. The only way to burrow down into the pile without the heavy equipment—which was currently occupied moving massive pieces of rubble—was to do the digging by hand. A bystander might think the process was a waste of time, something that moved too slowly, but it was surprising how fast the group could work. Any personal belongings recovered during the process were set aside for the survivors or for the family and friends of those who didn't survive. When this was all that was left of a loved one now gone, those few meager surviving items were of paramount importance.

Meg and Hawk had been assigned to part of the southern side of the pile. "Ready, Hawk? Find." Meg's voice sounded muffled behind her respirator, but Hawk clearly had no trouble understanding her command, as he put his head down and started to search.

Meg was helping him up and over a lip of concrete when a high-pitched buzzing met her ears, and her heart jumped into her throat. She stared at the drone, hovering twenty feet above her, and shook her head in disgust.

You're never going to be comfortable around that sound.

Not after the Mannew case, where that sound had heralded an imminent deadly explosion.

She wanted to make sure the drone was piloted by search and rescue looking for better visuals and not by a reporter looking for an angle on a story. Meg knew very well that victim recovery was happening at that moment; for the sake of the victims and the families, she wasn't going to allow this to be a spectacle.

"Hawk, hold." She pulled her radio off her belt and hit the TALK button. "Craig, Meg here. There's a drone hovering overhead. Can I get a confirmation this is a USAR drone and not media horning in on a story?"

There was a buzz of static; then Craig's voice crackled over the radio. "Stand by. Let me check."

Not wanting to waste time waiting, Meg clipped her

radio back into place as she threw the drone a sour look, then gave her dog the command to resume.

They were moving through an area filled with twisted and mangled rebar. Hawk managed to wind his way through it with relative ease, but Meg took considerably longer, the ragged steel ends catching on her coveralls as she twisted her body around and through.

"Meg, Craig here."

She pulled her radio off her belt again. "Meg here."

"I have confirmation the drone is ours. They're using it to search the exclusion zone. If something drops on the drone, we lose the equipment, but not a life."

"Makes sense. Thanks for the confirmation."

"Also, to let you know, the crane is going to do some work on the top of the pile, across from you. There's a large piece of roof slab USAR has asked to be removed as part of their strategy of starting at the top and working down, assuming that the greatest chance of voids, and therefore survival, is near the top and at the edges of the collapse. They're going to break from clearing widow-makers to do that. We're covering the edges now, but as soon as that slab is removed, I'd like you and Hawk to be the first on-site to check below it."

"Affirmative. Let me know if we need to change the grid while they're physically moving it, and when you want us to check it out."

"Roger that. Craig out."

As they continued the search, Meg kept an eye on the crane, ready to give the heavy equipment more space as it moved in and was attached to the sturdy cables USAR personnel had wrapped around the slab. When they were ready to lift, the call came over the radio to move back, and Meg, Hawk, and about forty USAR workers moved out of harm's way, giving the top of the pile and the entire path down to the dump truck on I Street NW a wide berth. It took less than ten minutes to raise the slab, confirm that the connections were solid and the crane was in control, and then slowly move the slab to the truck.

Meg watched it swing free of the pile before being lowered into the dump truck, where its several tons settled, making the truck bed lurch momentarily. Then the workers got the all clear, and everyone swarmed the pile again.

Meg, following Craig's directive, moved with Hawk up the south face of the pile, then farther up, to where the slab had once sat. "Hawk, find. This is all new territory. Find them."

Hawk put his nose down and climbed steadily higher.

Meg knew immediately he smelled something—from the perk of his ears, his short, rapid inhalations, and his high tail, it was clear he had the scent. She dropped her hand down onto her radio, getting ready to call for Brian for confirmation if Hawk alerted.

Hawk crested a toppled column, then squeezed low to shimmy under a twisted tangle of rebar and come out the other side. He put his nose down as soon he had all four feet on the top level, and moved forward as quickly as he could over the treacherous debris.

Then he leaped forward and started to dig.

Adrenaline punched through Meg. The only other time she'd seen Hawk skip the alert signal altogether and just start to dig in a search was at Arlington Cemetery, when they were looking for Sandy Holmes in a freshly dug grave. She and Brian had joined in with shovels, while Lacey had jumped in to join Hawk with her paws. Together they'd uncovered the newly buried coffin, but tragically, it had been too late. They'd been so close, maybe only a half hour late, which had made the loss hit them that much harder. So close, but so, so far.

She climbed after him, having to circle around the mangled steel—not able to slither under it as he had with her go bag on her back—and then boosted herself up another two feet until she was just below the top of the pile.

The surface in this location was compacted by the weight of the slab, comprised of smaller pieces broken by the combined force of the fall from the twelfth story and the slab crashing down. But if there was any chance of a void, there might still be life beneath.

Hawk certainly thought so. And she wasn't going to take the time to call Brian for confirmation when Hawk was already digging, trying to shift the smaller pieces with nothing more than his own paws.

She turned around to find one of the bucket brigades only about twenty feet away. "I need help here!" she yelled.

No one moved; they couldn't hear her behind her respirator and through the din of heavy equipment, chipping hammers, saws, rebar cutters, and concrete and steel dropping into sturdy plastic buckets.

She took a deep breath, then pulled her respirator down, stretching the elastic encircling her head, until the plastic mask cleared her nose and mouth. "I need some help here!"

Before she could snap the mask back into place, she registered the rancid mix of odors—concrete dust, diesel fuel, acrid chemicals, and death. It wasn't strong yet—it had only been a day, after all—but the unmistakable scent of decomposition rose from the pile, accelerated by the grievous injuries suffered by the victims. On top of the smell of human waste.

She looked down at her dog, still working frantically, and suddenly knew what they were going to find.

Still, until they knew for sure otherwise, there was always a chance.

She slid the mask into place as she waved an arm over

her head to several first responders, who turned at her call. Without waiting to see the response, because she knew they'd come immediately, she climbed up the rest of the way to join her dog, who was struggling to move the heavy materials. But he'd managed a shallow depression, and in it, Meg caught a glimpse of pale fingers and half a palm. The rest of the hand and the body that went with it were encased in debris.

Meg shrugged out of her pack, set it down about ten feet away, and dropped to her knees beside her dog. She stripped off her gloves to lay her warm fingers over a hand exactly as cold as she'd anticipated. Nevertheless, she yanked her glove back on and started moving rubble as a half dozen USAR workers joined her, dug around the hand, and freed it and then several inches of wrist and forearm below. She yanked off her right glove and pressed two fingers to the pulse point in the wrist, closing her eyes, concentrating on any movement under her touch.

Nothing.

She opened her eyes to find a thickset man wearing a black respirator and a hard hat crouching opposite her. The emblem on his jacket said he hailed from Maryland Task Force 1, and the name embroidered above the emblem said MARSHALL. She shook her head at him.

"Let me double-check," he offered, and she moved away so he could get in. Long seconds passed as he, too, searched for a pulse, until he raised his head and gave it a shake.

After standing, he turned to his team. "It's a recovery. Stanislowski, we're going to need a basket and a body bag." He surveyed the rubble surrounding them. "We're going to need a couple of Halligans and at least one chipping hammer."

Men peeled off to get the equipment required as he turned back to Meg. "Agent . . ." He trailed off.

Meg pushed to her feet. "I'm not an agent with the FBI. I'm a civilian consultant with the Human Scent Evidence Team. Just Meg is fine."

"Meg, I'm Derek Marshall with Maryland TF1. Can you call off your dog? We'll take over from here."

Meg was suddenly conscious that Hawk was still trying to rescue what he thought was a live victim. "Hawk, buddy, stop." Hawk slowed but didn't stop. "Talon, stop." She knew the use of his "Don't mess with me" name, the special name that required instant compliance, was overkill, but her dog was in overdrive right now. As far as he was concerned, the job wasn't done. More than that, why was everyone just standing there?

"Good boy," she praised as he stopped and stood, looking up at her, head tilted, clearly confused. "That's my boy. Come here, Hawk." When he came to stand beside her, she ran her ungloved hand over him, his fur gritty with concrete dust under her touch, and lavished him with praise for a job well done as she scanned the area around them. "While you're setting up, are we clear to check the rest of the area? In case you need to move anything? We don't want to miss a void."

"Thanks. That would be helpful."

With one last look at the victim's pale hand, Meg called Hawk to check the vicinity.

As she watched her dog working diligently to scent every inch around him, Meg realized where they were standing and which part of the original structure was under her feet. Now she knew why Hawk had found the victim buried in the rubble. According to the security video, they were over the part of the building that fell last. The part of the building that had stayed standing for perhaps as long as an additional ten seconds as the building swayed and twisted. Enough time for someone to know, or at least suspect, that they were in life-threatening danger. Enough time to break out in a sweat, and for fear pheromones to rise, before the building crashed to the ground and life ended. On top of that, surely there were injuries to the body, and injuries meant blood.

It was those compounds that Hawk had scented, that had made him frantic to find the person buried in the rubble. Meg had smelled only death, whereas Hawk had smelled life or, more precisely, a life in danger. And had reacted as quickly as possible in a bid to save that life.

He was a truly remarkable dog.

Hawk wasn't able to identify anyone else, though Meg made a mental note to scan the area again after the victim was removed and the crowd of USAR workers, who were possibly confounding any scent, was gone. They returned to the rest of their grid search, Meg keeping an eye on the recovery progress, watching as they uncovered a middle-aged woman to the waist, her twisted body packed into the crushed concrete. One quick look assured her that the woman hadn't suffered, that she'd died mercifully quickly as the building had fallen. That one look was enough, and she turned away from the body, bag, and basket, which would carry the victim away from her home one last time, and the dogged men and women who would complete that journey with her.

It wasn't the win she'd hoped for, even though she knew in her gut it was the kind of find they were overwhelmingly more likely to discover. At least it would bring closure to a family who was currently in agony, waiting for news about their loved one.

On her way in this morning, she'd seen the impromptu memorial that had sprung up at the Methodist church at the corner of Massachusetts Avenue NW and 9th Street NW, which was as close as anyone not involved in the rescue was allowed unless they lived nearby. Pictures of the missing, taped to the fence running around the eastern end of the church; hundreds of bouquets of flowers; handwritten cards with prayers and condolences; stuffed teddy bears and bunnies; and a continuous line of candles in glass holders, some with religious symbols, some with signs of peace and love.

It had broken her heart. Just as this discovery did. So much loss, and so much more still to go.

The radio at her hip crackled to life. "Brian to Meg."

"Meg here."

"Lacey's alerting. Can you come? C2 quadrant, near the bottom of the pile."

"Affirmative." She put her radio away. "Come on, Hawk. Maybe we'll get lucky this time."

It took five or six minutes to wind their way over to Brian, and when she arrived, he took one look at her, his eyes narrowing in suspicion. "You okay?"

"Yeah, it's just . . ." She shrugged. "When they moved that giant slab, Hawk found a victim. No confirmation needed, so I didn't call. Someone who died immediately, from the looks of things." She scanned the rubble. "Let's hope we do better this time. Start here?"

Brian called Lacey off to the side and up on a horizontal column, had her sit beside him. "That works."

It took Hawk a few minutes, but then he kept circling an angled section of slab before finally sitting near a filthy tuft of insulation.

Meg glanced at Brian, found him nodding. "Right here?"

"Yes." Brian pulled out his radio. "Craig, it's Brian. Lacey has alerted in my quadrant, and Hawk has confirmed. We need USAR." He outlined their exact position.

"Affirmative," Craig said. "I'll send a team to you now."

Meg pushed a broken piece of cabinetry out of the way and knelt down near the spot where both dogs had alerted. She grabbed a chunk of concrete and rapped it hard against the crushed body of either a washer or a dryer. "Hello! If you can hear me, call out." She waited for a moment, straining to hear any noise, and then tried again. "Hello? We're from search and rescue, and we're here to help you."

She turned toward Brian, but froze when she saw the dogs. They sat side by side, eyes laser focused on the debris where she knelt. Then Lacey let out a loud bark. Then another. Then Hawk barked.

Brian and Meg just stared at each other; then she rapped the chunk of concrete a few more times and pulled off her hard hat to press her ear to the metal of the appliance. She closed her eyes, concentrating. Then she thought she heard something.

Without moving, she looked sideways at the dogs. "Hawk, Lacey, speak!"

Both dogs barked and then fell silent as Meg concentrated. Then she heard it. A tiny, faint woof.

She sat bolt upright. "Brian, I can hear it!"

"What?"

"A dog. A dog is answering Hawk and Lacey. Switch places with me."

Brian and Meg swapped spots, and then Brian told the dogs to speak. His eyes sparkled as he, too, heard the faint response. "That's my Lacey-girl!" he praised. "You found a dog trapped in the rubble!" His gaze shot past the dogs to the team of six climbing the pile to them.

Twenty minutes later, after carefully moving concrete, wood, and steel and chipping through another slab, the USAR team pulled a filthy and trembling beagle from the debris pile. Both search dogs crowded around it, joyfully sniffing. The young dog was unhurt, though he was no doubt hungry and definitely dehydrated and edging toward hypothermic.

Meg and Brian offered to take charge of the dog. Brian picked him up and, with Meg's assistance, carried him down the pile. They made it down to ground level without any mishaps.

"I'll take him to triage and see what they want to do with him," said Brian, digging in his pack for Lacey's leash for the beagle.

"You do that. I'll go back to that area and make sure there isn't anyone else Hawk can scent," Meg offered. "It's unlikely, because the only reason he survived is he's small. A human wouldn't have survived in that space, but it's worth checking. Come on back when you're done."

"Will do."

Meg watched Brian, Lacey, and the beagle walk down the sidewalk toward triage and felt just a little bit lighter.

It was a small win, but in a search site with this level of devastation, every win, no matter how small, counted.

CHAPTER 12

Structural Analysis: The calculation of a structure's response to the stress of different external loads.

Tuesday, December 18, 1:32 PM
The Washington Post
Washington, DC

McCord sat in his cubicle, head down over his keyboard. He opened what was probably the eightieth tab in his browser and hoped the computer gods were on his side today and wouldn't crash his session just for kicks. A story was starting to form in his head, and he had the browser tabs to prove it.

Buildings in the developed world didn't simply fall down. So what had happened at Talbot Terraces?

Craig had told him the day before that he'd been lucky to make it into the site under the cover of chaos and Meg's identification, but that door would be closed for him today. And Craig was correct. He'd tried to get into the site, but every person was being vetted, and reporters were allowed no farther than the media tent, from which the collapse site couldn't even be seen. Not that rigid restrictions had stopped them—there had been a run on bookings at the Conrad for any room overlooking I Street NW, and news outlets had been using their expensive perches to track the rescue operations and supplement stories with aerial photos. If they hadn't been able to get a room, they'd paid surrounding businesses well for access to their upper floors or their roof.

There was no way to keep a site like Talbot Terraces entirely under wraps in the middle of the DC downtown core. There was always another building, a higher floor, a more direct line of sight from above.

His time on-site the day before had left McCord more shaken than he would have predicted. Then the release this morning of the security video capturing the collapse as it happened had only deepened his unease. Even before the firsthand accounts of the sound of what was potentially an explosion, McCord had been suspicious about the cause of the collapse, and his research had solidified his beliefs. Sure, structural collapses happened, but not to this extent, and with little or no warning, in a building of this age in that condition.

He'd spent considerable time looking for a similar incident anywhere in the world. There were hundreds of collapses with which to make comparisons, but somehow, none of them really fit.

The construction of a building could make it unstable, and sometimes a building or part of the building collapsed shortly after the completion of construction if the design had an inherent flaw. Or if there was a catastrophic construction error, such as occurred in 1981 with a building in Cocoa Beach, Florida, when the concrete forms were pulled from an upper floor after only a few days instead of the usual week or more. The final concrete pour had been in progress when the uncured concrete below buckled, unable to support the extra weight of the new concrete, and the building had collapsed. Eleven had died that day.

Earthquakes and landslides could topple or shatter a

building, as could extreme environmental pressures, like the heavy snowfall that had collapsed the roof of the Knickerbocker Theatre here in DC in 1922, killing ninety-eight people.

Old buildings, especially those not maintained or reno-vated, could deteriorate to the point of collapse, as hap-pened in Columbus, Ohio, when a three-story building more than one hundred years old started shedding exterior bricks not long before over half of the building collapsed. Existing buildings undergoing significant reconstruction could also be put under sufficient stress that a catastrophic collapse occurred.

None of these scenarios applied to Talbot Terraces.

Which had brought McCord around to collapses stem-ming from a terrorist attack. The Alfred P. Murrah Federal Building in Oklahoma City in 1995. The World Trade Center in 2001. Both incidents had been planned by men with an agenda, who had carried out their terrible plans, and hundreds or thousands had died.

The similarities weren't lost on him. Journalists had to look at every option, because there was no way law en-forcement was going to give any of them the inside scoop. Not even him, even if he pulled in every favor possible. And he'd tried, but from first responders on the scene to individuals at several levels of law enforcement and gov-ernment, if anyone knew anything, no one was talking. He might be able to sweet-talk information out of Meg, with their usual agreement in place that he stayed quiet until the FBI released him to go to print, but this time he doubted she'd have any kind of inside scoop. The powers that be were compartmentalizing information because the situation was too enormous, and that left Meg on the out-side.

Part of him knew it was simply too early. The entire focus right now, as it should be, was on finding survivors, if there were any left to find a full day after the collapse. The cause of the disaster would be fully investigated only after all the victims had been recovered and all evidence had been collected, right down to the bottom of the pile of rubble. The 2002 National Construction Safety Team Act put the investigation fully in the hands of NIST—the National Institute of Standards and Technology—due to the catastrophic loss of life, and he doubted they were even on-site yet. However, they would be shortly.

He turned to the list of residents released by law enforcement in an effort to identify the missing. The owners of the building had done what they could, putting together a list of owners of the units, but everyone knew the list included only a limited number of actual residents and certainly didn't include children, visitors, subletters, and anyone temporarily in the building, such as a delivery person. Family and friends had added to the list, as had residents who had left the building that morning and those who had escaped or who had been rescued.

He scanned the list on his monitor.

Immediately, several names leaped out at him. It shouldn't be a surprise, after all, that a luxury building in downtown DC, a stone's throw—albeit a long one—from the White House, would include the residences of some of the most important people in the country. Starting with the president's chief of staff, Karina Reilly. Anyone who wanted to send the president a message could conceivably do so through the death of his chief of staff.

Then there was Ansel Baumgarten, the CEO of Cohn Pharmaceuticals, a company with a reputation for keeping drug prices high and out of the generic market by a combination of secondary patents and frivolous petitions to the FDA and by restricting access to drug samples, thereby blocking generic manufacturers' ability to prove bioequivalence. As a result, lifesaving drugs had been kept out of the hands of hundreds of thousands who couldn't afford them, all while the company maintained sky-high profit margins, an aspect reflected in Baumgarten's yearly stock and cash bonuses.

Peter Garrison listed his primary residence in Talbot Terraces, but the high-profile criminal lawyer had a number of houses scattered across the country. Best known for his successful defense of a Hollywood actor accused of drugging his wife and then rolling her body into the swimming pool, where she drowned, Garrison had a rep for taking on big-money cases that brought him significant media attention—positive or negative, he didn't seem to care. It was all good to Garrison.

The last name that McCord instantly recognized was Dario Pasi, one of the top members of the United Steelworkers, for which he'd served as the international vice president for the past four years. A hard-ass through and through, Pasi was well known for his reach into federal politics, and that included the Senate and House leaders he had in his pocket. Given the current state of polarized politics, it was exactly the kind of thing that could make someone a target.

Any of these individuals could be targets, McCord thought as he scanned the list of names again, knowing there could be others he wasn't familiar with. But he kept coming back again and again to the overkill of bombing an entire building to kill one person. The risk of missing them altogether, unless you could guarantee they'd be there—and how could you do that?—the unbelievable carnage, the loss of property and, most importantly, the loss of other lives. That would require layers of callousness, blind hatred, or insanity. Or possibly all three together.

The more he turned it over in his head, the more it simply didn't make any sense. Why take the risk of attempting to bring down a building when something more direct would be infinitely more efficient? Sure, it would be a way to hide a hit, but at the huge risk of missing the target altogether. Not to mention, the kind of explosives needed for a job like this weren't available on your average street corner. Fortunately, he had contacts that could be his entry to the black market, where surely those explosives would be available and could have come from. Anything could be purchased if you knew the right people and if price was no object.

No matter where the explosives had originated, just having them wasn't enough to bring down a building. A knowledge of engineering and construction would be required. However, the whole structure had *not* fallen. If it was a domestic terrorism attack, and the goal had been to bring down the entire building, whoever was responsible had failed. Maybe whoever had made the attempt didn't have the knowledge required to complete the job competently.

If so, their incompetence had saved numerous lives. Thank God for small favors. But for that failure, the tragedy would have been much worse.

He opened a fresh document and yet another browser tab. He had a lot of work in front of him if he was going to sketch out the background of as many of the residents as possible and then look into what would be required to bring down a building of this size.

He put his hands on his keyboard and got down to work.

CHAPTER 13

Shoring: The temporary installation of posts or props to support a structure during renovation or repair or if it is in danger of collapse.

Tuesday, December 18, 5:24 PM
Talbot Terraces
Washington, DC

Webb bent over to peer down the tunnel. The light of his LED lamp cut through the inky blackness, illuminating the ragged hole at the far end. "I'm going in." Leading with the rolled sled held in both hands, he slid on his belly into the tunnel, pushing off with his boots, until his entire frame was inside.

It was narrow in the tunnel, and he was grateful he wasn't even remotely claustrophobic. As probies, firefighters got used to the claustrophobia that could come from wearing an SCBA mask, or they left the field. He was long used to wearing an SCBA mask and to enduring the isolating feeling of being in a smoky or flame-filled scene. The tunnel vision caused by the mask and helmet made you feel like you were all alone, even when you knew you had a crew of men and women behind you.

But this was very different. The tunnel was so narrow,

he could just barely get his shoulders between the shoring supports, and the razor-sharp freshly cut ends of rebar caught at any material near them. He would have been tempted to do a full commando crawl, but he couldn't take the risk of using his knees and feet to propel himself forward and kicking out one of the shoring posts, which might bring the whole tunnel down. All he could do was drag himself forward slowly using his elbows and forearms, pushing off with his toes as much as possible when he could find a toehold in the uneven floor.

It was quiet in the tunnel, quiet enough for him to hear his heart pounding in his ears from a combination of exertion and trepidation, so he filled the silence with his own voice to cheer himself on. "Hey, buddy. My name is Todd, and I'm coming in. Nearly there and then I'm going to help you get out of here." Taking his eyes off the tunnel floor in front of him, he looked up, letting the light wash toward the void space, where only darkness beckoned. "Can you hear me?" He held still for a second, but no longer when he didn't hear anything, and continued dragging himself forward. Another three feet, then six feet, then ten.

He looked up too swiftly and rapped his hard hat sharply against a chunk of concrete that wasn't cut back far enough. He swallowed the curse that rose to his lips and tried again. "Nearly there." He kept his voice cheerful, using the same tone Meg used with Hawk when she was trying to keep his spirits up as everything went to hell around them. "Hang on a little longer. If you're having trouble speaking, knock on something." He was drawing in breath to continue when two short taps reached his ears. "That's it. Hang tight. I'm coming."

Only about ten feet to go now. Ahead, a hole had been cut in an angled slab of concrete. The hole was about two feet across, but hopefully, that would be enough. If not, he was going to have words with the USAR crew member with the chipping hammer.

A sound cracked over his head, like a bullet blasting through concrete at lightning speed, and he automatically put his head down and pulled his hands, still clutching the McGuire sled, up to his hard hat as he squeezed his eyes shut. Breath sawing, heart jackhammering, he waited for the crushing blow.

But it never came, and after five seconds ticked by, he opened his eyes again. His gaze swung up to the ceiling. He didn't know what that sound was, but it was a kick in the pants to get moving before the dogs had two more victims to find.

He continued forward, his fear now slanting toward an edge of fury, driving him onward, powering his muscles to move more forcefully. Fury for the dead, fury for the anguish of the families. Fury that someone, somewhere, was responsible for this tragedy, for putting the lives of good men and women at risk. He held the fury close, letting it burn away the last of the fear, and used it to do the job that needed doing, to save one of the rare lives that might survive this disaster.

He got to the edge of the hole and was finally able to angle his head to illuminate the gap, giving him his first glimpse of the man trapped inside.

The void space was perhaps only four feet long, and the twentysomething man lay on his side in the fetal position on a ragged swath of carpeting on what had possibly once been his bedroom floor. He wore dress pants and a sky-blue button-down shirt, but no tie or shoes. *Looks like a staffer in the process of dressing for work at some politician's office.* His shirt was splattered and soaked in spots with blood, which had also run in rivulets down his face, from the right side to the left, as he lay trapped on his left side, his head tucked into the tight angle where a solid concrete slab was jammed against the shear wall. His right hand lay limp beside him, surrounded by crumbled dry-wall, and under his lax fingers lay the chunk of concrete he'd used to communicate desperately with the outside world.

Clock's ticking. Move it.

Webb fixed the light from his helmet on the man's face and was rewarded with a pained flinching of his eyelids, as the LED torch would have seemed blinding after a day and a half in absolute darkness. He lifted his head to direct the light toward the back of the void space. "Hey, buddy. I'm Todd. What's your name?"

"Kevin." The slightly slurred word was husky, pushed through parched, chilled lips.

"Okay, Kevin, I'm going to get you out of here. But I don't want to hurt you, and I can't examine you in there, so I need you to answer some questions for me." As he talked, Webb pulled off his heavy gloves and wound his right arm into the hole to find Kevin's exposed right wrist. His skin was much too cold to the touch, but based on the fact that he seemed relatively lucid—no way to tap SOS otherwise—Webb estimated his core temperature to be still above 80 degrees Fahrenheit. Definitely dangerous, but in no way past the point of no return. With a normal body temperature of 98.6 degrees Fahrenheit, a person was considered mildly hypothermic starting at 95 degrees Fahrenheit. The situation was getting serious by the time body temperature was in the eighties, and dire by the low eighties or upper seventies. Lower than that, especially for any amount of time, lay death.

Kevin wasn't there yet. But Webb could see he was badly affected simply from his temperature, and that was before taking any injuries into account. "Are you hurt anywhere? Do you suspect any bones are broken, or do you have any chest or gut pain? Back or neck pain?" As he talked, Webb took Kevin's pulse. Weak and rapid, as he expected, with his pulse sitting at 114 beats per minute.

"Arm is bad." Kevin took several shallow breaths and seemed to need to gather himself to continue. "Head took a knock."

"Did you lose consciousness?"

"I think so. But time and space got confused down here. In the dark. All alone."

Webb didn't want him to concentrate on that; he needed Kevin to focus on his freedom, which would help him push through the pain, fuzziness, and disorientation. "I bet that was hard. But we're going to get you out now."

"How many others got out?"

Definitely not going there. "I don't have a current count, but rescues are ongoing. Any other injuries?" Webb asked, trying to steer him back to his current situation.

"I think some ribs may be broken." Kevin stopped, tried to swallow, but had no spit to move in his mouth. "Hurts to breathe." He raised his head and pushed off the ground with his right hand, then let out a hoarse groan of pain and dropped down again.

Two things were clear to Webb—the man was in distress, but given the situation, Webb was going to need Kevin's help to drag him out of the void and into the tunnel. Even if Webb could get himself through the hole and into the void—which would be a challenge with all his protective gear—there wasn't room inside for two people. He couldn't pull Kevin out by both arms if one was broken, and he'd only dislocate Kevin's right shoulder if he pulled him by only one arm.

Kevin was going to have to take an active part in his own rescue. And that meant drugs to numb the pain.

It was risky giving him opioids when his respiration was depressed, but there was no help for it. They had to get out of there and preferably inside the next two minutes. If worst came to worst, he could counteract with naloxone, which was stocked in the med pack.

"Kevin, how much do you weigh?"

"One-eighty."

Webb reached into the pocket on the left leg of his bunkers, rooted around for a few seconds, and pulled out a prefilled syringe with attached needle. A quick calculation based on Kevin's body weight told him the full syringe would put him in the middle of the acceptable dosage range, which was perfect—enough for pain relief without further depressing his breathing or making him insensible when Webb needed him conscious and working in concert with him.

"Kevin, we need to do a few things to get you mobile enough to help me."

Kevin blinked at him owlishly, squinting and trying to focus. " 'Kay."

Webb shimmied closer, extended his arms into the hole and worked his head and shoulders through, then pulled the cap off the needle. "This is morphine. I'm going to inject it into your shoulder, because that's what I can reach. I'm going to do it through your shirt because there's no room or mobility to take it off. Hold still."

It was a stretch, but reaching forward with both arms, Webb grasped the top of Kevin's right arm, gripped the muscle firmly, and managed to get the needle in at the correct angle and the full dose delivered. Not having a sharps container handy, and not wanting to leave the exposed needle lying around when he still had the extraction to accomplish, he recapped the needle and jammed it back into his pocket.

Work fast, or we're in trouble.

"You should feel some pain relief immediately, which will increase over the next twenty to thirty minutes. But we can't wait that long. I need to stabilize your arm to be able to move you. I'm going to need your help to get you out of here. Do you understand?"

"Yes."

"Good man." Webb reached into another pocket and pulled out a flattened roll of bright orange, foam-covered aluminum. "I'm going to wrap your arm in this temporary splint." He angled his head to study Kevin's left arm and instantly identified the problem by the awkward angle of the forearm. "It looks like you've broken your radius and ulna, the two bones in your forearm. I need you to hold still. I'm going to be as careful as I can, but this is going to hurt like a bitch because we haven't given the morphine long enough. But we can't afford to wait." He kept up a steady stream of encouragement as he unrolled the foam-covered aluminum, eyeballed the forearm, folded back some of the length, then made a concave trough. He was about to get the splint into place under the arm when his radio squawked.

"Melnyk to Webb. Update."

Webb had to back partly out of the hole to access his left breast pocket and the radio inside. He pulled it out and hit the TALK button. "Webb to Melnyk. We're preparing for transport. Splinting a broken arm, then coming out. Will require the sled. Have paramedics standing by."

"Message received."

Webb slid the radio away, knowing Melnyk understood the actual message behind his sled reference—the victim wasn't capable of getting out himself, and Webb was going to have to drag him.

He bellied up to the hole again. "Let's get that arm set, and then we're going to move you. I'm going to do this as carefully as possible, but I'm not as close as I'd like, and any movement is going to be painful. Is the morphine kicking in?"

"A little."

"Good." Webb brushed chunks of drywall out of his way, then lay the concave splint alongside Kevin's forearm. "Take a breath and hold it." He stretched out as far as he could go, cursing his awkward position as he tried to be as gentle as possible. He slid one hand under Kevin's wrist and the other under his elbow, doing his best not to adjust the position of the bones. The breaks could lay as they were for now; the bones could be set by someone who had X-rays in front of them to guide their hands.

Even that slight motion had Kevin's breath hissing between his teeth.

This is going to be a success if he simply doesn't pass out. "I'm going to count to three. One . . . two . . ." He moved a beat early, knowing that if he hit three, conscious of it or not, Kevin would tense up and fight him even more. In one quick movement, he lifted Kevin's forearm off the ground and deposited it gently into the splint. But even with only minimal movement and under the effects of morphine, the young man still cried out in pain, then lay motionless, panting.

Getting him out of here and down the tunnel was going to be a challenge. Especially when the clock that had been ticking in Webb's head since he entered the tunnel was starting to scream.

"Kevin, you still with me?" Webb carefully closed the splint over his forearm, securing the arm inside. "We need to move, buddy, and I need you to help. Once you're out of this space, I'll do the rest, but I need you to do that to live. You want to live, right, Kevin?" At this point, Webb needed to put whatever pressure he could on this man, who was broken, concussed, hypothermic, dehydrated, and understandably not thinking clearly. Time to condense the situation to the life-and-death crisis it was in order to kick some adrenaline into action. That was all Webb would need, but it was absolutely required.

Kevin's eyelids fluttered and then stayed open. "Yes." The word was surprisingly clear.

Life would always try to find a way.

"I need you to turn yourself around a little and come through the hole headfirst. It's not very big, but they didn't feel they could make it bigger without risking the stability of this slab. I need you to bring yourself up to the hole, and then I can help from there. Once you're through, I'll do all the work."

Webb desperately wished he could have given Kevin a bolus of IV fluids, which would have considerably perked up his mental acuity. He had the needle, IV lines, and the bag of saline in his pockets, but now that he was here, there was no way to do it. And even if he could, there was no way to keep the needle from ripping out while he moved Kevin out of the void space, and then he'd have another problem on his hands, with a victim suddenly at risk of bleeding out.

"Kevin, can you do that for me?"

Kevin's only response was a grunt in the affirmative, but Webb would take it.

"You do that. Move slowly. Hold your arm close to your body to avoid jarring it. While you're getting yourself turned around, I'm going to lay out a piece of super-tough fabric, which I'm going to have you lie on. Then I'm going to pull you through the tunnel on it. Okay?"

"Yeah."

A creak and the sound of popping metal came from above. Webb's gaze jerked upward to stare at the concrete overhead. As his gaze dropped, he caught the terror in Kevin's eyes. "Move as fast as you can," he advised, but Kevin was already in motion, as if he'd been reminded of where they were and what their possible end could be.

Webb pulled back into the tunnel and unrolled the sled. Backing up, he laid it out. The extra material ran up the tunnel shore posts, and the long strip of strapping that ran down the middle third of the sled, with loops at each end, faced up.

He crawled over the sled as Kevin, with an agonized groan, managed to get his head and shoulders to the hole. The young man was breathing hard, holding his splinted left arm across his chest. But he was moving, despite the effort it required, for he knew his very life depended on it.

"Doing great." Webb gave him a rapid critical once-over. "How are your back and neck feeling?"

"Sore. I kind of feel like a building fell on me. But I can move."

Knowing that keeping your sense of humor at a time like this showed some serious backbone, Webb's estimation of Kevin rose considerably. "Great. Now through the hole we come, as fast and as smoothly as you can. I'll help from this side."

It took a full three or four minutes—and an incredible amount of pain—to get Kevin into the tunnel and onto the sled. As he lay down on the rocky surface, Kevin groaned, and then his body went limp as his broken arm fell to his side. His head lolled, and his eyes slid shut.

"You did it, buddy. Good job." Moving quickly, using the side handles on the sled and the two carabiners clipped on them, Webb attached the side of the sled to the central loop between Kevin's legs, securely packaging him. "It's going to be bumpy getting you down the tunnel, so I'm going to make sure your neck isn't injured." He pulled the long, narrow cervical collar from his pocket, slipped it under Kevin's neck, and secured it under his chin, locking his neck in place.

Webb pulled on his heavy gloves. Then, after grabbing the two handles on the front corners of the sled, he brought them together to hold in his right fist, raising Kevin's head and shoulders off the ground. After placing his left hand on the ground below him, he started to crawl backward on his knees and free hand. There was barely enough room for him to turn his head to look behind himself, but he managed a partial turn. Thirty feet away, lights and a number of faces peering into the tunnel greeted him.

"Coming out!" he yelled.

It was slow and difficult progress. Kevin's deadweight told Webb he'd lost consciousness, which was probably for the best, as the uneven ground felt sharp even through the reinforced knees of Webb's bunkers and glove. If he'd been conscious, Kevin probably would have passed out from the pain in his arm as he bumped over the rough surface. Webb had never done it before, but today speed trumped care. They needed to have been out ten minutes ago.

It was challenging for Webb as well, trying to crawl backward, mostly feeling his way, balancing on his knees and one hand, as he kept as much of Kevin off the ground as possible. His right arm was starting to shake, and he was thankful for every bicep curl, pull-up, lateral raise, and reverse fly he'd ever done. Strength training was a fire-fighting necessity—you had to have the strength to save not only your own life in a fire but also that of the man or woman standing next to you, even if it meant carrying them out of the fire. Or, in this case, a building collapse.

He turned to look behind him again, was pleased with their progress—only about ten more feet to go and they were free of the pile.

As he turned to look forward again, his lamp caught a dull flash of something metallic. Hesitating for just a second, Webb studied the object. and quickly realized he was looking at a jagged piece of a cell phone and its exposed circuit board nestled into a crevice near the floor of the tunnel. He turned back to the task at hand and continued another foot. And then he froze, as something that had been niggling at the back of his mind crystalized.

The fragment of cell phone. Unlike all the other debris he'd seen over the past two days, this wasn't pulverized or crushed, its edges flattened, twisted, and covered in concrete dust. It had clean lines, sharp edges, and the circuit board partially charred. As if the cell phone from which it came had shattered, blown apart by an explosion.

The morning's newscast rushed back to him.

Witness reports coming from individuals on the street at a distance at the time of the incident describe the sound of an explosion coming from the building immediately preceding the collapse. One witness characterized it as a boom coming from the parking garage below street level.

Did he just find evidence of a bomb?

"Hang on, Kevin." His right biceps sang with relief as he carefully lay Kevin down. He then braced his left hand by Kevin's hip, leaned forward, and peered into the crevice. The fragment of technology was jammed between a section of column and a tangled weave of rebar. Reaching in, Webb managed to get two gloved fingers around the curve of the protruding plastic casing, and with a couple of careful wiggles, he pulled it free. He held it up so it was fully illuminated by his LED lamp—it was definitely part of a circuit board, with some of the external plastic casing still attached. But it was notably scorched, and nothing else around where it had lain showed any signs of having been caught in the fires.

Keep it moving. Deal with this later.

He lay the piece down on Kevin's belly and was about to continue down the tunnel when it occurred to him that someone might need to see where he'd found the fragment. He dug in his pocket for the capped syringe and set it carefully beside the crevice to mark the spot. Then he picked up the sled again and inched his way to the tunnel entrance.

"You're just about there," Melnyk's voice instructed

from behind him. "A little farther . . . farther . . . That's it. The next time you move back, you'll be able to get a boot down. Then we'll get the backboard under him."

Another foot and Webb had both boots on the ground and was straightening with relief after so much time hunched in the tunnel. Hands came from all around, taking over for him, and as the sled was pulled into the garage, several men slipped the backboard underneath it to support Kevin's weight.

"Well done." Melnyk grinned and slapped Webb on the back as the garage resounded with cheers and hoots of success. "You got him."

"*We* got him." Webb returned his grin, relief at being free from the deadly weight of the pile twining in his chest with the elation of an unexpected live rescue. "Everyone played a part."

"But you got him *out*." Melnyk gazed locked on Kevin's abdomen. "What's that?"

"That's a good question." Webb carefully picked up the fragment and laid it in his gloved palm, then held it out.

The garage abruptly went quiet as first responders leaned in to study the piece.

"I found it close to the tunnel entrance, wedged in the debris near the ground. It caught my eye because in all that debris, it looked different. Not crushed, not flattened by pancaking concrete, but . . ."

"Exploded," Holt interjected, leaning in. "Charred. There have been reports suggesting there may have been an explosion before the building fell."

"Yeah, that crossed my mind. There are some clean plastic bags in the med pack. Can someone grab one?"

After sealing the piece of technology away, Webb followed four other firefighters as they carried the backboard with Kevin, still unconscious, to the gurney waiting in the driveway and transferred him using the McGuire sled.

Two paramedics, a male and a female, strapped him into place.

Webb gave them the rundown as the other firefighters returned to the garage. "Patient was lucid until he lost consciousness due to the pain of being moved. He's dehydrated and hypothermic. Reported head, arm, and rib injuries. He's tachycardic, respiration shallow and depressed. I didn't have the time to start a line, but I administered ten milligrams morphine sulphate IM to the deltoid before temporarily splinting the forearm. Looks like dual, closed radial and ulnar fractures."

"Temp is eighty-one degrees Fahrenheit," the male paramedic said.

"Pulse is 109," said the female. "We'll start warming in the ambulance. Heat's on, and we have blankets and warm saline and will start a line right away. Ready?"

"Ready. Let's move."

They each grabbed a side of the gurney and jogged it up the driveway to where an ambulance stood with lights flashing. They loaded Kevin, and then the female paramedic closed the doors, leaving her partner inside with Kevin, before she ran to the driver's door, climbed in, and took off, siren wailing.

Webb walked up to street level and stood in the cold air and rapidly fading light of day, exhaustion washing over him, leaving him wrung out. It had been a day of heavy physical work, followed by an emotional call to Meg, and then the most stressful extraction he'd ever done in his life. But they'd collectively saved a life, and that success shone through the fatigue.

He looked down at the bag still clasped in his hand. Maybe he'd found an important piece of the puzzle. If explosives really were involved, making the disaster a case of either foreign or domestic terrorism, it was going to be an FBI investigation. Craig Beaumont was on-site, and it made sense to pass the fragment off to him and let him determine next steps.

But first, he'd call Meg and let her know he was still alive and they had one more survivor to add to the tally sheet. One more in their favor.

He turned to the pile, glowing bright with emergency lighting and covered with rescuers. They'd been at it now for about thirty-four hours since first arriving on scene.

He had to wonder if Kevin would be the last victim they'd recover alive.

CHAPTER 14

Compressive Stress: External loads that squeeze a structural element, causing it to occupy a smaller volume.

Tuesday, December 18, 8:51 pm
Jennings/Webb residence
Washington, DC

Meg jerked when the stove timer went off, her reflexive hand gesture knocking over her nearly full wineglass, flooding the countertop with pale Riesling. She swore with enough force to have Hawk's head popping up from where he lay with his stuffed elf in his dog bed, which heavily layered guilt over irritation.

"I'm sorry, buddy. I didn't mean to startle you. Go back to sleep." She reached for paper towels and started mopping up.

At least she hadn't broken the glass, but it was the last of the wine. As she set the glass in the sink, she wondered how Todd would feel about her opening his bottle of eighteen-year-old Glenfiddich scotch.

In the end, it had been a truly miserable day. It had started with that horrific video of the collapse, followed by the outpouring of anguish at the memorial and Hawk's discovery of the woman. Their spirits had lifted with the discovery of the dog, but their luck had been short-lived, as multiple finds of human remains had followed, and the morning had gone straight downhill. Then the afternoon had been truly soul-sucking.

First, Hawk had alerted to a find, which had been confirmed by Scott and Theo. But the USAR team had uncovered not one intact deceased victim but two—a woman who looked not much younger than Meg and a baby who was only a few months old. The baby, dressed in a fuzzy shell-pink sleeper, lay in her mother's protective hold, as if her mother had tried to wrap herself around her child to protect her during their last moments. The child must have already been in her mother's arms, and at most, she only had seconds to do what mothers through the centuries had done—give her all trying to protect her child.

She'd died trying to protect her daughter. And the baby . . . another life gone before she'd had a chance to live.

The baby had hit Meg harder than any victim so far. The waste of life was a constant ache while they searched, and thoughts of half-read bedtime stories, birthday party planning that would never come to fruition, and grandchildren who would never be met and cradled were never far away, as she couldn't help but recognize all the lives ended in mid-step. But the loss of this one tiny child had stabbed deeper still.

The rescue operation was hard on everyone involved. The constant death and the violence of the collapse, which had left mostly remains in its wake, battered every one of them. She'd seen rescuers sitting in the Park at CityCenter, weeping, and others arguing over nothing, as tempers frayed and emotions ran high off the pile. On the pile, everyone was all business; off the pile, as soon as the rigid walls of duty relaxed even slightly, emotion had a chance to take over. And often did.

She thought she'd had it under control. Fury had clawed at anguish inside her as she'd fought to bury both deep, and she thought she'd succeeded. She and Hawk had moved on after those two victims, continuing the search, though she'd noticed that Hawk didn't stray as far from her as he had earlier in the day, as if he sensed she was riding the edge emotionally.

Then Todd had called, and her fear for him had nearly pushed her over the edge. She'd spent the next half hour going through the motions at best, every vibration under her feet thrusting a lance of terror through her with the thought that the pile was collapsing. His second call had come as a huge relief, but not even the news of the survivor had buoyed her spirits by that time.

When eight o'clock came, she'd fled the site, not waiting to say good night to Brian; instead, she'd sent a text saying she had to run and she'd catch him the next day.

Brian would have taken one look at her and known she was in a bad place. She just needed some time to find her balance again, that was all. She'd be fine tomorrow.

For no apparent reason, traffic was a snarl all the way home, and she spent that extra time in the SUV, frustratingly still or only crawling forward, fighting tears.

What was wrong with her today? This was so unlike her. Hawk, sensing her disquiet, kept sticking his head through the small window in the mesh to nudge at her shoulder with his nose. Trying to comfort.

However, she came home to a note from Cara on her counter, beside a fresh baguette, and a homemade lasagna for two in her fridge, ready for baking. As Meg slid the lasagna into the oven, she made a mental note to buy her sister flowers at her first opportunity for a kindness when she really needed it.

Forty-five minutes later, she pulled the lasagna out, covered it with foil to keep it warm, and put it back in the oven after turning it off, leaving the door cracked open.

Todd would be home soon. All she wanted was to eat and go to bed. Start over tomorrow. Maybe she'd find her center tomorrow, because she sure as hell had lost it today.

The front door opened. Todd's call came from down the hallway. "I'm home!"

She stepped into the front hallway and pasted on a smile she didn't feel. "Good timing. Dinner's ready, thanks to Cara."

"Can you hold it ten minutes? I'm filthy and need a shower. I'll be fast," he called, running up the stairs.

Of course he wanted to shower. He'd been inside the pile today, literally. She'd grabbed one herself after the lasagna was in the oven. Why was she so irritated because he reasonably wanted to clean up? Because it was making her day still longer?

She wished for the rest of her lost glass of wine.

The longer he was gone, the more her irritation grew. There was no logical reason for it, but anger warmed her more than the cold anguish of loss, so she let it simmer.

True to his word, he came down the stairs ten minutes later in black jeans and a gray crewneck sweatshirt, his hair still wet from the shower.

She had dinner ready to serve, so they sat down to eat. Todd filled the space between every bite with a play-by-play of the rescue and news of the possible bomb fragment. Part of Meg understood; she'd been there before herself—riding the high of a successful live rescue, pumped up on your own success and the success of the team. Especially now, when there was so much death, she understood how good it felt to concentrate on life. And she still couldn't bring herself to answer in more than monosyllables.

It was only once Todd put his fork down on his empty

plate that her quiet seemed to register with him. He reached forward to lay his hand over hers where it lay in a fist beside her plate. "You okay?"

She pulled her hand away and dropped it in her lap. "Fine. Just tired. Long day."

His eyes narrowed as he studied her. "It's more than that. You're mad. You're not even looking at me."

"Why would I be mad?" It was a stupid question, and she knew it, but she was buying time. She just wanted him to leave her alone, but he never did at a time like this. When he thought something was wrong, he'd keep poking and poking until he broke through.

"You'd need to tell me that."

"Nothing to tell." She picked up her plate and took it to the sink to rinse. *Maybe it's better to keep him talking about himself.* "Chief Koenig must be happy with how things went today."

"He is." He joined her at the counter, and she sidestepped so he could reach the sink. But he put his plate down and grasped her arm when she would have moved away. "What's going on?"

"Nothing. I'm just cleaning up after dinner."

"What did Luke call that? The 'all-purpose female answer'? Look at me." When she kept looking at the table, he caught her other arm and turned her to face him. "Look at me, please."

She set her jaw and raised her eyes to his.

"You *are* mad at me. Because of the tunnel rescue?"

She pulled out of his hold and backed away a few steps, putting some space between them. "You didn't have to be the one to do it."

From the way his face softened, it was clear he heard the fear she tried so hard to hide behind sharp words. "I'm sorry. I know it had to cut a little too close to home for you—"

"Too close to home? We were less than a mile from the site of that hoarder house fire. I felt like I was standing outside it all over again, watching it burn, knowing you were slowly dying inside, but this time I didn't have Chuck for support." Temper overflowed; now that she was talking, she didn't seem to know how to stop. "And that was after spending yesterday suspecting—correctly, mind you—that you were inside that building. It could have come down any second with you in it, and then I'd have been searching for your corpse in the rubble."

"It's my job. It's what I train for." His own temper was starting to fire as his volume built. "They needed someone who could do the extraction but could also assess the victim's medical status. The USAR guys couldn't do it, neither could any of the regular paramedics. They needed someone dual trained. Sometimes we have to do the job that needs doing. You would do the same. You *have* done the same. What about the Bowie Meat Packing Plant? You walked over a glass-littered I-beam with no one within thirty miles of you. Did I give you a hard time about it? No, because you did the job that needed doing. You did it as safely as you could with McCord in your ear, the same way I did with twenty rescuers behind me."

"Who wouldn't have had time to get to you if the pile had collapsed. Did you think of that?"

"And if you'd fallen off the I-beam—which you nearly did—you would have been dead the moment you hit the floor or the machinery below. Did you think of *that*?" He turned away from her, as if he couldn't stand to look at her anymore, and stood with his hands braced on the countertop, head bowed. Long seconds passed, and his white-knuckled hold gradually relaxed. When he finally spoke, his voice was quieter. "I'm sorry I scared you. That was never my intent."

As she stood beside the kitchen table, Meg's righteous fury drained away, no longer bolstered by his anger, leaving nothing behind but the anguish of the day. So many hours, so much effort, desperate to find life, but since the early hours of the rescue, no one had come out alive from the top of the pile. But so much violent death, victim after victim, most not even intact.

It was the stuff of nightmares.

She closed her eyes, trying to push back the wave of sorrow rising in her throat, but then all she could see were the pale, lifeless faces of the mother and child. She opened her eyes to her kitchen, blurry behind encroaching tears, and tried to frantically blink them away.

"I made a safety judgment call based on the prep work I'd seen. I honestly thought I could do it, and the clock was ticking," Todd continued, his back still to her. "Standing in that garage, staring at the ceiling, that roof collapse was top of my mind as well, but I had to push past it, or I wouldn't have been able to be part of the team. And when we realized we had a live victim so many hours after the collapse, well, we went into overdrive."

Meg grabbed the back of a chair, gripping tight enough that her nails likely left crescents dug into the wood, as she fought to control her breathing and swallow back tears. She couldn't do this; she couldn't break. How could she do her job, how could she continue the search, if she couldn't stand firm?

A single tear slipped past her defenses to slide down her cheek.

"We needed to get the guy out. I think he might be the last one we rescue alive. I think we all knew that. And we all wanted a piece of that life." He turned around, drawing breath to continue, but froze, his eyes locked on her face.

She pulled in a breath and held it, afraid if she let it out, all the pain would escape with it. And she'd shatter.

"Oh, Meg."

He started toward her, and she automatically took a step away, raising both hands to stave him off, but he ignored her, stepping into her, trapping her hands between them as he wrapped his arms around her and pulled her in.

The dam broke under nothing more than the gentle weight of his care, and as she clutched his shirt, the tears came. For relatives waiting for their loved ones, for entire families lost, for newlyweds just starting out, for seniors finally enjoying the freedom of their retirement. For promise and hopes and dreams . . . all snuffed out under millions of pounds of rubble.

For one tiny baby, so still and cold.

She barely felt it when he simply picked her up and carried her to the couch, but then she was in his lap, with the smooth glide of Hawk's silky fur against her as he pressed close. And between Todd's gentle comfort and Hawk's steadfast presence, she started to calm.

Finally, still slumped in Todd's lap, her head on his shoulder and one hand in Hawk's fur, she was able to catch her breath. She told him about the horrors of two days of searching the pile, and what she and Hawk had seen.

She talked out the pain and the horror. And when she had, she felt lighter.

She scrubbed a hand over her face. "I'm sorry."

"For what? For being human? For needing to release all that? You were trying to swallow it all, weren't you?"

"We need to be strong to show up at that site."

"We do. But sometimes, when all that death and pain

gets to you, you have to let it out to be able to face showing up to do the job again the next day."

"I haven't seen you do it."

"I haven't seen what you've seen. And guys tend to try
to macho their way through it, but it always comes out. I
like to use the punching bag at the firehouse gym to get
out my angst after a bad call. You know, the kind where
you lose a whole family even though you moved heaven
and earth to save them. You can bottle up that sadness,
and the guilt and second-guessing as well. Maybe if you'd
been two minutes sooner, that kind of thing. Or you can
go and hit something until your knuckles bleed."

She picked up his hand and ran her thumb over his un-
blemished knuckles. "I've noticed that a few times and
wondered at your overenthusiasm."

"You have to get it out somehow, or you'll snap. Now
you'll be ready to start fresh again tomorrow. I might feel
the same way today, except that rescue boosted the spirits of everyone involved. But I think it's going to have to
last us." He pulled back far enough to look into her eyes.
"Next time, will you tell me when you've had a nightmare of a day? Especially when I've made it so much
worse for you."

"I will, I promise." She rubbed two fingers over her
pounding temple.

"Headache?"

"After all that? In spades."

"What do you say we finish up here, get you some
Advil, then head to bed? We need to be in top form tomorrow."

"That sounds good. But first . . ." After turning his face
toward her, she kissed him. "Thank you."

"There's no need to thank me. It's what we do for each

other. Next time I'm going to lose it, you can hold the punching bag for me. Deal?"

Her laugh was watery. "Deal."

Later, walking up the stairs with him, Meg noticed that while Todd had taken in everything she'd said, and had talked about the rescue, he still hadn't shared what he'd seen in those first frantic hours inside the standing structure.

Maybe he wasn't as steady as he wanted her to believe.

CHAPTER 15

Built-in Supports: Beams that are fixed at both ends to provide structural stability by their ability to withstand all translational and rotational stresses. Also called encastre supports.

Wednesday, December 19, 9:25 AM
Washington Marriott at Metro Center
Washington, DC

"You ready?" Meg asked.

Cara sent her a sideways glance. "As I'm going to be." She looked down at Saki, who stood calmly at her knee. "So is Saki, though this is going to be different for her. She's never had to deal with grief on this kind of scale before. And stress. You can feel it from outside the room."

"Which is totally understandable. I can't imagine what they're going through."

"Hell is what they're going through."

"Yeah. But Saki's going to be great. She's such a pro."

"She really is. Though she's going to need every bit of that experience today."

Meg and Cara stood with their dogs in the gathering space outside the Washington Marriott's Junior Ballroom.

Inside was row after row of chairs facing the front of the room, which featured a number of displays—a drawing of the building, with different sections of the collapsed wing highlighted in different colors representing when each section fell; a schematic of the basic floor plan, with each apartment numbered and the fallen sections shaded in red; and an overhead photo of the pile, with different areas gridded off and numbered in a pattern, which Meg recognized as those she and the other dog and USAR teams had been searching. A makeshift lectern had been built using a chair and a number of stacked boxes, and on it sat an open laptop. Twin speakers flanked the front of the room, and a microphone lay on top of one, its cable coiled on the carpet.

Hundreds of men, women, and children occupied every chair, while more stood near the walls. A baseline hum of conversation filled the room, occasionally broken by a voice rising with an angry edge.

This was the family reunification center. Immediately following the collapse, friends and family had tried to get into the site, willing to do whatever was needed to help find their loved ones, wanting to pitch in themselves when they at first thought no one was moving fast enough. Officials hadn't allowed them onto the site but had recognized they needed a place for families and friends to gather as they waited for news. They'd chosen the Washington Marriott, less than a half mile away from the site but outside the restricted area. A location near the disaster site would make it easy for first responders who were working the pile but who were also needed for briefings to travel between the sites without losing excessive time. Three days in, organizers had fallen into a regular schedule of two briefings a day, at 9:30 AM and 5:30 PM, to update friends and family.

All the briefings were held by Deputy Fire Chief Ray Weinberg of DCFEMS Special Operations. Since this was not a job he felt comfortable giving any of his men and women, most of whom were busy at the site, he'd taken on the difficult task of dealing personally with the families. Todd had heard through the grapevine how the briefings were going, and had expressed admiration that Weinberg had decided he was the man for the job. And Meg had to agree. It was an emotionally grinding position. Working the pile was bad enough, but to come face-to-face with the raw and searing grief of the families, to have to deal with the anger that overflowed from frustration that things weren't moving fast enough . . . it had to be emotionally exhausting. Yet Weinberg intended to be here day after day, seven days a week, to lead every briefing until the last victim was found. They knew it could be weeks until the recovery was complete and every family had closure. His was not a task to be envied, but it was one to be respected.

Weinberg knew Todd's fiancée was with FBI K-9 search and rescue and had asked Todd if Meg might be willing to come to one of the briefings, as there had been questions about the use of dogs in the rescue. Todd had sent him to Craig for official approval, which Craig had immediately granted, and Meg had agreed to answer any questions the families might have. She'd also suggested that Cara accompany her. Cara had been at the site with Saki since the day before, mingling with the first responders during their infrequent and quick breaks, but therapy dogs hadn't been brought to the reunification center yet.

Saki was a charmer, a mini blue pit bull with a cleft upper palate that exposed her lower teeth and gave her a slightly goofy expression that instantly made humans comfortable around her. Short of stature, with a wide chest and stubby legs, she liked nothing more than to cuddle with people, and her soft fur and friendly manner never failed to bolster those experiencing life's many difficulties. Meg knew Saki would be an asset to both the organizers and the families because of her calming presence. Weinberg was happy for the assistance, admitting that, with everything else going on, they hadn't had time until now to arrange to bring dogs into the reunification center. If it went well with Saki, Weinberg would talk to Cara's therapy dog group about rotating in more dogs.

At first glance, the two dogs, in their navy work vests with yellow type, might seem to belong to the same organization. But a closer look revealed Saki's Canine Good Citizen vest and patch, whereas Hawk's vest clearly marked him as an FBI K-9. Several people had done a quick double take at Meg, Cara, and the dogs as they entered the lobby, but in a hotel full of grieving families and first responders running in and out at all hours of the day or night, no one had questioned two working dogs and their nearly identical handlers looking for the second-floor ballroom.

The hotel was still open for guests who had been previously booked, but it was not accepting any new bookings that were not related to the family and friends now meeting on the second floor. To distinguish family and friends, each was given a special wristband, and the second floor was now closed to everyone except officials leading the briefings, their support staff, invited first responders, and family and friends of the missing.

The second floor had become the central location for comfort, information, and services. On their way to the Junior Ballroom, Meg and Cara had passed doors labeled with laser-printed signs: GRIEF COUNSELOR – PLEASE KNOCK, METROPOLITAN POLICE DEPARTMENT, and MEDICAL EXAMINER'S OFFICE. Families could find out about the rescue operations, leave a DNA reference sample, be informed about the death of a loved one, and find counseling for their grief, all within approximately fifty feet.

Meg was impressed with the efficiency, but it was all just so tragic.

Now, standing outside the briefing room, the sisters were watching that tragedy play out in real time. It made Meg grateful she'd had her breakdown last night in the privacy of her own home, with her partner, and had followed it up with a good night's sleep. And some life-affirming time with Todd that morning. Her center was solid again, and with it, she'd be able to help those who needed her.

The people inside the briefing room ranged from squirming babies, held by pale mothers with shadowed eyes, to the elderly, seated with their walkers nearby. Signs of stress were everywhere, from the young woman clutching a travel mug so hard her knuckles shone white, to the middle-aged man who was frantically scrolling on his phone, looking for updates, to the silver-haired couple sitting absolutely still as they waited for the briefing to begin, holding hands, their faces blank masks, as if they already knew their loved one was beyond this world.

Meg had seen this before in her time with the Richmond PD. Some people just knew. They felt the void long before they received the confirmation from official sources. Still, they came to sit with the living, to hear word about the dead in a room pulsing with layers of sadness, shock, desperation, and resignation.

"Looks like they're getting ready to start, so I should go in," Cara said. "I'm going to mingle. I'll move around during the briefing if I can, and will stay as long as they need us afterward. Then I'll head to the site. You're going to go right back after?"

"Yes. Every minute we're not there searching is lost time

we'll never get back." Meg scanned the crowd, taking in the faces, all the overflowing emotion. "But this is important, so it's worth doing."

"It is. Good luck. I'll see you at home tonight?"

Meg nodded. "You and McCord can pop in anytime. Todd and I should be home around eight thirty. I'd like to touch base with McCord anyway. Find out where he's at with all this."

The sisters split up. Cara made her way to the rear of the room, where Saki immediately headed toward a child sitting on the floor, while Meg walked to the front of the room, where a number of uniformed officials had gathered. She recognized Weinberg by his DCFEMS officer's uniform of navy pants, long-sleeved white shirt, and black tie, and by his DCFEMS patch on his left shoulder. He was a little short for a firefighter but had the kind of wiry build that had surprising depths of strength and flexibility, which beat height any day in a crisis. His thick hair was almost entirely gray, and Meg placed him in his midfifties when she compensated for the wear and tear the last couple of days had likely done to him—the deep lines bracketing his mouth and the shadows under his eyes spoke to the stress and exhaustion hitting everyone involved seventy-two hours into the crisis.

Meg extended her hand as she walked up to him. "Deputy Chief Weinberg. Meg Jennings." She looked down at her dog as he stared up at the newcomer with bright eyes and a wagging tail. "This is my search-and-rescue K-9, Hawk."

Weinberg shook her hand. "Glad to meet you. Thank you for coming. It's my intention to answer every question posed to us by the families. I can handle most questions in real time myself. If not, my goal is to have answers for them by the next day, if possible. As you might imagine, the level of desperation is high, and they want to know every aspect of the operation. One of them yesterday asked about the dogs, thus my request to your SAC."

"I'm happy to help. I can't imagine the hell they must be going through. Whatever we can do to help alleviate some of that, we're all in."

"Thank you. We'll get started now. I need to review a few things, because they're desperate for the details. You'll be after that, because I don't want to slow you down too much. I know you're needed on-site." He started to turn away, then swiveled back to her. "If you could give Lieutenant Webb a message?"

"Of course."

"I haven't been able to reach out personally, so please pass along our thanks for a job well done yesterday. All our men and women are going above and beyond, but he went a step past that yesterday, putting himself in real jeopardy, and pulled out one of our few live victims. It's put me in a slightly better place today, because we actually have some good news to go with the bad. And we have plenty of that. Anyway, please pass along my personal thanks."

"I will. Thank you, Deputy Chief."

As Weinberg went to the microphone, Meg moved to stand closer to the wall behind him. She quietly told Hawk to sit, and then she stood at an angle so she could watch the crowd.

When Weinberg turned on the mic and stepped to where he could be seen by the laptop webcam, Meg realized the laptop was running a Zoom session so family and friends out of town could join the briefings.

"Folks." Weinberg waited as the room slowly quieted. "Good morning. I want to recap yesterday's activities, and then I'll bring you up to speed with any new activities since our last meeting yesterday, and then what the plan is for today." He took a moment to look around the room, meeting the eyes of as many people as he could. "I'd like to begin with this. In case you haven't heard about it on the news, yesterday, after our meeting had concluded, the combined efforts of DCFEMS and Virginia's Task Force 1 recovered Kevin Vaughn from under the rubble in the parking garage. They identified his location using listening devices and then tunneled under the pile to a void space. Mr. Vaughn was dehydrated, concussed, hypothermic, and suffering from several broken bones but is in stable condition in the hospital and will make a full recovery.

"Currently, our numbers stand at the following. Nine live rescues from the debris field—three from the building and six from the street. Seventeen dead—nine from the building and eight from the street. And seventy-nine unaccounted for.

"Now, along those lines, I need to go over a couple of things with you. I've been asked about notifications, and how you'll find out if one of your loved ones has passed. First of all, I'd like to remind you that unscrupulous people will take advantage of this situation and of your pain, which is unforgivable. But you can guard against it. Remember, the only real information is what you hear from me or other experts in this room. Anything new you hear from the media or from a friend who tells you they saw it on social media isn't true." A murmur ran through the crowd. "Not even something you read in the paper or hear on TV, not if you're attending every session here with us. We've made a commitment that no information will go out to the media until it has been shared with you here. Our teams understand that, too, and they know better than to talk to the media."

Only feet away, Meg made a mental note once again to

ensure anything she said to McCord went nowhere until he had the green light from Craig. He'd never wavered from their agreement of his silence in exchange for access to case information and FBI personnel for his eventual story, but this time it wouldn't just be the risk of getting her into trouble. A leak could cause irreparable damage to families who were already living a nightmare.

"Only trust what you hear here," Weinberg continued. "In fact, I'd recommend staying off social media altogether for now. And if your time comes to be informed of your loved one's death, that notification will come only from a Metropolitan Police Department detective. And it will only be done face-to-face. Someone may call to identify your location, but that actual notification will only come personally. They may find you here at the hotel, or at home, but they'll make personal contact. God forbid someone pulls this kind of stunt, but if you get a call telling you your loved one has been found deceased, don't believe it. It's not real." Weinberg loosed a sigh that, to Meg, carried with it anger at whoever might do such a cruel thing. But the truth was, it could happen; Weinberg knew it and wanted these people to be forewarned.

"On to activity on the pile. All the teams we discussed yesterday are on the pile, and searches are ongoing. One complicating factor has been a deep-seated fire that keeps reigniting under the pile. We had to suspend operations at one point in the early hours yesterday because of smoke obscuring the search areas under the artificial lighting. As I told you yesterday, they started digging in a north–south line between the A1 and A2 and C1 and C2 search areas."

Weinberg walked to the gridded overhead photo and drew his index finger down the map, from the midway point of the collapse on the north side straight down through the pile to the south side. "The trench is twenty feet wide and forty feet deep. So far, they've progressed about fifty feet and will be continuing today. The purpose of the trench is to make a firebreak in case the fire progresses that far. Without fuel the fire will die. We're removing that fuel."

He turned back to the overflowing crowd. "During the process of digging the trench, we found three victims. But I want you to prepare yourselves, because what I'm going to tell you will be difficult. For me to tell, and for you to hear. But remember at the beginning, we swore we would be absolutely honest with you no matter what. So, I'm being honest. We are finding a few victims, but what we're finding more often is human remains." A ripple undulated through the crowd, layered waves of cries, whispers, and whimpers, but Weinberg trudged on. "When we mark the map"—he indicated the gridded photo, which had nine red circles on it in specific places, several of which Meg recognized as the locations of Hawk's discoveries—"we're marking the position of only recovered victims. We can't count human remains, because they're not discrete victims."

Her heart aching with sympathy, Meg scanned the crowd. One woman in the front held her face in her hands, her shoulders shaking with quiet sobs. A young man on the aisle leaned into an older woman, perhaps his mother, whispering in her ear, as her face crumpled. A man behind her sat frozen, his face slack, with no comprehension in his eyes.

Because really, how could anyone inexperienced comprehend the forces at play here? Every family member in the room had to be picturing, at worst, their dead loved one buried in a pile of rubble. But as bucket crews cleared debris and the dogs were brought in to scent the new layers and alert on finds, nine times out of ten, additional digging did not find intact victims, but pieces of them—limbs or teeth or smears of blood or bodily fluids. Meg had seen it herself over the previous two days multiple times, and she and Hawk were only one team. Overall, it was the majority of what they were finding.

But to have to break that news to the families . . . Meg considered Weinberg, his stiff stance, the way his left hand clenched and unclenched the cord from the microphone, and the tightness bracketing his mouth. This was leadership. This was personally taking on what could be the worst job of this disaster, knowing you'd spend weeks drowning in the grief and anger directed straight at you with the ferocity of a shotgun blast, because people were suffering and had no one else to focus their fury on.

As if someone had heard her thoughts, sharp words broke out toward the rear of the room, and Weinberg strode partly into the crowd. "Folks. Folks! Look at me. Direct your anger at me or at the team. Not at your neighbor. They're not responsible for how things are being run. Up here." He pointed at his own chest. "Look at me."

The room quieted slightly, but Meg could still hear someone weeping. Cara moved up the side aisle to a young woman who sat a few chairs in, and Saki stretched out her leash to disappear into the crowd and go sit with her. The woman reached down to stroke her and take what comfort she could.

"I know emotions are running high," Weinberg continued. "They are for me too. But we're in this together. Right now, we're family. And family sticks together, works together. Gets through the rough patches together. Now . . ." He took a breath, gathered himself, and continued. "You remember yesterday, we asked that everyone who is a blood relation to anyone missing go down to the medical examiner's office a few doors down to have a reference

DNA sample taken? This is why we need those samples. There may be some people we can't identify, so we'll need to compare their DNA. If you haven't given a reference sample yet, please do so today." Weinberg stepped back to the front. "Truthfully, we're not finding as many voids as we had hoped. And those we do find are usually not more than eight inches deep."

Another murmur ran through the crowd, while someone from the back chanted, "No, no, no . . ."

"We're thankful we found Kevin Vaughn, but he was found in a void up against the stability of the standing shear wall. Into the wing of the building, because of the pancaking action of the floors as they fell, we're not finding voids of that size, and we're not finding many intact victims. But we won't give up hope. Kevin gives us hope, and we won't rest until we've searched the whole pile. So you know, when we do find remains, we are following protocol to the letter—making sure the area is clear and then collecting all the remains to go to the lab—and this is one reason why things are taking so long. Once the lab has them, they'll try to identify from clothing, jewelry, tattoos, dental work, or fingerprints, if any of those are possible. If not, DNA remains our best option. Please make sure we have your sample."

Weinberg glanced at Meg and then down at his watch, as if conscious of the time he was taking away from the team on the pile. "Quickly, I wanted to update you on the request we've had over the past few days to get closer to the disaster site. We've arranged to take you, two busloads at a time, to the Conrad, which has kindly allowed us access to their terrace that overlooks the site. We still need to organize who is going in which trip, but we'll start at two o'clock. We'll take names for everyone who is interested in going at the end of this meeting. Please note this will be a personal visit for family and friends only. There will be no media and no local or federal politicians there. This is simply for you to see the site and the rescue efforts.

"But I need to warn you—this is an active site with ongoing rescues. We don't want to lose time by stopping for this visit, so work will continue. You may see victims, or remains, being recovered. If you don't feel comfortable doing this, let us know and we'll try to accommodate you. But—and I can't stress this enough—we're going to get you to the Conrad and you can go only to the terrace. You can't leave the hotel. Anyone who tries to leave the hotel to get closer access to the site at ground level will be stopped, and subsequent visits will have to be canceled. It's a safety risk for you to be at the actual rescue site, so please, don't ruin this for everyone. Please stay with the group."

Weinberg waved Meg and Hawk over to him, and they moved to stand beside him.

"Yesterday you got to talk to one of the urban search-and-rescue members, and he told you all about the technology they use to hear voices or rhythms like tapping to find victims in the rubble. But he also said their best tool was the dogs, and someone asked if we could get a dog team in to explain how they work. This is Meg Jennings from the FBI Human Scent Evidence Team and her search dog, Hawk, and they've come to tell you about what they do." He handed Meg the microphone and then stepped into the wall of personnel who stood at the front.

Bet he's glad for the respite.

Meg scanned the crowd, taking in the faces, from hopeful to despairing to terrified, her heart aching for what they must be going through. "Good morning. As Deputy Chief Weinberg said, I'm Meg, and this is my dog, Hawk." She lay her hand on Hawk's head, and his tail beat a happy cadence against the carpet. "First of all, I want to say on behalf of everyone involved in the rescue operation, our hearts are with you. I can't imagine what you're going through, but know we're working as hard and as fast as humanly possible to get to anyone buried in the rubble. Yesterday's rescue? Kevin Vaughn? That was my fiancé, a firefighter/paramedic with DCFEMS, who medically stabilized him inside the pile and then pulled him out. Rescuers are willing to put their lives on the line to get to your loved ones. Have faith we're doing everything we can."

As she scanned the crowd, she found Cara and Saki. They'd moved on to a young woman holding a fussy toddler, who was now quiet, eyes wide, as she gently stroked Saki's head. Cara was whispering to the mother, who was nodding in response, her lips in a twisted, sad smile. "From a dog standpoint, it's not just the search dogs that help. We're using therapy dogs to help the first responders de-stress when they're on one of their short breaks. It's hard work out on the pile, physically and emotionally demanding work. Therapy dogs can help rescue crews go back to the job steady and a little more refreshed. And here, among you, we have another. I asked my sister Cara to come today with her therapy dog, Saki." From the crowd, Cara waved an arm over her head. "When the session is over, feel free to go see Saki. She's a wonderful, comforting dog who likes nothing more than to snuggle with a human."

As Cara sank down, Meg scanned the room. "Let me run you through how a search dog works at a site like this. Hawk and I arrived about a half hour after the collapse two days ago and have been here for a twelve-hour shift each day. There are other dogs who work the same shift we do, and more on the second shift, so dogs are always working the pile. Hawk is what we call a live find dog. They look for the living, for the lost and injured. His nose is about one hundred thousand times more sensitive than mine, and Hawk has been trained on a number of human scents, including blood and sweat.

"But the main thing Hawk looks for is skin cells. Everywhere we go, we drop about forty thousand skin cells each minute, which essentially leaves a path for a scent dog to follow. In a scenario like we have at Talbot Terraces, the scent dogs are looking for that same scent anywhere in the rubble, and especially a concentration of it. There are four live find scent dogs in my unit, and we were the first on the pile on Monday morning. The urban search-and-rescue teams arrived that afternoon and the next day, and they brought their own dogs, who are similarly trained."

Meg turned to the search grid photo. "Our teams are working together, so we're making the best possible use of the dogs. If any dog alerts on a scent, workers will come and concentrate on that area, so we have the dogs working in loose pairs so that each hit can be confirmed."

"What happens if the scent isn't confirmed?" The question came from somewhere in the crowd.

"Depending on the location and the strength of the first dog's alert, we may still divert crews to the area, because every area will have to be dug through, but if it's confirmed, then there's a rapid move to that area of the pile. The crews will come in and use large equipment, like a crane, to shift bigger pieces, if needed. Otherwise, crews will start digging and using concrete cutting tools to move debris and get into the pile. If needed, we bring the dogs back in to narrow the search or to confirm rescue crews are still in the right area. We don't want to waste time and effort by being in the wrong place."

"Wouldn't it be faster to use an excavator?" a male voice asked.

"A fair question," Meg said. "And one that makes sense, given the speed of using that kind of digging tool.

This isn't my area of expertise. That's what the urban teams do. But from what I understand, they have to balance out the type and weight of the debris, whether they can get an excavator close enough to that site—which can be hard if it happens to be in the middle of the pile—as well as how close to the surface any person might be. We have to be careful in general for the same reason. The whole point of the search is to find people in void spaces. It's paramount that we don't disturb those spaces, risking their collapse and injuring or killing whoever might be inside. That's why the number of people on the pile at any one time is limited. Right from the start, dogs got priority access, because they can steer the search.

"The other advantage with the dogs is they can get places we can't and can do it faster. Four feet and a lower center of gravity means they're sure-footed when we're struggling to climb over and around things. We train the dogs specifically for this, taking them to parks so they can practice on playgrounds and use stone fences as balance beams, keeping them in top shape and flexibility. That allows them to tackle a difficult landscape with confidence. We let them run free in the search area we're assigned, and if they get ahead of us and alert, that's okay, because they'll stay in place, signaling that alert, until we catch up with them."

"Is it dangerous for the dogs?" A female voice this time.

"Honestly, yes. They could cut their feet on the rough surfaces, get sliced by exposed metal or broken glass, have a fall, or be crushed by materials falling off the standing structure or by a piece of heavy machinery that isn't aware they're there. They're also breathing toxins we're not when we're masked, because they have to be able to scent to do their jobs. But this is what they do. To the dogs, it's kind of a game, and being able to find someone, like we did on Monday with Mark Casey, or to recover someone, as we did yesterday, so we could give a family closure, that's a win for Hawk. It's important work, and not without risk, but the risk is worth it. We work as safely and as quickly as we can. But rest assured, if the scent is there, the dogs will find it. In addition to the dogs, the urban search-and-rescue teams brought equipment with them that will help us hear if anyone is signaling to us in the pile. That's how Mr. Vaughn was found yesterday."

Meg looked quickly at Weinberg, who gave her a subtle nod. "I need to return to the site now so we can go back to work. If you come to the site this afternoon, watch for us or the other dogs. Watch how the teams all work together, using the specialized skills of each to work as a stronger unit. Our goal is to find your family members, and we won't stop until we do."

A smattering of claps and a chorus of thank-yous filled the room as she held out the mic for Weinberg, who took it and shook her hand with a low word of thanks.

"Hawk, come." After a quick glance at Cara, who smiled her goodbye, Meg stepped out into the hallway. The band of pressure around her chest eased slightly now that she was away from the families' expectations and their free-floating emotions. She didn't blame anyone in that room for their reactions to the crisis. She wasn't sure she'd do better; she would just have an inside angle into any incident through her connections in law enforcement and Todd's connections in firefighting.

The helplessness the families must be experiencing had to be overwhelming, and it overflowed as stress and anger. Weinberg completely understood that, and that intuition kept the briefings moving forward as he worked to keep everyone in the loop and to ease some of the anguish, if possible.

Inside the room, she heard Weinberg saying that the president had expressed a desire to meet with the families at the reunification center and that a visit was being arranged for some time in the next few days.

Meg looked down at her dog, who stood still at her knee, his warm brown eyes fixed on her face. "Come on, Hawk. The best thing we can do to help them is to get back to the site. And we'll do everything in our power to help them find closure."

CHAPTER 16

Progressive Collapse: The failure of a building's structural element that causes adjacent elements to fail due to the impact of additional load, leading to the runaway collapse of a large part of the structure or its entirety.

Wednesday, December 19, 11:41 AM
The Washington Post
Washington, DC

McCord rapped his knuckles on the door, beside the brass plaque that read MARTIN SYKES – EDITOR, and opened it at the call to come in from the other side.

The room beyond was a testament to the work of the *Washington Post*, with every wall covered with awards and framed copies of award-winning stories. Sykes, a solid man with a broad build and short steel-gray hair, sat behind a desk piled with papers and newsprint, but it was the other reporter and the stranger who sat opposite Sykes who captured McCord's attention.

"You wanted to see me?"

Sykes waved him in. "Yes. Come in and close the door. I want to bring you in on Prescott's work. Grab a chair."

McCord shut the door, then crossed to the round table in front of the window overlooking K Street NW and Franklin Park beyond. He paused for a moment, gazing across the park to the southeast, to where the collapse site was located, a mere four blocks from where he stood. From here, the downtown appeared entirely normal, as if unspeakable tragedy wasn't only minutes away. Upon turning away from the window, he dragged one of the chairs over to join the other two men.

Steve Prescott sat on the far side. McCord didn't know him well—he'd been at the *Post* for only about six months—but what he'd seen of his work was solid. He was about McCord's age, dressed in sneakers, jeans, and an untucked button-down shirt, and had pale skin and thinning reddish hair. The office scuttlebutt said he was never without a travel mug of coffee; McCord's gaze dropped to the floor to find a tall, covered mug beside his chair.

Never doubt the accuracy of office scuttlebutt. "Prescott."

"McCord."

The man between them was older, with a thin face and tidily cut hair, and was wearing a well-cut black business suit with a conservative charcoal tie. A leather briefcase leaned against his chair leg, and he held a tablet on his lap.

McCord stuck out his hand. "Clay McCord."

"Jack Burke." Burke shook hands with him.

McCord sat down, then looked expectantly at his editor.

"Mr. Burke has been working with Prescott on the Talbot Terraces collapse," Sykes said. "And since you were at the site itself on the day of the collapse, and because you've been looking at who might have been a target if the collapse was actually caused by explosives, I thought he might have some information that could help you."

"Appreciate that." McCord turned to Prescott. "You're making headway?"

"We've turned up some interesting things, yes. Immedi-

ately following the collapse, we gathered together technical details about the building," Prescott said.

"We?"

"Robbins, Sanz, and I together. We wanted to move
fast, and we worked well together on that lottery bribery
story, so with Sykes's approval, I pulled them in to help."

"You found something suspicious?" McCord asked.

"We had no idea. Ever seen building plans?"

"I have to admit I haven't."

"All the drawings and industry shorthand . . . We didn't
know what we were looking at. Or for. As a group, we figured out pretty fast we essentially needed a translator.
Then I remembered I knew someone in the field back
when I was working at the *Washington Times*. Remember
when that earthquake hit the DC area in August 2011 and
Hurricane Irene swept through a few days later? Remember the damage to the Washington Monument?"

McCord remembered the quake well. He'd been back
from Iraq for a few years by that time and had been standing in the newsroom when the quake hit shortly before
2:00 PM. The government had closed for the day, and all
buildings had been evacuated. Schools had closed, and
traffic chaos had ensued from so many people on the road
at the same time and from the smattering of traffic lights
knocked out. "Oh, yeah. I was in the old 15th Street NW
newsroom when the quake hit. Took them years to repair
the damage to the monument."

"It did. And just before it opened in 2014, I did a story
about the damage and repair work. Jack works for Ekhert
and Morrison and was my professional expert for that
story."

"We're an architectural firm," Burke supplied. "I do a
lot of building design, but I'm also a forensic engineer. I'm
the guy you send for if you need an investigation around
the failure of materials and structures."

"And you have ideas around what happened last Monday?" McCord asked.

"It's a bit soon for that. A full investigation will have to be launched, which won't happen until the rescue and recovery is complete, which could take weeks. NIST will handle the investigation, which could go on for years. But the materials Steve was able to gather has definitely raised some questions."

"Let me walk you through it from the beginning," said Prescott. "The building is thirty-one years old, and on the surface, there's no evidence of negligence. It's a luxury building, bringing in top dollar for residency, and has been well maintained. There are no complaints lodged with the DC Department of Consumer and Regulatory Affairs."

"In other words, it didn't collapse due to age or neglect," stated McCord.

"We haven't found any evidence to support that," Prescott replied. "Here are the basics. It's a twelve-story building, where most of the first two floors were occupied commercially, leaving the remainder of the shared space for the condo residents—the main lobby, security office, shared gym space, and a community room used for condo association meetings and the like, or could be rented out for special occasions. The luxury apartments were on floors three to twelve, and the terraced roof had a heated pool, hot tub, and several patio spaces with extensive gardens. Below the building was a two-level garage. The lower level was specifically reserved for building occupants and visitors, with elevator and stair access to the building, and the upper level was for public parking, to support the commercial enterprises in the building."

"That probably brought the owners a pretty penny," Sykes commented. "You know how terrible downtown parking is. And if they wanted people to come into their shops, they needed to give them somewhere to park."

"I'd assume there's a big mortgage on a ritzy place like that," McCord said. "That income would help balance some of it out."

"I'm sure that played into it," Prescott agreed. "But what's important for us here is the double garage structure. When the first stage of the collapse occurred, the middle section fell into the below-grade garage and out over the street. When the east wing fell, it continued to fill the garage but then also fell over the collapsed middle section."

McCord opened his mouth to speak, then stopped as the full import of Prescott's words struck home. "But that means . . ." He saw the building in his mind as it had been the day before; now he was trying to connect that visual with this new piece of information. "The debris pile is only about three stories high. But what you're saying is a large portion of the building is packed into two stories of previously open space underground. It's actually a five-story pile of concrete and steel."

"Yes."

"God. Which means anyone on the first floor is inaccessible at the bottom of that pile."

"Along with anyone who might have been getting into their car at that moment."

McCord stared at Prescott for a second as cold horror crawled down his spine. "I didn't think of that."

"Yeah, I know. I didn't either at first. Then it kind of hits you like a freight train, how little chance these people had. But back to the building itself. What we essentially have is a fourteen-story building now compacted into roughly five stories. And the big question is, What happened? That's what I've been working on."

"I've been doing some of that, too, and it's pretty clear from my research that something extraordinary happened."

"Agreed," said Prescott. "I wanted to get down to basics, so I went to the DC Department of Consumer and Regulatory Affairs and got a copy of the building plans. All the signed and sealed architectural drawings submitted for permitting, all the revisions, the construction plans, and the permits themselves."

McCord's eyebrows arched in surprise. "That was easier than it could have been."

"They're all public records, but yeah, sometimes they give you a hard time and let the red tape spin. Not this time. I was one of the first people to go looking for those records, but they said they're going to make scans of them public on the Internet, because there's going to be such a desire for access, and they don't have time to deal with individual requests."

"Everyone is going to have an opinion about them," Sykes muttered.

Prescott nodded. "I could have opinions about them myself. But we all know they'd be worth squat, because I'm a newspaperman and not a structural engineer. That's where Jack came into our investigation. Luckily for us, he can translate it all. We thought you'd want in on what it means."

"Hell, yes, I want in. This could be the biggest story to hit DC this year, but it's not just that for me. I got into the site yesterday, before it was locked down, so I was there, standing in front of the building hours after it fell. My partner, Cara, is on-site right now with her therapy dog, trying to help boost the spirits of the rescuers. My sister-in-law is in the FBI's Forensic Canine Unit, and they're on the pile every day, searching for survivors. And the dead." He met and held Prescott's gaze. "I'm invested. I'm up to my eyeballs in residents, sorting through who could have been a target if this was a targeted attack . . ." McCord turned to Burke. "Was it?"

"No one will be able to prove that definitively yet. It's

too early." Burke flipped open the cover of his tablet. "But I can paint you a picture. Let's start with the basics. The building went up in 1987 and is of reinforced concrete, plate-slab construction. That means it was constructed by pouring concrete in stages around two-way steel reinforcing bars, or rebar, and tying vertical columns into horizontal slabs. No steel beams and girders are used, just concrete and rebar. It's a more convenient way to build, especially in a concentrated downtown core, because you don't need the massive cranes required for beam and girder construction."

He angled the tablet toward McCord. "Steve sent me all the aforementioned information on the building, and I used it to do my analysis. The first thing to know is that there are three sets of plans. One from 1985 and two from 1986, with the final plans being the as-built final design plans submitted to the city to obtain the construction permit. But it's the difference between the plans, mainly between the second and final plans, that caught my attention. Here's where it gets technical."

"I can do technical."

"Excellent. There are two major differences between plans two and three. The first is in the support for the columns. Do you know anything about steel-reinforced concrete construction?"

"Nothing worth mentioning."

"Quick structural engineering lesson, then." Burke opened a blank document on his tablet and pulled out a stylus. "Let's say this is a basic column." He drew two parallel vertical lines, then drew two more vertical lines inside it. "Concrete has high compressive strength but low tensile strength, meaning it resists forces pushing in but doesn't do so well against forces trying to pull it apart. Rebar is added to provide that tensile strength, as well as to prevent cracking. Rebar is positioned inside the wooden form into which they'll pour the concrete, in a specific layout called a mat, held in precise conformation by steel supports before the concrete is poured. After it's poured, the concrete shrinks around the rebar as it cures, producing a solid support column. Rebar comes in lengths from twenty to sixty feet, so you need to use multiple pieces when you're building a multilevel structure like Talbot Terraces. To get sufficient strength from rebar, you can't lay the pieces end to end. Instead, you lay their ends side by side for a certain length, which we call 'lapping,' and the area where the two bars overlap is called a 'lap splice.' "

He drew some additional lines, each lining up precisely beside the end of an existing line, overlapping by an inch on-screen, and then drew a small loop around them to represent wiring them together. "This isn't to scale, but it gives you the idea. At all points in the design process, we have to keep in mind the regulations at the time of building, but back then, it was supposed to be a minimum twenty-inch lap splice, meaning ten inches of one piece of rebar overlapped ten inches of another piece of rebar." He drew a square bracket to the right of the lapped sections. "Does that make sense?"

"Yes," McCord said. "I assume that's not what they did?"

"Not according to the final plan. They did a six-inch lap splice instead."

"That's a pretty big difference. Three inches per piece, instead of ten. Is that a catastrophic error?"

"Not on its own, no. But it could mean that over time, you'd see accelerated cracking in those locations, especially under cold conditions. As a result, when under stress, the building wouldn't be as strong in that connection as it should have been."

"Did it happen at every location where overlapping occurred?"

"No, it happened in specific locations, which could

come into play, but we'll get into how that could happen. There are several bigger problems than the lack of lap, but I wanted to start with that so you had a feel for how the concrete is reinforced." He wiped the diagram from the screen and started again, drawing a column under a flat slab. "This is a typical column-slab configuration. To tie the column into the slab, the rebar is bent, so instead of going vertically through the slab, it has a ninety-degree angled turn into the slab and it ends there." He drew two pieces of rebar coming up from the column, then taking a sharp corner right or left into the horizontal slab. "That's normal, and that's what I see in the drawings. However, it's the rebar mat within the slab that caught my attention."

"There's something wrong with it?"

"There was a major change between the two plans in 1986. Within the slab, there are two mats of rebar—bottom and top. The bottom mat was designed on a regular grid pattern. The top mat was designed to reduce the risk of punching shear. Are you familiar with the term?" Burke's gaze flicked up to McCord.

"No, sorry."

"No need to apologize. It's an engineering term, so you may have never had cause to run into it. Punching shear is a failure in this kind of plate-slab construction where a column punches through a slab or the slab falls away from the column, leaving the column with no support at that location."

Burke picked up his stylus again. "Back to the rebar mats. I went over the bottom mat already—a standard grid pattern, with the bars running in two directions. The variance is in the top mat. In the 1985 and early 1986 plans, the engineer noted the amount of rebar and what size he wanted in the top mat, but specified he wanted twenty-five percent of the rebar clustered over the column.

For the purpose of this illustration, let's say this is the bottom mat, which would be positioned about one-fifth of the way into the concrete from the lower edge, running in two perpendicular directions to give the required tensile strength."

Above his sketch, he drew a two-way grid of evenly spaced lines. "But the top mat was supposed to have a grid pattern like this." He drew five closely spaced vertical lines that intersected with closely spaced horizontal lines, with wider spaced lines continuing on either side of the tight cluster in both directions. "This intersection point, where it's a tight five-by-five grid? That was to be placed directly over the column." He circled the precise placement in the column and slab diagram. "It would give significant structural stability and would highly reduce the risk of punching shear, because for the column to punch through, it would have to break all that rebar."

"But you're saying there was a change," McCord pointed out. "In the later set of plans?"

"Yes. I have no idea why, but that concentration of rebar specified in the early 1986 plans was removed in the later plans, and a regular grid, similar to the bottom rebar mat, was designed. Instead of concrete being poured around that tight concentration of ten pieces of rebar, there was at max two or four. That's a significant difference in stability."

"And would that cause a collapse?"

"It could contribute most certainly, given time and the corrosion of the materials. Now, this isn't a constantly exposed external construction, like an open multilevel parking structure, where the columns are exposed to the elements twenty-four-seven, three-sixty-five. But all building materials age, and all concrete absorbs water from rain, snow, or humidity, depending on where it is in the structure. That, in turn, leads to corrosion of the rebar within the concrete. When rebar corrodes, it expands, putting pressure on the concrete, causing it to crack. Ever been in a parking garage and you can see areas on the floor or columns where concrete has crumbled away, and you can see rusty rebar beneath?"

"Sure."

"That's called spalling. The concrete in those sections has cracked, leading to delamination, or the separation of the top layer or layers from the rest of the concrete. Now, I don't know that there were outward signs of concrete aging in this building. But all of this can be happening under the surface, leading to hidden weaknesses. And the parking garage of Talbot Terraces, though not directly exposed to the elements, was still exposed to increased moisture because it wasn't in a closed, temperature-controlled location."

"I doubt there was outward evidence of damage," Prescott said. "This is a luxury building with a rep for world-class residents and expensive buy-in prices. Except for what was going on in the parking garage."

McCord's gaze shot from Burke to Prescott. "What was going on there?"

"Hang on. I'll explain when Jack has covered the structural issues, because it all twists together. But it came out of the request for all the plans and permits. Jack, keep going with your structural analysis, and then we'll circle around."

Burke cleared the tablet screen again. "The other issue between the plans was the removal of a number of support beams."

McCord cocked his head slightly, studying Burke. "Beams, not columns?"

"Yes."

"I thought this building didn't have beams. It was columns and slabs."

"Overall, yes, but in special areas, especially in transition areas, sometimes additional support is needed. Do you know the difference between live and dead loads?"

"I can guess at that. A dead load is something that doesn't move, and a live load does."

"Correct. A dead load is something that will always be in place, be it a slab above, a parapet at the roofline, or a decorative concrete planter and everything inside it. A live load would be cars driving through and then parking in a parking garage. As design engineers, we design differently for dead and live loads, because dead loads are predictable and live loads are not."

"That makes sense."

"In this case, a transition was designed in the early 1986 plans for a step-down at the plaza level, over the parking garage, which stretched between Talbot Terraces and the Gerrard Apartments. At the bottom of the step-down, they designed some long planter boxes for use during the temperate times of the year. There were several restaurants on the south side of the eastern wing, and the plan was for them to have raised patios a step up from the plaza level. But that step-down in reality was a number of large, reinforced twelve-by-twenty-one-inch slab-drop beams running between the columns. Not only did they form the step-down, but they were also essential structural support overall."

"I assume from everything else you've explained that part of this support is missing?" McCord hypothesized.

"Not part." Burke shook his head, his lips a tight, disapproving line. "All. They're just gone in the later 1986 drawing, leaving that area at the same level as the plaza. But everything else was left in place as far as dead load goes, including the line of extremely heavy planter boxes. And no, before you ask, all of this wouldn't make the building collapse on its own."

"I assume none of this was to code at the time?"

"No. As you might imagine, what is considered code now was more relaxed back then, but this didn't even meet that."

"Why would they do that? I assume to trim costs, but surely it would be more expensive for the building to fall down and for them to lose the project, possibly while building it or later, and then get sued out of existence."

"Any developer will try to maximize their profits by minimizing their costs. Most of them have the building designed to the minimum code and then push any regulations as far as they can, but most of them stay within the law. And if they don't, often the contractor will push back, because an experienced contractor will know what's legitimate and what's not. In case of a disaster, anyone involved in the building—from the developer to the architect and/or design engineer, depending on if one or the other or both were required, and to the contractor—will all be sued, so it behooves each of them to check up on the others if they think something suspicious is going on."

"Seems logical." McCord leaned forward to see Prescott on the other side of Burke. "What was going on in the parking garage?"

"They were doing repairs," Prescott replied. "When we got the paperwork from the Department of Consumer and Regulatory Affairs, most of it was from when the building was being designed and built. But there was a permit for emergency repairs a little over a month ago. You have to put in a permit for certain renovations and repairs, including anything having to do with weight-bearing structural components. In the permit application, which was fast-tracked because it was an emergency, there was mention of a car accident. For a whopping three-dollar fee, we applied to the Records Branch of the Arrest and Criminal History Section of the Metro Police and received the accident report. Someone in the upper-level public parking spaces had some kind of medical emergency, lost control of their truck, and crashed into one of the support columns. According to the permit, the condo board of Talbot Terraces hired Solis Construction, a concrete remediation contractor, to shore up the area around the column and do the repairs."

"So even though the column took a significant hit, it didn't buckle," McCord stated.

"It didn't, nor should it have," Burke said. "Remember the live load issue? Parking garages are built to withstand higher loads because of it. Let's say you're designing a building, and you do the calculations for the residential part of the building, and eighteen-by-eighteen-inch columns are sufficient to manage the dead load. You're going to do different calculations for the live load in the garage, and you'll likely design something like twenty-four-by-twenty-four-inch columns through the garage and up through the first few floors before decreasing to that eighteen-inch size."

"So, the wider the column, the more rebar, the sturdier it is," McCord stated.

"Correct."

"Could the repair have damaged the column to the extent it started the collapse?"

"It shouldn't have. The concrete remediation company would have shored up the ceiling while the work was going on, and shouldn't have removed the posts until after the repair was complete and the concrete had cured. Even if they removed them early, considering the width of the surrounding columns, those columns should have been able to support the redistributed weight. You have to plan for that kind of contingency in parking garages, because it's not unthinkable to lose a column entirely due to a vehicular accident. We design for that." Burke studied

McCord, who sat drumming his fingers restlessly on his knee. "What are you thinking?"

"You keep bringing up these weaknesses but then say they wouldn't cause the building to fall on their own. Could they all act together?"

"Could they all simultaneously and spontaneously fail at the same time? Is that what you're asking?"

"When you put it that way, even I can hear that's an idiotic question," McCord muttered. "Because that has to be almost impossible."

"I'd say so, yes."

"So then I'm left wondering if someone could exploit any or all of these weaknesses to bring down the building."

"They'd have to get all the plans and study them enough to spot the differences. Then they'd have to know enough to *see* the differences, to understand them."

"We got all the permits and plans. You had the technical know-how to realize what it all means. If we could do it, so could someone else."

"Slow down a second, McCord." Sykes held up both hands to catch McCord's attention. "You're leaping to the theory that someone knew the building had a weakness and took advantage of it. *To bring down the building?* Why would someone do that? More importantly, we're looking at this building because it collapsed. Why would anyone target this building to the extent that they'd dig through all the permits and plans like we did? Because otherwise, there would be no way to know. It doesn't make any sense. It's much more likely this is an accident, or a serious design or construction flaw, rather than a plot to blow up a building."

McCord tipped his head in acknowledgment. "I hear you. And now we have someone here who can confirm the research I've done." He turned to Burke. "From what I can see, structures built in the developed world, with all our regulations and requirements, don't just fall down for no reason. There was no landslide, no hurricane, no tornado. The building has been standing for thirty-one years, and we have the opinion of a professional structural engineer that normal aging shouldn't have been enough to bring it down, even with these weaknesses.

"Yes, what I'm suggesting is the opposite of Occam's razor. This is *not* the most straightforward explanation. But I'm trying to tie things together. I have lists of the people living at the building at the time of the collapse. And while there are some big names there, including the president's chief of staff, it doesn't make any sense to bring down the whole building to get at one person when a bullet or explosives under a car would do the job more efficiently and with less risk of being caught. But the stories from eyewitnesses say they heard a boom just before the building came down." McCord leveled an index finger at Burke. "Let's say that beyond your current body of knowledge, you also knew explosives and demolition. Could you bring down this building?"

Burke reared back as if he'd been struck. "But I don't—"

"I know you don't. Hypothetical scenario. I'm not pointing a finger at you. Knowing what you know about the building, if you also knew how building demolition works, could you bring it down?"

Burke's eyes narrowed as he considered McCord. "You can bring down any building, even one newly built, with demolition explosives placed in the right locations." He held up a hand when McCord drew breath to speak, holding him off, as he took a few seconds to consider his answer. "If I was going to do it in an occupied building, I'd have to set the charges in columns I could access." He looked down at his tablet for a moment, where the five-by-five grid of rebar that hadn't been built was still displayed. "I'd pick columns that didn't have reliable structural stability, because I'd know the stress would be enough for them to fail. That would load weight onto the surrounding columns."

"Which are also inherently weak, so they'll fail," Prescott said.

"And once enough columns fail," Burke continued, "the slabs above will fail. As those slabs come down, you're left with what we call a 'slender column,' tall and skinny, with nothing at the midpoint for support, which will then buckle under its own weight. Which leads to a progressive collapse throughout the structure."

"Could it be done by targeting a certain number of weak columns?" McCord asked.

"Possibly." Burke's tone was guarded. "But to do that . . ."

"You'd have to either sneak around and not get caught, or you'd have to have legitimate access to the columns," said Sykes.

McCord could see the idea dawning in Sykes's eyes, the entire plan as it had come to him as soon as he'd heard Prescott's explanation.

"Like you would if you had to do column repair in the garage," Sykes continued.

McCord drilled an index finger in Sykes's direction. "There it is."

Sykes sat back in his chair and rocked a bit with the force of his landing, staring at McCord. "You think whoever did the repairs set the charges."

"If we're going with the theory that this was an intentional attack, yes. We need to know what they were doing specifically, when they got access, how long they had it for, and if they were still working on it." McCord swung around to Burke. "Could one column start the whole chain reaction?"

Burke took a moment to answer, but his opinion was telegraphed by a subtle head shake. "I'd have to do the calculations, but a single column seems unlikely. Buildings are constructed to protect from a single point of failure."

"Then you have to wonder if they had approved access to more than just that one damaged column." McCord paused, restlessly tapping his fingers together as his brain whirled. "Here's one other thing to think about. What if that accident . . . wasn't?"

"You mean there was no accident?" Sykes asked.

"Oh, no, they needed an accident to kick this off. What if it wasn't an accident, and there never was a medical crisis, but the column was hit on purpose? Note the person was driving a truck and not a Smart car. A big, heavy vehicle with a high profile to do maximum damage, but likely with a big crumple zone to protect the driver—"

"Let me get this straight," Sykes interrupted before McCord could continue. "You're suggesting an organized attack. Someone hits the column, necessitating repairs. Whoever wants to do the repairs makes sure they get the job and then sets charges to bring down the building. Detonate the charges and the building falls. Or part of it does. Does your theory say whether they planned to take down the whole thing?"

"My *theory*, as you call it, isn't that specific yet. But let's face it, if you want to bring down the whole thing and can't do it in one shot, you know you've essentially done it anyway. They're not going to leave what's left of the building standing indefinitely. It will all come down sooner or later, and whoever started it off doesn't have to take care of it himself."

"They may have suspected the elevator shaft was going to be a problem," Burke interjected.

"What do you mean?" asked Sykes.

"It's the reason the entire building didn't collapse.

There's a two-way shear wall around the elevator. You know that solid wall you can see where the building tore away? It's a structural element—a special reinforced wall poured in sections between each slab. It's built to resist forces that play against it in a perpendicular direction, like wind currents. The shear wall was built along the rear of the elevator shaft but also in a second direction along the sides of the shaft. When the rest of the building tore free, that shear wall combination stabilized the north–south wing of the building. It still took significant damage from the extreme forces at play, but it stayed upright. From the plans, there was a second shear wall built along one side of the stairwell in the wing that collapsed, but it ran in only one direction—"

"Wait," McCord interrupted. "That second shear wall. Was that why the wing fell in two sections? Why the end of the wing actually stayed standing for a few extra seconds?"

"Yes. The smaller, unidirectional shear wall tried to stabilize the east end of the structure, but it couldn't withstand the forces when it ran only in one plane."

"Do you mean if there had been a second, perpendicular wall, like there was around the elevator shaft, it might have stayed standing?"

"It's hard to say, but possibly. What's for sure, the way it was built, it couldn't do the heavy lifting required of it in that moment."

"Good to know while I'm trying to work out my theory."

"Does your theory have an explanation as to why someone did this?" Sykes asked.

McCord simply threw Sykes a nonplussed look. "I'm good, but I'm not that good. But this gives me a place to start." He stood and offered his hand to Burke. "Really good to meet you. Do you have a business card? I'm sure I'll have more questions."

Burke threw Prescott a sidelong look at his snort of laughter. "Of course." He pulled a card out of his inner breast pocket and handed it to McCord. "Call or text anytime."

"Thanks." McCord tucked the card between his first two fingers and then used it to throw a casual salute at Sykes. "Thanks for bringing me in on this. I need to make some phone calls."

McCord strode from the office. The first thing he was going to do was call Craig Beaumont and pass along this information so the FBI was looped into the possibility of sabotage. Then he was going to try to make contact with any survivors who had parked on the lower level of the parking garage and who had driven past the repaired column on the top level, in order to find out what they'd seen and if the repair work was still ongoing up to the day of the collapse.

He had the bit between his teeth now, and God help anyone who got in his way.

CHAPTER 17

Instability: The inability of a structure to remain in a state of equilibrium; when it is no longer able to successfully resist the forces of external loads.

Wednesday, December 19, 5:16 PM
Talbot Terraces
Washington, DC

A scream rent the air, an audible expression of a heart breaking in despair and agony.

"Hawk, stop." Meg dropped her gloved hand onto Hawk's back, and he held still, his head upturned and his eyes locked on her face. "That's my boy."

Meg followed the sound of the scream across the street to the Conrad. On and off through the afternoon, crowds of people had filled the fourth-floor open-air terrace. Trees were scattered over the terrace; their bare branches, wrapped with white twinkle lights, glowed as darkness settled around the site. Inside the site, double emergency lights on tall tripods had been set up around the perimeter, and extra lights had been carried up the pile to illuminate any area of interest.

From inside the brilliant wash of lights, Meg could only

barely see the outline of the family and friends of the lost at the railing on the Conrad's terrace. But she had no doubt that was where the scream had come from.

The rescue teams hadn't stopped working when the families arrived. That had been part of the discussion, to give the families private time to be as close as could be managed to their loved ones, to see the complexity of the site and the challenges the rescuers faced. But the majority of the first responders had argued it would simply take too much time, time they couldn't afford to lose at this stage of the rescue operation, as cold pushed at the bounds of survivability of anyone who might still be alive in the rubble. In the end, the incident control team had decided work would continue as the visits took place over the afternoon.

Meg thought it was the best decision. Even before her trip to the family reunification center, she'd heard word filter down that some of the families didn't think the rescue crews were working hard enough. Only a few of the searchers had expressed anger when they'd heard this; most, reasonably, had understood it was the reaction of people in unimaginable pain who felt absolutely helpless in a horrific situation. The teams continuing to work the pile—there were six teams on today, and the debris field buzzed with activity and was fully weighted at 150 personnel—was exactly what the families needed to witness. They needed to see the rescuers who had picked up and traveled hours away from their home state simply because their help was needed. This was search and rescue—you didn't question; you just showed up and got down to the work of saving lives.

By Meg's count, this was the third busload of family members coming to the site. The first group had arrived around two thirty and had stayed for about forty-five minutes. It had broken her heart to hear them calling for their loved ones, as if someone in the pile might hear a specific voice and make their presence known to rescuers. Meg wished it were that easy. If it were, they would have found everyone down here on day one and would be in cleanup mode by now.

If that were the case, Meg and Hawk wouldn't have spent most of their day finding human remains. The pile was now covered with a scattering of miniature red flags, each one representing the discovery of human remains they hadn't yet been able to document and collect, as the number of samples had grown so fast. Three additional intact victims had been found—one during the continued digging of the firebreak trench, two more as crews had moved debris as they worked their way down into the pile. As each layer was stripped off, it revealed new sites for the dogs to search and new potential discoveries. But they hadn't been the kind of discoveries anyone hoped to find.

Meg could see this was starting to wear on Hawk, and some of his usual nonstop enthusiasm was waning. And if this was affecting Hawk, she could only imagine how it must be affecting Lacey, who was a sensitive soul and took repeated search "failures," as Lacey would consider them, too hard. She knew Brian would be working diligently to keep her spirits up, as she would for Hawk.

So, she put some excitement into her voice and rubbed a hand down Hawk's back. "Okay, buddy, find them. Find them, Hawk. Just stay away from the edge of the trench. Neither of us is going over."

Hawk had just jumped onto what had once been a beautiful glass-fronted balcony with a stunning view of the nation's capital when Meg's radio buzzed to life. "Craig to all teams. I need everyone's attention right now."

Meg pulled her radio off her belt and activated the TALK button. "Meg to Craig. What's going on?"

"I need you all off the pile immediately. Full work stoppage."

"Hawk, stop." Hawk halted again and looked up at her with confusion for the repeated pauses in their search pattern. "Sorry, buddy."

Meg was about to question Craig's order when Brian beat her to it. "Brian to Craig. Can I get a confirmation on that? Everyone off the pile?"

"Yes. Off. Now."

The clipped commands and the stress behind Craig's tone told Meg something was very wrong. "We're getting off. Meg out."

"All teams, meet me in the Park at CityCenter, in the usual spot."

As the other teams signaled the receipt of Craig's order, Meg put her radio back on her belt. "Hawk, come. We need to find out what's going on."

They carefully made their way down the pile to street level, where they were directed through the tent city across the street, down New York Avenue NW, and then to the park. When Meg got there, Lauren, Scott, and their dogs were already at their meeting spot, but Craig was missing.

Brian, jogging up with Lacey, was the last to join the group. "What's going on?"

"No idea." Scott searched the crowd for their SAC. "Craig's the one who knows. Where is he?"

"I don't know." Meg scanned the small park, which was now filling with people as first responders came looking for incident command to explain what was going on and when they could get back to work. "I don't see . . . No, wait. Here he comes."

Craig appeared on the path, dressed in a ski jacket, his salt-and-pepper hair hidden under a woolen watch cap.

He headed toward them from the direction of incident command, lit by the glow of the Christmas light display. He wove quickly around others in the path to get to them. "Sorry. I was trying to get an update."

"What's going on?" Scott asked.

"The structural engineers are calling for a tactical pause. They have serious concerns about the standing structure. They've been monitoring its stability, and there was just what they consider a significant shift, so they wanted everyone off. Now that all work has stopped and the site is empty, they're checking it again to see how the building's stance has changed since Monday."

Meg pulled her collar closer to her jawline and bounced up and down on her toes a few times. The wind was picking up, the temperature was dropping, and the chill was making her cheeks ache. "Are they concerned it's going to fall? Is that why they called everyone off?"

"Yes."

Craig's curt response, lacking any embellishments, stopped them short.

"They're not being cautious," Brian said. "They think it's coming down."

"From what I understand," Craig said. "I think we're lucky no one's been killed."

"But it's seemed so stable." Lauren looked past Craig to where the standing structure was lit up in the twilight sky. "They've had crews in there several times. And I certainly haven't heard anything to make me think it was starting to lean."

"I bet if you hear something, it's already too late, and you won't be able to run fast enough," muttered Scott, but not quietly enough.

"That's the impression I got." Craig kept looking over to the incident command tent, as if he was expecting something.

"Are they going to make an announcement?" Meg asked. "Is that what you're waiting for?"

"That or more information." He turned back to the group. "Assistant Fire Chief Keenleyside may still be waiting on additional details. There's a team of structural engineers, and he wants consensus from them. But he's pissed."

Brian's eyebrows winged up in surprise. "At the engineers? Aren't they, like everyone else, doing the best they can under significant pressure?"

"No, not at the engineers. At himself. Though I'm not sure why. Keenleyside isn't clairvoyant, and as you said, the engineers are doing the best they can. The shift happened after a crane removed one of the larger slabs that overlapped into the exclusion zone. They wanted to get a drone over the area to check again for any sign of survivors. But when the crane pulled the slab off, things went to hell. It seems that ever since the collapse, the pile has been holding up the part of the building that's still standing."

"But . . ." Lauren's eyes were focused on Craig, horror in their depths. "But that means that every piece removed, every tunnel dug . . ."

"Brought it one step closer to falling on all of you, yes," Craig finished for her. "Every bucket of debris removed systematically weakened the structure's support."

The cold wind blowing into Meg's face had nothing on the chill that shot through her veins. She exchanged glances with Brian, saw the same thought in his eyes, but couldn't verbalize it.

Brian did it for her. "Yesterday Todd was in the tunnel they carved out of the pile, right near the shear wall."

"Which further compromised the stability of the pile," Craig confirmed. "They supported it to compensate for the weight of the pile, and it held. Is still holding. But as the standing structure leans farther . . ."

"There's no way it will be able to support that weight as well," Meg said. "Can they shore up the standing structure? Is that possible?"

"There's one other complicating piece of information." Craig's voice was flat, and Meg swore she heard defeat in his tone. "Have you seen the weather reports?"

"Gotta say, we've all probably been a bit too busy to catch them," Scott said.

"There's a nor'easter coming up the coast."

Meg suddenly remembered the newscaster from the previous morning, the one unsure of the direction of the storm's track. It sounded like that track was now set.

"This is way too early for something like that." Surprise laced Lauren's tone. "January would be a different story, but mid-December?"

"Welcome to climate change. Yes, it's early, but it's headed up the Eastern Seaboard, targeting DC tomorrow morning. Strong winds, freezing rain, heavy snow."

Lauren glanced up at the overcast sky that blocked any glimpse of stars. "If the engineers are worried about the pile shifting slightly and the whole thing coming down on its own, they must be terrified about what a winter storm would do."

"So much so, they're bringing it down tonight," Craig said. "They can't afford for the storm to bring it down and risk taking out the close-packed surrounding structures, like the Conrad, which could jack up the death rate."

The four handlers stared at him in shock.

Brian was the first to find his voice. "I mean, I know they were going to have to do that at some point, but tonight? Can they do it that fast?"

"That's the idea."

"They'll use explosives?" Scott asked. "Doesn't setting charges take planning and time?"

"The planning is already done. Incident command always knew there might come a time where they'd have to move fast to bring the rest of the building down, so they worked with the US Army Corps of Engineers to have a plan in place since day two. I don't think it will take much force to bring the building down, but there's definitely some skill involved in collapsing it into its own footprint, because otherwise the pile gets buried, and if there's anyone else alive left to find, we doom them forever. They also don't want to damage the surrounding buildings."

"When are they going to do this?" Meg asked.

"At 10:00 PM. They need time to bring in the explosives and to get in and set the charges. They'll also cover the existing debris pile with a large tarp to protect it during the implosion."

"It's safe to go inside the structure to set the charges?"

"Not really, but they know they have no choice. The building is coming down one way or another, and they'd like it to come down their way. The US Army Corps of Engineers will send in limited skilled personnel with explosives ready to be set at predetermined locations in order to take out individual columns in a specific order so that the building folds in on itself. While they do that, they'll have engineers actively monitoring the building, ready to give the order to get the hell out if needed. They're going to evacuate the surrounding buildings, in case things go sideways, but if all goes to plan, by ten thirty, everyone can go back to work on the pile."

"Minus the risk of the building falling on us."

Lauren's tone expressed the same relief Meg felt. After days of searching in the shadow of a building that could collapse at any moment, taking them with it, it would be an entirely different search once it was gone. And they'd be able to safely delve into the exclusion zone. Because of the temperatures, time was running out, but this might be just enough for a miracle.

"The surviving residents have been asking for days if someone could go in and retrieve some of their treasured belongings," Craig continued, "but this guarantees it won't happen. I feel bad for them when they've already lost so much."

"It's a good thing they ran the structure a second time on Tuesday to make sure there were no animals or people that were missed," Meg said. "It would be too dangerous to do that now."

"What can we do?" Scott asked, looking down at Theo, who sat at his side with his usual hangdog expression.

"I'm sending you all home. Nothing to do from now until the end of your shift. And when work picks up again after the demolition, it will be the B shift. Be here tomorrow, at 8:00 AM, to start again." When no one moved, Craig scanned their faces. "I know. I get it. But there's nothing else for you to do. Go home, get warm, and rest yourselves and your dogs. You've had an intense few days, and the break will do you good. Tomorrow is another day on the pile, and hopefully, we'll be able to get more done without the threat of the rest of the building hanging over you. At least until the storm really hits, likely closing the site temporarily."

The group broke up, and everyone headed to their vehicles, which were parked blocks away, out of the restricted zone.

Brian fell into step with Meg, their dogs between them. "I didn't get a chance to talk to you once you were back from the meeting at the Marriott. How did it go?"

The look she threw him wordlessly encapsulated the visit.

"That bad?"

"It wasn't good. I went with Cara and Saki, and Saki got right in there, doing her thing, because she instinctively knew people were hurting." She glanced sideways at Brian, met his gaze, knew she was safe being honest with him about the agony she'd witnessed. "It was awful. Hundreds of people there, every one of them in unbelievable pain, with some of that hurt and frustration running toward anger. They just feel so helpless. After they give a reference DNA sample, there's literally nothing they can do. And the waiting is unbearable."

Brian winced. "They know why they're giving the sample?"

"It was explained to them in black and white. Deputy Chief Weinberg is running the briefings and told them flat out that he's going to be brutally honest with them at all times. The only way for them to be assured they're getting the honest truth is if he never sugarcoats it for them. He told them today that most of what we're finding is human remains instead of intact victims. It was like they all took a body blow. Well, for most. There are a few that already know. You can see it in their eyes. They'll be there until it's official, but they already know their loved one is gone. They're the quiet ones, already lost in grief."

"I can't wrap my head around what they must be going through."

"You and me both. I think it's self-preservation for us not to be able to understand, because to truly understand would be agonizing." Meg looked over her shoulder, toward incident command, where first responders filled the streets as they were sent home to clear the site for the demolition. "I'm glad they're bringing the building down. We're running out of time. It's only a matter of days at most before they call it a recovery instead of a rescue, because anyone who survived the collapse won't survive the temperature."

"Then we'll be gone, and they'll send in the Victim Recovery Team."

"Yeah. I have a bad feeling that's coming quickly."

He rubbed her back in solidarity. "Then we do what we can as fast as possible. And we see if we can bring anyone else home."

CHAPTER 18

Implosion: A method of controlled demolition of a structure using strategically placed and timed explosives to ensure the structure collapses precisely into its own footprint.

Wednesday, December 19, 9:48 PM
Carnegie Library
Washington, DC

The Carnegie Library gleamed like a beacon in the dark night. Light shone through the wrought-iron grillwork in the arched windows and arrowed up in spears along the front facade of Vermont marble and Milford granite, causing the pale stone to glow. Wide, winter-dormant lawns stretched from the sidewalk to the building and alongside the stepped plaza leading to the southern entrance.

"Here should be good." Todd pushed through the gathering crowd to stop at the grassy edge of the sidewalk at the corner of K Street NW and 9th Street NW, Meg, McCord, and Cara following in his wake. He turned his back to the wind and pulled his knit fisherman's cap down more securely over his ears. "It's about as close as we're going to get. They're not going to let anyone past, not even those of us working the site, not until afterward." He pointed toward the intersection, devoid of traffic.

Twenty feet away, four Metro PD officers stood spread out along two police cars blocking 9th Street NW. They were dressed in heavy parkas, earflap hats, and thick gloves to ward off the cold wind. Past them, clearly visible beyond the triage, operations, planning, and logistics tents in the open parking lot, spotlit by industrial lighting, stood the debris pile and the standing structure just to the west.

Meg stepped closer to him, then pressed her shoulder to his, knowing they'd stay warmer if they stayed in contact. "No way. At this point, they have to be terrified someone might have snuck past them to get a better look."

"Or to try to get in one last time to get something out of the building. Well, maybe not now, with the demolition only about ten minutes away, but they were certainly pushing for it earlier."

Beside them, McCord put an arm around Cara and pulled her in against him, angling slightly so he blocked the wind with his body. "Surely no one's been allowed in there since Monday morning."

"No one but us," said Todd.

"You're certain nothing living is left in there?" McCord asked.

"Yes. No humans, no animals. Lots of precious possessions, though."

"You can understand the need to retain some of that," Cara said. "I'd be devastated if we lost everything and had no photos or family mementos. Even still, every foray into that building had to be dangerous."

"Especially after the structure shifted today," said Todd. "After that, no one was allowed in except the team of engineers who went in to set the charges. It was heavily guarded to begin with, more so after charges were placed."

"When did they clear the site?" McCord asked.

"At about five thirty," Meg said. "We were actively searching when they called it because they considered the building that unstable. They didn't want any more debris removed, because they thought that might be enough to topple it. They stopped all work and moved everyone blocks away. Once the building is down, though, they'll be on-site within a half hour. What a relief that will be."

"Being able to search without the building overhead?" Cara asked.

"Yes. We've had to maintain a zone of exclusion all along, so there are sections we've never been able to search. The teams on the night shift will start with those areas to see if anyone has been missed." Meg's cell phone rang. Clumsily, she pulled it out of her pocket with her gloved hands. Brian's face grinned up at her from the screen. She pulled off a glove with her teeth and swiped to accept the call, then jammed the phone between her shoulder and ear as she tugged her glove on. "Hey, where are you?"

"I was going to ask you the same thing," said Brian. "We're on the sidewalk at the bottom of the library's front walk, on the south side."

"You're not far, then. We're at the corner of 9th and K."

"Be right there." The line went dead.

Shivering, Meg jammed her phone in her pocket, then pulled her collar in tighter, hunching her shoulders against the cold. "They're just down the street." Her exhaled breath fanned out in a diaphanous cloud. "That leading cold front certainly moved in fast. The temp must have dropped twenty degrees since this morning."

"It sure feels like it," Todd said. "And they don't expect the storm until tomorrow morning. Come here." His gloved hands on her hips, he pulled her in so her back was against his chest as he blocked the wind with his larger frame. "Stay out of the wind."

"Thanks. I'd offer to be your windbreak, but I wouldn't block much of it for you, big guy." She threw up an arm, waved over her head. "There's Brian and Ryan."

"I'm impressed you can tell that's who it is," McCord said. "To me, we look like anonymous blobs in all this winter gear."

"You guys found a good spot," Brian said when he and his husband reached the group.

"Todd led the way," Meg said. "Even when he's out of his turnout gear, he still has that first responder intensity, and people sense they should get out of his way."

"Handy." Brian turned and looked down the street toward what was left of Talbot Terraces, staying quiet for a minute. "It's been only a few days, but I'm used to the pile with a hundred people on it. Now it looks so deserted and forlorn."

"It won't be for long," Todd said. "Not if they want everyone back to work about thirty minutes after the demolition. They'll let the worst of the dust settle, and then they'll be back at it."

"The families will be pleased." Cara tucked her scarf in closer to her throat. "They've been begging rescuers to search the exclusion zone."

"You've talked to the families?" Ryan asked.

"I've been here with Saki, trying to comfort the rescuers, and Meg and I went to the family reunification center this morning. Both groups are beyond stressed. The families because their loved ones are missing, and some of them mistakenly think the rescuers aren't doing enough, and the rescuers because they're working as hard and as long as humanly possible—truly backbreaking work too—and all they're finding right now is human remains."

Brian's grim expression spoke more clearly to that shared experience than words could. "I guess we're lucky we have our own built-in therapy dogs. We don't have to go looking for one."

Cara laid a gloved hand on his forearm and gave it an understanding squeeze. "That's a mixed blessing, and you know it. Because while you can lean on Lacey, it's more work for you to keep her spirits up when she gets discouraged."

"And she does," Meg said pointedly. "More so than Hawk. Don't think we can't see the extra work you're putting in there."

"He really is." Ryan affectionately shoulder-bumped Brian. "He comes home from an exhausting twelve-hour shift and then bathes and babies Lacey before I can get him to stop to eat a bite himself. He doesn't shut down until she does."

"I'm glad she's resting at home and isn't here now." Brian's gaze scanned the packed crowd. "Too many people. She might accidentally get hurt."

"And we can't help in the search if one of our dogs is injured," Meg said. "I thought there would be some people here, but I didn't think it would be this many."

"People are drawn in by tragedy," stated McCord. "It's why people rubberneck at traffic accidents. It's their survival instincts kicking in. They're wondering, 'Could that happen to me, and, if so, how could I come out of it alive?' "

"I think on top of it, people also feel for the families of the victims. They're showing support with the memorial up a block, at that church, but also here. It's not just the spectacle of it all."

Meg glanced at Todd, who remained quiet. His head was turned toward the disaster site; his eyes were fixed on the standing structure. He hadn't expressed why he'd wanted to come tonight, after a long day here already. She hadn't questioned him directly, and originally she'd had no plans to go herself when she could have followed along by watching any local or national newscast. However, when he'd said he was going to go, she hadn't hesitated to accompany him. He'd been her rock last night; she would be the same for him if he needed it. McCord had already planned to go as part of his continuing coverage for the *Post*, but once Cara had heard Meg was going, she'd agreed to tag along. They'd left their four dogs hanging out together in Cara's living room, by the Christmas tree, had dressed themselves to ward off the chill, and had headed downtown.

Meg had texted Brian to say they were going, and Brian had said he and Ryan would come as well. It was a matter of sticking together and supporting each other through everything at this point.

They were all here because Todd wanted to come. They were all going through enough that Meg hadn't wanted to pry; if he wanted to talk about it, he would, but so far, he hadn't, even after last night. After being together for more than a year and living together for six months, she understood how Todd ticked. Firefighters in general had to deal with a lot of crises. No one called 911 and asked for the fire department because everything in their lives was going smoothly. Everything involved loss. Loss of a home due to fire, a vehicle following an accident, a loved one following a medical call. The job was constant stress. And while firefighters were pragmatic people, they still felt the full brunt of the constant barrage of rage and sorrow that came their way.

Thus, Todd's strategy around the punching bag.

Todd wasn't a talker, but eventually, if something was really bothering him, he'd bring it up. He'd talked about the positive outcome of the single survivor from the garage but had been mostly silent about his experience inside the standing structure. Even though he'd ridden the high of the live find last night, Meg knew the other experiences had to be weighing on him once that high dissipated. On top of that, Todd didn't have his usual team structure for support. The DCFEMS firefighters were absolutely a team, but as opposed to the shift he worked with at the house, alongside men and women he'd come to trust with his life as well as his emotions, shifts at the Talbot Terraces site were made up of a mix of personnel from DCFEMS and different firefighter and USAR groups. She knew the end result could be feeling like you were working in isolation, even as you were surrounded by fellow rescuers.

Meg suspected those experiences, both inside the building and under it, needed to come full circle for Todd. Needed closure. He needed more than to just watch it on TV. He needed to see the building fall, to hear it, knowing he'd done everything he could, including putting his own life on the line for the victims, alive and dead, as well as their families. She knew he'd done everything. The courage it must have required to climb into the pile, knowing it could end his life at any second, was immense. She knew it, even if he hadn't discussed that aspect of the operation.

Craning her neck, she looked back at him, her nearly six-foot frame putting her close to his own height, so they were almost eye to eye. "You okay?" She kept her voice a little low as her best shot at a private moment in this undulating crowd.

His gaze broke from the building and shifted to her. "Yeah." He started to look away, but she shifted against him, drawing his gaze down. When she simply stared at him in silence, eyebrows raised, he said, "Mostly."

"You might feel a little steadier if you talked about it

some. Trust me, I know. Last night you watched what can happen when you don't talk about it."

"Yeah, maybe. I feel like I'm still processing. I just . . ." He stopped, considered his words. "Want to see this through. I was there at the beginning; I feel like I need to be there at the end, you know?"

Her gloved hand closed over his where it still rested against her hip. "Yeah, I know."

Two loud alarm blasts filled the air.

"That's the five-minute warning," Todd said for the group.

Around them, the crowd seemed to pack in tighter, as if everyone was leaning forward in anticipation. The noise level lowered, the throng talking in hushed tones now, with long glances in the direction of the disaster site. About half of the people held their cell phones, ready to capture the final collapse of Talbot Terraces. Meg couldn't imagine wanting to capture the footage for her own use, because she knew already it wouldn't be anything she'd want to revisit. And if, for some strange reason, she ever wanted to, she knew this was being covered by many different news organizations from multiple angles, from the street to surrounding rooftops, to the Conrad's south-facing suites.

At 9:59 PM three alarm blasts sounded, and the crowd became nearly silent.

Meg still stood in front of Todd, her gaze fixed on the building. Her heart was pounding so hard, she was sure he could feel it through the layers of their coats. She knew it was silly—there was no danger here for her or for those she considered family, either by blood or by bond, who surrounded her. But still, the anticipation was palpable. She could see it, too, in Brian, who stood with his weight on one leg as he bounced his other heel.

She jumped at the first explosive boom, which was

quickly followed by others in sequence. A fraction of a second pause and then another series of booms as the building seemed to shudder. The north end of the structure dipped and then collapsed straight down, and the rest of the building followed it, with a roar so earsplitting that even a full block away, Meg found herself shrinking back into Todd. As the building broke apart, some of the shattered windows caught and reflected the light in brilliant, transient sparkles, before the whole structure dropped into a massive cloud of pulverized dust and debris. Meg knew as long as she lived, she'd never forget the rumble and shudder beneath her feet as millions of pounds of concrete and steel crashed to the ground, and the way the thunder of the collapse echoed back to them from the glass, steel, and concrete facades of every building for blocks.

In the background, camera shutters clicked as photographers attempted to capture the sheer speed of the collapse in a series of still images.

Then it was quiet, with the spotlights shining on billows of dust as they rose into the air and spread out across the disaster site.

"That's it, then," Cara breathed.

"At least for the structure," Meg said. "Now we need to wait for the dust cloud to settle. As long as the storm hasn't already hit hard, we're on duty at eight tomorrow morning, and we'll keep going until the weather makes it too dangerous to keep working."

"I can't help feeling we've closed a chapter tonight," Brian said. "The story isn't over, but we're moving on."

"You think they're going to move to recovery soon?" asked McCord.

"I think so. Then it will be out with the live find dogs, in with the cadaver dogs. We'll have to see how fast they make that transition. It's coming. You can feel it. No live finds since the second day, and that one was a miracle. There just aren't the spaces we need to support life." Meg stepped away from Todd, then turned to face him. "Seen enough?"

"Yeah."

"Let's head out as soon as we can get out of this crowd." Meg tossed a last glance at the heavy cloud that hung suspended over the now larger debris pile. "We'll be back soon enough."

CHAPTER 19

Punching Shear: The rapid failure of the connection point between a reinforced column and a slab, caused by concentrated local loads. As a result, the connection shears, and the column punches, or breaks through, the slab, leading to its collapse.

Thursday, December 20, 9:12 AM
The Washington Post
Washington, DC

"Hey, McCord."

McCord dragged his eyes away from the article he was reading on his monitor to the woman who stood outside his cubicle, holding a half-empty coffee cup. She was dressed casually in faded jeans, a mauve kangaroo-pocket hoodie, and red high-top sneakers. She wore her too-bright-to-be-natural red hair pulled up into a messy bun, with a pencil sticking out. He was willing to bet she'd jammed it there when her hands were full and forgotten all about it.

It was Cynthia Redmond, another investigative reporter with the *Post*. He hadn't worked with her often, but when he had, he'd found her smart, intuitive, and driven. "Hey, Cynthia."

"Got a minute?"

"I'm trying to do some work before I pack up to get home before that storm really gets going. Freezing rain so far, and it's going to get worse. But yeah, I can make some time." He grabbed his coffee cup and raised it halfway to his mouth before he realized it was empty. "Walk and talk?"

"You bet. I could use a refresh."

McCord led the way through the maze of bullpen cubicles toward the narrow galley kitchenette on the far side of the floor. He gave a silent word of thanks when he saw the coffeepot still had enough in it that he wouldn't have to make a fresh pot. That task would fall to the next unlucky soul who came for coffee. He poured coffee for himself, then topped up hers. "What's up?"

"I think I've learned something odd that could impact the story you're writing about Talbot Terraces."

McCord froze momentarily as he was about to set his mug down on the counter, then continued the motion. "Define *odd*."

"Something I'd consider unbelievable, but what do I know?" Cynthia added cream and sugar to her coffee and then leaned against the opposite countertop. "I hear you're looking at why the building came down."

"I've been trying to figure out what happened. If it wasn't a structural accident, could it have been sabotage or terrorism? If so, I feel like I'm getting nowhere on a motive. I've reviewed the list of residents and those who died or are still missing, and I can't substantiate any reason for anyone to bring down the building to get at one particular person."

"What if a person isn't the target? What if it's the building itself?"

McCord crossed his arms over his chest and stared at

her, as if he could divine her meaning if he focused on her long enough. "Come again?"

"I think the building was the target."

"The building . . . Why would the building be the target? Surely not for the insurance, because the first person or group the insurance company is going to look at— hard—is the beneficiary."

"No, not for the insurance. I actually wasn't looking for anything having to do with Talbot Terraces. I just stumbled over it and then thought you'd be interested because you're on the collapse investigation. I'm currently working on a story about conspiracy theories. What they are, how the initial story moves, how it gets embellished, and why some people consider it God's own truth. I've been looking at a bunch of different stories that are going around. And one of them involved Talbot Terraces."

"In what way?"

"You know our immigration system is screwed up to the point where it sometimes feels like no one is winning. Not us, not the immigrants. Definitely not anyone trying to apply for asylum."

"Not my usual beat, but yeah."

"Some people feel with the drop in the birth rate, we're going to need immigration to keep all our jobs filled. Others think immigrants are coming into the country exclusively to steal our jobs."

"I've seen both sides of that argument take essentially the same data set and use it to fit their established beliefs."

"Me too. Now, there are some people who think foreigners are being smuggled into the country to make an end run around that system."

"With what proof?"

"Stop thinking like a logical newsman," Cynthia said, with an index finger scold. "The people who believe some of these stories do so blindly. They don't need proof. What they need is outrage. Rile someone up, get the outrage machine going, especially using social media, and some people will believe whatever story you tell them that feeds into their worldview.

"In this case, the story is that, borrowing from the Civil War, there's a new, modern Underground Railroad. But instead of transporting black people to the northern states or to Canada, this one is transporting immigrants into the United States. The point of the railroad is to get these American citizen hopefuls away from the border states, which have the facilities to deal with illegal aliens, and move them deep into the center of the Lower Forty-Eight, where they can disappear. And like the Underground Railroad did in the Civil War, this new one has stops where immigrants can stay for a cooling-off period, wait for fake papers to be created, that sort of thing. The conspiracy theory points to Talbot Terraces as one of those stops."

"Define *stops*. Like, they get food and water and move on, or they live there, waiting for any search for them to cool off?"

"The latter."

"That's ridiculous. The building was at capacity, with owners who overwhelmingly lived in their own condos as residents. I can tell you from everything that's been made public by the building owner, the condo association, and word filtering through from the families, most of the people who lived there owned those apartments. Sure, there were a few that were rentals, but that was *not* the majority of the apartments. Not to mention this is a luxury building. If this railroad was actually real, no one would pick an expensive luxury building to use as a halfway house. The theory just doesn't make sense."

"But that's the thing. Inside the echo chamber, it doesn't have to make sense. For whatever reason, these people believe it."

"What's the theory, then? That they brought down the building to take out that stop on the railroad?"

Cynthia shrugged. "I don't have a theory, but it struck me that someone should know about this other than just me. And, you know . . . you have those contacts . . ."

"You mean Meg Jennings and Craig Beaumont at the FBI?"

"Well, yeah. I know Metro PD started off with this case, but if the building was brought down by explosives, then it's domestic terrorism. And that's FBI jurisdiction."

McCord covered his thinking time as he drank more coffee, then swirled the dark liquid in his mug, trying to work out this new angle in his head. "It makes zero sense to me logically, but putting that aside, it's the first thing I've heard for why anyone would want to hit the whole building that tells a complete story. I thought about the insurance angle, but if the person responsible was going to get a payout, they'd have to find a way to guarantee they wouldn't get caught, otherwise there'd be prison time instead. It's way too big a risk and too high a death toll just for cash, no matter how greedy people are. But something they'd consider a moral reason . . . that's something people could get behind and act on, even at risk to themselves. And while we might not agree with the reason, the be-all and end-all is people will take risks, like putting their own lives on the line to help perfect strangers. Or to stop something they consider harmful to others."

"Extreme altruism, you mean. Like when a guy is walking his dog, sees a house on fire, and runs in to rescue the family."

"But with a spin, if that's what we're looking at here. An individual or group who was so invested in a cause to save one particular faction, they sacrificed another entirely. So, what group or individual are we looking at here?"

"I can't say they were responsible, but the group talking

about it calls itself the Brotherhood of Libertas. Libertas, which is Latin for *freedom*."

"What do you know about them?"

"Almost nothing. That's the problem. I've just scratched the surface on this one, but considering the location they discussed, I felt I needed to bring it to you right away. Finding out more about them is going to take some serious time. These are the kind of folks who hang out on the dark web, and they're incredibly suspicious of anyone new to them, in case it's law enforcement. Often, anyone new to them needs to know someone already in the group in real life who can vouch for them, or at least needs to have an established identity on the dark web in similar groups. Not to say sometimes law enforcement doesn't get in, anyway, but it's less often. Their constant suspicion works to keep them safe."

"Which means it's going to be a lot harder to find out anything about them." McCord drained his mug and then raised it to Cynthia with a nod of thanks. "I appreciate the intel. I'm going to try to run with it, if that's okay."

"That's my intent. It's a small part of my story. It could be your entire story. What are you going to do?"

"Not sure yet." McCord walked to the sink, rinsed his mug, upended it, and shook most of the water out. "I'm going to grab my stuff and head home to work from there before the storm really hits. Supposed to be a doozy—sudden temperature drop, flash freeze, blizzard conditions."

"It's a good thing they brought that building down last night. Did you see it?"

McCord recalled the brief flash of cold white spotlights on glass and concrete as the building crumbled. "I was there."

"You went down? Wasn't it a zoo? Just a bunch of people rubbernecking?"

"It was a zoo, and yes, there was the rubbernecking

component, but it wasn't just that." He could still hear the quiet words of the stranger standing beside him, intended only for her God's ears. *Eternal rest grant unto them, O Lord, and let perpetual light shine upon them. May they rest in peace. Amen.* "Some were there to stand for the dead. Some of the first responders were there to see this stage of the rescue and recovery through. It wasn't all for the thrill of a building demolition." He pushed off the counter. "Thanks again, Cynthia. Get yourself home and out of the elements before it gets kicking out there."

"Will do. Later, McCord."

McCord strode back to his cubicle, saved his document to the network drive where he could access it from home, and shut down his desktop computer in case of power blips. Then he gathered everything he needed into his laptop bag, shrugged into his jacket, and headed out.

Still, he couldn't stop thinking about the kind of mind who would find killing possibly hundreds of your own countrymen and destroying hundreds of millions of dollars in property an acceptable exchange for keeping foreigners out of your country. Surely that wasn't possible.

Nevertheless, something in McCord—something that grew with each step down the hallway—said it could be.

CHAPTER 20

Hidden Beam: An additional construct of reinforced steel, hidden within the rebar mats of a slab so as not to expand its depth, that acts to increase the total load resistance of the structural element.

Thursday, December 20, 10:37 AM
Jennings/Webb residence
Washington, DC

McCord practically blew through the doorway on a flurry of snow as he stepped into Meg's foyer.

Cody shot through the door and was poised to bullet down the hallway, but Cara's single-word command of "Mat!" had him glumly plopping to sit on the front mat as Cara, Blink, and Saki followed him in before McCord shut the door.

Meg waited for them in the front hallway, a towel already in hand, and she bent down to wipe the snow from Cody's paws. "There you go, buddy. Go find Hawk." Before Meg could turn to Saki, Cody was gone. She glanced up at McCord, who rolled his eyes. "Does he ever slow down?"

"Almost never." McCord unlaced his boots and stepped

out of them. "But at least he's a better listener now." He slipped out of his jacket and shook the snow out over the front mat. "Mudroom?"

"Yes, please. Okay, Saki, you're done. Blink, honey, come here."

With the dogs dry and the winter gear left in the mudroom, they gathered around the Christmas tree and the blazing fire Todd had built in the fireplace.

Cara sat down in the armchair. "It's absolutely miserable out there."

"The freezing rain has turned to snow, and it's really starting to blow." McCord dropped into Meg's recliner. "They cleared the site and sent you home?"

"They never brought on the A shift," Meg said from the kitchen. She set mugs of coffee, cream, and sugar on a tray with a plate of Christmas cookies. "Todd, Hawk, and I were getting ready to head to the site when Craig called and said to stay home. Todd got a text to the same effect a few minutes later. The storm was coming in, and they were already getting freezing rain. One of the B shift crew had a fall about a half hour before shift change because of the degrading conditions and was taken to the hospital with minor injuries. The powers that be decided it was too dangerous to have anyone on the pile under icy conditions like that, so when the B shift ended at 8:00 AM, they closed the site down." She carried the tray to the coffee table. "Help yourselves."

Cara leaned forward to add cream and sugar to one of the mugs. "Where's Todd?"

"Upstairs still." Meg sat down on the couch. "He was calling George Washington University Hospital for an update on Kevin Vaughn."

Cara settled into her chair with her coffee, wrapping both hands around her mug for warmth. "They'll tell him that?"

"Kevin himself will. Incident command passed his extension on to Todd, figuring they owed him that much. He tried to make contact with Kevin last night, before we came out for the demolition, but he was in surgery." A noise in the hallway drew her eyes to the kitchen doorway, and Todd walked through in jeans and a red-plaid flannel shirt. "Did you make contact this time?"

"Yes. He's doing okay. I'm reading between the lines a bit from what he told me, but it sounds like they confirmed a Grade 3 concussion. The ulna was broken twice in a closed, segmental fracture, and the radius once. They used surgical plates and screws to stabilize the breaks. Two of his lower ribs are fractured, and then there's the multitude of bruises and contusions. But no internal bleeding, and while he was hypothermic and dehydrated, they got him stabilized with warm saline and heated blankets."

"That man is unbelievably lucky," said McCord. "He was standing in the right place at that exact moment, fell into a perfect three-dimensional placement of rubble, was attuned to the sound level of the pile, and was able to signal when it was quiet and then actually be heard. That wouldn't have happened without all that specialized equipment."

"Without a doubt," Meg agreed. "The dogs' hearing beats ours hands down, but even they wouldn't have been able to pick that up. He's also lucky he was relatively accessible, toward the outside of the pile and not smack in the middle of it."

Todd snagged a coffee and sat down on the couch beside Meg. "The people who were trapped in the middle of the building are the ones they're finding now while digging the firebreak. In that area, there are no voids, at least none big enough to support life. Kevin's advantage was to fall near the shear wall. Though our tunneling next to it likely helped weaken the standing structure."

"There was no way to know that at the time," Meg said. "But when I think of what could have happened . . ."

Todd dropped his hand over hers and squeezed. "It didn't. To any of us, as it turns out, and all of us could have been killed. From those in the building to those in the garage, to those on the pile. Did you hear about any recoveries last night?"

"Craig says they pulled out five more bodies from the exclusion zone last night and found more remains."

"What are the chances anyone is still alive in there?" Cara asked.

Meg and Todd exchanged glances, and then she extended an open palm to him. *You take this one.*

"Approaching zero, would be my guess." Todd paused for a sip of coffee. "And after this storm . . . The human body can survive for only so long as the temperature drops. With these sustained temps, if there's anyone left, I'm afraid they're not going to survive." He met Meg's eyes. "Do you agree?"

"Yes." She looked over to where Hawk played with a red rubber figure-eight toy near the tree as Cody tried to catch one end of it to join in a tug-of-war. "I think finding Kevin was a miracle. Take him out of the equation, and we haven't recovered anyone alive since about eight hours post-collapse. Everyone pulled out alive on that first day was at the edge of the collapse, with relatively little weight above them, was in the top sections of the pile, or was in a car, again near the edge of the rubble that flowed out into the street. No one on foot on the street survived. As the heavy equipment removed the edges of the pile on the street, and the farther in they went, the worse it was. No one survived the initial collapse.

"I think that's going to be the overall story. People haven't died waiting for us. They never survived the first minutes of the event. The video shows the building collapsed from the bottom, with each floor crashing down on top of the one below it, to then have another layer crash down on it. We're lucky if we're finding voids of more than just a few inches."

Her gaze rose to the Christmas tree, festively decorated with bright ornaments and shining lights. "There's going to be some devastated families this holiday season. With multiple empty chairs at the table for some." She turned her hand over, linked fingers with Todd. "It's kind of a reminder of how fast things can turn and never be the same again. And to appreciate what you have while you have it." She smiled as Todd raised their joined hands to his lips and kissed the back of her hand.

"Those families yesterday, at the reunification center . . . It was heartbreaking." Cara dropped a hand down to Saki, where she sat beside Cara's chair, and stroked her head softly. "Saki was great. And really helpful to a bunch of people who were seriously hurting. The whole situation, it's agony for them. Honestly, I think those who were informed about a death early will have it easier. For them, it's over. They have closure. They aren't waiting, their lives suspended, not knowing and unable to move forward. For those sitting in that room twice a day, waiting for any kind of news, it's agony now and will almost certainly be agony later. At least those who already have closure can start the process of coming to grips with their new reality. Their only question now is why it happened."

Knowing McCord was working this story from a multitude of different angles, Meg turned to him, only to find his distracted gaze focused on the fire as the fingers of his left hand ran restless circles over the edge of the recliner arm. After working so many cases with McCord, she was familiar with his many moods. When he became totally distracted, chances were excellent he wasn't paying attention because his brain was moving a mile a minute, worrying away at a story lead. "That's a good question, isn't it, McCord?"

Three beats of silence passed.

"McCord?"

McCord's head jerked toward Meg. "What?" He had the grace to look sheepish. "Sorry. Woolgathering."

"Must be some pretty interesting wool. What's on your mind?"

"One of my colleagues came to me with a story angle today."

"About the collapse?" Todd asked.

"Not directly. But about the building. She's working on a story about conspiracy theories. In her research, she learned about a theory that includes Talbot Terraces. Which seems suspicious to me."

"What do you mean?"

"We keep hearing about conspiracy theories, many because they're so damn unbelievable. But really, how many are there? The big ones make the news when some violence stems from one of them, but are there really that many that take hold and spread nationwide? That capture the passion of those who believe this kind of stuff? A couple dozen? So, when she brought me this story about Talbot Terraces, something clicked for me. I'd spent days trying to figure out if this could have been done on purpose. Then through publicly available sources, I learned about the weaknesses in the structure from shortcuts taken during construction, which I told you about yesterday. And now this." McCord turned to face Todd. "You found what could be a bomb component, which led TEDAC to investigate."

"Wait," Cara said. "TEDAC? I feel like I should know what that is."

"The Terrorist Explosive Device Analytical Center," said Meg. "They're the scientific arm of any IED investigations in the country. It's run by the FBI and the ATF but uses people from the Departments of Defense and Justice, as well as intelligence organizations. When you need support for explosives evidence, they're the people to call, so we did. They came right away. Top-notch lab too. If anyone can get us answers, they can."

"Do you know how TEDAC's investigation is coming along?" asked McCord.

"I don't. But I can ask Craig for an update. I know it's early—the investigation has barely started—but they're going to be pushing hard. They'll have experts looking at the materials and the lab types running chemical profiles on any residue they found." She pulled her phone out of her pocket. "Let's find out." She zipped off a quick text to Craig. "Keep going. I'll interrupt when I have something."

"Sure. This is the story she came to me with." McCord went through the story about the modern Underground Railroad and smuggled immigrants.

"It seems pretty far-fetched to me," said Meg when McCord finished outlining what he knew. "Why would anyone believe that?"

"That's because you're a logical person who seeks verification," said Todd. "Not everyone is like that. One of the guys in the firehouse, for instance, this is the kind of thing he might buy into. Terry O'Dwyer."

It was a name Meg recognized. A man she'd met only briefly, who'd seemed pleasant, but she knew he'd been problematic to the department a few times in his dealings with the city's residents. "Ah."

"O'Dwyer tends to fall for conspiracy theories like this, without looking for much in the way of verification. Especially if the story comes from someone he trusts and involves the government. He has his friends he follows on social media, and if it comes to him that way, he might consider it the absolute truth."

"But would he do anything with the information?" McCord asked. "That's the other wrinkle. They would need not only to believe the story but then to act on it. And have the skills and access to explosives."

"I've worked with O'Dwyer for years. I find it hard to believe he'd do something like this. He also doesn't have the technical skills. On top of that, and this is just my gut reaction, he was in my crew right after the collapse, when we were the first units on scene and first in the building. I saw the faces of my crew, and there was shock and disbelief on every one of them. He's been there daily, and I've seen his rage and sorrow. He may have some far-out ideas about things and is likely in the 'I did my own research' crowd, but he's not a bad person. He's definitely not this kind of bad person."

"It blows my mind that anyone would be so convinced by this story they'd bring down a building, with no concern for the lives inside." When McCord sighed, Meg said, "What? Does it all seem so obvious to you?"

"Not at all. But there are those who are sucked in by social media and network opinion bubbles that only reinforce an existing confirmation bias. No, my problem is that since Cynthia has brought this up, it's been gnawing at me."

"I knew something was bothering you." Cara's raised eyebrows said she expected him to spill. "I was waiting for you to finish working it out in your head before I poked at you."

The smile McCord gave her was one of gratitude. "You know me so well. And know what I need."

"You're lucky to have me," she said, with a wide grin. "Now can I poke at you?"

"You don't have to poke. It's just all this talk about baseless conspiracy theories, and the idea that this one theory might have possibly killed a hundred or so people, makes me look at those of us in the journalism field. I know some of the development of these theories is because of us. It could be one of us talking about a theory on national air as if it were fact. It could be that so many of us want the news to be balanced in a time of political division, so we give air to both sides, and that can include this kind of information, again giving it weight, as if it were real."

"But you don't do that," protested Cara.

"No, you don't," Meg agreed. "Maybe I didn't catch every story you wrote before I met you, though I know I read some of your pieces. But since getting to know you, I've read them all. Sometimes, I admit, to see how you portray the Human Scent Evidence Team." She raised a hand before he could speak. "And you've always been fair; I have no complaints. Though I still wish your photographer hadn't caught me and Hawk after the Whitten Building bombing, but that's not on you. You always center every story around the truth as you uncover it, and it doesn't matter what side it reflects, if there is one, because you're just telling what happened. How others read your story and what they take from it isn't on you."

McCord nodded and drank more coffee before setting the mug down on an end table. "I know that logically, but part of me still feels some responsibility, because it's my profession as a whole that isn't handling this stuff as well as it could. And maybe the real issue there is that we don't have enough information on the details of this kind of story—who started talking about it, where their information came from, whether there are any actual witnesses, et cetera, et cetera—to debunk it."

"Do you have enough information from your colleague to dive into this?"

"No. I have what I told you."

"Where can you find more on this stuff?" Todd asked. "The dark web?"

"No doubt, but I don't have the background for that. What I need is someone who knows their way around the Internet, especially the dark corners. Someone experienced with online groups, preferably hate groups, and who knows how to camouflage himself so he's not an instant giveaway as a plant. Someone . . ." McCord trailed off, still staring at Todd.

Todd returned a questioning look. "Someone . . . ," he prompted.

"Give me a second." McCord pulled his phone out of his pocket and started scrolling through his contacts. "I just thought of something. Or, rather, someone."

"You know someone familiar with the dark web?"

"Maybe. I went to college with this guy. Rob Tucker. He should have been years behind me in school, but he was this supersmart, super-techy guy who just blew through school. This guy has the kind of smarts where you have to reel him back in a conversation because he's ten steps ahead of you, so far ahead that you can't see the path he took to get there. I'd have to do that, and I don't consider myself stupid."

"And he hangs out on the dark web?"

"I have no idea, but the guy is a computer geek through and through. Last I heard, he was working in the Computer Forensics Unit of the Massachusetts State Police in Essex County. I'd bet, in his job, this is the kind of thing he needs to be familiar with, and he possibly dips his toe into that world now and then." He stopped scrolling. "And there he is." He drummed his fingers on the arm of the recliner, his lips pursed and brow furrowed in thought.

"You want to call him?" Cara asked. "And you have his number?"

"I'm seriously thinking about it. And as long as it's still the same cell number as before, then, yeah, I have it. I mean, mine hasn't changed, and most people keep the same number for decades. It's worth a shot. Now, he may be busy and might not have time to give us a hand."

"Which you won't know unless you ask," Todd pointed out. "Do it. What do you have to lose? Worst he'll say is no. Unless he has direct ties to the Brotherhood of Libertas and is going to sell you down the river, there's no downside."

"No, there isn't." Solid certainty backed McCord's tone now. "Let's give it a try." He dialed the number from his contacts list and put the phone on speaker.

The phone rang three times before a distracted voice came on the line. "Tucker."

"Tucker, hey. It's Clay McCord calling."

There was a second of hesitation; then the voice came back with considerably more enthusiasm. "McCord, man, how you been?"

"I've been good. You?"

"Can't complain. You still slogging away at the *Post*?"

McCord chuckled. "Some days it definitely feels like that. Yeah, I am. And that's actually why I'm reaching out to you. I'm looking for a little help with a story. You still working for the Massachusetts State Police?"

"You bet."

"You still . . ." McCord paused, weighing his words, then deciding to go for it. "Walking that thin line when it comes to hacking?"

A snicker came down the line. "You know too much about my past, McCord. Why are you asking?"

Meg sent McCord a raised-eyebrow pointed look. Everyone in the room had noted that Tucker didn't answer the question.

"I'm going to be straight with you, Tucker. Because I need help. Your kind of help."

A few seconds of silence, then, "Go on."

"I'm working on a story about the Talbot Terraces collapse in downtown DC. I'm sure you've heard about it on the coast?"

"Yeah. Awful."

"It is. I'm neck-deep in it by proxy as well. My sister-in-law is an FBI K-9 handler, and she's been out on the pile since the morning of the collapse, looking for survivors. My brother-in-law is DCFEMS and spent the first day inside the standing structure, rescuing those who were trapped."

"Christ. I can't imagine."

"It's a nightmare. My angle on it has been investigating what happened."

"I'm hearing explosive components were found."

Really? Meg mouthed to McCord, who glared back. She mimed zipping her lips and throwing the key over her shoulder.

"That's interesting," McCord said. "That's supposed to be kept quiet while the investigation is ongoing, because the evidence is unsubstantiated."

"That's the kind of information that moves like wildfire through law enforcement ranks and divisions. You'll note the story still isn't out though. We know to keep our mouths shut. So . . . you got something concerning the explosive?"

"Not yet, but I have a potential story about why that could help my investigation But I can't convincingly go where the story takes me."

"And that is . . . ?"

"The dark web."

"Ah . . ." The glee in Tucker's voice was unmistakable. "And that's why you came to me."

"Yeah. I knew this wasn't the job for me. I wouldn't be able to pull it off with the kind of confidence that would open doors. Honestly, I wouldn't know where to go. And I know we haven't been in contact much over the past few years, but when it came to something like this . . ."

"You need the Wizard. I hear you. Fill me in."

McCord sat back, grinning and shaking his head with amusement, which Meg took to mean this was the Tucker McCord had been expecting.

"A colleague came to me with some information she'd learned while doing a story about conspiracy theories." McCord did a quick rundown of the theory. "You got all that?"

"Sure do. Any ideas around who's involved?"

"A group called the Brotherhood of Libertas."

Silence for a moment, then a curse.

McCord went stiff in the recliner. "What? You know them?"

"Oh yeah, I know them."

"You sound alarmed. Why don't I know them if you sound alarmed?"

"Because this is what they do. They move around in the shadows. They aren't involved in rallies or protest marches. They stay on the down-low, off the grid, so to speak, so people don't know what they're about."

"Would they be promoting a theory like this?"

"Promoting and acting on something like this is right up their alley."

"Damn. Is this something you could help us with? Can you find a way into that world?"

Tucker's laugh was full of confidence. "Don't need to find a way in, as I'm already there. You can't just drop in on these types of people when something big happens. They'll be instantly suspicious. You have to be there already, have a reputation, be a known commodity, and then you can make headway."

"And you're already that known commodity?"

"I am. Because the dark web is often one of our best ways to know when something horrific is coming down the pike, I keep a hand in. I have a persona, and I hacked a bunch of records to insert myself into events. Plus, I have a record with the Massachusetts State Police, which comes in handy for street cred."

"All of which is false."

"The whole ID is false. But that's who they believe I am."

"And you didn't hear anything about this attack ahead of time?"

"No, but the dark web is a big place, with millions of active users. You try to keep your ear to the ground, but it's impossible to police everything all the time."

"Understandable. Knowing all this, though, could you nose around? See if the Brotherhood of Libertas has anything to do with Talbot Terraces? Because—let's lay it out—if they had no trouble leveling a building and possibly killing a hundred or so people, and it looks like they got away with it, they won't hesitate to do it again. No Underground Railroad has only one stop."

"Leave it with me. I have some time today, before the Pats play tonight. I'll do some nosing around."

"Still following the Patriots, huh?"

"To my dying breath."

"Then I appreciate you fitting me in around their schedule. Next time I'm in the Boston area, I owe you a drink."

"I'll take you up on that. Give me a day or two and I'll call you back. That work for you?"

"Absolutely."

"Later then." And Tucker was gone.

McCord dropped his phone into his lap. "That sounds promising, as a start at least."

"He sounds like a character," Cara commented. "The 'Wizard'?"

"It was his college nickname. There wasn't anything Tucker couldn't do with a computer, no site he couldn't hack into. I think as a country, we're lucky he turned that devious brain of his to law enforcement instead of crime, or law enforcement as a whole would have a serious problem on their hands."

Meg's cell phone dinged, and she picked it up, then read the screen. "It's Craig." She looked up to meet McCord's eyes. "There's a meeting being called for tomorrow about the explosives investigation. He wants us to take part and will update as to the time when it gets worked out. It sounds like it's going to be multi-departmental, so my guess is they've found something definitive."

"You'll keep me in the loop?" McCord asked.

"As always."

It would be good to finally have something proactive to work on. It might not be anything that would involve the dogs, but Meg would be happy to pass the baton to the investigative team to get them off and running. As it was, she had a feeling that she and Hawk were about to hand off to the Victim Recovery Team once the site was deemed a recovery instead of a rescue operation.

If moving forward meant admitting there was no one left alive to find, then she would be more than happy to focus on the need for justice. Someone was responsible, and she was determined they'd pay for what they'd done.

CHAPTER 21

Structural Elements: Load-bearing components of a building, including beams, columns, walls, floors, the foundation, and the roof.

Friday, December 21, 9:25 am
Fourth-floor conference room, J. Edgar Hoover Building
Washington, DC

"This feels wrong." Brian pulled out one of the chairs around the long rectangular table, beside a line of dark-suited agents clustered around the end. "We should be out there. Our dogs aren't useless yet." He sat down and pulled himself up to the table. "Lacey, down." He pointed at the wall behind his chair.

Meg took the chair beside him, then glanced behind her to see Hawk lying down against the wall next to Lacey, so they were nose to nose, before she needed to give the command. "Good boy, Hawk." She swiveled forward to face the table. "And I agree. I know they announced this morning they've moved from a rescue to a recovery, but honestly, they could have kept us."

"Especially Lacey and Hawk. They trained only a few months ago on decomposing human remains for the water searches. They're familiar with it. Maybe Rocco and Theo aren't, but these two are. They called it because of no more chance of survival due to the cold weather, but because of those temps, how much decomp is going on? The victims might still smell mostly like live finds."

"Agreed. It's not like we're working in the summer heat. I texted Craig after he let us know about the change in operation, and I recommended he send Hawk and Lacey out at the very least, if not all of us. We're not otherwise deployed. Why not use us? We know the chances of us finding anyone alive is approaching zero, but is it *truly* zero?"

"Especially when the option is sitting in the office, waiting for the next deployment. I'd rather be out helping." Brian looked down at Lacey. "Though I know it's rough on my Lacey-girl. She takes it so hard when there aren't live vics to find. Still, I'd rather hide one of the firefighters in the pile to keep her going than take her out of the equation."

"I hear you."

The door to the conference room opened, and three more agents entered, followed by a tall man, with short dark hair and a lean, athletic build, who wore khaki cargo pants and a black Henley, a German shepherd at his side. Greg Patrick, a member of the Forensic Canine Unit's Explosives Detection Program, had been an army explosive ordnance disposal specialist before his honorable discharge at the end of two tours of duty. Using his existing skills, he'd pivoted to training dogs to detect the explosives he was so familiar with. Ryder was his current K-9 partner.

Greg raised a hand to Brian and Meg in greeting before pulling out a chair across from them on the far side of the table. "Morning."

"Morning." Meg returned the gesture. "I see lots of agents from the Critical Incident Response Group, but are we expecting someone from TEDAC too?"

"Not from TEDAC itself, but we have their lab results so far. SSA Mona Byrne from the Critical Incident Response Group is coming up to share them with us."

"That's an impressive turnaround at the lab."

"To say those samples got kicked way up to the top of the list is an understatement. Mona rode the lab to make sure they stayed there too. I like Mona—she's efficient and doesn't stand for anyone else's inefficiency. Lots of suits here already. Who else are we expecting from our group?"

"Craig is coming, along with Lauren and Scott."

Craig came in at that moment, followed by Lauren, Scott, and their dogs. He stopped behind Greg's chair and looked across the table to Meg and Brian. "I talked to incident command today, and they're happy to have you all on the pile, joining the Victim Recovery Team, as long as you're not needed for another deployment."

Relief flowed through Meg, reinforcing in her own mind how invested she was, though she suspected they wouldn't find anyone else alive, which she knew would be hard on them. It was crucial to bring all the victims home; their families deserved nothing less. "Thank you. We'll head back after this meeting."

Within a few minutes, every chair around the table was taken, and a few more agents stood, their backs against the walls.

Mona Byrne sat beside Greg, a brown file folder on the table in front of her. She had a fine bone structure, and her sandy hair was cut short to wisp around her face. The black pantsuit she wore over her slender frame was pure no-nonsense, which, Meg discovered as soon as Byrne opened her mouth, matched her attitude.

"Thank you all for coming." Byrne looked around the room, and her gaze finally settled on Craig. "SAC Beaumont, thank you and your team for all your work at the site thus far. I'm sure it's been difficult on multiple levels."

Craig gave her a nod of acknowledgment. "Thank you. It's been a challenge, but one the teams are more than capable of meeting. Do you have the lab results from the cell phone fragment Lieutenant Webb discovered?"

"That and the few others. Though I suspect we're lucky we found it when we did, and that Lieutenant Webb realized it simply didn't look like other artifacts of the collapse and was therefore a resident's personal property. Greg, can you outline what was found in the debris?"

"Sure." He scanned the room. "I think I've met most of you, but for those I haven't, I'm Greg Patrick, part of the Forensic Canine Unit's Explosives Detection Program." A fond smile curving his lips, Greg looked down at Ryder, who lay beside his chair. "And this is my German shepherd, Ryder. As usual, Ryder did most of the heavy lifting. So, when Lieutenant Webb brought out the fragment of a cell phone, he wisely bagged it. He was gloved the whole time, so there was no DNA cross contamination. Not knowing what to do with the fragment, he took it to SAC Beaumont, who then called me in. If Ryder alerted on it, then we needed to get into the pile to see what other evidence there might be. And Ryder alerted on it immediately."

"Confirming some type of explosive," Scott stated.

"Yes. Then the question was, What else was in the pile? There were two options. Go over the pile and pull out anything the explosive detection dogs alert on or go into the tunnel and see what else is there. I volunteered to go into the tunnel." Greg looked across the table to Meg. "Lieutenant Webb is your fiancé?"

"Yes."

"And he volunteered to go in and pull that guy out? All the way to the end of the tunnel?"

"Yes."

"I take my hat off to him. That took guts."

"Sounds like we should take our hats off to you. You did it too."

"Not nearly as far and for not nearly as long. But I don't mind saying, it was terrifying. Every little creak, every groan, every echo of a saw working the pile above . . . I was sure it was going to come down on us. My fitness tracker probably thought I was in cardiac arrest the whole time I was in there. Ryder, on the other hand, was his usual Energizer Bunny self and was totally in the zone. We had to adapt a bit, as you can imagine. I needed to get a feel for what he was alerting on, but there was very little room, so I had crawl backward. The crew in the garage helped me work my way into the tunnel feetfirst, and then Ryder followed, facing forward. The site of the discovery was estimated to be about ten feet inside the tunnel, but I was letting him lead the way as I inched backward. I could tell he was already picking up on explosive residue right from the start."

"When you're in a site like that, with residue spread all around but in low concentration, that's not enough for him to alert?" asked an agent at the far end of the table.

"We train the dogs to be sensitive to faint scents, but to zero in on the more concentrated ones. As you can imagine, following any bombing, trace residue of the explosive gets blown everywhere. And depending on the explosive used, I mean *everywhere*, over significant distances. We simply can't collect everything for testing. Ideally, we need to find the pieces of the actual explosive device. The one someone built, which could have chemical taggants, tool marks and, if we're lucky, latent fingerprints."

"You can get fingerprints off bomb components that survive the explosion?" Brian asked. "That seems . . . incredible."

"Not all the time, but it can be done, depending on the size of the fragment and its condition," said Byrne. "And if you think that's incredible, this will blow your mind. Sometimes, if we're extraordinarily lucky, we can find DNA on those same fragments."

"That does blow my mind. Did you find that here?"

"Let's go through this from the beginning," Greg said. "And we'll get to the results in time."

Brian huffed out a breath of frustration, and Meg gave him a placating look and patted his hand.

"As I said, I could tell Ryder was in the zone from the moment we entered the tunnel. He might have picked up more in the garage in time, but this area clearly had a greater concentration. I let him lead. As long as he wanted to push forward, I crawled backward. Webb had described the spot to me and had said that he'd marked it with a syringe with a bright orange cap, so I couldn't miss it. I pushed past it, hoping Ryder would alert there. And he did, though not his usual alert, as he couldn't sit. But he knows not to bark. We train them not to, as depending on the explosive, you don't want vibration of any kind. Instead, he gave a quiet whine at the spot where the phone fragment had been stuck.

"But just above that and a little farther in, Ryder wanted to jam his snout into a small gap between concrete slabs. Needless to say, I wasn't going to be moving pieces of concrete out of the way for better access, because I was afraid of doing anything to unbalance the pile or the supports, which could have been deadly. It was tricky, but I got in there with my flashlight, and I'd brought some tools with me, and managed to pull a bit of wiring out from that gap."

Byrne opened the folder, flipped through a few pages, and pulled out a color photo, which she handed to Craig, who sat beside her. He took a long look, then passed it to Scott. When the photo circled the table to Meg, she held it between herself and Brian so they could both see. Sitting next to a black-and-white ruler measuring both inches and centimeters—with a white label that had the acronym TEDAC and a string of digits, which Meg took to be the case file number—was a half-inch piece of two wires twisted together, their red-and-yellow sheaths battered and scorched, with copper ends protruding.

"What specifically are we looking at?" Meg asked. "I mean, Ryder alerted to it, so it came from the device, but what would it have done?"

"It's part of an IED's blasting cap assembly," Greg said. "And I know that because shortly after and a bit farther down the tunnel, he alerted on the cap itself, which I found under some plumbing. Mona?"

Byrne pulled another photo from the folder, which was also passed around the table. Two truncated red-and-yellow wires, identical in type to those in the previous photo, were attached to a narrow silver cap, the ends of which were peeled back in ragged, razor-sharp petals.

"As you can see," Greg continued, "the end of the blasting cap, which is built more solidly, survived the explosion with a bit of the wiring still attached."

"I'm amazed it's still intact," Brian said.

"You have to remember what high explosives do. They don't grind objects to powder. They shatter them because of the high pressures they produce. So we usually find bits of the casing, wiring, or blasting cap. If detonation cord is used, we don't usually find it, just traces of the pentaerythritol tetranitrate explosive it's composed of, because the cord explodes and the casing burns up. But with what we have, the type of bomb is forming for us. A cell phone in proximity to the explosion. Wires. An electric blasting cap."

"A cell phone that sets off an explosive with a phone call," Meg hypothesized.

Greg nodded. "That's it."

"What was the explosive?"

"That's where the lab comes in." Byrne took over the explanation. "Greg collected the fragments Ryder hit on, as well as some small bits of debris, which were likely from a part of the building that was close to the bomb when it exploded. The lab sampled everything and ran it all through the mass spectrophotometer to determine the chemical composition of the trace evidence." She picked up a report and scanned down it before flipping to the second page. "Ammonium nitrate, ethylene glycol, sodium nitrate, nitrocellulose . . ." She looked up and scanned the room. "Nitroglycerin."

"That sounds like dynamite," Craig said.

"That's because it *is* dynamite. The one thing about dynamite, as opposed to something like C-4, is it doesn't have a chemical taggant that would allow us to track it back to the manufacturer and, potentially, to who purchased it. But because TEDAC is good, and because they have detailed chemical profiles of most commercially available explosives to assist in materials identification, they've already identified that precise blend. It's a product called MaxBlast, sold by McArthur Blasting Supplies. McArthur provides explosives and accessories for roadwork, construction, mining, and quarrying."

"Commercially available, meaning anyone can buy it?" Lauren asked.

"Once you've applied for an explosives license or permit on the ATF E-Form 5400 and been granted said license. Only then can companies sell you explosives, and needless to say, everyone has to track it, down to the last stick of dynamite. I'll be paying a call to McArthur Blasting Supplies, which is in Baltimore, later today."

"This seems like a good start," said Craig. "Are you going back into the pile to look for more?"

Greg shook his head. "Even with the standing structure

down, there's still too much risk of the pile collapsing on anyone inside it. Incident command knows we're looking for additional evidence, but knows that evidence needs to be in either of the garage levels. If they're removing debris from the top down, it may take them at least a few weeks to reach those levels, but they're happy to work with us. If that means having the explosive detection dogs go over each layer of the pile a couple of times a day, then that's fine. Eventually, they'll reveal all the debris, and we'll make sure the USAR crews know what we're looking for."

"Normally, in the case of an explosion," Byrne explained, "we'd take a lot more evidence from the scene immediately, looking for blast damage to help us put the scene back together before the explosion occurred. This would help us pinpoint the location of the explosion, assuming there were no surviving witnesses. If a car explodes, killing the person inside, but a witness sees it from two blocks away, that witness can tell us a lot about what happened, and we don't have to put so much of the incident together strictly based on evidence. In this case, we have witness reports of the sound of an explosion from down the street. Unfortunately, most of the people who had the best eyewitness view of what happened did not survive the building collapse. So, to start, we're looking at the recovered physical evidence."

"Did you get fingerprints?" Brian asked.

"The lab guys have a way of bringing up latent prints using cyanoacrylate fuming and a fluorescent dye called BY40, as long as the temperature of the blast stayed below about 900 degrees Fahrenheit. They brought up a print this morning. It's a partial, but it looks clean, and it may be enough for sufficient points of comparison. If we're lucky, the perp is in the system. If not, we can confirm at time of arrest."

"DNA?"

"They're going to try for DNA, but that's going to take some time. However, it's worth the effort since that's the superior method of identification. We get DNA and it's an open-and-shut case when it gets to court."

"Do you have a feel for how they brought the building down?" asked one of the Critical Incident Response agents from where she stood against the wall. "Would dynamite be enough to do it?"

"Dynamite is kind of an odd choice," Byrne said. "It's a high explosive, but there are others that create greater pressure waves and do more damage. Maybe it was all they could get? C-4 would have worked better, but it has extremely limited use, mostly military, and is monitored even more closely. And it has a taggant, so it's traceable."

Meg and Craig exchanged glances. Meg knew that McCord had taken the information about the design weaknesses to Craig, who had taken it to Peters, who had passed it to incident command. But now that information seemed doubly important.

"Or maybe that was all that was needed," Meg said. "Because they had some inside information."

Greg's gaze locked sharply on her. "What do you mean?"

"My sister's partner is Clay McCord." Meg paused, waiting for recognition, but none showed in his eyes. "Remember the Mannew bombings? Remember how he contacted an investigative reporter to publish his messages?"

Recognition dawned in Greg's eyes. "That guy?"

"That guy. He's worked a few of our cases with us and has a history of being really useful as far as digging out information. This time, it's not just him digging but also several other *Washington Post* reporters. When Talbot Terraces fell, they went to work pulling building plans and construction permits. They also brought in a structural engineer to explain all that information to them because they're not familiar with building design or construction, so they wouldn't know if something was off if it was staring them in the face."

"Was it?"

"It was. Long story short, there were significant shortcuts taken when the building went up. Things like insufficient rebar added to columns and slabs at connection points, or major structural elements simply left out."

"This engineer thinks this is why the building came down?" Byrne asked. "It collapsed under its own weight?"

Meg shook her head. "No, he thinks someone might have taken advantage of these inherent weaknesses to bring the building down. These are publicly available plans and permits. You can apply to get them from the DC Department of Consumer and Regulatory Affairs. I'm sure there's a run on them now, but would there have been in the past? If not, you'd think we could find out who else was interested in those plans. Keeping that in mind, and with what you've told us today, would it make sense that dynamite was used, because that's all that would be needed considering the weaknesses? Craig, did McCord send you the schematics from the engineer?"

"Just before this meeting," Craig confirmed. "I can pass them on to you, Mona."

"I'm thinking I'd rather have a meet with this structural engineer," Greg said. "Could that be arranged? Between him and me, I think we could figure this out."

"And there's one other piece of information you probably don't have yet," Meg continued. "There was a car accident in the garage about a month before the collapse. A driver in a pickup truck had some sort of medical incident and hit one of the columns, damaging it, which required a company to come in to do the repair ASAP. Do you think it would be useful to know more about the accident?"

"Hell, yes."

"No, I mean right now." Meg turned to Craig. "I can

call McCord. He was looking into this, and I know he was going to be talking to one of the condo survivors this morning. Worst that will happen is he won't answer his phone."

"Call him," Craig said. "Time is of the essence."

Meg pulled out her cell and called up McCord's number, then typed it into the triangular teleconferencing unit in the middle of the table. The sound of a phone ringing came through the speakers.

McCord answered on the third ring. "Hey, what's up?" He sounded a little out of breath.

"Hey. You're on speaker with Craig, all four dog teams, Greg Patrick from the Explosives Detection Program, and Supervisory Special Agent Mona Byrne and a number of agents from the Critical Incident Response Group. They've been sharing some information about the explosives discovered in the parking garage. We're looking for an update on who you've talked to specifically about the parking garage."

There was a beat of silence, and Meg could hear the question McCord was trying not to ask because of the strangers in the room.

Apparently, Craig could hear it too. "Standard agreement, McCord. We'll share the data on the explosives in exchange for your information about the garage reconstruction, knowing you'll keep it confidential until we release you."

"Sounds good." There was the sound of a car door shutting before McCord's voice returned, now sounding constrained inside his vehicle. "I just left talking to two of the surviving residents, one of whom happens to sit on the condo board at Talbot Terraces. An older couple, Tom and Trudie Beecham, had lived in 407 for coming up on twenty years, which is why Tom sat on the board. He was retired, had the time, and was invested in maintaining the sanctity of their building. Anyway, Tom and Trudie left that morning at about seven forty-five to do their usual mall walking at Gallery Place before it opened for business, and then they'd normally stop for a coffee and a muffin before coming home, but they got word of the collapse. DCFEMS got their shih tzu, Gracie, out to safety, but that was all they had other than her purse, his wallet, and what they were wearing. They're staying at their daughter's home in Georgetown. They're early risers, so they asked me to come and have coffee with them at eight thirty this morning."

"It sounds like they walked to the mall," Brian stated. "Did they have a car? Did they use the garage?"

"Yes, to both of those. Like the rest of the tenants, they parked on the lower garage level but had to drive through the upper level to get in and out of the tenant parking area. While Tom didn't notice much, because he was always the one driving, Trudie took note of everything. She saw the damaged column shortly after it happened. Said it was bad, that whatever hit it must have hit it hard, and concrete had crumbled away right down to the steel bars inside in a section that affected about a quarter of the column height. But by the next day, someone had already been in, and metal supports had been installed around the column. About a week later, work started on that column first and then spread to a number of others, shoring them up, doing some sort of work, and leaving them wrapped in black plastic. She assumed to keep it protected while the concrete cured—"

"Wait," Craig interrupted, "what other columns?"

"Apparently, the repair guys found some areas where other columns were starting to age, and minor repair work was needed," McCord said. "The condo board was told they could spend a little money now or a lot of money later, so the board hired them to do repair work on other columns now, as it would save them money in the long run. The condo board is always struggling to get residents to pony up the cash for building improvements, so the board jumped at the chance of a smaller repair cost."

"Greg Patrick here. This other repair work gave these guys cover to actively work on those columns, and possibly any others in the area. And unless the condo board came down to check the building blueprints, they might not have realized that they were 'working on' columns outside the repair contract. Could Trudie identify which ones were being worked on?"

"She could. Because we had copies of the building plans, I took along a copy of the two garage levels. She didn't have anything to say about the lower level but specified on the upper level plans which column had been hit as well as the other ones that were worked on."

"We want a copy of that," Craig said.

"It's yours. Now, the concrete remediation company that sent the repair guys, that's another story. We know, again from permits, the company the board hired is Solis Construction, concrete remediation specialists. In fact, Solis was in such a rush to get the work done, they paid extra for the accelerated plan review for the repair permit, stating it was emergency work. According to their website, which looks very fancy, they do concrete repair and restoration, balcony repairs, concrete waterproofing, masonry, polyurethane crack injection, and high-rise building restoration. They also do underground parking garage restoration, including support column repair. As I said, it's a very fancy website. Wonderful photos, nicely organized."

"I'm hearing a *but*, McCord," Meg said.

"Yeah, it's a big one. The company doesn't exist. It's not registered anywhere, their phone number leads nowhere, and when you go to the address, it's an empty lot."

"It's a front."

"Yup. But when you run a Google search for *concrete repair*, it pops up twice at the top of the search results, once in a sponsored ad and once as the number one search result. Tom wasn't involved in finding them but knows the president of the board called them, and they lowballed the job and were instantly available with the needed shoring materials that day, beating off anyone else. And once they were in for the damaged column, they offered a lowball cost on the rest too."

Scott made a grumbling sound in the back of his throat, drawing Meg's eyes.

"Don't buy it?" she asked.

"It seems risky. I'm getting the whole implied tale—that the car accident wasn't an accident but was planned to do the damage to a specific column, weakening it so it required repairs. But how could Solis Construction be assured of getting the job? If they don't get the job, the whole plan—whatever that plan might have been—grinds to a halt."

"I've been thinking about that too," said McCord. "The accident blew up on social media, even if it wasn't covered in the *Post*, so I think had a call not come into Solis that day, they'd have called the condo board themselves. They wouldn't have gone to this length to lose their chance at it at that point. And if that wasn't their plan, they must have had some other contingency plan in place. I assume they had a burner phone they used for untraceable calls, which they've now destroyed, so no phone contact at that number. Does this fit into what you guys have learned?"

Meg glanced at Brian to see a smile curving his lips. He'd caught the subtle fishing for details as well.

Greg looked at Craig, who nodded and pointed at the teleconferencing unit.

"We've found trace evidence and components of dyna-mite-based bombs," Greg said. "And your information fits in perfectly. The mediation work gave them cover to drill holes for the dynamite, likely near the tops of the columns, where the column-slab connections were weakest."

"Any chance that could have been captured on security footage?" McCord asked. "The dynamite would have had to be stored off-site, but it was a swanky building and should have had great security."

"I'll find out," said Byrne. "If it exists, we'll get it. Greg, go on."

"The dynamite would be triggered by an electric blast-ing cap powered and activated by a cell phone. But now, with this updated information, that more than one column may have been actively involved, I have a theory. At first, I thought this might have been sympathetic detonation—when the concussive shock wave from one explosive going off is enough to set off an adjacent explosive. But I think that might be too unpredictable. There's no absolute guar-antee it would work. Then I thought of something else. Ever heard of simultaneous ring?"

Meg shrugged. "No."

"It's a phone function. With it, you can place a single call to multiple phones, all with different numbers, at the same time. People use it in business all the time. They'll forward their calls using simultaneous ring to a number of different phones. Whoever picks up the phone gets the call. But in this case, I don't think that's the goal."

Puzzle pieces were falling into place for Meg, and she could suddenly see Greg's theory. "You're thinking multi-ple bombs, each on its own column and each with its own cell phone, all called at the same time, all going off at the same time."

"Taking out multiple weak connections at the same

time. They'd all go off simultaneously, and the end result would be what sounds like a single, bigger explosion."

"From what the engineer explained," McCord said, "as those column and slab connections were severed and the slab fell, it would leave too much load on these now 'slender columns,' and they'd buckle. With no support beams in place to support the load, you'd hit the point of no return, more slabs would come down, and the collapse would progress. First, all the floors in that section, and then the short shear wall in the east end holds on for a few seconds before it collapses, taking the end of the wing with it. But the main shear wall held, and that's why part of the building stayed standing."

"Whether they planned to bring the building down or fatally wound it, I'm not sure," Greg said, "but what they did was damned effective either way." He sat back heavily in his chair. "So that's the how. We still need to confirm, but that combined series of events lines up in my head perfectly. Now we need to figure out the why."

Meg stared at the teleconferencing unit, torn over whether to ask McCord for an update on Tucker. But when McCord stayed quiet, she took her prompt from him. "Thanks, McCord. We appreciate your time and will let you go."

"No problem. Hey, when your meeting is over, can you give me a call? Maybe from Craig's office?"

Craig simply cocked one eyebrow but nodded.

"Can do. Talk soon." Meg ended the call.

The conference room meeting ended with promises from Greg and Byrne about supplying full reports, and from Craig about passing on McCord's marked building plans. Then Brian, Lauren, Scott, and their dogs headed to the site, while Meg, Hawk, and Craig headed for his office.

Craig closed his office door behind them. "So . . .

McCord is working on something he doesn't want to share with everyone yet?"

"He's working on the why but has called in some help to do it and doesn't want to get them into trouble. Not that I think it would, but I understand him keeping a confidence."

"Someone on the shady side of the law?"

"That's just it. Not at all. In fact, he's one of us."

"Well, let's call him and see."

Meg placed the call and put it on speaker. "McCord, it's Craig and me. What's up?"

"I have an update, and I need to bring Craig into the loop." He quickly explained the basics of what was going on as Craig sat motionless behind his desk.

When McCord wound down, Craig snagged the phone out of Meg's hand and asked, "Can you get in here right now?"

"I can. Do you need something special?"

"You're going to explain all this to EAD Peters."

"Peters?"

Meg stifled a smile at the touch of fear in McCord's voice, even though she completely understood it. Saying Peters was a hard-ass was an understatement. The only time McCord had met him was at the Hoover Building during the Stevenson case and then immediately after it at Meg and Cara's place for a party. But he'd heard Meg's stories, including two suspensions that came directly from Peters.

"Yes, Peters," Craig confirmed. "Come down now, McCord. I'll get us in." Without another word, he ended the call, handed the phone to Meg, picked up his office phone, and dialed an extension.

"Dylan, it's SAC Beaumont. I need to see EAD Peters this morning, preferably in about thirty minutes. Top priority. Yes, I'm sure. Top. Priority. That will work. Thank you." He hung up his phone. "With what McCord has, it's time for the big guns. Definitely Peters, likely also Detective Lieutenant Harper from the Massachusetts State Police."

Craig met Meg's eyes, and she saw foreboding in their depths.

"There's another target. We've been on the clock all this time but had no idea. And now we have to race to catch up before another tragedy occurs."

CHAPTER 22

Shop Drawings: All the detailed design plans, illustrations, and diagrams created by or for the contractor, to be used during the active building phase of a structure.

Friday, December 21, 10:58 AM
EAD Peters's office, J. Edgar Hoover Building
Washington, DC

McCord jogged down the hallway toward where Meg and Hawk waited. "Am I late?" He paused, hands on hips, and sucked in air. "Sorry. Got caught in traffic. The chaos with the closure around Talbot Terraces has radiated pretty far outward, so I had to park blocks away and sprint in."

"You're not late. Catch your breath."

Bracing the heels of his hands on his knees, McCord bent over, only to come nearly nose to nose with Hawk, whose tail thumped in happy greeting on the carpeted floor. "Hey, buddy. Good to see you." He gave himself a half dozen heavy breaths and then straightened, giving the dog a quick stroke as he went. "I'm ready." He shot Meg a sideways glance. "Is he going to eat me alive?"

"He's more bark than bite. And in this case, you're bringing us reliable intel. On top of that, you don't work for him. He can't suspend you. Come on. Craig's waiting inside." Meg pushed open the solid wood door with EXEC-UTIVE ASSISTANT DIRECTOR ADAM PETERS –CRIMINAL, CYBER, RESPONSE, AND SERVICES emblazoned on the brass name-plate. "Hawk, come."

She led the way into a modest outer office with only enough room for two chairs, one of which was occupied by Craig, and Peters's assistant's desk and chair.

Craig stood as soon as they entered. "Ready?" At their nods, he turned to the young man behind the desk. "We're all here now."

"Just one moment." The young man picked up the phone. "SAC Beaumont and his team are here, sir. Yes, sir." He put down the phone. "You can go in."

Craig went through the door first, and Meg heard McCord's quietly mumbled "Great" just before she stepped over the threshold, and had to try hard not to go in smiling.

Slender, bald, and wearing glasses, Peters was one of the most unassuming men Meg had ever met. At least until he looked at you with those laser-beam blue eyes, which con-veyed intelligence, intuition, and absolute control. One of the youngest executive assistant directors in Bureau his-tory, Peters had used his undeniably plain looks and aver-age build to let people underestimate him, only to sucker punch them with the force of his personality and the machinations of his wily mind. Meg understood the man they were dealing with, but it occurred to her that maybe she'd sold McCord a little too much of the control factor and not enough of the team player aspect of Peters's per-sonality. She knew bringing Peters in at this point would only ease their way into the investigation. McCord was expecting the boom to fall.

Three chairs sat in front of Peters's L-shaped desk— there was one more than usual, Meg had cause to know. After all, there'd been only two when she'd been called on the carpet after disobeying a direct order from Craig. It had been to save a life—successfully—but she'd still disobeyed an order.

Craig took the right-hand chair and looked at Meg and McCord, then at the other two chairs. They both wordlessly sat down.

Peters sat back in his chair, steepling his hands together, and tapped his index fingers. He fixed Craig with a steely stare. "I had a meeting with the Cyber Division pushed back a half hour because I understand you have something described to me as 'top priority.' I don't like having others changing my schedule at their whim. This better be good."

"It is, sir. It's about the Talbot Terraces collapse. You remember Clay McCord from the *Washington Post*?"

"The favored reporter from the Mannew case. Did you know, Mr. McCord, that we seriously considered you a suspect for a while in that case? Because of that communication?"

McCord's spine stiffened, and he drew himself up. "I suspected as much right from the beginning, but we weren't going to hold back the messages just because it put me in the line of fire."

Peters's eyes narrowed on McCord, but he nodded ever so slightly. "I assume you have something you want to pass on to us? Or else Beaumont and Jennings wouldn't have brought you."

"I do. I'm sure you know almost every investigative reporter in the city has been on this and only this story since last Monday."

"I would imagine."

"I got a tip from one of the few reporters who isn't working on the story. She'd run across information on Talbot Terraces when she was researching a story on conspiracy theories."

Peters's eye roll left no one in the room questioning his

opinion of that topic. "My hatred of conspiracy theories aside, how does Talbot Terraces play into one?"

"There's a story going around about an Underground Railroad for immigrants. It brings them in, gets them settled away from the borders, where they can take honest American jobs away from . . . well . . . honest Americans. Talbot Terraces was rumored to be a stop on the railroad. A place for immigrants to be hidden in apartments, out of sight, until the coast was clear to move them along. Or lose them in DC. Another aspect of this is that the story is being told by the Brotherhood of Libertas."

It was clear that for all Peters's previous irritation at having his morning hijacked, they had his attention now. "I know about them." Peters's eyes cut to Craig. "Cyber's had them on the watch list for years, but they're devious and hard to pin down. Nearly impossible to infiltrate."

"I'm about to make you extremely happy, then," McCord continued. "But let me run this in order, so you have the whole picture. I'd been working on motive for bringing down the building, but nothing seemed to fit. We had numerous well-known people in the building, though many of them had already left that morning to go to their high-profile jobs. But even if they'd been the target, why would you go to the trouble of bringing down a building to try to get one person who might have walked out of said building ten minutes before it fell? It made zero sense and was way over-the-top overkill."

"Sir, there's something else you might not know about yet, because we literately just learned of it ourselves," Craig interjected. "TEDAC has identified not only bomb components in the building debris but also trace evidence of dynamite. The building didn't fall on its own."

"Confirmation of terrorism. Definitely our case, then." Peters gave Craig a single nod, which Meg read as a "Good call" guy nod on this meeting.

"There's more around that as well," said McCord. "The building plans and permits are public records, and we got copies and consulted with a structural engineer. There were structural weaknesses in the building, which meant less dynamite was required, and taking out only a minimal number of columns could do the catastrophic damage they needed. I'm not sure how much detail you know, so let me run through it quickly." McCord took Peters through the design weaknesses, the accident that required repair on a column, and the additional column work. Then he sat back and waited while Peters absorbed it all.

There was a full thirty seconds of silence while Peters ran the details in his head before he finally spoke. "First of all, excellent work, Mr. McCord. The Bureau appreciates you bringing this to us rather than making a splash on the front page. Does your editor agree with that choice?"

"He doesn't know it all yet, but he'll agree when he does, because he knows we'll have unprecedented access to the FBI for interviews for our story."

" 'He doesn't know it all yet,' " Peters repeated as he scanned their faces. "You came here instead because time is of the essence." He leaned forward, intensity radiating in every bunched muscle. "What don't I know?"

"When I talked to my colleague, she said she wasn't able to dive into this story, because she didn't know how to get around the dark web. More than that, she knew she'd never learn anything, because everyone would know right off she was an outsider. That's when I looped Rob Tucker in."

"I don't know the name. He's here at the Bureau?"

"No, he's in the Computer Forensics Unit at the Massachusetts State Police in Essex County. He and I went to college together. Tucker is younger than me, but he graduated high school early and started college young. He was a total computer whiz. Even back then, he could hack into anything. He could have been a great criminal. He joined law enforcement instead."

"We like it when they do that. You contacted him?"

"Yes. I explained the whole thing. Tucker said he'd be willing to nose around a bit. He already has an established fake persona on the dark web, complete with a criminal record care of the Massachusetts State Police, so he's a known commodity. He agreed anyone new wouldn't be able to find out anything, because no one would let them in. But he was already there, so the Brotherhood of Libertas wouldn't be instantaneously suspicious, especially when he was stroking their egos about their success with Talbot Terraces."

McCord shifted in his chair slightly to pull his notepad out of his back pocket. He pulled out the pen and flipped to the middle of the pad, to a page where the scrawling blue-ink script ended. "And that's how he found out about the larger picture of the Underground Railroad. And the other targets."

"Targets?" Peters stressed the word. "Plural?"

"Plural. Tucker is going to send me a picture of the map he saw, but the essentials of the conspiracy theory are this. They say immigrants are coming over the border on foot through Canada. It's the longest undefended international border in the world, at over 5,500 miles. Across that span, there are only about one hundred official border crossings, and they're not all manned twenty-four-seven, three-sixty-five. And there are lots of places where you can walk across the border in the middle of nowhere.

"These immigrants are walking over the border under the cover of night and have specific small-town locations in which to meet to get onto the beginning of the railroad. From there, they're transported by those in the chain, by car or by van, to larger locations, where they're given fake

IDs so they can move around freely and buy bus and train tickets to go to the next location. Big cities house the main stops on the railroad. Because they want big cities, where strangers can get lost, they avoid the Midwest, sticking more to the coasts. On the Eastern Seaboard, it's DC, New York City, Boston, Pittsburgh, Cincinnati, and Charlotte. Out west, it's Seattle, Portland, Salem, Reno, and San Francisco. The railroad doesn't go too far south, because they don't want to mix with those trying to come through the southern border, where there's already a significant problem."

"That's already a big area. Do they have targets in each of those cities?"

"They supposedly don't have intel on all of them. That information is coming from Brotherhood of Libertas members and those from similar groups, from what they hear in the local chatter and what they supposedly see with their own eyes."

"When you go out looking for something specific," Meg said, "you can often find it, even when it's not really there."

"Totally. They're biased. And outraged at how unfairly they're being treated in many aspects of their lives, most of which they feel they have no control over, because 'The Man' is in charge. But this . . . this they feel they can help with. It gives them the power to take back some of their own."

"Even though people die and millions of dollars in property damage racks up, this seems legitimate to them?" Craig asked.

"Apparently so."

"Where are the targets?" asked Peters.

"Tucker is sending me a list of buildings that are allegedly stops on this Underground Railroad. But the one you need to know about is called the Wilmott, a twenty-story apartment building in the heart of Pittsburgh. Not a luxury condo building like Talbot Terraces, but it holds more apartments."

"We need to get information on that building ASAP," Craig said.

"Tucker has some of that information already. He . . . uh . . ." McCord looked up at Peters, who simply waved his hand in a circle, as if to say, "Go on." "He hacked into the city systems to get a look at their records. The building went up in 1992 and is also of concrete slab construction. It has two hundred twenty apartments. He doesn't know the occupancy rate, but he's assuming it's quite high."

"Note that the Wilmott isn't that far from DC," Craig pointed out. "Or at least a lot closer than to Portland or San Francisco. What do you want to bet their plan is to use the same people, the same materials supply chain for the explosives, and the same general procedure, since it worked the last time?"

"You'd win that bet," said McCord. "A similar underground garage accident happened yesterday."

Peters went ramrod straight in his chair. "I need everything this Tucker has immediately. And I need agents from the Pittsburgh field office on-site now. Do we need to evacuate the building?"

"Tucker doesn't think we do. They wanted to get the process at the next building started before anyone could figure out what had happened to this one. They figure they'll get one, or maybe two more buildings, down this way before someone actually figures out how they're doing it."

"Did they think we wouldn't be able to put it together?" The sneer in Peters's tone was biting.

"I would say so. And to give credit where credit is due, not just you, but us. We pulled the plans and permits. If I can make a suggestion?"

"Of course."

"Get in touch with Jack Burke from Ekhert and Morrison. He's the structural engineer we've been working with. He seems solid, and he's already up to speed on this story. Get the Wilmott plans into his hands. Better yet, get him and a team he trusts to the building itself. Fly them out, since time is of the essence. Get them to evaluate and shore up the building and advise about evacuation." He paused while Peters made a note on the yellow legal pad at his elbow. "At this point, you need a known commodity, not someone who wins a request for proposal and you have no idea who they are and whether they could have nefarious intentions."

"That's smart. The other thing I want to do is make contact with Tucker's commanding officer. Tucker's infiltrated the group now, and he's our best source of knowledge. We don't have the time to bring in someone else and can't risk them not being accepted. Not when we have a sure thing already. Essex County, you said?"

"Yes. Tucker guessed you'd want to do that, so he sent all the information you need. His commanding officer is Detective Lieutenant Nicholas Harper." McCord rattled off a phone number, which Peters noted. "Have you dealt with them before?"

"The Massachusetts State Police, yes. Essex, no. But I don't foresee any trouble. Not once they get the whole story and a rundown of how their officer has been a great assistant. When it's made clear what we're trying to avoid, that Boston could be next, and"—he pinned McCord with a sharp look—"when they're assured they'll get credit for the operation in none other than the *Washington Post*, I'm sure they'll be accommodating."

"I'm the one writing that story, so let me assure you, that'll happen."

"Is there any danger to Tucker?" Meg asked. "He's the one worming his way in. I know they're not meeting in person, but if anyone is able to track him electronically, it could be a threat to him."

"Believe me, I asked him. He laughed at me." McCord shrugged. "I guess we can only take him at his word that he's bouncing through international servers, or some such thing I couldn't follow, to hide his location."

In his pocket, McCord's muffled phone sang "We're Off to See the Wizard."

Meg looked at him pointedly. "Let me guess, that's your ringtone for the Wizard?"

"The Wizard?" asked Peters.

"Tucker's nickname in college. I gave him his own ringtone for all communication because I don't want to miss anything in real time." McCord pulled his phone out, opened his text messages, and scanned a new one from Tucker. "Now we have another angle. He's been tracking group members by their IP addresses. They apparently don't mask their IP addresses the way he does. There are several who don't strike him as being overly tech savvy, but he's gone after one in particular because he's the one who's always discussing structural aspects of the building. He thinks this guy is the construction expert, possibly even a concrete remediation expert. Who can he provide this information to?"

"Me, immediately," said Peters. "Send him this email address." He recited it to McCord as he typed it in. "Tell him I'm waiting for it." He swiveled in his chair toward the desktop computer on the short arm of the L-shaped desk and brought up his email. "He's just sending the one for now?"

"Yes, he says he's going after others, but it may take more time."

"I need to call his commander ASAP, before he finds out

about this in some other way. But first . . ." Peters picked up his phone, punched in an extension, then waited. "Masalis, it's Peters. I need you and the boys to be ready to trace an IP address in a couple of minutes. We have a potential lead in the Talbot Terraces bombing. Yes, bombing. TEDAC has confirmed. I'll forward the information to your email within the next few minutes. Work fast. I want to be hitting up a judge for a search warrant within the hour." He put down the receiver without formally ending the call.

"That should light a fire under them," Craig said in a casual tone.

"It always does." Peters's computer made a soft ding. "And there it is." He opened the email, scanned it, and forwarded it before he turned to McCord. "There are a few different avenues we're going to investigate all at the same time. Give me the number of the structural engineer." He wrote down Burke's information as McCord recited it. "Next, the name of the concrete remediation company. Solaris?"

"Solis," McCord corrected, and, after flipping to the correct location, read out their information from his notepad.

"You'll get a report from Mona Byrne with TEDAC's findings," Craig said. "They've already identified the type of dynamite used and the company that produces it. She's going there now to find out who's purchased that product, to try to trace it. They're also looking at the cell phone fragment, though I doubt they're going to make headway there."

"Agreed. It's likely a mass-produced burner phone."

"Greg Patrick's theory is that a number of burner phones set off each dynamite charge simultaneously. Called from a burner phone. All one hundred percent untraceable."

"They'd be stupid to do otherwise," Peters said. "Belief

in this insane theory aside, everything they've done here is *not* stupid. It's all carefully planned and calculated."

"It's been the perfect meeting of minds," McCord commented.

The laser-like blue eyes fixed on McCord. "Meaning?"

"It's doubtful one person organized all of this. Too much expertise is involved. It's unlikely the expert in building design is also the expert in concrete remediation is also the expert in explosives. The first two skills could go together—it would actually make sense if they did—but the last is less likely. You may be looking at one person running the show, or you may be looking at a couple of people."

"Is Tucker going to be able to tell us more about that?"

"He's going through older messages and trying to talk to people, trying to figure out what's going on. Not in an 'I'm law enforcement, so spell it all out to me' kind of way, but more of a 'Wow, you guys are amazing. How did you do it?' kind of way."

"Appeals to their egos." Peters shook his head. "They always love it when someone does that. Playing the sycophant is a great way in. Okay, next. Those plans you and your colleagues got ahold of . . ."

"They've been posted online because of the demand to see them," McCord said.

"That's good, but we need to know who else asked for them before that happened. How did you guys get them?"

"Copies of the permits and plans came through the Department of Consumer and Regulatory Affairs. You have to make an online account to access the permits, and the plans could be accessed online or in person. But the problem with both of those access channels is that fake information could be provided. A burner phone number and a transient email address and all that information could be yours. You might be able to track them that way eventually, but likely not fast enough to stop plans already in motion. You might have better luck with the garage security footage."

"They have footage to catch them in action?"

"Maybe," Craig clarified. "They're looking into it. If we're lucky, and security footage was uploaded to the cloud and wasn't kept on-site, the cyber types might be able to do facial recognition. Mona and her agents are handling that too. There are a lot of balls in the air right now."

"I like balls in the air. All we need is one caught, and we could have a lock on a suspect. Additional balls are great, but I'd be happy to start with one. The most important thing is to stop any further tragedies. The rest can be worked out later to substantiate the case in court." Peters looked down to where Hawk lay beside Meg's chair. "Are you needed at the collapse site?"

"Yes. It's a recovery now, but we'd rather be down there helping if we're not needed somewhere else."

"Tough job. It's a recovery, so they aren't expecting any more survivors."

"No, sir. But there are victims to bring home and families that need closure."

Peters studied her unblinkingly for several long seconds. "Then you need to do what you need to do, and the FBI is happy to provide support for that important function. Well done, Jennings. Please pass on my thanks to the other members of your team."

"Yes, sir. Thank you, sir." She looked down at Hawk as she stood. "Hawk, up. Come. We have work to do."

McCord and Craig followed her out, and as they went through the doorway, they heard Peters already on the phone, reaching out to the Massachusetts State Police. "This is Executive Assistant Director Adam Peters of the

FBI. I'd like to speak to Detective Lieutenant Harper. Yes, I'll hold."

Craig quietly closed the door behind them. "Wouldn't you love to be a fly on the wall in Detective Lieutenant Harper's office? That could be quite a surprise for him."

"Hopefully, there won't be any pushback or trouble for Tucker." Concern crumpled McCord's brow. "I just needed a hand going somewhere I couldn't manage on my own."

"Oh, I wouldn't worry about that." Craig's words were rock solid with surety.

"No?"

Craig laughed. "You just spent time with Peters. Do you really think he's going to let go of an asset like Tucker? No way."

"It's not just letting go of an asset. It's Tucker not getting in trouble with his commanders for bailing my ass out."

"That's not going to happen," Meg said.

"No," Craig agreed, "it's not. Tucker could be the lynchpin in the case. Now, the real question is, Will the info he's providing be enough for us to track down the son of a bitch running this group? And can we stop them before they kill again?"

CHAPTER 23

Yield: The point at which materials under stress will deform permanently.

Saturday, December 22, 2:06 PM
Talbot Terraces
Washington, DC

Meg had been following the case all day, with Craig providing up-to-the-minute updates to the teams out on the pile.

Meg expected the message in the first text, though it surprised her how fast the investigation progressed:

IP address led to Internet provider. Search warrant with judge.

It wasn't even an hour later when the next group text came through.

Search warrant signed. Agents dispatched to ISP.

There was no place for the dog teams in this part of the investigation, so Meg was glad Craig was staying on top of its progress and keeping them in the loop. All the rescuers were invested in this case, but because of everything McCord and Tucker were doing, she was much more aware of what was going on. She'd filled the other teams in on the bare bones, but Brian had spent his entire break picking her brain, so he now knew everything she did.

When her phone dinged next, she was working with a team after Hawk had alerted on a scent, so she ignored it. Then several additional alerts came in. After confirmation from one of the USAR dogs, Pennsylvania TF1 moved in, and more human remains were discovered.

Yet another red flag.

She scanned across the pile, across a sea of identical flags, each location waiting for a retrieval team to properly collect the remains, which would go to the medical examiner's office. It felt like it was taking entirely too long to process each site, but Meg also understood the pressure the teams were under and the care they insisted on taking. They'd bring home everyone they could, and if that meant taking the time to process each site carefully, then that was what they'd do. No one would be lost to the process of clearing the site.

Her phone alerted again, reminding her she was behind on updates. "Hawk, come." She led him away from the USAR team to a level section of slab so she could pull off her gloves and take out her phone.

She scanned down unread texts from Craig.

ISP is cooperative because of warrant. Has provided name and home address of suspect. Jerome Meyer.

Agents redirecting to Meyer's address.

Meyer in custody. Computer equipment seized and going to Cyber.

Bringing Meyer in. Interview at the Hoover Building tonight, once lawyer arrives.

Meg switched to the private conversation between herself and Craig and fired off a text. **I want to observe tonight. And I want to bring McCord.**

Craig's response was immediate and exactly what she expected. **You can't bring media to this.**

I can if you clear it. If he hadn't brought Tucker in, we'd be nowhere and hundreds more might have died. She waited a moment and then added, **It's the least we owe him. So many cases, he's come through for us. He nearly died in August. What has he asked of us in return?**

The long minutes of silence that followed told her she'd made her point. Craig was either mulling or had gone up the chain to clear it, something else Meg expected. Peters had to clear this, or it wasn't happening.

She knew there was a good chance Peters would block the request. Truthfully, that was the most likely outcome. But she'd seen something in Peters's eyes earlier today—recognition of the advantage of collaboration. Law enforcement was sometimes its own worst enemy. People didn't talk to law enforcement, because they were scared of cops, and when push came to shove, that was exactly what FBI agents were. But McCord, with his fingers in so many pies, including some in the underworld, could find out things they couldn't, entirely changing the face of cases, like the sex trafficking ring in Virginia and the Mob trade in blood diamonds in Philadelphia. Not to mention how his knowledge of the Civil War and his ability to correctly determine urbex sites had allowed Meg and Brian and the dogs to save multiple lives.

They owed it to him.

"Come on, Hawk. Back to work."

The text came ten minutes later. It was short and to the point but gave her a little kick of triumph as she stood on the pile, amid the remains of tragedy.

Tell McCord to meet us at the Hoover Building after shift.

Whatever she could do to speed this case along, not only to find justice for the lost still waiting beneath her dust-covered boots but also to save those innocents who were unknowingly threatened, made her pushiness acceptable, in her opinion. Who knew what else McCord could do to help? And if not in this case, then in the next. As far as she was concerned, keeping McCord invested was only to their advantage.

She sent off a quick text to McCord. **Suspect in custody. Interview tonight at the Hoover Building. Have cleared the way for you to observe. Meet me there at 8:15, after my shift. Don't be late.**

She didn't even have time to pull on her gloves before McCord responded with a single emoji—the one with wide eyes as the head exploded.

Hours later, McCord stood beside Meg in the observation room at the J. Edgar Hoover Building. It was one of the rare occasions when Hawk wasn't at her side—Meg had been able to get word through to Todd, and he'd taken Hawk home in her SUV for a bath and dinner while she'd eaten an energy bar as she walked to the Hoover Building, and would come home with McCord.

Meg and McCord stood at a two-way mirror that looked through to a stark, utilitarian interview room containing a table with an embedded silver restraint bar, four chairs, and several wall-mounted cameras, to record all interactions with the suspect from different angles.

McCord leaned in so the other half dozen agents and supervisors in the room couldn't hear. "Am I going to be allowed to record this?"

"Absolutely not. If I was you, I wouldn't even be seen making notes. You're here. Let's not push it. Peters wouldn't like it."

"Someone would snitch on me?"

"He may be here himself. I've been in this room with him before. Unless they send him in with Meyer. Peters is known for his interrogation skills. He can get people to say all sorts of things they wish they hadn't." The door opened, and Meg's gaze shifted to over McCord's shoulder. "Or maybe they're keeping him for the B Team, because he just walked in. They must be about to start."

She nodded a greeting at Peters, who stayed on the other side of the room, and then she kept an eye on the open doorway. "I was expecting Craig to come. Maybe he got held up back at the site." Through the large window, the door to the interview room opened, and a dark-suited agent led in a man with his hands cuffed behind his back. The man was wearing battered steel-toe boots, heavy brown work pants smeared with pale splotches of dried material, and a gray plaid shirt over a faded black T-shirt. The man's eyes swung from side to side, and Meg would have thought he was strategically cataloging everything in the room, except his eyes never rested on anything for more than a fraction of a second.

He's terrified. Good.

Meg had watched plenty of interviews over her years in the Richmond Police Department and then the FBI and was familiar with the bravado a lot of suspects used to bluster their way through an interview. This one wasn't showing it. The agent steered Meyer into one of two chairs on the far side of the table, then had him lean forward so he could unlock one cuff and attach it to the restraint bar.

"We're waiting on your lawyer's arrival," the agent said. And then left the room.

Long minutes passed as Meyer sat in the chair on the other side of the glass, his eyes ever moving. He managed to hold himself still for about a minute, but then he started to vibrate—first his heel began to bounce, and then his fingers began drumming the tabletop.

The door to observation opened, and Byrne came in, carrying a file folder, followed by an older man in a dark suit and tie. Meg recognized him but didn't think they'd ever met.

Byrne walked up to the window and studied their suspect through it. "Looks like he's simmering nicely."

"Is his lawyer not here?" Meg asked.

"Oh, he's here. We wouldn't want a suspect to not have his legal representation." Byrne's smile was sly. "We're just ensuring he's taking the scenic route to get here. We're keeping Mr. Meyer on ice until he arrives."

Meg looked back at the scene, seeing Byrne's calculation. "He's rattled. You're trying to let him unravel a little more."

"Damn straight. If this guy had anything to do with that horror four blocks away, I want him more than rattled. Then I want him to sing like a canary, so we can stop this from ever happening again." She half turned to the man beside her. "Lance, have you met Meg Jennings? She's with Beaumont's Human Scent Evidence Team."

"I haven't had the pleasure. SAC Lance Shaff." Shaff put out his hand but was already scanning the room. "Where's your partner?"

"At home, having a bath and a good meal with my fiancé. However, I came straight here after our twelve-hour shift on the pile. If there's concrete dust in my hair, that would be why."

Shaff's congenial expression melted away, and his face went tight with compressed lips and flat eyes. "That must be a difficult job. Thank you for continuing with it. I understand your teams were relieved of duty but are continuing to work the pile anyway."

"Yes. Until we're needed elsewhere, we'd prefer to keep searching. A few days ago, I went and talked to families at the reunification center. It was . . . excruciating to watch. They're in unfathomable agony. Whatever we can do to help that . . . well, it's still not enough, but at least it's something." Meg peered into the interview room, where Meyer sat, shoulders hunched and head hanging low, his hands clenched together. "It's why I wanted to come. And why I wanted to bring Clay McCord. Mona, you spoke to McCord this morning in our meeting."

Byrne turned to study McCord, and her gaze settled on his visitor badge. "You're the guy from the *Washington Post*. The one who helped put the pieces of Talbot Terraces and the Underground Railroad together."

"With several other reporters. On a story of this size, it's always a team effort. But yes, that was me this morning. And don't worry. I'm only here to observe. I'm not going to release anything I hear from that room. Craig Beaumont worked out permission for me to be here on the basis that I wasn't going to publish the interview. He understands it will help me write a fuller story in the end. Once the FBI gives me the green light."

Byrne stuck out her hand, and McCord reflexively reached out to shake. "Please pass along our thanks to the rest of the team, including Mr. Tucker. We owe all of you so very much. To say that information broke this case wide open is an understatement." She let go of his hand. "And we're going to trust in your confidentiality."

"You can trust him," Meg said. "We do."

"Good to know. Oh, by the way, we ran Meyer's prints against the partial print on the phone fragment. No match. But we knew he wasn't acting alone. Now we need to find out who he was working with." Byrne's attention was attracted to the interview room when the door opened and a tall blond man in an impeccably cut charcoal suit and a burgundy tie stepped in, his eyes taking in his client's restlessness. "That looks like my cue to get started. Let's go, Lance. I don't want to give them any time to discuss."

As the door to observation closed behind them, everyone gathered around the window, and one of the agents turned up the control for sound from the other room.

Byrne came through the interview room door, with Shaff behind her. They took the two empty chairs facing the men; then Byrne folded her hands serenely on the file folder and met Meyer's eyes. "This interview is being recorded. I'm Supervisory Special Agent Byrne, and this is Special-Agent-in-Charge Shaff. We're from the Critical Incident Response Group. Please state your names for the record."

"Jerome Meyer."

"Donald Powell."

"Thank you. Mr. Meyer, you were Mirandized in the field, but I'd like to review your rights. You have the right to remain silent." Byrne went through all the Miranda warning. "Do you understand your rights as I have explained them to you?"

Meyer kept his eyes down and nodded.

"Mr. Meyer, if you could verbally answer the question for the record?"

"Yes."

"Mr. Meyer, you're currently charged under District of Columbia law with the manufacture and possession of a weapon of mass destruction, detonation of a weapon of mass destruction, placing explosives with intent to destroy or injure property, malicious destruction of property resulting in death, and multiple charges of first-degree and attempted murder. Under federal law, you're charged with stolen explosive materials, unlawful storage of explosive materials, and prohibited shipment, transportation, receipt, possession, or distribution of explosive materials. To start. The US attorney is still considering the case. But this will be enough for us to hold you, likely without possibility of bail, as I'm sure any judge would consider you a flight risk."

Meyer went a pasty shade of white with a tinge of green, which made Meg think he had no idea what he was getting into. *This one doesn't seem like the brains of the operation. More like a patsy, someone easily swayed to a cause, who got carried away. Until he was hung out to dry.*

"Wait. I didn't do all that." There was an unmistakable note of desperation in Meyer's tone that overlaid a quaver of fear.

"We didn't say you did it all singlehandedly, Mr. Meyer, but you were involved. Many of those charges will net you personally around thirty years each, if not more. If you're found guilty of all those charges, you'll be behind bars for decades." Byrne leaned forward slightly for emphasis. "Likely for the rest of your life."

"You can't—"

"Jerome." Powell laid a hand on Meyer's forearm for a moment. "SSA Byrne, we're not here for you to threaten my client."

"I'm hardly threatening him, Mr. Powell." Byrne smiled, but it had an edge to it. "That's the US attorney's job. I'm just passing along the list of charges he's laid out after considering the case. All those lives lost, Mr. Powell. Yes, there's also catastrophic property damage, but the lives . . . so many gone. That's all the jury is going to remember. What's going on right now, the rescuers and the dogs out on the pile, frantically searching for life. It's going to be essentially impossible to find a jury member across the country who won't start the court case with some sort of bias toward your client, no matter now neutral they'll try to be."

"Mr. Meyer, SSA Byrne has laid out what's at stake for

you," said Shaff. "The best thing you can do is be honest with us. We're not averse to a conversation with the US attorney, maybe to discuss reducing some of those charges, but there would have to be *significant*"—Shaff leaned hard on the word—"information provided by you to allow us to sit down with him. Let's start with this. You're a trained concrete surface repair technician?"

Meyer glanced uncertainly at Powell, who nodded. He looked back at Shaff. "Yeah."

"Who do you currently work for?"

"I'm unemployed."

"Who *did* you work for?"

"Fuller Construction. But they laid me off and—"

Powell jumped in, cutting Meyer off. "Just answer the question, Jerome. That's all they need."

Behind the glass, McCord leaned down to murmur to Meg, "I don't think this guy is the sharpest knife in the drawer. He's going to give away enough information to hang himself if he keeps that up."

"Definitely not sharp, and the agents know it. More than that, he's scared. Sometimes you have a fight on your hands in an interview, and sometimes they fold almost immediately because they're desperate to save themselves. I have a feeling this guy is the latter kind."

"How long have you been laid off?" Shaff continued.

"About three months."

"Did they give you cause for the layoff?"

"Too many guys, not enough work."

"What exactly does a concrete surface repair technician do?"

For a moment Meyer seemed to forget his fear, in his contempt for what he clearly saw as an idiotic question. "What do you think we do? We repair concrete."

Powell's lips tightened, but he said nothing. Apparently,

he knew it didn't always play to a suspect's best interest to antagonize the cops.

But Shaff's expression didn't change. "What kind of jobs? And what goes into that kind of work?"

"We have to make the concrete, make sure the mix of materials is right. Install forms for pouring concrete. Seal the concrete after it's cured. Repair areas where the concrete has spalled ... uh ... crumbled, stripping away the old concrete and adding fresh."

"Not only do you repair concrete, but you lay fresh concrete as well?"

"Yeah."

"You can take plans from an engineer and turn it into a building using reinforced concrete?"

"Yeah."

"And you understand what the design shorthand in those plans means?"

"Yeah."

"Is there a point to this questioning?" Powell interrupted. "We could provide a copy of his résumé, if that would save you time."

"This will do fine," Shaff said, without missing a beat. "Mr. Meyer, when you saw the plans for Talbot Terraces, did you spot the weaknesses right off?"

"I ... I ..." Meyer's eyes were swinging around the room again, as if he was looking for an escape. Then he went still. "No."

Byrne flipped open the file folder, turned around the top piece of paper, and slid it across the table toward Meyer.

McCord leaned in closer to the glass. "That's the plans for Talbot Terraces. They have Burke's markings on them. That should be the upper level of the parking garage."

"Do you recognize these plans, Mr. Meyer?" Byrne asked.

"No."

"You hardly looked at them. Want to try again?"

Meyer picked up the paper, and Meg could practically hear him counting to ten in his head before he set it down. "Never seen it before."

"What about this one?" Byrne slid another piece of paper over.

"Not that either."

Byrne picked up both pieces of paper and then spent several long seconds tapping them upright on the tabletop to line them up before meticulously laying them in the file folder, over several other pieces of paper. "Mr. Meyer, are you aware that we have your electronics? That our computer experts are looking into your online activities? That we know about the Brotherhood of Libertas, and that the Rodbuster3471 account can be traced to your home address, where you live alone? And that those same computer experts will tie you directly to that account?" She flipped the folder closed with enough force to communicate to Meyer she'd had enough. "Our case is open and shut on those charges. If you're going to continue to lie to us, you're wasting our time, and we'll communicate with the US attorney to proceed." She sat back in her chair and fixed Meyer with an unblinking stare.

"This is it," Meg said. "This is where either he plays ball, and we can possibly get ahead of this, or he's prepared to go down with full charges."

"If he goes down with full charges," McCord murmured, "it's because the people he worked with will kill him if he talks."

"They'd have to get to him in prison."

McCord gave her a single raised eyebrow.

"Yeah, yeah, it happens, I know." Meg turned to the window, where Meyer sat, sweating. His heel was jiggling again, and while the green tinge had left his complexion, a flush now rode high on his cheekbones. "Looks to me like he's starting to crack."

Meyer leaned toward his lawyer, and all Meg could hear was furious whispering.

Then Powell sat back and faced the two officers. "My client would like to propose a deal."

"What kind of deal?" asked Byrne.

"His cooperation for a greatly reduced sentence. We want all the explosives charges removed."

"Do you, now? In exchange for what?"

"He'll give you the name of the man responsible for organizing the bombing. And will explain how it was set up and what his role was. But he wants those charges gone. He had nothing to do with the explosives."

"I'll have to inquire if the US attorney is willing to agree to this request. Keep in mind, if I get an agreement on this, and your client does not provide real and salient information that leads to a break in this case, the deal is off and those charges are still in play."

"I understand."

Byrne turned to Meyer. "Do *you* understand, Mr. Meyer? This all rests on you."

"Yeah. I understand."

"Then, if you'll excuse us for a few minutes, we'll pause this interview."

Byrne and Shaff left the room, and all sound cut out, even though Meyer and Powell had their heads together, talking furiously.

"What happens now?" McCord asked.

"They're standing in the hallway, on the phone with the US attorney, who I guarantee has been waiting for their call," Meg replied. "They knew it would come to this. The first solidly reliable suspect arrested in a case like this?

They were always going to use him to flip on everyone else. It's an acceptable trade in their opinion. Not that it's going to do Meyer much good."

"What do you mean?"

"Even if they get rid of the weapons of mass destruction charges, that still leaves him with malicious destruction of property and all those first-degree murder charges. He'll still never see the light of day. But maybe Powell thinks first degree won't stick for Meyer and there's a chance he may get only a couple of decades for a lesser charge. From Meyer's perspective, it's likely worth the trade-off. And this isn't a gang case, like the last interview I witnessed, when Giraldi went down without making a peep. He knew the Mob would reach him from outside and his life was forfeit if he talked. This isn't the same kind of group. Powell doesn't have the same concerns for Meyer and will likely be advising him to save his own skin."

"And if he gives you a name? Or names?"

"They'll go after them tomorrow. Maybe even tonight, if they can discover their location or locations fast enough. With the Wilmott already under attack, there's zero time to waste." Motion caught Meg's eyes as the interview room door opened again and Powell and Meyer broke apart. "That was fast."

"Well, as you said, the US attorney was waiting for their call."

Inside the interview room, Byrne and Shaff took their seats again.

"Mr. Meyer, you have a deal," Shaff said. "The US attorney is willing to drop the explosives charges, pending significant information from you that leads to further arrests. And he doesn't mean someone online who helped pick the building. He means the person who spearheaded the attack, as well as whoever assisted in planting the explosives. Are you in agreement?"

Meyer nodded, paused, and answered verbally before he could be corrected again. "Yeah."

"Then let's start with the most important question. Who organized the attack on Talbot Terraces?" Shaff asked.

"Levi Bragg."

"And who is Mr. Bragg?"

"Bragg did stuff with explosives in the army. When he came back stateside, he got a job at a quarry where they make crushed stone and fill. Unionville Quarry. He does their blasting. They're up in the Piedmont, so lots of rock."

"Did Mr. Bragg acquire the dynamite for Talbot Terraces?" Byrne asked. "We know it came from McArthur Blasting Supplies, but they sell to many road, construction, and quarry companies, so we haven't been able to narrow down that particular dynamite."

"Yeah. He said they have to track all their supplies, but it's easy to say you use more to blast than you really do, and you pocket the rest in small batches so no one notices. Do it long enough, and you end up with a decent store of explosives. That's what we used. Unionville had no idea their explosives weren't all used up."

"Was the accident with the truck in the underground garage planned? Or was it really an accident?" Shaff asked.

"Planned. That was Chip Carter. He wasn't thrilled about messing up his RAM 3500 by hitting that column, but he did it. He knew what was at stake."

Byrne looked like she wanted to change tacks, go after motive, but she kept herself on topic. "Mr. Carter rammed the column."

"Yeah."

"There was no medical emergency."

"No."

"Who told him what column to ram?"

Meyer remained silent, then glanced sideways at Powell, who nodded, but still Meyer hesitated.

"Let me remind you that the deal is not set, Mr. Meyer," said Byrne. "It's all or nothing. And that will require you admitting to your role in the attack."

Meyer huffed out a sigh, his lips twisted in reluctance. Then he gave in. "I told him. Bragg got the building plans and had me look to see how we could bring it down. The idiot architect made some really stupid structural choices. Made our job easy."

"You knew about the reduced lap splice, the lack of rebar concentration over the columns, and the missing support beams?"

Meyer jerked in surprise at the familiar professional language. "You know about that?"

"You're not the only one who can read building plans, Mr. Meyer. Did you intentionally target those areas?"

"Yeah."

"How did you ensure Solis Construction was the one to come in and make the repairs?"

Judging by his expression, Meyer was figuring out that the FBI knew a lot more than they'd initially let on. "Bragg and Ian Richardson went to the trouble to make up a website. Really fancy. Stole pictures and text from a bunch of other real websites. It looked good. Richardson is a computer geek, and he knows SOE—"

"SEO," Shaff corrected. "Search engine optimization."

"Yeah, that. He set up the site so it would be at the top of a Google search. Made sure it was clear it was a local family business. Better Business Bureau stamp. Solid-looking company. And then they bought a Google ad to make sure Solis showed up at the top of the page twice. The condo board called the day of the accident."

"What were you going to do if they didn't call you?" Byrne asked.

"Bragg had some plan. He was going to give it to the next day and follow up himself, say he saw a story about the collapse on Facebook, or something like that. All he needed to do was get into the request for proposal, and then he was going to undercut anyone else by a lot. But they called him first. You can rent shore posts, so I did that, came over, and set them up. It was overkill, but it made it look serious to the condo board. Bragg was with me that day, and we did a review of the other columns in the upper garage. They were all fine, at most only a little surface delamination, but we told them it wasn't good, and would they like a quote for that repair work as well? Since doing it now would save them a lot of money downstream if they let it get worse. They went for it."

"You caught them at a time of 'crisis,' though it was a crisis of your making," Byrne said, "and they were already panicked, so they bought in. And you made the price worth their while."

"Yeah."

"How did you set the charges?"

"We hung tarps to curtain off each column and closed down the visitor parking spots in that area. Put up more shoring supports so people would think the area was weak and to stay away. Bragg brought the dynamite and set the charges. Drilled holes in the columns and slid the dynamite in so the explosions would shatter the columns and sever the rebar. Used burner phones wired to the dynamite for remote detonation. The day before, we left the columns wrapped in black plastic and took down the shoring supports. Told the condo board the columns were set and structurally sound, but we'd leave them wrapped to continue curing for another week, and then we'd return to remove the covers."

"How did the remote detonation work?" Shaff asked.

"Dunno. That was Bragg's bit. I had nothing to do with it. Something with the phones is all I know."

"How many columns did you target?"

"Eight."

"Did you expect the whole building to fall?"

"Yeah. With the columns I picked, it was going to trigger a progressive collapse. What I didn't count on was the strength of that shear wall. I didn't think it would keep part of it standing. Either way, the end result is the same. It's down."

Byrne went motionless, and Meg could see in her expression the decision that she now had enough information that she was willing to anger Meyer. "And your goal was to kill every person in that building."

"No."

"Then what was your goal?"

For the first time, fury overrode the fear in Meyer's eyes. "To do our part. To stand up for America. To stop the flow of illegals into the country."

Meg's gaze wasn't on Meyer, but on Powell. From his wide eyes, parted lips, and the way he pulled back a few inches from his client, Meg knew he was learning something shockingly new. Something he didn't like. Disgust flashed in his eyes, and then it was gone, covered by a bland professional veneer. But Meg had seen it.

"You want to know why I lost my job?" Meyer ranted. "Because they hired someone cheaper than me. Under the table. Not a citizen."

Byrne pinned Meyer with a laser-focused stare. "You justify the death of hundreds because you were laid off?"

"It's not just me. It's thousands of people, and it will only get worse. These people are here *illegally*, and no one seems to care. If we don't stand up, who will?"

"Why Talbot Terraces? Why was taking out an entire building the key to this plan of yours?"

"It's one of the stops."

"The stops on what?"

It poured out of Meyer then, all the vitriol, all the hate, all the warped nationalistic pride. All the confirmation that the imaginary railroad was exactly why they'd rained terror down on DC, and why so many families would never be the same.

By the time Meyer had talked himself out, color rode high in Byrne's face and her jaw was set, as if clenching it would keep her from saying the wrong thing when they now had Meyer exactly where they wanted him.

Shaff saw it, too, and took the lead. "Mr. Meyer, I think we have everything we need from you for now. One of the agents will take you to holding before your transfer to the central detention facility."

"What about my deal?"

"That's for the US attorney to work out with your lawyer. End of interview."

Byrne and Shaff left the interview room, Byrne still not having said another word.

"So that's it?" McCord asked as the buzz of conversation rose in observation.

"For now. They have Bragg's name and his workplace. They'll be able to get his home address from government records, and they'll want to go after him immediately. They'll also track down Richardson and Carter, but Bragg's the one they'll want first."

"Think he's a flight risk?"

"Oh yeah. We need to find Bragg before he hears Meyer's been taken into custody. Think of what he's responsible for. If Bragg goes into the wind, there's a good chance he'll head for Cuba or some other non-extradition country, and then we'll never get our hands on him." The fury in Meg's tone cut like a newly sharpened blade and matched the fury burning in her gut.

She looked back into the interview room as an agent cuffed Meyer's hands behind him. The righteous anger had drained away, and Meyer looked like a scared little boy again. "Every single one of them needs to pay for what they've done. Meyer's never going to see the light of day again as a free man. Bragg is next."

CHAPTER 24

Deflection: The displacement of a structural element from its original position due to external forces.

Sunday, December 23, 6:08 AM
MD 27 N
Germantown, MD

Meg sightlessly reached for the travel mug in the SUV's console cup holder and bumped hands with Brian as he did the same. "Sorry."

"No worries." Brian pulled her cup out and handed it to her. "Clearly, we both had the same thought."

"That it's too damned early to be on the road, so coffee is a necessity? Oh yeah. How are the dogs?"

Brian looked through the mesh separation behind them. "They're both sleeping. Lucky puppers."

"I told you to close your eyes and catch a catnap." Meg took a quick glance behind her, getting a glimpse of Hawk, eyes closed, his muzzle on his front paws. "Or dog nap, as the case may be."

"And leave you to drive on your own through these on-and-off whiteout conditions?" Brian peered out at the bare trees that lined one side of the road and the smattering of houses on the other, set far back from the road. A gusty northwest wind whipped through, bringing fresh snow and stirring up the drifts left from the nor'easter, making driving treacherous for seconds at a time as visibility dropped to near zero.

"Luckily, we have those flashing lights in front of us to help guide the way." Meg took another sip from her cup, then held it out for Brian to take so she could put her hand back on the wheel. In sections where farmers' fields sandwiched the highway, and the wind was particularly strong, she needed both hands white-knuckling the wheel to keep them in their lane. It was a truly nasty day, unusually cold and snowy for so early in the winter season. "What are they forecasting for the high temp today?"

"Here?"

"That's the only temp that matters to us currently."

Brian checked the weather app on his phone. "Five degrees Fahrenheit."

"Son of a—"

"But right now it's a balmy minus two. This is what we get for heading up into the mountains in winter."

"I don't know what to say to that."

"I'm sure you'll have some choice words when we get out of the SUV. I'm sure I will too."

If this arrest came down to an extended search with the dogs, it was going to be brutal out there for all of them.

Craig's call had come at just before four thirty that morning, leaving her scrambling in the dark for her cell phone, which lay facedown on the bedside table. By the time she'd grabbed it, Todd was also awake and reaching for the bedside lamp.

She hadn't even looked at the ID on the screen. Had just accepted the call. At this hour of the morning, there was a 98 percent chance she knew who it was. "Hello."

"It's Craig. They're sending agents out to Bragg's place, and I want you and Brian to go."

She was awake now and tossing back the covers. "I need five minutes to dress and feed Hawk. Where are we going?"

"Just outside of Damascus, Maryland. Bragg lives up in the Piedmont, relatively close to the quarry where he works. We want to apprehend him before he's up and hears about Meyer."

Todd was on his feet and motioned to the dog and then downstairs—he'd let Hawk out and then feed him.

She mouthed, *Thank you*, and started pulling out fleece-lined yoga pants, a thermal long-sleeved shirt, and a heavier sweatshirt for over top. After putting Craig on speaker, she started stripping out of her pajamas. "Who's going?"

"Mona is bringing a team of agents. But he's up in the mountains, surrounded by woods and farmland. She wants you to come in case he gets around them, especially in the dark. I told her she could have both you and Brian. Two teams would be better than one, especially in challenging weather."

Meg stifled a groan. "Is the weather going to be a challenge?"

"Yes. Snow is falling, and the winds are picking up. You'll be about eight hundred feet above sea level, so the winds will have a kick. And it's always colder up there."

Meg pulled on her yoga pants. "Is it smart to do this in the dark? Wouldn't it be better to wait until daylight?"

"That idea has been floated, but they're worried about any word getting through. They'd rather be there before six thirty at the latest to catch him in bed or just out of it. The idea is to get there, and then they can always pause if they need to. But they want you and Brian to be with them, and it's nearly an hour away."

"Have you called Brian?"

"No, he's next."

"Tell him I'll pick him up on my way to the Hoover

Building. Tell Mona I can be there, even with stopping for Brian, by five o'clock at the latest, possibly sooner. Tell Brian not to take the time for coffee, because if I know Todd, he's already got a pot going and will have travel mugs out for both of us."

"Will do. I'm going to text you a photo of Bragg, so you know who you're looking for. Tucker pulled it off one of their forums. Call if there's anything else. Otherwise, we'll keep you updated out in the field."

The photo came in seconds later. In it, Bragg stood in a black T-shirt and black cargo pants, a handgun in a holster at his hip and an American flag hanging from the short pole he angled over his shoulder. He had a gray beard that needed a trim and a black ball cap on backward, with a small laurel wreath stitched in gold above the back strap. He was big and muscular, and his expression clearly said, *Bring it on.*

They were ready to roll, coffee and all, before five o'clock, but it took a little longer for the agents to be ready. The caravan was on its way by 5:10 AM. They held the sirens but used lights to get out of town, and then again as needed as they made their way up the George Washington Memorial Parkway in Virginia, up I-495 into Maryland, and then from I-270 to MD 27, which would take them most of the rest of the way.

Meg and Brian were the last vehicle in the convoy, and they had their orders—stay a block away, out of sight; be ready to take up the chase if needed, but only if needed. Both handlers were prepared with everything they might need for a cold-weather chase: flashlights, satellite phones with GPS in case of spotty cellular communication, a thermos of lukewarm water for the dogs, a thermos of hot coffee for Meg and Brian, extra dry gloves and socks, and their usual high-energy dog food and energy bars. In addition to their own winter gear, they'd both brought boots for the dogs and canine coats, instead of their usual FBI work vests. They had to be prepared to be out in the winter weather for a considerable amount of time, though they both hoped the apprehension would be much more straightforward than that.

They were also both carrying their sidearm, in case it wasn't a straightforward apprehension. And they would be wearing thermal tactical gloves, which they could use in the field even at these temperatures.

They'd both rather be over- than underprepared.

Another blast of wind shook the SUV, and a gust of snow hid the vehicle in front of them, flashing red-and-blue lights and all. Meg took her foot off the gas and hovered it over the brake, letting the SUV coast for a few seconds, until the gust died down and the vehicle in front appeared again.

Brian checked the map on his phone. "We're getting close now. He's at the end of Sugarloaf Drive, which is just off MD 27. Should be there in under five minutes."

"Have you got a satellite view?"

"Yes."

"What are we looking at?"

"If he rabbits? Trees and farmers' fields. He's at the end of the street, and his house is half in the trees. Beyond is more forest, breaking into a field, then either more trees or fields, depending on which direction he picks."

"He'd pick away from MD 27 and civilization."

"Agreed. There's lots of lack of civilization for him to pick from, but there are also some smallish towns. Mount Airy to the north, Germantown to the south. Hey, Germantown. If he heads there, maybe we can go visit the Old Montgomery County Jail. Nothing but great memories there, right?"

If her eyes had been lasers, he'd have been burnt to a crisp. "Oh, yeah, that was a great jaunt. Nothing like fighting a perp four stories up on an open walkway that disintegrates out from under your feet, so you fall a whole story. Concussion number two right there."

"Yeah, on second thought, not a great memory. Anyway, if Bragg is eventually going to head for civilization, he's going to make for Frederick, which is big enough to get lost in."

"The question is, Once he's aware of the agents, will he guess they brought dogs? His approach to escaping will change if he thinks there are dogs."

"Which could be to our advantage as long as he stays on foot in the hills. The moment he carjacks a vehicle, we're no use anymore."

"Which means we need to catch him before that happens."

Meg's phone rang, and she punched the steering wheel button to accept the call. "Jennings."

"It's Mona. We're nearly there."

"Where do you want us?"

"There's a church with a big parking lot just past Sugarloaf, on the right-hand side of MD 27. We'll park the vehicles there, then go in on foot. You can wait there and be on hand in minutes if we need you."

And stay in the warm. "Sounds good," Meg replied. "Are you going to wait for sunrise to go in? Or go in now and get him out of bed?"

"We're going to make the call when we get there."

"Okay. We'll follow you to the church. We'll suit up the dogs, so we're ready to move when needed, then will wait for word. Good luck."

"Thanks."

Five minutes later they were pulling into the parking lot.

Security lights mounted high on the redbrick church dimly lit the snow-covered asphalt as vehicles pulled in to park in a line. Agents poured out, already in winter gear. Armed with flashlights, they jogged across the road and down Sugarloaf Drive.

"Let's get the dogs ready to go," Brian said.

One at a time, they climbed out of the SUV, gathered their gear from the back hatch, then stood in an open door leading to the K-9 compartment, getting their dog dressed in coat and boots, before bringing their go bags into the front. Then all they could do was wait.

When they heard the barrage of gunshots, even from down the street and over the wind, they decided waiting any longer would be a mistake. They gathered their gear and their dogs and sprinted across the road. When they hit Sugarloaf, they saw a group of agents in the scattered light of an overhead streetlight, sheltering behind a car at the end of the street, as shots rang out. Two agents popped above the car from opposite ends and fired a burst of rounds before ducking down again.

"We can't get close to that." Brian's words were nearly whipped away by the wind. "We can't risk the dogs."

"Agreed. But we can get a bit closer and be ready to move, if needed. If he has them pinned down out front, and he knows the back forty's out his back door, I don't think he's going to wait to take them out."

"We could circle around behind, but we may as well wait until they've cleared the house."

"Agreed. A piece of dirty laundry each and the dogs will be on his trail. It's lousy conditions for a search for everyone, but that may play to our advantage. He may not be able to get far on foot, and we'll be behind him the whole way. Come on. Let's take shelter behind that stand of cedars up ahead. It will block us from view and cut this wind."

They waited out of sight and slightly out of the bitter wind as the end of the street went quiet. After they'd waited about five minutes, Meg peeked around the cedars to find the end of the street deserted. "I can't see them. They must have moved up to the house. I still don't want to get closer yet. Not until they've cleared it. If they have him, I'll happily go back to the SUV and blast the heat."

"I'll race you to it." Brian's shoulders rode high toward his ears. He wore a knit cap over his dark hair, with the hood of his ski jacket pulled up and over his cap. As he sank down farther into the high collar of his jacket, all that showed were his nose, his green eyes, and the lower edges of his eyebrows.

She knew she showed the same minimal amount of skin.

When her phone rang a minute later, she had to slip off her tactical gloves to get the phone out of her pocket. "Jennings."

"It's Mona. He's gone. The tracks lead out the back door and disappear into the woods. Can you follow?"

"Yes. We're actually only a half block away; we came when we heard the firefight. But I need you to do something for us. We're coming, and we have plastic bags. I'll give you the bags, then I need you to find me two pieces of dirty laundry—a sock or underwear will be perfect. It can't be clean laundry—it must be worn. I need you to turn the bags inside out and pick up the items with the bags, not touching them yourself, and then turn the bags right side out around the items and seal them. The dogs will use his scent to track him. We're on our way. Meet us at the front door. Don't let anyone follow him out the back. Leave the trail pristine." She ended the call and put her phone in her pocket. "Let's go."

Bragg's house was the last on the street, where cracked

asphalt gave way to a short gravel driveway. A battered and faded red mailbox stood at the edge of the street, and an older model black pickup truck stood in the upper reaches of the driveway. Thirty or forty feet beyond was a plain redbrick bungalow with a pale gray shingled roof, unadorned save for an American flag blowing in the wind over the front door. That same front door stood wide open; the battering ram used to force it leaned against the wall nearby.

One agent filled the front door. When he spotted the dog teams, he called into the front hallway, "Byrne. The dogs are here."

Meg handed the bags to Byrne. A few minutes later, Byrne returned, holding two bags, each with a sock.

"Does this work?"

"Perfect."

Meg and Brian each took a bag.

"We'll stay in touch," Meg said. "Either by cell or sat phone, if we lose the signal. We both have your number saved in both phones. Hawk, come."

"Lacey, come."

They jogged around to the rear of the house, to where a line of tracks led from the back door. From the size of the boot prints and the length of the gait, they knew Bragg was a tall man with big feet and was running flat out.

But he'd be no match for two trained search teams, teams that jogged five miles several times a week to stay in shape for long-distance running. Teams that did parkour just as often, keeping the dogs in top condition to manage any terrain.

Meg opened her bag and gave Hawk the scent while Brian repeated the process with Lacey. "Hawk, this is Bragg. Find Bragg." She closed the bag and tucked it into the outer pocket of her go bag. Then checked to make sure her sidearm was securely in place at her right hip before meeting Brian's eyes.

He gave her a nod. They were ready.

"Hawk, find Bragg."

"Lacey, find Bragg."

The dogs put their noses down and immediately picked up the scent, which ran straight along the trail of boot prints.

The hunt was on.

CHAPTER 25

Chase: An open vertical space in a structure, such as an elevator shaft, a mechanical space, or a space cut to accommodate pipes or electrical wiring.

Sunday, December 23, 6:56 AM
Damascus, MD

The dogs took them directly into the forest that surrounded the rear of the house, exactly as Meg had expected. Bragg had to have known the best way to escape without law enforcement out front seeing him was to get lost in the woods. His only risk would have been if law enforcement encircled the house, but if he'd detected them early, he would have known they didn't have the chance. Pin them down out front while you got ready to leave, even if that preparation was no more than boots, gloves, and a heavy jacket, fire off one last volley, and make your escape.

If he hadn't taken the time to make those preparations, it would be a very short chase. Even dressed as she was, it was brutally cold, and Meg was worried about Hawk, though being involved in an active search would certainly help both of them to stay warm. Already Meg felt the relief of getting her blood pumping and the warmth it brought to her extremities. As long as they kept moving, they should be fine. If they had to stop for any period of time, they could be in serious trouble.

How had Bragg detected Byrne and the agents so early in the operation? Security system? He'd already been awake and had seen movement? Meg hadn't heard a dog bark, so she didn't think that was it. Her money was on a perimeter intrusion detection system along the outskirts of the property. He was at the far end of the street, so there would be little need for anyone to be on foot around his property, except perhaps for mail delivery, which would go only as far as the bottom of the driveway and would never occur at this hour, especially on a Sunday. If the system alerted Bragg only inside the house but had no outward sign of alarm, he could have been aware of them the moment they set foot on the outskirts of his property, even if the alarm had wakened him at this early hour.

However it had happened, Bragg was in the wind. Literally.

Even so, the dogs were hot on his heels. Hawk and Lacey ran side by side on their extended leads as Meg and Brian easily jogged behind them. They wove around trees and thick scrub, following no path except that left by Bragg's boot prints.

Bragg would know he was leaving a trail a five-year-old could follow, so Meg knew he'd have to find a way to hide his tracks. "He may try to head for one of the major roads," Meg said. "There's no way he's stupid enough not to think he's being followed."

"He probably doesn't think he's being followed by dogs. But yeah, if he hits a major road that has been plowed or is completely windswept, he'll think he has a better chance of hiding his escape. But he's going the wrong way for that. I studied the map to figure out how he could take off. If he wanted roads, he needed to go north. He's going west."

"Toward Frederick." Meg's breath was starting to come a little harder now but was still comfortable for talking.

"Yeah. If that's his plan, he may not have wanted to detour onto the roads. It's only about fifteen miles to Frederick as the crow flies, and it's mostly farmers' fields between here and there, and basically all downhill. There are a few suburban areas down the mountain, but he could skip every one of them by sticking to the fields."

They burst out of the trees into a long, narrow field, a panorama of white broken only by a tall, spindly wooden pole that carried the power lines running parallel to MD 27.

Brian's steps faltered for a moment, and then he called for Lacey to stop. "Unless this is how he's going to do it."

Meg looked out over the field as the wind whipped around her, stabbing its tiny icy knives into the exposed skin of her face.

The field was a smooth wash of snow. The boot prints were gone.

It was a reminder to both of them that they were trailing someone who knew the area intimately and had formulated an escape based on that knowledge.

"He knew the winds up here would obliterate his footprints," Meg called over a particularly strong gust that blew a flurry of snowflakes around them.

"Then he didn't count on the dogs. But we need to keep our eyes open. There's always a chance he's waiting in the woods to pick off anyone who guesses which way he went."

"Agreed." Meg patted the grip of her Glock 19. "But we won't be guessing. Hawk, find Bragg."

"Lacey, find Bragg."

The dogs took only a few seconds to zero in on the scent again, picking it up even under the covering of snow. And they were off, arrowing straight down the field for the bank of trees on the far side. The snow was deeper here, in some areas coming up to mid-shin on Meg, and moving through it was much more challenging.

It was a relief to step into the woods, as the wind lessened inside the thick cluster of trees.

"Damn!" Brian exclaimed. "That wind is brutal."

"It sure is." Meg pointed to the boot prints, which seemed to have stepped out of nowhere. "The dogs are on target."

"Like we expected anything else."

The dogs curved their path to the north, and soon they were running alongside a narrow, frozen creek as it ran downhill. They stayed on that path for over a half mile, keeping to the trees along the downward slope. While they were still following clear boot prints, Bragg was nowhere in sight.

When the creek curved toward the south along with the ground, leveling out slightly, they stepped out into a field. When the wind-driven snow settled momentarily, they could see this field was much larger, large enough that they'd be completely exposed while crossing it if he lay in wait on the far side. They could take the dogs around the perimeter, try to stick to the trees, but if he didn't traverse the field, they'd lose time trying to pick up his scent again.

"Let the dogs lead?" Brian asked, seeing the same danger.

"Yeah, but let's be ready." She changed the lead from her right hand to her left and pulled her Glock from its holster. "I don't like how exposed we are here, though the whiteout conditions play to our advantage for cover. We still need to be ready for anything. We can't help the dogs, they have to follow the trail, but I'd recommend we zigzag behind them."

"Yeah. Harder to hit a moving target."

They hit a different problem about halfway across that field, as Hawk started to slow and then paused to paw at his nose.

"Hawk, stop." Meg holstered her Glock and caught up to her dog, then instantly realized his problem. His snout was covered with ice and snow, as his humid breath had been freezing instantly around his mouth and nostrils. "Oh, buddy. Let me help." With her gloved fingers, she broke up the caked-on snow and ice, and his breathing instantly eased. "Brian . . ."

"Doing it. Lacey's having the same problem. Those short inhalations they have to do while scenting is making them ice up faster than when they're breathing normally."

As he straightened, Meg got a good look at his face. "She's not the only one having issues. You're pinking up like you're easing toward frostbite."

"You too. Not much help for it unless we're going to give up."

"We are *not* doing that."

"My feelings exactly. He gets away from us now, he may never be found, and all those people won't get any justice. No way."

Meg held out a gloved fist, and he bumped his to hers. "Let's keep going, then." She pulled her Glock again. "Hawk, find Bragg."

"Lacey, find Bragg."

As they moved across this field, deeper in all directions, Meg noticed the dogs start to drift apart a little and even start the back-and-forth undulation of scent cone trailing. They'd moved from direct scent path tracking to a more heads-up air scenting and trailing technique, compensating for the strong winds, which not only buried the boot prints but also blew the scent particles wide. The dogs still had the trail—judging from their behavior, there was no doubt—but it was weaker here.

They paused in a narrow strip between encroaching trees to wipe their dogs' noses quickly again. Everyone was breathing heavily now, even though they were all in top shape.

"Look at that." Meg indicated the boot prints, which reappeared briefly before disappearing into the next downward-sloping field. The steps were short and seemed to stagger, in contrast to the long, straight strides outside Bragg's home.

"He's tiring," Brian panted. "If we're finding slogging through this deep snow against the wind a good workout, he may decide those fifteen miles to Frederick aren't doable. In which case, he may try to break into a home along the way."

"That would be risky. If he aims for one of those small clusters of houses, they're tiny neighborhoods, where he could be seen. Unless he goes for an isolated farmhouse."

"That could be a big error. Farmers keep rifles handy in case anything gets into their livestock or tries to mess with their property. That could be asking for a firefight. They also tend to keep dogs, something else he might not be willing to take on, because if he shoots a dog, he attracts attention, and right now, he wants to lay low. It's why we're prepared to take him on, but I don't think he's going to shoot at us unless he's forced. It just identifies him to everyone around him. Ready?"

"Ready."

They came to a country road, but the dogs crossed over it and into the next field, making Meg thankful many of the properties in this area were unfenced. A farm lay to their right, the gray steel silo and red barn rising out of the snow up a slight rise, but the scent path took them wide of the main buildings.

They were just cresting the rise when the dogs abruptly cut to the right instead of continuing downhill. Meg scanned down the hill to see if the dogs had missed anything. From their current position, they could see for miles when the gusting snow died down momentarily. All that lay below was field after unending field of snow, ending miles away in the gray smudge of neighborhoods leading up to the outskirts of Frederick.

"I don't see any movement down below," Meg called.

"Me either. Maybe he changed direction because he realized it's too exposed to go that way."

They followed the dogs to the north, back into a clump of trees, then out and under a transmission tower carrying high-voltage power lines. Across one more field and then they came to a wooden fence enclosing acres of farmland. The dogs stopped, panting, and Hawk looked up and whined.

"He went over," Brian said. "The trail stops here. Think the dogs can parkour over, like we did at Bethlehem Steel, wearing all this gear and those boots and in this much snow? Going to be a challenge to take a run at it through this drifting."

"I think we're about to find out. Want to be springboard again?"

"Sure. If it ain't broke, don't fix it. Climb over."

Meg holstered her Glock, grabbed the top rail, and stepped up on the bottom rail. It was an easy up and over for a human, but the dogs were going to need a little assistance. She jumped down, and landed in the soft snow on the far side. "I'm ready for them. Hand me your bag."

Brian wiggled out of his go bag and handed it over the top rail to Meg, who set it down against a fence post. "Let's give them a good fifteen feet to take a run at it.

Lacey, Hawk, stay." He and Meg moved down the fence; then Brian turned away from his dog, bent over, bracing his gloved hands on his knees, and called, "Lacey, over!"

Lacey took off at a run, bounding through the snow, sending it spraying, and then leaped. She landed on Brian's back, skidding as her boots didn't get enough traction on his slick jacket, but she still managed to push off to sail over the fence. It wasn't graceful; instead of arcing smoothly over the fence as she had at Bethlehem Steel, she went over more like a flying squirrel, with all four legs extended, but she managed to pull in and land with a skid into the snow on the far side. She found her feet and shook herself off, snow flying in all directions.

"Well, that wasn't pretty, but it got the job done," said Meg. "Hawk, you're next. Hawk, over!"

Hawk sprinted for Brian, hit his back, and managed to push off again with a little more grace than Lacey, but his landing was definitely less coordinated, as he slipped and face-planted into the snow. But he bounced to his feet again, shaking off snow, his tail wagging.

"They obviously thought that was fun," Brian said as he scaled the fence. "Good for them. This search is brutal. I'm glad someone is finding something to enjoy. Let's get the show on the road. I'm beginning to not be able to feel my cheeks." He pulled out his bagged sock and offered it once more to Lacey and then to Hawk. "Lacey, find Bragg."

"Hawk, find Bragg."

The dogs made a beeline across the field, and as they crested a small rise, Meg pulled back on the lead at the sight of a long, low building in the middle of the field. "Hawk, stop. Brian."

"I see it. Why is that all the way out here?"

"I bet it's for storing hay. This field is fenced, which

tells me they have livestock, likely cows. They'd be kept in the barn in these temps, but the rest of the year, they'd be out in the field all day. The farmer would keep hay bales stored in the field to feed them here in place in good weather, rather than driving them all the way to the barn." She met Brian's eyes. "If there's hay in it still, it's going to be well insulated from the wind and snow. It's still going to be cold, but if he's suffering from frostbite, and we don't know what he's wearing, it would be a place to shelter."

"If he's exhausted from trying to stay ahead of anyone pursuing him, then he might shelter there to rest for a few hours. Or longer. What farmer is going to visit an isolated outbuilding in this weather when there are no cows anywhere near it? But wouldn't it be locked?"

"Why would they lock it? All the way out here and holding only hay? There's no need. He could walk right in. I don't see any windows on this side. They likely pack in the hay along the long walls, so why risk a leaky window and moldy hay? But there will be windows on the front and back to let in light, because they're not going to run electricity all the way out here for hay storage. He may be watching through them." Meg studied the building, angling her back to the wind but bracing against the force of the gusts. "I have an idea. Turn around."

Brian turned his back to her, and she rooted through the front pocket of his go bag for the satellite phone, which she knew he kept there.

"Let's assume we have no signal, so we'll use the sat phones. You follow the trail to this side of the building. If the trail leads to the front, don't follow it if there's any chance of being seen. I doubt he'll hear us over this wind, but be super quiet anyway. I'll take Hawk around to the far side to make sure the trail doesn't lead away from the building. I'll stay low under the back windows." She turned around so Brian could pull out her satellite phone. "Silence your phone, and then text me when your side is clear. I'll do the same. Once we don't think he's gone anywhere else, we'll call in backup. If he tries to make a break for it, we'll take him at that point, but I don't want to get into a firefight with him where the dogs have nowhere to go and could get hurt."

"Sounds sensible."

They both silenced their phones, then commanded their dogs to continue the search, adding the command "quiet" so they understood the change in search parameters. They split up about twenty feet from the structure, and Meg and Hawk circled around the back, and Brian and Lacey skimmed along the side. Hawk responded to Meg tightening up the lead and to her hand signal to go left, but she could tell he was confused, because she was taking him out of the scent plume. Lacey, on the other hand, was clearly still in it.

Meg was even more sure Bragg was inside the outbuilding.

They came to the back corner of the structure, and Meg stopped Hawk with a hand gesture. She leaned around the corner to find a wide window that filled the middle section of the back wall, but they had easily four feet below the window in which to scurry. Another hand signal had Hawk moving forward, and Meg crept behind, bent almost double, keeping her shoulder nearly to the wall. They were slow and virtually silent, only the slight squeak of snow under Meg's boots giving them away. As the wind spun a flurry of snow to surround her, stealing her breath, she was sure they were silent to anyone inside. Around the far corner, the side wall was an unbroken stretch of steel, as expected.

They crept around toward the front of the building, Hawk never indicating he was in the scent cone. Meg gave him the hand signal to stop and stay, and she crept toward the front of the building. She inched ever so slightly past the corner, just far enough for one eye to peer around, and found two windows and a set of double-wide doors. A surge of triumph warmed her when she also spotted a half-buried boot print in front of the doors.

Bragg was inside, and the proof lay in the lee of the building, which was slightly protected from the wind. The print would be gone in minutes, but their skilled canines had kept them doggedly on his trail, allowing them to finally run him to ground.

Meg pulled back around the corner and took out her sat phone to find a message from Brian already.

Trail ends here. Boot print at door. He's inside.

Her fingers were clumsy with cold, and it took her a couple of tries to get the message typed out. **Agreed. Texting Mona our GPS coordinates. Wait as close to the front as you can. If you hear a door open, we'll have to move on him. Otherwise, we wait.**

She sent off a text to Byrne with the GPS coordinates of their location. Then she took more time, knowing the agents would be in motion, to give a longer breakdown of the setup—where they were, the safest way to approach, and what they might expect to find inside. She forwarded everything to Craig to keep him in the loop. Then she curled around Hawk as bone-chilling cold set in with the lack of movement, trying to shelter and warm her dog in any way she could.

It felt like the longest fifteen minutes of her life. She'd anticipated reacting to the cold, but the unexpected ferocity of her shivering and teeth chattering rattled her frame, even as the wind continued to buffet them. She didn't hear anything from Brian but knew if his fingers were losing sensation, as hers were, he wouldn't be able to type anything.

Worst of all was her concern for her dog—she couldn't tell how cold he was, because if he was shivering, she couldn't feel it over her own. Guilt layered over worry that she'd put him in this position, even though she knew very well there was nowhere else he'd rather be than out on a search with her. But if the cold cost him an ear or a paw, she'd never forgive herself.

A text came in from Byrne saying she and the agents were on-site and were approaching. Meg hated to do it, knowing it would only make him colder, but she gave Hawk the hand signal to lie down in the snow, and then she lay over him. If it came down to a firefight, the only way they'd hit her dog was through her, and she was going to make them as small a target as possible.

She never heard the agents' approach, only the yells of "Federal agents! Get your hands in the air!" as agents streamed into the structure.

Not a single shot fired.

Minutes later, a hand shook her shoulder, and she looked up to find Byrne crouching before her. Minutes after that, Meg, Brian, and the dogs were hustled into one of the SUVs parked nearby, which was blessedly warm and dry. As she clumsily stripped off her gloves, her fingers barely working, she couldn't hold in the whimper of pain. But all that mattered was getting her dog out of his winter gear and letting his feet warm as hot air flowed from the heating system. Her fingers struggled with the fastenings, just as Brian's did, but they stripped the dogs out of their wet gear and tossed it all in the back of the SUV.

Meg studied Brian's face. His cheeks had gone from pink to the white of frostbite setting in, but when she reached out to press two fingers to his cheek, a touch of pink diffused into the depressed tissues.

"I can feel that." Brian dragged off his cap and unzipped his jacket, though it took him three tries to do it. Then, pushing the sides of his jacket apart, he let his head fall back on the seat. "Do I need to poke your face?"

"No. I'm getting pins and needles everywhere now, including my cheeks, so I'm okay. I've never been colder, but I welcome the pain, because that means my nerves are coming back."

"Todd's going to be unimpressed."

"I'm glad Todd's not here to see this right now. By the time we're in DC, we'll both be back to normal."

The passenger side door opened in the front, and Byrne climbed in, then slammed the door behind her. "Sweet Christ, I've never been so cold." She took in Meg and Brian and had the grace to blush. "Sorry. That's a dumb thing to say when you and your dogs nearly froze to death out there."

"Not dumb at all," Brian countered. "We get it. It's *cold*."

"Is Bragg contained?" Meg asked.

"He didn't even put up a fight. Too exhausted, too cold. He had boots but not a great jacket. No hat, no gloves. He ran too fast to dress properly for the weather, and that was his downfall. Pretty sure his fingers and ears are frostbitten. He had a handgun and tried to use it, but his hands weren't working properly, because of exposure. It was an easy arrest on our part—a lot harder on yours. Thank you. We wouldn't have been able to track him without you. If he'd been able to shelter here for a while to warm up and get his second wind, we might never have caught him."

"Always bet on the dogs," Brian said. "They never steer us wrong."

"Never," Meg agreed, stroking a hand over Hawk's warming fur as he thumped his tail against the floor mat. "They're the very best of us."

They'd done it—they'd closed the circle and caught the man responsible for spearheading the unspeakable tragedy of Talbot Terraces.

There would be more arrests to come, and more of the lost to bring home, but the path toward healing had begun.

CHAPTER 26

Topping Out: A construction rite celebrating the completion of the structural phase of a new building. The celebration can include placing an evergreen tree, called a "topping tree" or a "construction Christmas tree," atop the structure to symbolize the safe and successful completion of the structure's framing.

Monday, December 24, 7:07 PM
Jennings/Webb residence
Washington, DC

Meg pulled the red sweater over her head and tugged it down so that it lay snug over her hips. She picked up the long gold chain that lay on her dresser, and the glass pendant swung free. After slipping the chain over her head, she centered the pendant to lie over her breastbone and then ran her fingertips across the embedded swirls of electric blue, black, and soft gray before closing her fist around it.

Miss you, Deuce.

As if sensing her wistfulness, Hawk rose from where he lay under the wide window and came to bump against her knee. She looked down to find Hawk smiling up at her, his tongue lolling and his tail undulating his entire rear end.

Bending, she ran a hand down his back and then pressed a kiss to the top of his head.

"You know, buddy, some people are lucky to find a heart dog. And here I am, beyond blessed to have two. I wish you'd had a chance to meet Deuce. He would have loved you. You would have been such buddies." She straightened, releasing the memory pendant that contained a swirl of Deuce's ashes, a piece she'd had made following his death while pursuing a suspect on a dark, rainy night in Richmond. "Now, let's go have a party."

She slipped gold hoops into her ears and ran her hands under her dark hair to fluff it out over her shoulders. Then she stood and stared at her motionless reflection in the mirror.

"That isn't a look that says, 'Bring on Christmas!' " said Todd from where he leaned one shoulder against the bedroom doorjamb. "It's Christmas Eve, and your family is going to hit the doorstep anytime. It's a happy occasion. Why the pensive expression?"

"I've been thinking."

He flashed her a quick grin. "Uh-oh. Sound the alarm. She's been thinking." He walked to her, took her hand, and drew her down to sit with him on the end of the bed. "Seriously, though, what's going on?"

"Do you remember how you said on the day of the collapse you were fine with whatever wedding plans I made, as long as I was still going to marry you?"

"Yes."

"What if I want to toss everything we've already agreed to? Cancel the venue, the florist, the photographer. Would you still be okay with that?"

"As long as you still want to marry me, yes."

"We'll lose our deposit."

"I can live with that." He took both of her hands in his. "I want this day to be special for you. That will make it special for me. If you think what we've already arranged isn't it, and you know what is, then let's talk about it."

"You're really going to be that reasonable?"

"I really am. It's not always the case, but for many men, they know from the get-go the wedding is more for the bride than the groom. *I* know it. I want you to have what would make the day special for you. I'm just happy to show up because we're going to make that commitment to each other."

"Then what if we got married at Cold Spring Haven?"

His eyebrows shot skyward. "At your parents' rescue?"

"Yes." When he stayed silent, his narrowed eyes locked on hers, she pushed on. "You think it's weird."

He shook his head slowly. "Not at all. Lots of people have backyard weddings, which is what this would essentially be. With a horse, an emu, probably a litter or two of kittens, and some orphaned baby deer. Is that what you really want?"

The corner of her lips twitched. "Well, the deer might not get a personal invitation, but . . . yes. I think it is."

"Is this still about the original plan being 'too much'? Because of Talbot Terraces?"

"Honestly, no, I don't think so. This has actually been coming on for a month or more. It just got kicked into overdrive with all the emotion of the past week. Even as I was making decisions on people and places, there was this little voice in the back of my head telling me it wasn't a good fit. I think I got carried away."

"How much of that was Cara getting carried away?" Todd's tone was light, making it clear he didn't blame Cara.

"That might have been some of it, as we egged each other on. But once I stopped to think about it, the more and more I thought it wasn't *us*. The collapse simply held that feeling under a magnifying glass, clarifying it. It's not that all that finery wouldn't be lovely, but when it comes down to it, you and I are practical people with close friends and family, and I think we'd be happier celebrating the official start of our life together as husband and wife with that smaller group, not with two hundred of our acquaintances." She frowned, studying the crease between his brows. "What?"

"I think you're pretty smart. I was happy giving you the big, flashy wedding if that's what you wanted, but it wasn't sitting solidly with part of me. This . . . this plan for something smaller and intimate . . . I like it. A lot. What are you thinking?"

"Something simple. But simple doesn't mean it can't be lovely. Keep the guest list shorter, maybe more like seventy-five than two hundred. Outdoors, with a tent in case it rains, but under the sky if it doesn't. Maybe an arbor. Just Cara and Emma as my attendants."

"With Luke and Josh as mine."

"Exactly. A simpler dress, a more country feel to the whole affair."

"More relaxed." He grinned and nodded slowly. "Yeah, I like it. Much more than the original idea." When she looked skeptical, he laughed. "Yes, I said I liked the other idea. What I liked was it seemed to make you excited. But this . . . this *I* like. And after dinner, we can kick off our shoes and have our first dance barefoot in the grass." He gave her a mock leer. "Sexy."

She laughed and gave his shoulder a push, but then laid her head on it. "Another thought. We booked for August because that's what they had available. If we're doing it at the rescue . . ."

"We don't have to wait. I like that too. What are you thinking?"

"What about May? When the trees are blooming and before it gets too hot?"

"I think that would be really nice."

"Good. Should we tell them tonight?"

"Ask them, you mean."

"I'm assuming Mom and Dad won't have a problem with it, but you're right. Ask them tonight."

"They're all going to be here. I think it's the perfect time." As she lifted her head from his shoulder, he caught her chin lightly in his fingers, studying her face. At her raised eyebrows, he ran his thumb over her cheek. "Just making sure there are no lasting traces of your adventure yesterday. No signs of frostbite."

"Not on Hawk either. We're lucky there. He didn't have nearly the amount of cold-weather gear I did, and I was worried about his ears and paws. Which is why I was trying to keep him warm with what little body heat I had, and keep him out of the wind while we waited." At the sound of his name, Hawk came over and bumped their hands with his nose, wagging his tail happily. "Hi, buddy. Yes, let's go downstairs. Cara, McCord, and the dogs will be here shortly."

Twenty minutes later found them downstairs in the kitchen, putting finishing touches on the appetizers spread out on the table, while hors d'oeuvres warmed in the oven. Across the room, the Christmas tree sparkled in jewel tones, and the snap and crackle of a roaring wood fire warmed the space.

"Hello!" Cara, McCord, and the dogs stepped into the front foyer on a chill gust of wind.

"Come on in!" Meg called. "McCord, get that door closed. It's freezing out there, and I'm done with freezing this week."

"Totally understandable," Cara said, toeing off her boots and bustling down the hallway, her arms full of a giant platter of Christmas cookies and squares. "Though it will keep our snow and will guarantee a white Christmas. Which we'll be happy to look out on from inside, where it's warm and dry."

The pack of dogs shot past them to frolic in the family room, where Hawk and Blink immediately settled into a tug-of-war with a red, green, and gold rope that Meg couldn't resist giving her dog as an early present.

Cara set the platter down in one of the few empty spots on the table. "What can I help with?" She looked around the kitchen. "It all looks pretty much ready to go."

"It pretty much is," Meg replied. "I expect them any minute now. They called about twenty minutes ago, saying they were getting close."

McCord squeezed a six-pack of craft beer into the already overloaded fridge. "Traffic is crazy, with people trying to get places for Christmas Eve. Probably slowed them down. Not to mention just finding parking on this street."

"Always a challenge." Meg held up two wineglasses. "Cara?"

"You bet. I'm not driving tonight. Crack it open."

Three sharp knocks sounded from the door as Meg was pulling the cork on a bottle of Pinot Grigio. She was about to set down the wine bottle, but Cara waved her on as she headed for the front foyer. "Don't you dare stop. I'll get the door. Pour one for Mom while you're at it."

Down the hallway came the calls of greeting, along with stomping feet and the sound of suitcases rolling.

Meg leaned over to peer out the kitchen door. At the end of the hallway, Cara still had her arms around her mother, and her father was shucking off his parka. Two large wheeled suitcases were lined up against the wall. "Are you moving in?" she called.

Her father strode down the hallway with a grin and caught her up in a huge hug. "Would it be so bad if we did?"

She wrapped her arms around him and inhaled the scent that was so quintessentially Jake Jennings—a mix of hay, miscellaneous animals, and the spice of his cologne. It seemed like the scent of the rescue was so much a part of him, even showering never totally scrubbed him of it. "Nah. I'd have someone to walk Hawk when the weather is lousy."

He gave her one more squeeze and released her to step back. "Nice try. I mean, we could have left the second suitcase at home, but then there'd be no presents for you."

"And I'd have had to kill him." Eda Jennings stepped in between her husband and daughter to hug her eldest. "And that would be so messy, especially around the holidays."

Meg patted her mother on the back and chuckled. "So practical."

"Always." Eda planted a kiss on her cheek, then turned to Todd. "Todd." And walked into his arms.

Meg turned to find her newly adopted sister, Emma, headed straight for her. "Hey, you."

Emma wrapped her arms around Meg and practically bounced them up and down. "I'm so happy we're here!"

"Was the drive that bad?"

"Wasn't terrible until we hit the beltway. Then it was nuts." Some of her enthusiasm dimmed. "You don't need to be at the collapse site tomorrow, do you?"

"No. Those of us celebrating Christmas were relieved at five o'clock. Those not celebrating, or who wanted to continue, will keep working the site, though for two days, it will be only one shift. Then we're all back on the twenty-sixth to continue the recovery operation. But enough about that for now. Come and grab a drink. Mom, I've already poured wine for you. And we have lots of food. I mean *lots*. Please don't leave me with all this food."

Emma giggled. "I'll do my best."

Fifteen minutes later, the entire group settled in the family room, with new presents added to the tremendous pile under the tree as Christmas music softly played in the background and dogs sprawled, snoozing, everywhere. Except for Cody, who sat motionless, watching every bit of food move from McCord's plate to his mouth.

McCord looked down at his dog. "You're pathetic." He glanced at Meg. "He got dinner, I swear."

"I believe you. I don't think he's ever going to stop trying to steal your dinner, even though you deny him every time."

"Hope springs eternal," said Eda. "He needs to take a lesson from Saki."

Everyone looked to where Saki lay asleep, her back pressed against Cara's leg where she sat on the floor by the fire.

"She knows better," said Cara. "Honestly, I'm not sure this one"—she head-cocked in Cody's direction—"will ever truly grow up. Some goldens take a long time."

"Some never do," Meg said. "My money is on Cody being that kind."

"I'm not taking that bet," McCord mumbled around a mini egg roll.

"So, what's new on the wedding planning?" asked Emma from the floor beside Cara. "Have you been looking at dresses?"

"Emma," Eda scolded gently. "Meg's been busy lately, and I'm sure hasn't had a moment to think about the wedding."

Meg took in Emma's slightly crestfallen face and gave her a bright smile. "Actually, I have been thinking about the wedding. And that includes the dresses." She met Cara's eyes. "We've done a lot of planning. Just know I appreciate all the time you've given me on this. I've enjoyed it."

Cara stared at Meg, her eyes narrowed, her head tilted at a slight angle, but she stayed silent.

Meg took Todd's hand, felt the strength of his grip in return, and turned to her parents. "We've decided . . . well, mostly me, but Todd is one hundred percent behind me . . . that the wedding we had planned isn't right for us."

Emma sat bolt upright, her eyes wide. "You mean you're canceling it?"

"Not the wedding, just the version of it we'd originally planned, as a big event here in DC." She turned to her parents. "With your agreement, we'd like to have our wedding at the rescue."

It wasn't often that Eda Jennings was at a loss for words, but she seemed stunned into silence.

"At Cold Spring Haven?" Jake clarified.

"Do you own more than one rescue?" Meg winked at him. "Yes, at Cold Spring Haven."

"Are you sure?" Eda found her voice, and her tone was half caution, half hope.

Meg turned to find Todd's warm eyes fixed on her face. He nodded his agreement, and she turned back to her parents. "We're sure. We'd like to have the wedding there, outside, surrounded by the animals and the rolling hills. We want to keep it smaller, with just our closest friends and family there. And we'd like to move it up to May. Because now we don't need to wait. What do you say?"

Her parents shared one of those unspoken mind melds using only their eyes—which had always amazed Meg—before Eda said, "We'd love it."

Getting up, Meg moved to hug both of her parents. "Thank you," she whispered in her mother's ear. "It'll be like being married at home . . . because it is."

Eda kissed her cheek as she pulled back, all smiles. "We're thrilled. Truly. But you know it will be more work for us to do it this way."

"It will totally be worth it. You in?"

"I wouldn't miss it for the world."

"And we'll help," Emma chimed in. "Right, Cara?"

Cara slung her arm over Emma's shoulders and grinned at her mother. "I wouldn't miss it for the world," she echoed.

"I would hope so." Meg sat down and picked up her glass of wine. "Starting with the two of you being my attendants."

Meg had to hold back a laugh when Emma's eyes nearly bugged out of her head. *"Seriously?"*

"Seriously. Which means we need to talk dresses." She gave Cara a small, apologetic shrug. "And I need to start from scratch on my wedding dress. The ones we were looking at . . ."

"Are all wrong for this," Cara agreed. "But we can do it."

"You got that right." Leaning forward, Meg extended her glass, and Cara touched hers to it with a musical chime.

Then Meg settled back as her mother, Cara, and Emma started to discuss the possibilities excitedly.

In the background, Judy Garland's smoky contralto broke through a lull in the conversation.

Through the years we all will be together if the fates allow . . .

So many families gathering tonight would have an empty chair and would be feeling the agony of a lost life, a lost love. So much pain, so much loss, and all because someone had told a story that wasn't true to drum up outrage for their personal cause. It made Meg's heart ache thinking of all those gone, long before their time.

"Hey, you in there?"

Realizing Todd's face was only inches from hers, she blinked to bring him into focus. "Yeah." She kept her voice low as the joy of the season spun around them. "I was just . . . thinking about all the people who are gone and the families who are missing them tonight. Two weeks ago they were all planning the holiday season together. Now those families are ripped apart and will never be the same again."

He put an arm around her shoulders, pulled her in against his solid warmth. "I know it's hard. Trust me, no one knows better. But you can't get lost in it, or every loss is a body blow, over and over, until you're drowning in others' agony and won't be capable of helping when you're needed most. For here, for now, stay with us. Stay with me."

She'd given her all to help guide the lost from darkness into light. Those she couldn't bring to the light had been beyond anyone's help before the first rescuer had set foot on the pile.

Todd was right—she'd done all she could; now it was time to stay here, in this moment.

With one last wish for comfort for the families of the lost, she turned away from the darkness and back to the joy and light.

Back to her family, to their love, and to the peace of Christmas.

Acknowledgments

For the first time, I'm stepping out from behind the Sara Driscoll pseudonym. In the past, Ann Vanderlaan and I wrote the acknowledgments together as Sara, though we thanked our own separate people. This time, it's just me.

The first person to acknowledge is Ann. Over the years of writing the FBI K-9s, she slowly passed on much of her boundless knowledge about dogs and canine nose work. No one anticipated her sudden passing, but I'm beyond grateful to her that she left me prepared to tackle the FBI K-9s alone. *That Others May Live* is not the first book I wrote on my own—I can thank the NYPD Negotiators series for that—but there is so much specialized knowledge required to portray the dog teams accurately that I had some concern about the technical aspects, not to mention that I also took on the task of the chapter titles and definitions, something that had always been exclusively Ann's domain. Many, many thanks to Ann for all her work on the series up to now, which allowed me to accept her baton and carry it over the finish line for both of us.

I could not have written this book convincingly without the assistance of Josh Porter and his Building Integrity YouTube channel. Josh is a structural engineer in Florida, and immediately following the collapse of Champlain Towers South, he started a series of videos analyzing what went wrong with the building that led to the collapse. Josh's goal was not to assign blame but to examine scientifically the building's plans and the photo evidence following the collapse to explain the progression of the disaster. Not only did Josh's clear and concise explanations teach me an immense amount about structural engineering and building design, but they also allowed me to apply some of those insights to Talbot Terraces to produce a realistic situation. Thank you, Josh, for your extensive virtual lessons. Rest assured, any engineering errors in this book are mine alone.

For the first time in seven books, I had a new editor at Kensington, and I admit I felt a little trepidation at the change, especially at a time when the writing process would already be different. But from the first conversation with James Abbate, the connection was immediate, and I knew I was in great hands. James, you instantly jumped in with both feet and have been an absolute joy to work with. Throughout the entire process, I appreciated your organization and efficiency and always felt like we were on the same page. It has been an undeniable pleasure to collaborate with you, and I look forward to our continuing teamwork in the future.

My agent, Nicole Resciniti, has gone above and beyond for me lately. Ann's passing left us with some unexpected legal aspects that needed to be wrapped up for me to continue writing the series solo, and she took on every challenge with good humor and efficiency. Nicole, I can never manage all this without you, but this time, more so than ever! Also, thanks to the Seymour Agency support team of Marisa Cleveland and Lesley Sabga for assisting with communications and promotion.

As always, the talented people at Kensington Books have been wonderful. Kensington's art department, helmed by Louis Malcangi, did an amazing job on a cover that I knew from the start would be a challenge simply because of the content and complexity of the scene. Communications and publicity were once again deftly handled by Jesse Cruz, Larissa Ackerman, Lauren Jernigan, Kristin McLaughlin, Alexandra Nicolajsen, Vida Engstrand, Kait Johnson, and Sarah Beck. Many thanks to the entire Kensington team for their camaraderie and support.

Finally, my critique team—Jenny Lidstrom, Jessica Newton, Rick Newton, and Sharon Taylor—thank you for your extra help on this one. Not only did you do your usual detailed critique work, but you did it under the tightest time constraint yet. I don't know how to sufficiently thank you, but know the final product of this book is possible only because of your constructive criticism and suggestions. Sharon, a special thanks to you for your in-depth analysis of voice and emotional impact, and especially for that last-minute, thirty-six-hour extra read!

—Jen J. Danna, writing as Sara Driscoll